Gertrude F. H. Atherton

Patience Sparhawk and her Times

A Novel

Gertrude F. H. Atherton

Patience Sparhawk and her Times
A Novel

ISBN/EAN: 9783337349165

Printed in Europe, USA, Canada, Australia, Japan

Cover: Foto ©Andreas Hilbeck / pixelio.de

More available books at **www.hansebooks.com**

PATIENCE SPARHAWK

AND HER TIMES

A Novel

BY

GERTRUDE ATHERTON

AUTHOR OF "A WHIRL ASUNDER," "THE DOOMSWOMAN,"
"BEFORE THE GRINGO CAME," ETC.

JOHN LANE: THE BODLEY HEAD
LONDON AND NEW YORK
1897

M. PAUL BOURGET,

Who alone, of all foreigners, has detected, in its full significance, that the motive power, the cohering force, the ultimate religion of that strange composite known as " The American," is Individual Will. Leaving the ultra-religious element out of the question, the high, the low, the rich, the poor, the man, the woman of this section of the Western world, each, consciously or unconsciously, believes in, relies on himself primarily. In the higher civilisation this amounts to intellectual anarchy, and its tendency is to make Americans, or, more exactly, United Statesians, a New Race in a sense far more portentous than in any which has yet been recognised. As M. Bourget prophesies, destruction, chaos, may eventuate. On the other hand, the final result may be a race of harder fibre and larger faculties than any in the history of civilisation. That this extraordinary self-dependence and independence of certain traditions that govern older nations make the quintessential part of the women as of the men of this race I have endeavoured to illustrate in the following pages.

G. A.

Patience Sparhawk and Her Times

BOOK I

I

"Oh, git up! Git up! Did you ever see such an old
slug? Billy! *Will* you git up?"

"What's the use of talking to him?" drawled a
soft, inactive voice. "You know he never goes one
bit faster. What's the difference anyhow?"

"Difference is my mother wants these groceries for
supper. We're all out of sugar 'n flour 'n beans, and
the men's got to eat."

"Well, as long as he won't go, just be comfortable
and don't bother."

"I wish I could be as easy-going as you are, Rosita,
but I can't: I suppose it's because I'm not Spanish.
Guess I've got some Yankee in me, if I am a Californian." The little girl leaned over the dash-board of
the rickety buggy, thumping with her whip-stump the
back of the aged nag. Billy was blind, uncertain in
the knees, and as languid as any *caballero* that once
had sighed at *doña's* feet in these dim pine woods.
As far back as Patience could remember he had never
broken his record, and his record was two miles an
hour. In a few moments she set the whip in the socket
with an irritable thump, wound the reins about it, and
sat down on the floor beside her companion. For

some reason best known to themselves, the girls preferred this method of disposition when Billy led the
way, — perhaps because he had an errant fondness for
the roughest spots of the rough road, making the high
seat as uneasy and precarious as thrones are still ; perhaps because Patience rebelled at habit, and in all her
divagations was blindly followed by her Spanish friend.

Billy ambled up and down the steep roads of the
fragrant pine woods on the hills behind Monterey, and
the girls gave him no further heed.   Patience's long
plait having been shaken loose in her wild lurches over
the dash-board, she swung about, dangled her legs out
of the buggy, and commanded Rosita to braid her hair.
The legs she kicked recklessly against the wheel were
not pretty.   They were long and thin, clothed with
woollen stockings darned and wrinkled, and angled off
with copper-toed boots.   She wore a frock of faded
gingham, and chewed the strings of a sunbonnet.

" Don't pull so, and do hurry," she exclaimed as the
Spanish girl's deft slow fingers moved in and out of the
scanty wisps.

" I 'm not pulling, Patita, dear, and you know I can't
hurry.   And I 'm just thinking that your hair is the
colour of ashes."

" I know it," said Patience, gloomily, " but maybe
it 'll be yellow when I grow up.   Do you remember
Polly Collins?   When she graduated she had hair the
colour of a wharf rat, and when she came back from
San Francisco the next year it was as yellow as the hills
in summer."

" I don't care for yellow hair," and Rosita moved
her dark head with the slow rotary motion which was
hers by divine right.

"Oh, you're pretty," said Patience, sarcastically. "You want to be told so, I suppose — There! you pulled my hair on purpose, you know you did, Rosita Thrailkill."

"I didn't, Patita. Don't fire up so." And Rosita, who was the most amiable of children, tied the end of the braid with a piece of tape, rubbed her blooming cheek against the pale one, and was forgiven.

Patience drew herself into the buggy and braced her back against the seat. Her face had little more beauty than her legs. It was colourless and freckled. The mouth was firm, almost dogged, as if the contest with life had already begun. Her brows and lashes were several shades darker than her hair, but her eyes, wide apart and very bright, were a light, rather cold grey. The nose alone was a beautiful feature, straight and fine ; and the hands, although rough and sunburned, were tapering and slender, and very flexible.

In her red frock, the highly-coloured little Spanish girl glowed like a cactus blossom beside a neglected weed. Her plump face was full of blood ; her large dark eyes were indolent and soft. Patience's eyes comprehended everything within their radius in one flashing glance ; Rosita's, even at the tender age of fifteen, looked unswerving disapproval of all exertion, mental or physical.

"I wonder if your mother is drunk?" she asked in her slow delicious voice.

"Likely," said Patience, with frowning resignation. "But let's talk of something more agreeable. Isn't this perfume heavenly?"

The dark solemn woods were ravishing with the perfumes of spring, the perfume of wild violet and lilac and lily, and the faint sweet odour the damp earth gives up as the sun goes down. From above came the strong bracing scent of the pines. Now and again the wind brought a salt whiff from the ocean. No birds carolled, but the pines sang their eternal dirge.

"What's your ideal?" demanded Patience.

"Ideal? What ideal?"

"Why, of man, of course."

"Oh, man!" contemptuously. "I have n't thought much about men. I don't read novels like you do. I wish somebody would die and leave me a thousand dollars so I could live in San Francisco and have a new dress every day and go to the theatre every night. Miss Galpin says we must n't think about boys, and I don't — perhaps because the boys in Monterey are so horrid."

"Boys? Who said anything about boys?" The chrysalis elevated her patrician nose. "I mean men."

"Well, you're mean to turn up your nose at boys. They like you a good deal better than they do me, and a good many of the other girls."

"That's funny, is n't it? and I not pretty. But I suppose it's because I talk. You just sit still and look pretty, and that's not very entertaining. I read in a novel that men like that; but boys have got to be entertained. Goodness gracious! Don't I know it? When I was at Manuela's party the other night in my old washed muslin frock and plaid sash, did n't I talk my throat sore to make them forget that I was the worst dressed girl in the room and had the most freckles? Of course the girls did n't forget — nor some other things — " with a bitter lowering of the lids —

" but the boys did.   Somehow I feel as if men would always be my friends, if I'm not pretty."

" What do you know about men, anyhow?   You're only fifteen, and you've never met any but old Mr. Foord, and the farm hands and store keepers, who," aristocratically, " don't count."

" Have n't I read novels?   Have n't I read Thackeray and Dickens and Scott and ' Jane Eyre ' and ' Wuthering Heights ' and Shakespeare and Plutarch's Lives, and the life of Napoleon and Macaulay's ' History of England ' and Essays — those all ain't novels, but they write about men, real men, too.   I've made my ideal out of a lot of them put together, and I 'll never marry till I find him."

" Well, I 'd like to know where you 'll find him in Monterey," said the practical Rosita.   " Miss Galpin says you 're too romantic, and that it 's a pity, because you 're the brightest girl in the school."

" Did Miss Galpin say that? "   Patience took a brass pin out of her frock and extracted a splinter from her thumb with a fine air of indifference ; but the pink flooded her cheek.   " She 's always reading Howells and James, and says they 'd keep anybody from being romantic.   But that 's about all I 've got, so I think I 'll hold on to it."

The sun dropped below the horizon as they jolted out of the woods and down the steep road toward Carmel Valley.   They reached a ledge, and Patience, forgetful of hungry men and an irascible parent, called : " Whoa ! " to which Billy responded with an alacrity reserved for such occasions only.

" I never get tired of this," she said.   " Do you? "

" It 's pretty," said Rosita, indifferently.   " Why are

you so fond of scenery — nature, as Miss Galpin calls
it — I wonder? "

"I don't know," said Patience, and at that age she
did not. She was responsive but dumb. She gazed
down and out and upward with a pleasure that never
grew old. A great bleak mountain loomed on the
other side of the valley. It was as steep as if the
ocean had gnawed it flat, but only the peaceful valley
lay under; out in the ocean it tapered to an immense
irregular mass of rock over which the breakers leapt
and fought. Carmel River sparkled peacefully beneath
its moving willows. The blue bay murmured to the
white sands with the peace of evening. Close to the
little beach the old Mission hung its dilapidated head.
Through its yawning arches dark objects flitted; mould
was on the yellow walls; from yawning crevice the
rank grass grew. Only the tower still defied elements
and vandals, although the wind whistled through its gap-
ing windows and the silver bells were no more. The
huts about the church had collapsed like old muscles,
but in their ruin still whispered the story of the past.

"Isn't it splendid to think that we have a ruin!"
exclaimed Patience.

"It's a ruin sure enough; but there's uncle Jim.
He must think we're dead."

A prolonged "Halloa!" came from the valley, and
Patience, with a sigh, bade Billy "Git up," which he
did in the course of a moment.

"Halloa, you youngsters, why don't you hurry?"
cried a nasal voice. "I've been waiting here an hour."

"Coming," said Patience. "It's too bad he had
to wait."

"Oh, he smoked and swore, so he's all right," said

Rosita, who had not taken the trouble to reply. None of the girls was allowed to visit Patience at her house ; but Mrs. Thrailkill, who was fond of her daughter's chosen friend, and pitiful in her indolent way, often allowed Patience to drive Rosita as far as the branching of the roads, where the Kentucky uncle met his niece and took her to his farm.

In the dusk below a wagon and two horses could be seen, and a big man under a wide straw hat, sitting on the upper rail of a fence, his heels hooked to the rail below. Patience inferred that he was chewing tobacco and expectorating upon the poppies.

"Well, I reckon!" he exclaimed as the buggy reached the foot of the hill. "You two do beat all. Do you s'pose I 've got nothing better to do than moon round pikes waiting on kids like you? How 's your ma, Rosita? Well, Patience, I won't keep you — much obliged for giving my lazy Spanish niece a lift. Come on now; supper 's ready 'n after."

The two little girls kissed each other affectionately. Mr. Thrailkill lifted Rosita down, and Patience turned Billy in the direction of a fiery eye and a dim column of smoke under the mountain. The evening seemed very quiet after the rattle of Mr. Thrailkill's team had become a part of the distance. Only the roar of the surf, the moaning of the pines, the harsh music of the frogs, the thousand vocal mysteries of night — not a sound of man. Patience, after her fashion, rehabilitated the Mission and peopled the valley with padres and Indians ; but when Billy came to a sudden halt, she sprang prosaically to the ground and let down the bars of her mother's ranch. After she had replaced them she took hold of Billy's bridle, and endeavoured, by jerks and expostulation, to induce him to move more rapidly. The road now lay through a ploughed field stretching gloomily on the east to the horizon, where the stars seemed dropping into the dark. Cows roamed at will, or lay heavily in their first sleep. Here and there an oak thrust out its twisted arms, its trunk bent backward by ocean winds. The house soon became plainly outlined, a long unpainted wooden story-and-a-half structure, the type of ranch house of the second era. Castilian roses clambered up the un-painted front. Clumps of gladiolus, pinks, and fuschias struggled with weeds in the front garden. Beyond was a number of out-buildings.

When Patience reached the porch she dropped Billy's bridle, lifted out the sugar, and stepping to the kitchen window, looked through it for a moment before opening the door. Her mother was very drunk.

II

THE room into which Patience frowned was a large rough kitchen of the old familiar type. The rafters were festooned with cobwebs, through which tin cans and aged pails were visible, and an occasional bundle of rags. The board walls were unplastered and un-painted. Out of the uneven floor, knots had dropped to the cellar below. The door of a cupboard, built against the wall with primitive simplicity, stood open, revealing a motley collection of cans, bottles, and cracked dishes. Pots and pans were heaped on a shelf traversing two sides of the room. A table was loaded with odds and ends, in the midst of which place had been made for a lamp.

Over a large stove a woman was frying bacon and eggs. She wore a brown calico garment, torn and smudged. Her fine black hair, sprinkled with ashes, hung raggedly above magnificent dark eyes, blinking in a crimson face. The thin nostrils and full mouth were twitching. In her ruin she was still a beautiful woman, and she moved her tall bloated form with the pride of race, despite the alcohol in her veins.

On a broken chair by the stove sat a young man in the overalls and flannel shirt of a farm hand. His hair was clipped to his skull with colourless result; his large red under lip curved down into a yellow beard. In a long low room adjoining the kitchen a half dozen other men were seated on benches about a table covered with white oilcloth and chipped crockery. They also wore overalls and flannel shirts; and they were bearded and seamed and brown. The Californian sun soon burns the juices out of the flesh that defies it.

Patience flung open the kitchen door and threw the sugar on the table.

"Oscar," she said peremptorily to the man by the stove, "take Billy round to the barn and put him up, and bring in the flour and the beans. They're under the seat." The man went out, muttering angrily, and she turned to her mother, who had begun a tirade of abuse. "Keep quiet," she said. "So you're drunk again? I thought you promised me that you wouldn't drink again for a week. Where did you get it?"

"Couldn't help it," muttered the woman, cowed by the bitter contempt in her small daughter's eyes, and thrusting a long fork into the sputtering fat.

" Where did you get it ? "

" Could n't help it."

Patience opened the package of sugar with a jerk, and filling two bowls with the coarse brown stuff carried them into the next room and set them at opposite ends of the table. The men ceased talking as she entered, and saluted her respectfully. They felt vaguely sorry for her ; but they were afraid of her, and she was not a favourite with them. Her mother, " Madge," as they called her to a man, they worshipped, despite or because of her peccability. They went down before her deathless magnetism, her coarse good nature, her spurious kind-heartedness. It was only when very drunk that she became violent and vituperative, and even then she fascinated them. Patience told herself proudly that she had no attraction for "common men " — that she repelled them. Not being a seer, she was saved the foreknowledge of a fatal gift in operation.

She took the large coffee-pot from the back of the stove and filled the men's cups with its thick fluid. Her mother's rolling eyes followed her with a malignant sparkle. She was afraid of her daughter, and resentment had eaten deep into her perverted nature. Patience filled a plate with bread and apple sauce, and went into the parlour to eat her supper in solitude. She took all her meals in this room, which with little difficulty she appropriated to her exclusive use : it was very small. She kept it in fairly good order : she was not the tidiest of children. But the old brussels carpet was clean, barring the corners, and the horsehair furniture had been mended here and there with shoe thread. As it still prickled, however, Patience had made a cushion for the clumsy rocker out of an elderly gown which she had found in a trunk in the garret with other relics of finery. She occupied the rocker impartially whether eating or reading. The marble-topped table also served for dining and study.

In a forlorn old bookcase were her only treasures, the few books, mostly classics, which John Sparhawk had reserved when a succession of failures had forced him to sell his library to Mr. Foord. In one corner was a large family Bible on a small table. It was old and worn. Its gilt edges shone dimly through a cobweb of infinite pains.

On the papered walls were two large coloured photographs of Mr. and Mrs. Sparhawk, taken apparently when each was close on thirty years. The woman's face bore traces of dissipation even then, and the red mouth was very sensual. But the cheeks were still delicate and there were no bags under the large flaming eyes. The bare neck and arms and half revealed bust were superb; the poise of the head, the curve of the short upper lip, the fine arched nostril, were the delicate insignia of race; the pride stamped on every feature was that of birth, not of defiance. The man had a slender upright figure and a finely modelled head and face. The deeply set eyes were cold and piercing, but between the stern curves of the mouth there was much passion. Patience had studied these faces, but she was as innocent as if she had been bred in a cloister, and their mystery baffled while it allured her.

She ate her supper with a hearty appetite. Her mother's lapses, being accepted as part of the routine of existence, rarely depressed her spirits. Nevertheless she frowned heavily as turbulent sounds pierced the thin partition, not so much at her mother's iniquity, as at the prospect of being obliged to wash the supper dishes. The expected crash came, and she ran into the kitchen. Her mother lay prone. Two of the men lifted her immediately and carried her up the narrow stair. Patience sullenly attacked the dishes. She dumped them into a large pan of hot water, stirred them gingerly with a cloth fastened to a stick, drained the water off, poured in a fresh pailful, and dried them hastily. She filled the frying-pan with water and set it on the hottest part of the stove to cook itself clean. Occasionally she coughed with angry significance : the men in the next room were invisible behind a grey fog of their own puffing. She spattered her clean pinafore, blackened her hands, and devoutly wished herself alone on a desert island where she could live on cocoanuts and bananas. At such times she forgot the few compensations of her unfortunate life and felt herself only the poverty-stricken drudge, the daughter of Madge Sparhawk.

III

WHO Madge Sparhawk was before she married the Yankee rancher had at one time been an absorbing topic for dispute in Monterey. One gossip averred that she had been the dashing leader of the lower ten thousand of San Francisco, another that she had come from the Eastern States as the mistress of a wealthy man who had wearied and cast her off; a third confidently affirmed that she had been a brilliant New York woman of fashion who had gone wrong through love of drink, and been sent under an assumed

name to California by her afflicted family; a fourth
swore that she had been an actress, a fifth that she
had been the high-tempered queen of a gambling
house. On one point all agreed: she was disreputable,
and John Sparhawk was a fool to marry her. However, they were somewhat disappointed that they saw
so little of her. They were not called upon to snub
nor tolerate her. She rarely came into the town; never
excepting on horseback with her husband, when her
splendid beauty drew masculine Monterey from its
perch on the fence tops,—where it sat and smoked
and murmured the hours away,—and gathered it about
her, stirring the diluted rill of *caballero* blood.

As far as the little world of Monterey could learn
through the gossip of servants, she was a helpful wife
to a devoted husband who patiently strove with the
fiend that possessed her. When he was killed by the
accidental discharge of a gun her grief was so violent
that only a prolonged carouse could assuage it. Sub-
sequently she recovered, and with occasional advice
from Mr. Foord attempted to run the farm. As John
Sparhawk had made no will, she was her child's legal
guardian, the absolute mistress for eight years of what
property her husband had left. There was a little
ready money, the dairy was remunerative, and the ranch
well stocked. But that was five years ago. Her habits
had grown upon her; the ranch was mortgaged and
run down, the stock decreased by half.

Patience had rebelled heavily at her father's death,
and wondered, with childish logic, why, if one parent
had to die, it could not have been her mother. Her
father's manner had been cold, repellent, like her own;
but that his nature was deep and passionate even her

young mind had never doubted. She felt it in the close clasp of his arms as he held her before him on his horse when galloping about the ranch ; in his sudden infrequent caress ; in the strong pressure of his hand as they wandered through the woods or along the shore at night, not a word spoken between them.

It was not until after his death that she made acquaintance with her social separateness. He had begun her education himself. Her only girl companion was Rosita Thrailkill, the niece of a neighbour, whom her father would not permit her to visit in Monterey. John Sparhawk's only friends were the Thrailkill brothers and Mr. Foord, an elderly gentleman, who had lived in Monterey under the old régime, lost his fortune in the great Bonanza time, and returned to the somnolent town to end his days with his library, the memory of his dead Spanish wife, and a few old friends, world-forgotten like himself. He lived in the dilapidated Custom House on the rocks at the edge of the town, and Patience had ruled his establishment since her baby days. It was the only house in Monterey she was permitted to enter, and she entered it as often as she could. A hundred times she had sat with the old gentleman on the upper corridor and listened to the story of the capture of Monterey by the United States fleet in 1846 ; stared breathlessly at the crumbling fort —the *castillo*—on the hill above Junipero Serra's cross, as Mr. Foord verbally restored its former impregnability.

He told her tales of the days of light and life and joy when Monterey was the capital of the Californians, and the Americans were not yet come, — stories of love and revenge and the great free play of the primitive

passions, unpared by modern civilisation. For her
those old adobe houses in the town were alive once
more with dark-eyed *doñas* and magnificently attired
caballeros. Behind the high walls of the old gardens
fans fluttered among the Castilian roses and dueñas
stealthily prowled. The twisted streets were gay again
with the court life of the olden time, the grand parades
of the governors, the triumphant returns from the race
on the restless silver-trapped steeds.

Every house had its history, and Patience knew them
all. She wandered with Mr. Foord along the dusty
streets, lingered before the garden walls, over which she
could see and smell the nasturtiums and the sweet
Castilian roses. But gone were the *caballeros* and the
doñas. They lay in the little cemetery of the *padres*
on the hill, over beyond the yellow church which
marked a corner of the old *presidio*, and well on the
road to a great hotel whose typical life was vastly different from that old romantic time. They lay under
their stones, forgotten. The thistles and wild oats
rioted under the gnarled old oaks. The new-comer
never paused to glance at the worn carvings on the
thick rough slabs.

Behind the garden walls a few brown old women
lived alone, too practical to brood upon an enchanted
past. Cows nibbled in the *plaza* where once the bull
and the bear had fought while the gay jewelled people
screamed with delight. Gone was the tinkle of the
guitar, the flutter of fan, the graceful woman hasten-
ing down the street half hidden in her mantilla, the
lovely face behind the grating. The screaming of the
sea-gulls, the moaning of the pines, the roar of the surf,
alone remained the same, careless of change or decay.

Wooden houses crowded between the old adobes. Most of the Spanish families were half American: their women had preferred the enterprising intruder to the indolent *caballero*. Arcadia was no more. The old had kissed the hand of the new, and spawned a hybrid.

After John Sparhawk's death, Mr. Foord persuaded his widow to send Patience to the public school. The little girl was delighted. She had looked with envious longing at the stone building, painted a beautiful pink, which stood well up on the hill at the right of the town and was still known by the imposing name of Colton Hall; it had been built by the first American *alcalde*, and was a court house for a brief while.

But it was not long before Patience learned the bitter lesson that she was not as other girls, despite the fact that at that time she was well dressed and that she drifted naturally to the head of her classes. School girls are coarse and cruel. Children are the periodical relapse of civilisation into savagery. These girls of Monterey excluded Patience from their games and recess conversations, and intimated broadly that her mother was not respectable.

At first Patience gave them little heed. She loved study, and was of a wild happy nature beneath her prim exterior. Moreover, Rosita was her loyal friend; and one of the older girls, Manuela Peralta, who had a kind and independent heart, sheltered her as much as she could. But Patience was too bright and observing to remain long in ignorance of her hostile environment. When the awakening came her young soul was filled with rage and bitterness. The full meaning of their innuendoes she was too ignorant to understand, but that she was regarded as a pariah was sufficiently evident.

Little as she loved her mother, a natural impulse sent her to her only remaining parent with the story of her wrongs. Mrs. Sparhawk became violently indignant and shortly after very drunk. The subject was never mentioned between them again; nor did Patience speak of it with any one but Rosita, whom she regarded as a second, beloved, and somewhat inferior self. But her soul cried out for the strength that only a man's strong soul can give to woman at any age; and the man that had prayed to live and defend her lay with the forgotten Californians on the hill.

Mr. Foord divined her trouble, and did what he could to make her life endurable, although her shy reserve forbade any intimacy beyond the old friendship. Miss Galpin, her teacher, made no secret of the fact that Patience was her favourite scholar, and encouraged her to study and read and forget.

Patience indulged in no further outbreak, even to herself. She cultivated a cold and impassive exterior, an air of rigid indifference, and studied until her small head ached. She was not old enough to analyse; it was instinct only that made her assume callousness; but in her young vague way she grappled with the social problem. She did not approve of Mrs. Sparhawk any more than others did; but Mrs. Sparhawk's daughter behaved herself, and stood at the head of her classes, and had been assured again and again that she "looked like a little lady;" therefore she was at a loss to comprehend why Patience Sparhawk was not as good as other girls. There was Panchita McPherson, who lied profusely and whose mother sat in the sun all day and baked herself like an old crocodile, while her husband sat on the fence by the Post Office and smoked a pipe from the first of January until the thirty-first of December. Yet Panchita was of the *haute noblesse*, and treated Patience as she would a rag-picker. Francesca Montez never knew a lesson and was so vulgar that she brought the blush to Patience's cheek; but she lived in an adobe mansion which once had been the scene of princely splendour, and gave two parties a year. The American girls had not even the prestige of the past; they could not reckon up a great-grandfather between them, much less peeling portraits of *caballeros* and trunks of splendid finery; but they were bright and aggressive, and made themselves a power in the school.

As Patience grew older she compelled the respect of her mates, and they ceased to annoy her. The consciousness of social supremacy never faded, not for an instant; but even tying a tin can to a dog's tail becomes monotonous in time, and they had numberless little interests to absorb them. If Patience had been a rollicking emotional child she would doubtless have kissed herself into popularity and been treated to much good-natured patronage; but she scorned placation, and grew more reserved as the years went by. She accepted her fate, and discovered that there were times and hours when her mother, schoolmates, and social problems could be forgotten. Her spirits were naturally buoyant, and her mind grew philosophical; but as Mr. Foord once observed to Miss Galpin, "her start in life had been all wrong, and it would matter more with her than with some others."

IV

AFTER Patience had put the kitchen in order she went up to her room. She slept at one end of the house, her mother at the opposite. Several of the hired men occupied a dormitory between; the rest slept over the dairy.

She lit her candle and began to undress, then extinguished the flame suddenly and went down stairs and out of the house. She felt sullen and heavy and depressed, and knew the remedy.

The moon was at the full; the great ploughed fields were a sea of silver; the dark pines on the hills opened their aisles to cataracts of crystal, splashing through the green uplifted arms. Strange shadows moved amidst the showers of cold light, twisting rhythmically under the touch of the night wind.

Patience loved nature too passionately to fear her in any mood or hour. She sped over the rough field, climbed the fence, and walked hastily toward the Mission, pausing now and again to inhale the rich perfumes of Spring. The ruin looked like the skeleton of a mammoth caught in a phantom iceberg. Even the dark things that haunted it were touched to beauty by the silver light pouring through the storm-beaten rose window over the massive doors, into the abysms between the arches.

Patience skirted the long body of the church with haste; mouldering skeletons lay under the floor, and like all imaginative minds she had a lively horror of the dead. She entered the open doorway and ascended the steep spiral stair in the tower.   The steps were cut from solid stone and were worn by the trampling of many feet.   As she neared the top she called, —

"Tu wit !   Tu woo !" and was promptly answered.

As her chin appeared above the floor of the little room, where the moonlight came through hollow casements, an old grey owl, a large wise solemn owl, advanced from the wall with slow and stately step ; and despite his massive dignity there was expectancy in his mien.

"Poor Solomon," said Patience, contritely.   "I forgot your supper."   She climbed into the room and attempted to pat his head ; but when he saw that the hand was empty, he flapped his wings, and turning his back upon her, retired to the wall, blinking indignantly.

Patience laughed, then sighed, and sank on her knees before the low window overlooking the ocean.   The blue bay still whispered to the white sands sparkling like diamond dust in the moonlight, the yellow stars winking in its clear depths.   But the ocean was uneasy, and hurtled reiterantly in great deep-throated waves at the rocky shore as if its giant soul were in final rebellion against this conventional war with a passive foe. About Point Lobos its voice waxed trumpet-toned.   It shouldered itself into mighty waves and tossed the spray into writhing shapes.   Everything else was at rest.   The great forces of nature were the angry prisoners of the tides.   The moon grinned in his superior way.   The little stars seemed to say : "Up here we are quite composed, and as vain as pretty women.   If you would only keep quiet you would make such a fine large looking-glass."

As Patience gazed out upon the beautiful scene, her young mind shifted its impressions.   She forgot her life, and began to dream in a vague sweet way. Not of a lover. Despite the fact that she had manufactured a composite which occupied a pedestal in her imagination, she thought little about love. Her reveries were a wandering of her ego through the books she had read, environed by the nature whom she knew only in lovely profile. Had she lived her fifteen years on the sterile plains of Soledad, she might perhaps have been as harsh and bitter as its sands, her soul as grey, so susceptible was she to the subtle influence of great externals. But Monterey had saved her, and on nights like this she felt as if she too were flooded with crystal light, now and again clouded by something which perturbed, yet vibrated like the music of the pines.

When in a particularly romantic mood, she imagined herself Mariana in the "Moated Grange," or hummed "The Long Long Weary Day," and tried to feel sad, but could not. She never felt sad in her tower, with the owl on guard and the slighted dead in the church below. Sometimes she took herself to task for not having a proper amount of sentiment, but concluded that no one could be unhappy when so high above the world and all its hateful details. Occasionally she looked longingly at the perpendicular mountain : it was many times higher than her tower; but she was a lazy little thing, and would not climb.

As she knelt, gazing out on the ocean, or up at the spangled night, she was a very different-looking being from the sharp practical child that had exhorted old Billy and berated her mother. The loosened hair clung softly about her pale face, whose freckles the kind moon with his white brush painted out. Her mouth had relaxed its stern lines. Her eyes were full of the moon's shimmer, and of something else, — the struggling light of a developing soul.

Patience's soul had taken care of itself and showed virility in spite of the forces at war against it. What the little battling spark strove for, puzzled Patience even at that unanalytical age.   Religion — Christianity, to be more exact — said nothing to her; it appealed to no want in her; even the instinct was lacking.   John Sparhawk had clung to the rigid faith of his fathers with a desperation which Patience, child as she was, had half divined. He had had prayers night and morning, and compelled his daughter to learn her catechism and many chapters of the Bible. After his death Mr. Foord took her to church on Sunday mornings and occasionally read her a little lecture. She listened respectfully, but felt no interest.

Nevertheless, when alone in her tower at night, when she had set her foot on its lowest step with deliberate intent to get as high above the earth as she could, she was conscious of an upreaching of the spiritual entity within her, a wordless demand for the something higher and holier of which the supreme beauty of the Universe is symbolical.

V

THE next morning, Patience, after helping her convalescent parent to get breakfast, stood on the porch debating whether she should go over to Mr. Thrailkill's ranch and see Rosita or spend the day in Mr. Foord's library.

The scholars of Colton Hall had a week's vacation, and how to make the most of seven long days of freedom in exquisite spring weather was a serious question.

As she hesitated she bethought herself of Solomon. She ran to the safe, and gingerly extracting a piece of raw meat wrapped it in a newspaper, and went over to the Mission. The owl had not moved, apparently, from the spot where he had taken his indignant stand the night before. When he scented the meat, however, he walked majestically forward, and taking no notice whatever of Patience, began at once upon the meal she spread at his feet.

Patience had decided in favour of the library, and started leisurely for Monterey. The ocean rested heavily after its labour of the night, swinging forward at long intervals with deep murmur, or throwing an occasional iridescent cloud of spray about Point Lobos. The keen air sparkled under a flood of golden light. The earth was green with the deep rich green of spring. Great bunches of it sprang from even the ragged mountain side, and long blades struggled to life between the broken tiles of the old Mission. Patience crossed the valley through beds of golden poppies and pale blue baby-eyes struggling with infantile pertinacity to raise themselves above the waving grass. She plucked a poppy and held her nose in the great cup that covered half her face. She liked the slight languor its heavy perfume induced.

She climbed the hill, and the woods shut out the world. Patience forgot her destination and wandered happily and aimlessly in the dim fragrance. She plucked some pine needles, and rubbing their juices free pressed her hands about her face.   On the whole she preferred their pungent freshness to the poppy.

After a time she began to skip over the carpet of yellow violets and to sing in a high childish treble.   She was only a happy little girl with her lungs full of oxygen, her veins warmed by the sun, her heart exhilarated with the surpassing beauty of the morning.   She threw pebbles at the squirrels and laughed loudly when they scampered up the stately trees.   Spiritual problems did not trouble her, and social trials were forgotten.

She dawdled away the earlier hours of the morning in the woods, then descending the hill on the town side, regained her severe and elderly demeanour.   The ocean was not visible here, but a bay bluer than sapphire curved into sands whiter than marble dust.   The sun shone down on the red-tiled white adobes, on the high garden walls pink with Castilian roses, as gaily as in the old Arcadian time.   But alas! it shone also on cheap wooden cottages and shops which had invaded even the hill on the right, where once a few stately mansions stood alone.

The town was very quiet.   It was always quiet. Some holy unheard voice seemed ever saying "Hush!" As Patience walked down Alvarado Street to the Custom House, she saw a slender brown woman watering the roses behind her garden wall.   She had been the belle of Monterey in her time, "La Tulita," and tradition had it that she still watered a rose-bush which General Sherman had planted.

On the next block several dark lads sat on a fence in the approved Montereño style, smoking *cigaritos*.   As Patience passed they lifted their caps as gallantly as ever *caballero* had done, although they did not fling them at her feet.

She saw no one else until she reached the Custom House. Mr. Foord stood on the corridor that overhung the rocks. He was a large round-shouldered man, with a benign face the colour of aging marble and a brow of the old time intellectual type. The eyes behind his spectacles were dim and kind. The lower part of his face was humorous and stern. He wore a silk hat, a well-brushed suit of broadcloth, and carried a gold-headed cane.

"You're going to town!" cried Patience.

"I am," he said smiling, "and I suppose you are going to read your eyes out in the library. Well, I'll not be back until to-morrow, so you'll have things all your own way. Tell Lola to cook you some dinner. I must be off."

"Bring me a box of candy," she commanded, as she stood on tiptoe to give him the little peck she called a kiss. It was her mark of supreme consideration.

He promised, and she went into the library, a large room opening on the corridor, where many a great ball had been given in the days before and after the Americans came. A half dozen old-fashioned bookcases, crowded with books, stood against the walls of the low room. The books were bound in spotted calf or faded cloth, black cloth with peeling gilt letters. One large case contained John Sparhawk's library, and Patience knew that it was practically hers. The floor was covered with a thick red carpet. A large easy-chair was drawn before the deep fire-place, in which a huge log crackled: it was still winter within adobe walls.

"Altogether," thought the philosopher of fifteen, as she flung her sunbonnet on the floor, "I guess that so

long as I've got my tower and the woods and this room,
I'm not so badly off as some."

She roamed about the room, opening the doors of the
bookcases in turn.   One case had been filled with
books selected for her especial use, but Mr. Foord had
not forbidden her the freedom of the others, being
wiser than many guardians.   Nevertheless, certain books
were placed on top shelves, their titles concealed
beneath the moulding of the case, and Patience had
looked speculatively at them more than once.   To-day
they exerted a peculiar fascination.   And it was rarely
that she was alone in the library.

She possessed an investigating and tentative mind, and
this forbidden territory appealed eloquently to her
unruly will.   But to get them out was not an easy task.
They were tightly packed, and the moulding was like
unto a prison bar.   But Patience was a person of
resource.   She gave one of the books a smart thump,
and it slanted inward.   She inserted her thumb under
its lifted edge and worried it out.   It was a small
volume bound in black, its lettering worn away.   She
opened it and glanced curiously at the titlepage.
"Boccaccio's Decameron" winked invitingly.   The
pages were spotted with yellow.   The drawings looked
as if the stories might be reasonably interesting.

Patience curled herself in the deep window-seat,
quite sure that she had found a treasure.   The book had
a furtive and apologetic air.   "I have grown old, at
least," it seemed to say.   "I am but an elderly rake,
and can only mumble of the past."

She read a few stories, then put the book back in its
place with a resentful shove.   Being wholly without the
knowledge for which Eve pined, the stories were stupid

and meaningless to her. She took down a thick volume bound in ragged calf. On the back was one large word, "Byron." The leaves of this book were spotted too, but on the leaves were poems, and she loved poetry. Even when it was uninteresting she enjoyed the rhythm. She returned to the window-seat, and child-like, looked at the pictures first. The portrait of Byron she fell in love with immediately, and knocking her composite off its pedestal, lifted that proud passionate face to the station of honour.

There was an immense-eyed picture of the Bride of Abydos which she thought looked like Rosita, and one of the Corsair dashing in upon his segregated love : —

"My own Medora, sure thy song is sad!"

Francesca and Paola gazed at each other across a table : —

"That day no further leaf we did uncover."

A castle which looked older than the book loomed massively from the page : —

"Lake Leman lies by Chillon's walls."

Never having heard of Byron, she was unable to enlarge her knowledge at once with his most celebrated creations ; but she liked the looks of Conrad and Medora, and plunged into their fortunes. She read every line of the poem, and when she had finished she read it over again. Then she stared at the breakers booming to the rocks on the opposite horn of the crescent, her eyes expanded and filled with a wholly new light. She might be unlettered in woman's wisdom, but the transcendent passion, the pounding vitality of the poet, carried straight to intuition. The insidious elixir drifted into the crystal stream. That incomparable objectivity

sang the song of songs as distinctly into her brain as
had it gathered the sounds of life for twenty years.
Her cheeks were flushed, her eyes were bright. She
felt as if she were a musical instrument upon which
some divine unknown music were vibrating; and as
she was wont to feel in the tower — but with a substratum of something quite different. She was filled
with a soft tumult which she did not in the least comprehend, and happy. She looked almost beautiful.

After a time she read "The Bride of Abydos," and
dreamed over that until she discovered that she was
hungry. She had forgotten to order dinner, and went
to the kitchen to beg a crust.

Lola, large, unwhaleboned, vibrating porcinely with
every motion, her brown coarsely moulded face beaming with good nature, her little black eyes full of
temper and kindness, her black hair in a neat small
knot, an unspotted brown and yellow calico garment
secluding her person, stood at a sink in a kitchen as
brilliantly clean as a varnished boot. Even the corners
shone like glass, Patience often observed with a sigh.
The two tables were scrubbed daily. The stove was
black, the windows white. Not a pan nor a dish save
those in the sink was in sight.

Patience made a sudden dash, a leap, and alighted
on Lola's back, encircling the yielding waist with her
supple legs. The woman emitted a hoarse shriek, then
laughed and pinched the legs. Patience plunged her
cold hands into the creases of Lola's neck, gathering a
quantity into the palms. She was unrebuked. There
were a few persons that loved Patience, and Lola was
of them.

"*Pobrecita!*" she exclaimed. "You are cold, no?"

"*Mucho frizo*," murmured Patience, sliding the back of her hands down the mountainous surface of Lola's. "And hungry, *madre de dios.*"

"Hungry? You no have the dinner? When you coming?"

"Hours ago, Lola. How cruel of you not to call me to dinner! How mean and piggish to eat it all yourself!".

"Ay, no call me the names. How I can know you are here *si* you no tell? Why you no coming here straight before going to the *librario?*"

"I forgot, Lola *mia;* and then I became — interested. But do give me something to eat."

"*Si.*" And with Patience still on her back Lola waddled to the cupboard and lifted down the remains of a corn cake rolled about olives and cheese and peppers.

"An *enchilada!*" said Patience. "Good."

Lola warmed the compound, and spread a napkin on a corner of one of the tables; then, suddenly unloosening Patience's arms and legs, tumbled her headlong into a chair, laughing sluggishly as she ambled off. Patience ate the steaming *enchilada* as heartily as had Byron never been. In a moment she begged for a cup of chocolate.

"*Si,*" said Lola, "I have some scrape already;" and she brewed chocolate in a little earthen pot, then beat it to froth with her *molinillo.* Patience kicked her heels together with delight, and sipped it daintily while Lola stood by with fat hands on fat hips in reflex enjoyment.

"Like it, *niña?*"

"You bet." Then after a moment she asked dreamily: "Lola, were you ever in love?"

" *Que !* Sure. Was I not marry? Poor my Pedro !
How he lika the *enchilada* and the chocolaty; and
the lard cakes and the little pig cooking with onions.
And now the worms eating him. Ay, yi !" and Lola sat
herself upon a chair and wept.

VI

As Patience walked home through the woods subse-
quently to a long afternoon with Byron, she was hazily
sensible that she had stepped from one phase of girlhood into another. She had an odd consciousness of
gazing through a veil of gauze upon an exquisite but
unfamiliar landscape over which was a dazzle of sunlight. She by no means understood the mystery of her
nature as yet; she was technically too ignorant; but
instinct was awake, and she felt somewhat as when she
had drained the poppy cup for long. She was in that
transition state when for the first and last time passion
is poetry.

She arrived home in time to get supper. Mrs.
Sparhawk was unexpectedly sober, and very cross.

" My land, Patience Sparhawk !" she exclaimed, as
her daughter opened the door and untied her sunbonnet, "seems to me you might help cook dinner in
vacation instead of being off all day reading books or
playing with that Spanish girl."

" Seems to me," said Patience, restored to her
practical self, " that as you 're twice as big as I am and
twice as strong, you 're pretty well able to get it yourself. And as it 's your fault there ain't any servant in

this house, I don't see why I should make one of myself for you. Seems to me you 're fixed up."

Mrs. Sparhawk blushed, and smoothed her hair consciously. The hair had been washed, and was decorated with a red bow. She wore a garment of turkey red calico with a bit of cheap lace at the throat and wrists. Her face was plastered with a whitewash much in vogue. She looked handsome, but evil, and Patience stared at her with an uneasiness she was not able to analyse. She turned away after a moment.

" I 'd put on an apron," she remarked drily. " You might get spots on that gorgeous window curtain dress of yours."

At that moment the man Oscar entered the room. He uttered a note of admiration which made Patience turn about sharply. He was gazing upon Mrs. Sparhawk's enhanced charms with an expression which Patience did not understand, but which filled her with sudden fury.

"Here !" she exclaimed roughly, "go into the dining room until supper 's ready. This kitchen ain't big enough for three."

The man moved his eyes and regarded her angrily.

" Who 's boss here?" he demanded.

" It 's not your place to ask questions. You 're hired to work outside, and when you come into this house there 's only one place for you. Now go into the other room." Her eyes were flashing, and she had drawn up her shoulders. The man backed away from her much as dogs do when cats give warning.

" That girl gives me a chill. I hate her," he muttered to his mistress.

3

Mrs. Sparhawk gave a loud laugh which covered her embarrassment, and slapped him heartily on the shoulder. "Go in, go in," she said. "What's the use of family quarrels?"

The man slunk away, and Patience went about her work with vicious energy. She fried liver and baked biscuits while her mother stirred the steaming cherries and brewed tea. When supper was ready she filled Oscar's plate first and served him last, not hating herself in the least for her spite and spleen. After Mrs. Sparhawk had taken her place at the head of the table even her exuberant beauty could not dispel the frown on the hired man's brow, until, to Patience's disgust, she divined the cause of his surliness, and deftly exchanged her plate for his.

VII

THAT night Patience did not go to her tower, but wandered over the dark fields, a drooping forlorn little figure in the crawling shadows. She felt dull and tired and disheartened. By nine o'clock she was asleep. She awoke as fresh as the morning. When Mr. Foord returned from San Francisco in the afternoon he found her curled in the easy-chair by his fire. She started guiltily as he entered, then tossed her head defiantly, let Byron slide to the floor, and went forward to kiss him.

As he was about to take the chair she had occupied he espied the fallen volume. He lifted it hastily.

"What is this?" he demanded.

Patience blushed furiously, but set her lips with an expression he understood.

"It's Byron, and I'm going to read it all. I've read a lot."

He shifted the book from one hand to the other for a moment, his face much perturbed. Finally he laid it on the table, merely remarking: "Sooner or later, sooner or later."

Patience offered him a piece of the candy he had brought her; but he preferred his pipe, and she perched herself on the arm of his chair and ate half the contents of her box without pause. She had not yet learned the subtle delights of the epicure, and to enjoy until capacity was exhausted was typical of her enthusiastic temperament. When she could no longer look upon the candy without a shudder she climbed to the old gentleman's shoulder and scratched his bald pate with her ragged nails. It was her emphatic way of expressing gratitude, and beloved by Mr. Foord above pipe and *enchilada*.

Patience took Byron home with her that evening, Mr. Foord merely shrugging his shoulders. After supper she read until dark, then hid the book under the bed and went over to the tower. She ran up the twisted stair, and astonished the owl by clasping him in her arms and kissing him passionately. He manifested his disapproval by biting at her shoulder fiercely. She shrieked and boxed his ears smartly. He flapped his large wings wildly. A battle royal was imminent in that sacred tower where once the silver bells had called the holy men to prayer. But Patience suddenly broke into a laugh and sank on her knees by the window, while Solomon retreated to the wall, and regarded her with a round unwinking stare, brooding over problems which he did not in the least understand.

Patience brooded also, but her lids drooped, and she barely saw the beauty of ocean and rock and spray. The moon was not yet up, and the half revealed intoning sea was full of mystery.

She was conscious that her mood was not quite what it had been during her last visit. All of that was there — but more. She felt higher above the earth than ever before, but more conscious of its magnetism. Something hummed along her nerves and stirred in her veins. Her musings shaped to definite form, inasmuch as they assumed the semblance of man. Inevitably Byron was exhumed for duty; and if his restless soul were prowling space and Carmel Valley, his famous humour, desuetous in Eternity, must have echoed in the dull ears of roaming shapes.

Beside the white face of the child was the solemn and hebraic visage of the owl. Some outworn chord of Solomon's youth may have been stirred by his friend's tumultuous greeting, for he had stepped, with the dignity of his years, to her side, and stood regarding, with introspective stare, the reflection of the rising moon.

Patience did not see him. She was gazing upon Byron, whose moody passionate face was distinctly visible among the stars. Alas ! her vision was suddenly obscured by a hideous black object. A bat flew straight at Carmel tower. Patience sprang to her feet, tossed her skirt over her head, and fled down the stair. The owl stepped to the stair's head and gazed into the winding darkness, his eyes full of unutterable nothing.

VIII

ON Monday school re-opened, and Patience was late as usual. She loitered through the woods, conning her lessons, having been too much occupied with her poet to give them attention before. As she ascended the steps of the schoolhouse the drone of the Lord's Prayer came through the open window, and she paused for a moment on the landing, swinging her bag in one hand and her tin lunch-pail in the other.

She was not a picturesque figure. Her sunbonnet was of faded blue calico dotted with white. The meagre braid projecting beneath the cape was tied with a shoe string. The calico frock was faded and mended and much too short, although the hem and tucks had been let out. The copper-toed boots were of a greyish-green hue, and the coarse stockings wrinkled above them. The nails of her pretty brown hands looked as if they had been sawed off. But the eyes under the old sunbonnet were dreamy and happy. The brain behind was full of new sensations. In the sparkling atmosphere was an electric thrill. The day was as still as only the days of Monterey can be. The pines and the breakers had never intoned more sweetly.

A voluminous A—men! startled Patience from her reverie. She went hastily within, hung her bonnet and pail on a peg, and entered the schoolroom, smiling half deprecatingly half confidently, at Miss Galpin. The young teacher's stern nod did not discompose her. As she passed Rosita she received a friendly pinch,

and Manuela looked up and smiled; but while traversing the width of the room to her desk she became
aware of something unfriendly in the atmosphere. As
she took her seat she glanced about and met the
malevolent eyes of a dozen turned heads. One girl's
lip was curled; another's brows were raised significantly, as would their owner query: "What could
you expect?"

Patience blushed until her face glowed like one of
the Castilian roses on the garden wall • opposite the
window.   "They've found out about Byron," she
thought.   "Horrors, how they'll tease me!"

School girls have a traditional habit of "willing" each
other to "miss" when in aggressive mood. To-day
some twenty of the girls appeared to have concerted to
will that Patience should forget what little lore she had
gathered on her way to school. Patience, always sen-
sitive to impressions, was as taut as the strings of
an Æolian harp from her experience of the past week.
Such natures are responsive to the core to the psycho-
logical power of the environment, and once or twice
this morning Patience felt as if she must jump to her
feet and scream. But even at that early age she divined that the sweetest revenge is success, and she
strove as she had never striven before to acquit herself
with credit.

All morning the silent battle went on. Miss Galpin,
who was beloved of her pupils because she was pretty
and dressed well, was a graduate of the San Francisco High School, and an excellent teacher. Frankly
as she liked Patience she had never shown her any
partiality in the schoolroom; but to-day, noting the
antagonism that was brought to bear on the girl, she

exerted all her cleverness to assist her in such subtle fashion that Patience alone should appreciate her effort. In consequence, when the morning session closed, Patience wore the doubtful laurels and the bad blood was black.

As the girls trooped down into the yard Rosita laid her arm about Patience and endeavoured to lead her away. Manuela conferred in a low tone with the foe, voice and gestures remonstrant. But there was blood in the air, and Patience squared her shoulders and awaited the onslaught. Incidentally she inspected her nails and copper toes.

Several of the girls walked rapidly up to her. They were smiling disagreeably.

" Can't you keep her at home? ". asked one of them.

" Think she 'll marry him?" demanded another.

Patience, completely taken aback, glanced helplessly from one to the other.

" What do you mean?" she asked.

" Come, Patita," murmured Rosita, on the verge of tears.

Manuela exclaimed : " You are fiends, *fiends!*" and walked away.

" Mean? Do you mean to say she got off without you knowing it?"

" Knowing what?" A horrible presentiment assailed Patience. Her fingers jerked and her breath came fast.

" Why," said Panchita McPherson, brutally, " your mother was in here Saturday night with her young man and regularly turned the town upside down. They were thrown out of three saloons. Can't you keep her at home?"

Patience stared dully at the girls, her dry lips parted. She knew that they had spoken the truth. She had gone to bed early on Saturday night. Shortly afterward she had heard the sound of buggy wheels and Billy's uncertain gait. Many hours later she had been awakened by the sound of her mother stumbling upstairs; but she had thought nothing of either incident at the time.

Panchita continued relentlessly, memories of many class defeats rushing forward to lash her spleen : " You 'll please understand after this that we don't care to have you talk to us, for we don't think you 're respectable." Whereupon the other girls, nodding sarcastically at Patience, entwined their arms and walked away, led by the haughty Miss McPherson.

For a few moments Patience hardly realised how she felt. She stood impassive; but a cyclone raged within. All the blood in her body seemed to have rushed to her head, to scorch her face and pound in her ears. She wondered why her hands and feet were cold.

"Come, Patita, don't mind them," said Rosita, putting her arm round her comrade. "The mean hateful nasty — *pigs !*" Never before had the indolent little Californian been so vehement; but Patience slipped from her hold, and running through a gate at the back of the yard crouched down on a box. Rosita's words had broken the spell. She was filled with a volcano of hate. She hated the girls, she hated Monterey, she hated life; but above all she hated her mother.

After a time all the hate in her concentrated on the woman who had made her young life so bitter. She had never liked her, but not until the dreadful moments just past had she realised the full measure of her inheritance. The innuendoes she had not understood, but it was enough to know that her mother had disgraced her publicly and insulted her father's memory. Her schoolmates she dismissed from her mind with a scornful jerk of the shoulders. She had beaten them too easily and often in the schoolroom not to despise them consummately. They could prick but not stab her.

The bell rang ; but she had an account to settle, and bonnetless she started for home.

Mrs. Sparhawk was sitting on the porch reading a novel when Patience walked up to her, snatched the book from her hand, and flung it into a rose-tree. The woman was sober, and quailed as she met her daughter's eyes. Patience had walked rapidly under a hot sun. Her face was scarlet, and she was trembling.

"I hate you!" she sobbed. "I hate you! It does n't do any good to tell you so, but it does me good to say it."   .

The girl looked the incarnation of evil passions. She was elemental Hate, a young Cain.

"I wish you were dead," she continued. "You 've ruined every bit of my life."

"Why — what — what — " mumbled the woman. But the colour was coming to her face, and her eyes were beginning to glitter unpleasantly.

"You know well enough what. You were in town drunk on Saturday night, and were in saloons *with a farm hand*. To make a brute of yourself was bad enough — but to go about with a common man! Are you going to marry him?"

Mrs. Sparhawk laughed. "Well, I guess not."

Patience drew a quick breath of relief. "Well, that's what they're saying — that you're going to marry him — a man that can't read nor write. Now look here, I want one thing understood — unless you swear to me you'll not set foot in that town again I'll have you put in the Home of the Inebriates — There! I'll not be disgraced again; I'll do it."

Mrs. Sparhawk sprang to her feet, her face blazing with rage. "You will, will you?" she cried. She caught the girl by the shoulders, and shaking her violently, boxed first one ear, then the other, with her strong rough hands. For an instant Patience was stunned, then the blood boiled back to her brain. She screamed harshly, and springing at her mother clutched her about the throat. The lust to kill possessed her. A red curtain blotted even the hated face from sight. Instinctively she tripped her mother and went down on top of her. The crash of the body brought two men to the rescue, and Patience was dragged off and flung aside.

"My land!" exclaimed one of the men, his face white with horror. "Was you going to kill your ma?"

"Yes, that she was," spluttered Mrs. Sparhawk, sitting up and pulling vaguely at the loose flesh of her throat. "She'd have murdered me in another minute."

Patience by this time was white and limp. She crawled upstairs to her room and locked the door. She sank on the floor and thought on herself with horror.

"I never knew," she reiterated, "that I was so bad. Why, I'm fifteen, and I never wanted to kill even a bird before. I wouldn't learn to shoot. I'd never drown a kitten. When the Chinaman stuck a red-hot poker through the bars of the trap and burnt ridges in the live rat I screamed and screamed. And now I've nearly killed my mother, and wanted to. Who, who would have thought it?"

When she was wearied with the futile effort to solve the new problem, she became suddenly conscious that she felt no repentance, no remorse. She was horrified at the sight of the black veins in her soul; but she felt a certain satisfaction at having unbottled the wrath that consumed her, at having given her mother the physical equivalent of her own mental agony. Over this last cognisance of her capacity for sin she sighed and shook her head.

"I may as well give myself up," she thought with young philosophy. "I am what I am, and I suppose I'll do what I'm going to do."

She went downstairs and out of the house. She passed a group of men; they stared at her in horror. Then another little seed from the vast garden of human nature shot up to flower in Patience's puzzled brain. She lifted her head with an odd feeling of elation: she was the sensation of the hour.

She went out on Point Lobos and listened to the hungry roar of the waves, watched the tossing spray. Nature took her to her heart as ever, and when the day was done she was normal once more. She returned to the house and helped to get supper, although she refused to speak to her equally sullen parent.

IX

IT was several days before the story reached Monterey. When it did, the girls treated Patience to invective and contumely, but delivered their remarks at
long range. The mother of Manuela said peremptorily
that Patience Sparhawk should never darken the doors
of the Peralta mansion again, and even Mrs. Thrailkill
told the weeping Rosita that the intimacy must end.

Miss Galpin was horrified. When school was over
she took Patience firmly by the hand and led her up
the hill to her boarding-place, the widow Thrailkill's
ancestral home. The long low adobe house was trav-
ersed from end to end by a pillared corridor. It was
whitewashed every year, and its red tiles were renewed
at intervals, but otherwise the march of civilisation had
passed it by. Mrs. Thrailkill, large and brown, with a
wart between her kind black eyes, and a handsome
beard, was rocking herself on the corridor. When she
recognised the teacher's companion she arose with great
dignity and swung herself into the house.

Miss Galpin led Patience down the corridor to a
room at the end, and motioned her to a chair. Several
magazines lay on a table, and Patience reached her
hand to them involuntarily; but Miss Galpin took the
hand and drew the girl toward her. The young
teacher's brown eyes wore a very puzzled expression.
Even her carefully regulated bang had been pushed upward with a sudden dash of the hand. She was only
twenty-two, and her experience of human nature was
limited. Her ideas of life were accumulated largely

from the novels of Mr. Howells and Mr. James, whom
she revered; and neither of these gentlemen photo-
graphed such characters as Patience.   It had probably
never occurred to them that Patiences existed.   She
experienced a sudden thrill of superiority, then craved
pardon of her idols.

"Patience, dear," she said gently, "is this terrible
story true?"

"Yes, ma'am," said Patience, standing passively at
Miss Galpin's knee.

"You actually tried to kill your mother?"

"Yes, ma'am."

Miss Galpin gasped.   She waited a moment for a
torrent of excuse and explanation; but Patience was
mute.

"And you are not sorry?" she faltered.

"No, ma'am."

"Oh, Patience!"

"I'm sorry you feel so badly, ma'am.   Please don't
cry," for the estimable young woman was in tears, and
mentally reviling her preceptors.

"How can I help feeling terribly, Patience?   You
break my heart."

"I'm sorry, dear Miss Galpin."

"Patience, don't you love God?"

"No, ma'am, not particularly.   Leastways, I've
never thought much about it."

"You little heathen!"

"No, ma'am, I'm not.   My father was very religious.   But please don't talk religion to me."

"Patience, I don't know what to make of you.   I
am in despair.   You're not a bad girl.   You give me
little trouble, and I've always said that you had finer

impulses than any girl I've ever known, and the best
brain. You ought to realise better than any girl of
your age the difference between right and wrong. And
yet you have done what not another girl in the school
would do, inferior as they are — "

"How do you know, ma'am? I never thought I
would. Neither did you think I would. You can't
tell what you'll do till you do it."

Miss Galpin was distracted. She resumed hurriedly :

"I want you to be a good woman, Patience, — a good
as well as a clever woman. And how can you be good
if you don't love God ? "

"Are all people good the same way ? "

"Well, it all comes to the same thing in the end."
Miss Galpin blessed the evolution of verbiage.

"Are all religious people good ? "

"Certainly."

"These girls are religious, especially the Spanish
ones, and they've behaved to me like devils. So have
their mothers, and some of them go to five o'clock
mass."

"Girls are undisciplined, and mothers often have a
mistaken sense of duty."

"You are good, and Mr. Foord is good," pursued
the terrible child. "But you'd be just as good if you
were n't religious. It's born in you, and you're refined
and kind-hearted. Those people are just naturally vulgar, and religion won't make them any better."

Miss Galpin drew the girl suddenly to her lap and
kissed her. "I'm terribly sorry for you, dear," she
said. "I wish I understood you better, and could help
you, but I don't. I never knew any one in the least
like you. I worry so about your future. People that

are not like other people don't get along nicely in this world.   And you have such impulses !   But I love you, Patience, and I 'll always be your friend.   Will you remember this ? "

Patience was undemonstrative, but she kissed Miss Galpin warmly and arranged her bang.

" Now, let 's talk about something else," she said. " Are you going to get up those private theatricals for the night that school closes ? "

Miss Galpin sighed and gave up the engagement. " Yes," she said.   Then, hesitatingly : " Do you wish to take part ? "

" No, of course I don't.   I 'll have nothing more to do with those girls than I can help.   You can bet your life on that.   But I can help drill Rosita.   What 's the play ? "

" I 'll read it to you."   Miss Galpin took a pamphlet from a drawer and read aloud the average amateur concoction.   Rosita was to take the part of an indolent girl with the habit of arousing herself unexpectedly. In one act she would have to dash to the front of the stage and dance a parlour breakdown.

" I am afraid Rosita cannot act," said Miss Galpin, in conclusion, " but she is so pretty I could n't leave her out."

" Rosita can act," said Patience, emphatically. " I 've seen her imitate every actress that has been here, and take off pretty nearly every crank in Monterey.   And Mrs. Thrailkill can teach her one of the old Californian dances — and a song.   Rosita has a lovely voice, almost as pretty as a lark's."

" Really?   Well, I 'll talk to Mrs. Thrailkill and persuade her to forgive you, and then you can come here every afternoon and drill Rosita. And now will you promise me to be a good little girl?"

"Yes, ma'am — leastways I'll try. Good-bye," and Patience gave her a little peck, seized her sunbonnet, and went hurriedly out.

"I suppose," she thought as she sauntered down the hill, "I'd better go and have it out with Mr. Foord. It's got to come, and the sooner it's over the better. Poor man, I'll make it as easy for him as I can. It'll be harder on him than on me, for I'm used to it now."

The old gentleman was walking up and down the corridor as she turned the corner of the custom house. He looked very yellow and feeble, and supported himself with a stick.

"Oh, Patience!" he exclaimed.

For the first time Patience felt inclined to cry, but her aversion to display feeling controlled her. She merely approached and stood before him, swinging her sunbonnet.

"Don't let us talk about it," he said hastily.   "I have something else to say to you. Sit down."

They sat down side by side on a bench.

"You know," the old gentleman continued, "I have a half-sister in the east — Harriet Tremont, her name is — in Mariaville-on-Hudson, New York. She is the best woman in the world, the most sinless creature I ever knew, yet full of human nature and never dull. She is very religious, has given up her life to doing good, and has some eccentric notions of her own. She writes me dutifully twice a year, although we have not met for thirty, and in her last letter she told me she intended to adopt a child, rescue a soul as she called it, and furthermore that she should adopt the child of the most worthless parents she could discover in her work among the worthless. Since — lately — I have been thinking strongly of sending you to her. You must get away from here. You must have a chance in life. If you remain here you will grow up bitter and hard, and the result with your brain and temperament may be terrible. You are capable of becoming a very bad or a very good woman. You are still young — but there is no time to lose. Should you care to go?"

"Of course I should," cried Patience, enchanted with the idea of an excursion into unknown worlds. Then her face fell. "But I should n't like to be adopted. That is too much like charity."

"Is the ranch entirely mortgaged?"

Patience nodded.

"Well, let us look at it as a business proposition. You will be little expense to her — she is fairly well off; and one more in the household makes no appreciable difference. You will attend the public schools with the view to become a teacher, and when you are earning a salary you can repay her for what little outlay she may have made. Do you see?"

"Yes. I don't mind if you look at it that way."

"I 'll see your mother in a day or two. You don't think she 'll object, do you?"

"Object? What has she got to say about it?"

"A great deal, unfortunately. She is your legal guardian. But she does n't love you, and I think can be persuaded. I shall miss you, my dear. What shall I do without my bright little girl?"

Patience nestled up to him, and the two strangely assorted companions remained silent for a time watching the seagulls sweep over the blue bay. Then Mr. Foord drifted naturally into the past, and Patience grew romantic once more.

X

THAT night Patience felt no inclination for either bed or tower. She wandered over the field, entered the pine forest, and walked to the coast. The tall straight trees grew close together; their aisles were very gloomy. From the ground arose the ominous voices of the night, and the wind in the treetops moaned heavily. But Patience was not afraid. She revelled in the vast dark silence, and felt that the world was all her own.

As she left the forest she saw great clouds of spray tossed high into the starry dark, heard the ocean rush at the outlying rocks, breaking into mist or leaping to the shore. The sea lions were talking loudly; the sea-gulls, huddled on the high points of the coast, scolded hoarsely.

On the edge of the forest was a cabin. Patience walked toward it. She knew the old man that lived there. He was evidently awake, for the open window was yellow with light. As she passed it on her way to the door she glanced within. Her skin turned cold; her hair stiffened. A sheeted corpse lay on the bed. Candles burned at head and foot. Patience, brave as she was, abjectly feared the corpse. She believed that she could survive a ghost, but she knew that if shut up with a dead body for ten minutes she should go mad. To-night she would have fled shrieking were it not that the room had a living occupant.

In a chair beside the bed sat a man gazing at the floor, his chin dropped to his chest. He wore rough clothes, but they were the affectations of the gentleman, not the garb of the dead man and his friends. Nor had Patience ever seen so noble a head. The profile was beautiful, the expression mild and intellectual, and most melancholy.

Patience forgot her terror as she wondered who the stranger could be; but in a moment it was renewed tenfold. Down the ocean road from Monterey came a wild hideous yell. The man by the corpse raised his head apprehensively, rose as if to flee, then sank wearily to his chair again. The clatter of hoofs on the hard road mounted above the thunder of the waves. Patience staring into the dark suddenly saw the leaping fire of torches, and a moment later tall figures riding recklessly. The yelling was incessant and demoniac.

"The man murdered Jim and they're lynchers," thought Patience. She glanced about wildly. A small tree stood near. She scampered up the trunk like a squirrel, and hid in the branches. None too soon. In another moment those terrible figures were screaming and gesticulating before the hut.

The smoky flames revealed an extraordinary sight to Patience's distended eyes. These men were bearded like the men of modern civilisation, even their hair was properly cut; but they wore the garments of Greece and Japan, flowing robes of white and red; one dark sinister-looking being upheld a glittering helmet.

Patience rubbed her eyes. Did she dream over her Byron? But no mortal, none but the sheeted dead,

could have slept and dreamed in that infernal clamour.
Only the man by the bed sat immobile. He did not
raise his head. Out of the pandemonium of sound
Patience at last distinguished one word: "Charley!
Charley!" If "Charley" were the man within the
hut he gave no sign; nor when they threw back their
heads and as from one throat gave forth a rattling
volume of ribald laughter.

Suddenly Patience, who, seeing no rope, began to
recover her courage, noticed that one of the men had
ridden beneath her tree, taking no part in this singular
drama. Once he turned his head, and an aquiline
profile, fine and strong, with black hair falling above
it, was sharply revealed against the red glare. Impulsively Patience leaned down and touched his
shoulder. He looked up with a start, and saw a small
white face among the leaves.

"What on earth is this?" he asked. "Is it a
child?" His voice was rich and deep, with a gentle
hint of brogue.

"What are they?" asked Patience. "Are they real
devils, or only men? And are they going to kill him?"

The man laughed. "I certainly should ask the same
question if I had not happened to come with them.
Oh, they won't do any murder, unless they happen to
frighten some one to death. They're members of the
Bohemian Club of San Francisco — newspaper men and
artists — who are down here on a lark."

"Who's the man in there by him, and why do they
yell at him so?"

"Oh, he is a solitary spirit, a man of genius. He
got tired of them and gave them the slip to-night.
This is revenge."

"They have the Estrada house on Alvarado Street," said Patience. " I heard they were here." Then she noticed that her companion wore the common garb of American civilisation. " Why are n't you rigged up, too?" she asked.

" Oh, I 'm hardly one of them. I 'm only an Eastern man — a New Yorker — and am staying at Del Monte for a day or two. I rode over to see them this afternoon, and they insisted upon my staying for dinner. What on earth are you doing here by yourself at this time of night?"

Patience explained. Then she added wistfully, " I shall be frightened to death going home through those woods alone. I 'll imagine that that corpse and those dreadful-looking men are behind me at every step."

" Just drop onto my horse and I 'll take you home. I 'm pretty tired of all this." He raised his arms and lifted her down, placing her in front of him. " Lucky I had an English saddle," he said, and as he bent his head Patience could see that he was smiling. "Oh !" he added abruptly, " I have seen you before. Now — tell me where to go."

Patience directed him, and they cantered away unobserved.

"Where did you see me?" she asked, "and how odd that you should remember *me* !"

"You have wonderful eyes. Although I 'm an Irishman I won't go so far as to say they are pretty, but they look as if they had been born to see so much. It would be difficult to forget them. Upon me soul you are actually trembling. Did you never have a compliment before?"

" Never ! And I guess I 'll remember it longer than you remember my eyes. Where did you see me?"

"I was standing at the window of the house in Alva-rado Street when you came along from school with a dozen or more of the girls. You all stopped to gaze at a passing circus troupe, and — I noticed you first because you stood a little apart from the others."

"I usually do," said Patience, drily.

He did not add that, attracted by the eagerness of her gaze and her rapid changes of expression, he had asked who she was, and that a Montereño present had related the family history and her own notable per-formances in no measured terms. "She's got bad blood in her and the temper of Old Nick himself. She'll come to no good, homely as she is," the man had concluded. "Curious enough, the boys all like her and would spark her if they got a show; but she's hell-set on gettin' an education at present and does n't notice them much."

Patience made him talk on for the pleasure of hear-ing his voice. "Are you a real Irishman?" she asked.

"Well, I've been an American for twenty years, but there's a good deal of Irish left in me yet, especially in me tongue."

"I'd keep it, if I were you. It's nicer even than the Spanish. Do you think our voices are horrid?"

"I think that if you'd pitch yours a little lower it would be an improvement," he said, smiling. And Patience registered a vow which she kept. In after years when great changes had come upon her, her voice was envied and emulated.

As they left the forest and entered Carmel Valley Patience pointed to her home, then suddenly took the reins from his hand and directed the horse toward the Mission. The waning moon hung over the ocean, and the Mission stood out boldly.

"Come up to my tower," said Patience; "the view is *something!* That will be your reward. I never took any one there before."

"All right," he said, "I may as well make a night of it." He tethered his horse and followed her up the spiral stair.

"Solomon is not here," she said regretfully. "He's out foraging. Now!"

The young man walked to the window and inspected the view. Patience regarded him with rapt admiration. He was tall and strong and well dressed. She had never dreamed that anything romantic could really happen to her; and as she was sure that it would be her last experience as well as her first, she suddenly felt depressed and miserable, her imagination leaping to the finish.

He turned and met her eyes. "What are you thinking of?" he asked.

But Patience was too shy to tell him, and asked him if he liked the view.

"It's a jolly view and no mistake. You're not a happy child, are you?" he added, abruptly. With the enthusiasm and spontaneous kindness of his Irish blood he had conceived the idea of dropping a seed in this plastic soil, and was feeling his way toward the right spot.

"I don't know that I am," said Patience, haughtily. "I suppose some of those people told you things."

"Well, they did, that's a fact. But you mustn't get angry with me, please, for upon me word I like you better than any one I've met in California."

"Don't you live here?"

"My home is in New York, and I return to-morrow."

"Oh! Well, I don't see how I should interest you."

"You do, though, and that's all there is to it. I'm neither as cautious as an Englishman nor as practical as an American — though God rest the two of them; I mean nothing to their detriment. But there's a force in you, and force does n't go to waste, although it's more often than not misdirected. I can feel yours myself; and I'm told that you're the cleverest girl in the town as well as the proudest and most ambitious. Now, what do you intend to do with yourself?"

"I suppose I'll be a teacher; and if Mrs. Sparhawk has no objections I may go East soon and live with a religious old lady."

"Well, that's not so bad; only I doubt if that life will suit you any better than this." He put his finger under her chin and turned her face to the light. "I am a lawyer, you know," he added, "and features and lines and curves mean a good deal to me. You've got a good will, begad, and like all first-class American women, you'll keep your head up until you drop. And you have all her faculty of beginning life over again several times, if necessary. You'll never rust nor mould, nor write polemical novels if things don't go your way. You've got a good strong brain behind those eyes, and although you'll make mistakes of various sorts, you'll kick them behind you when you're done with them, begin over and be none the worse. Remember that no mistake is irrevocable; that there are as many to-morrows as yesterdays; that only the incapable has a past. It is all a matter of will as far as the world is concerned, and ideals as far as your own soul goes. No matter how often circumstances and your own weakness compel you to let go your own private ideals,

deliberately put them back on their pedestal the moment
you have recovered balance, and make for their attain-
ment as if nothing had happened. Then you'll never
acquire an aged soul and never lose your grip. Can
you remember all that? "

" You bet I can."

He laughed. " I believe you. I might add : Don't
love the wrong man, but I'll not throw away good
advice. You'll not be wholly guided by reason in
those matters. I will merely say, Rub the first experience in hard and let a long while elapse before your
second, or it will be the greater mistake of the two.
Your reactions will be very violent, I should say. Well,
I'll be going now."

" I'd rather you'd stay and talk."

" Would you? Well, being a lawyer, I know where
to stop. Besides, I'll have all those fellows after me if
I stay too long. We'll doubtless meet again. The
world is small these days."

Patience followed him reluctantly down the stair, and
he walked beside her across the valley, leading his
horse. When they reached the farmhouse he shook
hands with her warmly, wished her good luck, and rode
away. She ran up to her room, and, lighting a candle,
transcribed his words into an old copybook.

XI

Miss Galpin expostulated with Mrs. Thrailkill to such
effect that Patience spent two hours each afternoon in
the family garret rehearsing Rosita while the astonished

rats took refuge in the chimney. Patience could not act, but she had dramatic appreciation and an intellectual conception of any part not beyond her years. Rosita was not intellectual, but, as Patience had discerned, the spirit of Thalia was in her. She quickly became enamoured of her unsuspected resources and at the prospect of exhibiting herself on a platform. Not only did she rouse herself to something like exertion, but she faithfully followed the instructions of her strenuous teacher and discovered a talent for posing and little tricks of manner all her own. Her mother taught her the song and dance, which were to be the sensation of the evening.

It was on the fourth day that Patience, returning home late in the afternoon, met Mr. Foord in the woods. The old gentleman looked sad and perplexed, and Patience sprang upon the step of his buggy and demanded to know what was the matter.

"It's very odd," he said, "but she won't let you go."

"Won't let me go?" cried Patience, furiously. "Well, I'll go anyhow."

"You can't, my dear. The law won't let you."

"Do you mean to say that the law won't protect me from that woman?"

"I am afraid she has the best of it." He recalled the woman's angry cunning face, as he had pleaded with her, and shook his head. "You see she was never in the town in that condition before. The men out there are so devoted to her that — so she has informed me — they would swear to a man that they had never seen her drunk. And, you see, she's never abused you —the only time she struck you she had provocation

—you must admit that. You are under her control until you are eighteen, and I don't see that we can do anything. I'm very sorry. I never felt so defeated in my life."

" But for gracious goodness sake why won't she let me go? I'm no good to speak of about the place, and she certainly is n't keeping me for love."

" Well — I think it 's revenge. She remarked that she had a chance to pay up and she 'd do it."

" I 'll just run away, that 's all."

" The law would bring you back, and arrest me for abduction."

" I hate the law," said Patience, gloomily. "Seems to me I 'm always finding something new to hate."

" You must not hate, my child," and he quoted the Bible dutifully, although in entire sympathy with her. " That is what I am so afraid of — that you will become hard and bitter. I want to save you from that. Well, perhaps she 'll relent. I shall see her again and again. I must go on, Patience."

She kissed him and walked sullenly homeward. As she entered the kitchen her mother looked up and laughed. Her face was triumphant and malignant.

"You don't go," she said. "Not much. I 've got the whip hand this time and I 'll keep it. Here you 'll stay until you 're eighteen — "

Patience turned abruptly and ran upstairs. As she locked her door she thought with some satisfaction: "Now that I know myself I can control myself. If I 'd jumped on her then she 'd have fallen in the stove."

As her imagination had not dwelt at great length upon the proposed change the disappointment was not as keen as it might have been, much as she desired to leave Monterey.   Moreover, she was occupied with Rosita and the coming examinations.   And did she not have her Byron?   She rose at dawn and read him. In the evening she went over to the tower and declaimed him to the grey ocean whose passions were eternal.   The owl, who regarded Byron as a great bore, closed his eyes when she began and went to sleep. Sometimes — when the sun rode high — she sat upon the rubbish over Junipero Serra's bones, and with one eye out for rats and snakes and tarantulas, conned a new poem.   She liked the contrast between the desolation and death in the old ruin and the warm atmosphere of the poetry.   As often Byron was unheeded, and she dreamed of the mysterious stranger who had so magnetised her that she had forgotten to ask his name.   She had only to close her eyes to hear his voice, to recall the words which seemed forever moving in one or other chamber of her mind, to see the profile which she admired quite as much as Byron's.   As for the voice, it had a possessing quality which made her understand the wherefore of the thrilling notes of the male bird in spring-time.   She invested her ambitious young lawyer with all the dark sardonic melancholic fascinations of Lara, Conrad, Manfred, and Don Juan.   The wild sweet sting of spring was in her veins.   Her mind was full of vague illusions, very lovely and very strange, shifting of outline and wholly inexplicable.

XII

On the afternoon of the last day of school several of the girls decorated the hall with garlands and flags. Carpenters erected a stage, and Patience arranged the " properties." When the great night arrived and Monterey in its best attire crowded the room, no curtain in the sleepy town had ever been regarded with more complacent expectation. The Montereñas were thoroughly satisfied with their offspring, and performances of any sort were few.

The programme was opened by Manuela, who wore an old pink satin frock of her mother's cut short and trimmed with a flounce of Spanish lace. Her brown shining face looked good will upon all the world as she recited " The Wreck of the Hesperus." Then came a dialogue in which all the little participants wore white frocks and crimped hair.

Meanwhile, in the dressing-room, Rosita was limp in Patience's arms.

" Oh, Patita ! " she gasped, " I can't ! I can't ! I 'm frightened to death ! What shall I do ? "

" Do ? " cried Patience, angrily, who was so excited herself that she pumped Rosita's arms up and down as if the unfledged Thespian had just been rescued from the bay. " Do? You must brace up. When you get there you 'll be all right. And you *must not* get stage fright. Rosita, you *must* make a success. Remember you 've got the star part. Don't, *don't* make a fool of yourself."

"Oh, if you could only hold my hand," wailed Rosita.

"Well, I can't, and that's the end of it. Now! brace up quick." The prompter was calling in a loud whisper, —

"Miss Thrailkill, be ready when I say, 'Life.'"

"*Ay, dios de mi alma,*" almost sobbed Rosita.

Patience dragged her to the wings and held her there. When the cue was spoken she gave her a hard pinch, then a shove. Rosita gasped and disappeared.

Patience slipped round into the audience, her heart in her throat, her eyes black with excitement. If Rosita broke down she felt that she should have hysterics.

At first Rosita had nothing to say. Upon entering she had merely to fling herself upon a divan in an indolent attitude whilst the others carried on a spirited dialogue. Patience saw that she had managed to get to the sofa without falling prone, but also observed that her bosom was heaving. Nevertheless, when her time came she managed to drawl her lines, although with as little expression as she told her rosary. Patience stamped her foot audibly.

But as the play progressed it was evident that Rosita was recovering her poise. When she finally had to come forward she moved with all the indolent grace of her blood, and delivered her little speech with such piquant fire that the audience applauded loudly. And with that clatter of feet and hands a new light sprang into the Spanish girl's eyes, an expression half of surprise, half of transport. From that time on she acted in a manner which astonished even her instructor.

She looked exquisitely pretty. Her white rounded

neck and arms were bare. Her black soft hair hung to her knees, unbound, caught back above one little ear with a pink rose. Her dress was of black Spanish lace covered with natural roses. On her tiny feet she wore a pair of black satin slippers which had belonged to her grandmother and twinkled many a time to the music of El Son.

When, upon being twitted with her indolence, she suddenly sprang to the front of the stage, and after singing an old Spanish love-song to the music of her own guitar, danced El Son with all the rhythmic grace of the beautiful women of the old gay time, she was no longer an actress but an impersonator. The more the delighted audience applauded the more poetically she danced, the more significantly her long eyes flamed. Once when the applause deafened she swayed as if intoxicated. As the dance finished, her red lips were parted. She was panting slightly.

When the curtain fell Patience rushed into the dressing-room and embraced her rapturously. " Rosita ! " she cried, " you were simply, mag-*nif*-icent."

Rosita, who was trembling violently, hung about Patience's neck.

" Oh, Patita ! " she gasped. " I was in heaven. I never was so happy. You don't know what it is to have a hundred people thinking of nothing but you and applauding as if they were mad. Oh, I 'm going to act, act, act forever ! I never want to do anything else. And is n't my skin white? I wish I had two necks and four arms."

XIII

THE next morning prizes were distributed. Patience took most of them, but Rosita was still the sensation of the hour, although she had not passed an examination. At noon she had a luncheon party. She sat at the head of her table in a white dotted Swiss frock and Roman sash, and talked faster than she had ever talked in her life before. Altogether she was by no means the Rosita of twenty-four hours ago.

Mrs. Thrailkill had prepared a luncheon of old time Spanish dishes, and hovered, large and brown and placid, about a table loaded with chickens under mounds of yellow rice, *tamales*, and *dulces*. Patience, between Manuela and a young cousin of Rosita's, was not unhappy. Her prizes lay on the window seat, she liked good things, and was infected with the gaiety of the hour. True, she wore her old muslin frock and a plaid sash made from an ancient gown of her mother's, and the rest of the girls looked like a bed of newly blossomed flowers; but at fifteen the spirits rise high above trifles.

When she started for home she was as light of heart as her more favoured mates; but in the wood a dire affliction smote her. One of her teeth began to ache. She had seen her mother many times with head tied up and distorted face, and had wondered scornfully how any one could make a fuss about a mere tooth. Now, however, when her own suddenly felt as if impaled on a needle, she uttered a loud wail, and ran toward home as fast as her legs could carry her. She found her mother similarly afflicted, and a bottle of drops on the kitchen table. Mrs. Sparhawk condescended to apply the remedy, and the agony left as suddenly as it had come.

After supper Patience went over to her tower, and as ever floated between Carmel Valley and the stars, enveloped with warm ether, which swirled to towers and turrets inhabited by a projection of herself which she saw only as a lover. Unfortunately all this rapture was enacted in a strong draught. Even Solomen uttered a sound once or twice which resembled a sneeze. Again Patience's tooth was punctured by a red-hot needle. Her castles vanished. She caught her cheek with her hand, stumbled down the winding stair, and flew across the valley, the needle developing into a screw.

The house was quiet, the kitchen dark. She lit a candle and searched frantically for the drops. They were not to be found. Then it occurred to her that her mother must have taken them to her room, and she ran up the stair.

XIV

At dawn next morning Patience found herself on the summit of the mountain behind the house. Her progress thither had skimmed the surface of memory and left no trace.

The sea was grey, the sky was grey. A grey mist moved in the valley. Beyond, the wood on the hill loomed in faint black outline. The birds in the trees, the seagulls on the rocks, the very ocean itself, were

5

locked in the heavy sleep of early morning. Once, from the tower of the Mission, came the plaintive hooting of the owl.

After a time Patience plucked a number of stickers from her stockings, and wiped blood from her torn hands with a large leaf wet with dew. She clasped her hands inertly about her knees and stared down upon the ocean. Horror was in her sunken eyes. The skin of her face looked faded and old. Her nose and chin were as pinched as the features of the dead. She did not look like the same child. Nor was she.

Her eyes closed heavily, her head dropped. She roused herself. She felt that she had no right to do anything again so natural as to sleep. But suddenly she toppled over and lay motionless ; until the sun sent its slanting rays under her eyelids. Then she stretched herself lazily, rubbing her eyes, and smiling as children do when waking. But the smile froze to a ghastly grin.

She raised herself stiffly and descended the mountain, clinging to the brush, the stones rolling from beneath her feet. She ran across the valley and plunged into the pine woods, but did not linger in those fragrant aisles.

When she reached the edge of the town she paused and half turned back ; but there was one thing she dreaded more than to meet the people of Monterey, and she went on.

She skirted the town and made her way toward the Custom House by a roundabout path. She passed a group of boys, and averted her head with a gesture of loathing. One boy, a gallant admirer, ran after her.

"Patience !" he cried, "wait a minute." But Patience took to her heels and never paused until she reached the Custom House. The perplexed knight stood still and whistled.

" Well," he exclaimed to his jeering comrades, " I always knew Patience Sparhawk was a crank, but this lets *me* out."

Patience stood for a few moments on the rocks, then went slowly to the library and opened the door. Mr. Foord sat by the fire. He looked up with a smile.

" Ah, it 's you," he said. " I 'm very proud of you. — Why, what 's the matter? "

Patience, her eyes fixed on the floor, took a chair opposite him.

" What is it, Patience? "

She did not look up. She could not. Finally she moved her face from him and stared at the mantel.

" I 've left home," she said. " I 'd like to stay here for a while."

" Why, of course you can stay here. I 'll tell Lola to put a cot in her room. But what is the matter? Has your mother been drinking again? "

" I don't know."

" Has she struck you again? "

" No."

" Well, what is it, my dear child? You know that you are always more than welcome here ; but you must have some excuse for leaving home."

" I have an excuse. I can't tell it. Please don't say anything more about it. I don't think she 'll send for me."

" Well, well, perhaps you 'll tell me after a time. Meanwhile make yourself at home."

He was much puzzled, but reflected that Patience

was not like other children; and he knew Mrs. Sparhawk's commanding talent for making herself disagreeable. Still, he was shocked at her appearance; and as the day wore on and she would not meet his eye, but sat staring at the floor, his uneasy mind glimpsed ugly possibilities. At dinner she ate little and did not raise her eyes from her plate, although she made a few commonplace remarks.

At four o'clock Billy, the buggy, and a farm hand stopped before the Custom House. The man handed a note to Lola, asking her to give it to Patience.

The note read:

You come home — hear? If you don't, I'll see that you do.

M. SPARHAWK.

Patience went out to the man, who still sat in the buggy. "Tell her," she said, looking at Billy, "that I'm not going home, — not now nor at any other time. Just make her understand that I mean it."

The man stared, but nodded and drove off.

XV

AT midnight Patience was awakened by a frantic clamour in the street. "Those dreadful Bohemians," she thought sleepily, then sat up with thumping heart.

"They say your name, _niña_, no?" said Lola, whose sonorous slumbers had also been disturbed.

Patience slipped to the floor and looked through the window. The moon flooded the old town. The ruined fort on the hill had never looked more picturesque, the pines above more calm. In the hollow near the blue waters the white arms of Junipero Serra's cross seemed extended in benediction. The old adobes were young for the hour. One might fancy Isabel Herrara walking down from the long house on the hill, her *reboso* fluttering in the night wind, old Pio Pico, glittering with jewels, beside her.

And in the wide street before the Custom House, surrounded by a hooting mob, the refuse of the saloons, was a cursing gesticulating woman. Her black hair was unbound, her garment torn. She flung her fists in the face of those that sought to hold her.

"Patience Sparhawk!" she shrieked. "Patience Sparhawk! Come down here to your mother. Come down here this minute. Come, I say," and a volley of oaths followed, greeted with a loud cackling laugh by the rabble.

Patience saw Mr. Foord, clad in his dressing-gown, go forth. She flung on her clothes hastily and ran down the stair. Her mother and Mr. Foord were in the kitchen.

"Oh, she 'll come back," Mrs. Sparhawk was saying. "I 'll see to that. How do you like a row under your windows? Well, I 'll come here every night unless she comes home. You 'll put me in the Home of the Inebriates, will you? Think she 'll like to have that said of her mother when she 's grown up? Not Patience Sparhawk. I know her weak point. She 's as proud as hell, and I 'm not afraid of going to any Home of the Inebriates."

Patience pushed open the door. "I 'm going with you," she said. "Now get out of this house as fast as you can."

"Oh, Patience," exclaimed Mr. Foord. His old cheeks were splashed with tears.

"Oh, I'm so sorry. I'm so sorry," said Patience, her hands clenching and quivering. "I didn't think she'd do this, or I wouldn't have stayed. What a return for all your kindness!"

"Patience," said the old gentleman, "promise me that you will come to see me to-morrow. Promise, or I shall not let you go. She can do her worst."

"Well, I'll come."

She ordered her mother to follow her out of the back door that they might avoid the expectant mob. Mrs. Sparhawk walked unsteadily, but received no assistance from her daughter. If she had fallen, Patience could not have forced herself to touch her. Had the woman been a reeling mass of physical corruption, a leper, a small-pox scab, the girl could not have shrunken farther from her.

They did not speak until they ascended the hill behind the town and entered the woods. Patience never recalled that night without inhaling the balsamic odour of the pines, the heavy perfume of forest lilies, without seeing the great yellow stars through the uplifted arms of the trees. It was a night for love, and its guest was hate.

No more terrible conversation ever took place between mother and daughter. After that night they never spoke again.

XVI

THE next morning Patience, after breakfast, carried a
pair of tongs and a newspaper up to her room. She
spread the newspaper on the table, then with the
tongs extracted Byron from beneath the bed and laid
it on the paper. She wrapped it up and tied it se-
curely without letting her hands come in contact with
the cover. That same afternoon she carried the book
to the Custom House and threw it behind a row of tall
volumes in one of the cases. Long after, Mr. Foord
found it there and wondered. He was not at home
when she arrived. When he returned she was deep in
his arm-chair, reading Gibbon's " Rome." He was
not without tact, and determined at once to ignore the
events of the previous day and night.

" What ! " he exclaimed, " are you really giving
poor old Gibbon a trial at last? And after all your
abuse? But perhaps you won't find him so dry, after
all."

" I wish to read what is dry," said Patience. " I 'm
going to take a course in ancient history."

" No more poetry and novels ? "

"Not a line." She spoke harshly, and compelled
herself to meet Mr. Foord's eyes. Her own were as
hard and as cold as steel. All the soft dreaming light
of the past two months had gone out of them. They
were the eyes neither of a girl nor of a woman. They
looked the eyes of a sexless intellect.

Patience had done the one thing which a girl of
fifteen can do when crushed with problems; she had

twitched her shoulders and flung them off. She comprehended that her intellect was her best friend, and plunged her racked head into the hard facts which required utmost concentration of mind. The sweet vague dreams of the past were turned from in loathing. If she thought of them at all it was with fierce resentment that she had become conscious of her womanhood. The stranger was thrust out of memory. She went no more to the tower. The owl hooted in his loneliness, and she drew the bed-clothes over her ears. When she walked through the woods, to and from the town, she recited Gibbon in synopsis. She spent the day in Mr. Foord's library, returning home in time to get supper. She did her household duties mechanically, and the eyes of mother and daughter never met. The man Oscar kept out of her way.

Miss Galpin had gone to San Francisco and would return no more : she was to marry. Rosita was visiting in Santa Barbara. Manuela, now a young lady, was devoting the greater part of her time to the Hotel Del Monte, where the flower and vegetables of San Francisco gather in summer. She went up to the tanks in the morning and to the dances in the evening ; and informed Patience, one day as they met on the street, that she was having a perfectly gorgeous time, and had met a man who was too lovely for words.

The long hot days and the foggy nights wore slowly away. Patience grew thinner, her face harder. Mr. Foord did his best to divert her, but his resources were limited. She peremptorily forbade him to allude to the romance of Monterey, and he took her out in his old buggy and talked of Gibbon's " Rome."

Once they drove through the grounds of Del Monte,

— the trim artificial grounds that are such an anomaly in that valley of memories. On the long veranda of the great hotel of airy architecture people sat in the bright attire of summer. Matrons rocked and gossiped; girls talked eagerly to languid youths that sat on the railing. It was all as unreal to Patience as the fairyland of her childhood, when she had hunted for fays and elves in the wood. She stared at the scene angrily, for the first time feeling the sting of the social bee.

"A vain frivolous life those people lead," remarked Mr. Foord, who disapproved of The World. "A waste of time and God's best gifts, which makes them selfish and heartless. Empty heads and hollow hearts."

But Patience, gazing at those girls in their gay dainty attire, the like of which she had never seen before, experienced a sudden violent wish to be of them, empty head, hollow heart, and all. They looked happy and free of care. The very atmosphere of the veranda seemed full of colour and music. Above all, they were utterly different from Patience Sparhawk, blessed and enviable beings. Even the frivolity of the scene appealed to her, so sick unto death of serious things.

XVII

ONE day, late in September, Patience, as usual, left Monterey at half past four in order to reach home in time to cook the supper. Nature had smiled for so many successive days that she wondered if the lips so persistently set must not soon strain back and reveal the teeth. The sun, poised behind the pine woods, flooded them with yellow light. As Patience walked through the soft radiance she set her teeth and recalled the chapters of Thiers' " French Revolution," through which she had that day plodded. But her head felt dull. She realised with a quiver of terror that she was beginning to feel less like an intellect and more like a very helpless little girl. Once she discovered her curved arm creeping to her eyes. She flung it down and shook her head angrily. Was she like other people?

Mingling with the fragrance of the pines it seemed to her that she smelt smoke. She hoped that her woods were not on fire. She walked slowly, indisposed as ever to return home, the more so to-day as she felt herself breaking.

" I wish the sun would not grin so," she thought. " I 'll be glad when winter comes."

The smell of smoke grew stronger. She left the woods. A moment later she stood, white and trembling, looking down upon Carmel Valley. The Sparhawk farmhouse was a blazing mass of timbers. A volume of smoke, as straight and full as a waterspout, stood directly above it. Men were running about. Their shouts came faintly to her.

Patience pressed her hands convulsively to her eyes. She clutched her head as if to tear out the terrible hope clattering in her brain, then ran down the hill and across the valley, feeling all the while as if possessed by ten thousand devils.

" Oh, I 'm bad, bad, bad ! " she sobbed in terror. " I don't, I don't ! "

As she reached the scene the roof fell in. She

glanced hastily about. The men, withdrawn to a safe distance, were gathered round the man Oscar. One was binding his hands and face. As they saw Patience they turned as if to run, then stood doggedly.

" Where is she ? " Patience asked.

There was an instant's pause. The crackling of the flames grew louder, as if it would answer. Then one of the men blurted out: " Burnt up in her bed. She was drunk. We was all in the field when the fire broke out. When we got here Oscar tried to get at her room with a ladder, but it was no go. Poor old Madge."

Patience without another word turned and ran back to the woods. She ran until she was exhausted, more horrified at herself than she had been at any of her unhappy experiences. After a time she fell among the dry pine needles, her good, as she expressed it, still trying to fight down her bad. She felt that the demon possessing her would have sung aloud had she not held it by the throat. She conjured up all the horrible details of her mother's death and ordered her soul to pity; but her brain remarked coldly that her mother had probably felt nothing. She imagined the charred corpse, but it only offended her artistic sense.

Finally she fell asleep. The day was far gone when she awoke. She lay for a time staring at the dim arches above her, listening to the night voices she had once loved so passionately. At last she drew a deep sigh.

" I might just as well face the truth," she said aloud. "I'm glad, and that's the end of it. It's wicked and I'm sorry; but what is, is, and I can't help it. We're not all made alike."

XVIII

PATIENCE was once more installed in Lola's room. Mr. Foord applied for letters of guardianship, which were granted at once. But as he had feared, she was left without a penny. He wrote to his half-sister, asking her if she would take charge of his ward. Miss Tremont replied in enthusiastic affirmation. Miss Galpin invited Patience to spend two weeks with her in San Francisco, offering to replenish the girl's wardrobe with several of her own old frocks made over.

Those two weeks seemed to Patience the mad whirl of excitement of which she had read in novels. She had never seen a city before, and the very cable cars fascinated her. To glide up and down the hills was to her the poetry of science. The straggling city on its hundred hills, the crowded streets and gay shop windows, the theatres, the restaurants, China Town, the beautiful bay with its bare colorous hills, surprised her into admitting that life appearèd to be quite well worth living after all. When she returned to Monterey she talked so fast that Mr. Foord clapped his hands to his ears, and Rosita listened with expanded eyes.

" Ay, if I could live in San Francisco ! " she said, plaintively. " I acted all summer, Patita, but I got tired of the same people, and I want to go to the big theatres and see the real ones do it. I 'd like to hear a great big house applauding, only I 'd be so jealous of the leading lady."

Patience was to start, immediately after Christmas, by steamer for New York. Mr. Foord spent the last

days giving her much good advice.   He said little of
his own sorrow to part from her.   Once he had been
tempted to keep her for the short time that remained
to him, but had put the temptation aside with the sad
resignation of old age.   He knew Patience's imperative
need of new impressions in these her plastic years.

The day before she left she went over to Carmel to
say good-bye to Solomon.   He flapped his wings with
delight, although he could not see her, and nestled
close to her side in a manner quite unlike his haughty
habit.   Patience thought he looked older and greyer,
and his wings had a dejected droop.   She took him
in her arms with an impulse of tenderness, and this
time he did not repulse her.

"Poor old Solomon," she said, "I suppose you are
lonely and forlorn in your old age, but this old tower
would n't be what it is without you.   It 's too bad I
can't write to you as I can to my two or three other
friends, and you 'll never know I have n't forgotten you,
poor old Solomon.   Oh, dear!   Oh, dear!   I wonder
if owls do suffer too.   You look so wise and venerable,
perhaps you are thinking that lonely old age is terrible
—as I know Mr. Foord does."

Solomon pecked at her mildly.   Her gaze wandered
out over the ocean.   She wondered if a thousand years
had passed since she had dreamed her dreams.   Their
very echoes came from the mountains of space.

When she went away Solomon followed her to the
head of the stair.   She looked upward once and saw
him standing there, with drooping wings and head a
little bent.   The darkness of the stair gave him vision,
and he fluttered his wings expectantly, as she paused
and lifted her face to him.   But when she did not

return he walked with great dignity to his accustomed place against the wall, nor even lifted up his voice in protest.

The next morning Rosita accompanied her to the station and wept loudly as the train approached. But Patience did not cry until she stood in her stateroom with Mr. Foord.

BOOK II

BOOK II

I

PATIENCE watched the dusty hills of San Francisco, the sparkling bay alive with sail and spar, the pink mountains of the far coast range, the brown hills opposite the grey city, willowed and gulched and bare, the forts on rock and points, until the wild lurching of the steamer over the bar directed her attention to the unhappy passengers. In a short while she had not even these to amuse her, nothing but a grey plain and empty decks. At first she felt a waif in space; but soon a delightful sense of independence stole over her, of freedom from all the ills and responsibilities of life. The land world might have collapsed upon its fiery heart, so little could it affect her while that waste of waters slid under the horizon.

The few passengers came forth restored in a day or two. A husband and wife and several children did not interest Patience; neither did the captain's wife, in whose charge she was. A young girl with a tangle of yellow hair under a sailor hat was more inviting, but she flirted industriously with the purser and took not the slightest notice of Patience. Her invalid mother reclined languidly in a steamer chair and read the novels of E. P. Roe.

The only other passenger was an elderly gentleman who read books in white covers neatly lettered with

6

black which fascinated Patience. She was beginning to
long for books. The invalid lent her a Roe, but she
returned it half unread. As the old gentleman had
never addressed her, did not seem to be aware of her
existence, she could hardly expect a similar courtesy
from him.

She was glowering upon universal stupidity one
morning when he appeared on deck with a carpet bag,
from which, after comfortably establishing himself in
his steamer chair, he took little white volume after
little white volume. Patience's curiosity overcame her.
She went forward slowly and stood before him. He
looked up sharply. His black eyes, piercing from their
shaggy arches, made her twitch her head as if to fling
aside some penetrative force. His very beard, silver
though it was, had a fierce sidewise twist. His nose
was full nostrilled and drooped scornfully. The spectacles he wore served as a sort of lens for the fire of his
extraordinary eyes.

" Well? " he said gruffly.

" Please, sir," said Patience, humbly, " will you lend
me a book? "

" Book? I don't carry children's literature round
with me."

" I don't read children's literature."

" Oh, you don't? Well, not ' The Chatterbox,' I suppose ; but I have nothing of Pansy's nor yet of The
Duchess."

" I would n't read them if you had," cried Patience,
angrily. " Perhaps I 've read a good many books
that you have n't re-read so long ago yourself. I 've
read Dickens and Thackeray and Scott, and," with
a shudder, " Gibbon's ' Rome ' and Thiers' ' French
Revolution.' "

"Oh, you have? Well, I beg your pardon. Sit down, and I 'll see if I can find something for a young lady of your surprising attainments."

Patience, too pleased to resent sarcasm, applied herself to his elbow.

" Why are they all bound alike? " she asked.

"This is the Tauchnitz edition of notable English and American books. How is this?" He handed her a volume of Grace Aguilar.

" No, sir ! I 've tried her, and she 's a greater bore than Jane Austen."

" Oh, you want a love story, I suppose? " His accentuation was fairly sardonic.

" No, I don't," she said with an intonation which made him turn and regard her with interest. Then once more he explored his bag.

" Will this suit you? " He held out a copy of Carlyle's " French Revolution."

Patience groaned. " Did n't I tell you I 'd just read Thiers' ? "

" This is n't Thiers'. Try it." And he took no further notice of her.

Patience opened the volume, and in a few moments was absorbed. There was something in the storm and blare of the style which struck a responsive chord. She did not raise her head until dinner time. She scarcely spoke until she had finished the volume, and then only to ask for the second. For several days she felt as if the atmosphere was charged with dynamite, and jumped when any one addressed her. The owner of the Tauchnitz watched her curiously. When she had finished the second volume she told him that she did not care for anything more at present. She leaned over the railing

most of the day, watching the waves.   Toward sunset
the gentleman called peremptorily,—

" Come here."

Patience stood before his chair.

"Well, what do you think of it?" he demanded.
" Tell me exactly what your impressions are."

" I feel as if there was an earthquake in my skull
and all sorts of pictures flying about, and exploded
pieces of drums and trumpets, and kings and queens.
I think Carlyle must have been made on purpose to
write the French Revolution.   It was — as if — there
was a great picture of it made on the atmosphere, and
when he was born it passed into him."

" Upon my word," he said, "you are a degree or two
removed from the letters of bread and milk.   You are
a very remarkable kid.   Sit down."

Patience took the chair beside him.   " He made my
head ache," she added.   "I feel as if it had been '
hammered."

" I don't wonder.   Older heads have felt the same
way.   What 's your name?"

"Patience Sparhawk."

" Tell me all about yourself."

"Oh, there is n't much to tell," and she frowned
heavily.

"Don't look so tragic — you alarm me.   I 'm convinced there is a great deal.   Come, I want to know."

Patience gave a few inane particulars.   The old
gentleman snorted.   " It 's evident you 've never been
interviewed," he said grimly.   " Now, I 'll tell you who
I am, and then you won't mind talking about yourself.
There 's nothing so catching as egotism.   My name is
James E. Field.   I own one of the great newspapers of

New York, of which I am also editor-in-chief. Do
you know what that means? Well, if you don't, let me
tell you. It is to be a man more powerful than the
President of the United States, for he can make
presidents, which is something the president himself
can't do. He knows more about people's private affairs
than any of intimate relationship; he has his finger on
the barometer of his readers' brain; he can make
them sensational or sober, intellectually careless or
exacting; he can keep them in ignorance of all that is
best worth knowing of the world's affairs, by snubbing
the great events and tendencies of the day and vitiating
their brain with local crimes and scandals, or he can
illumine their minds and widen their brain cells by not
only enlarging upon what every intelligent person should
wish to know, but by making such matter of profound
interest; he can ignore science, or enlighten several
hundred thousand people; he can add to the happiness of the human race by exposing abuses and hidden
crime, or he can accept hush money and let the sore
fester; he can lash the unrest of the lower classes, or
chloroform it; he can use the sledge hammer, the
rapier, and the vitriol, or give over his editorial page to
windy nothings; he can demolish political bosses, or
prolong their career. In short, his power is greater than
Alexander's was, for he is a general of minds instead of
brute force."

"My goodness gracious!" exclaimed Patience. ·
"What sort of a paper have you got?"

He laughed. "Wait until you've lived in New
York awhile and you'll find out. Its name is the
'Day,' and it has made a president or two, and made
one or two others wish they'd never been born. By

the way, I didn't tell you much about myself, did I? The auxiliary subject carried me away. I'm married, and have several sons and daughters, and am off for a rest — not from the family but from the 'Day.' I've been round the world. That will do for the present. Tell me all about Monterey."

With consummate skill he extracted the history of her sixteen years. On some points she fought him so obstinately that he inferred what she would not tell. He ended by becoming profoundly interested. He was a man of enthusiasms, which sometimes wrote themselves in vitriol, at others in the milk of human kindness. His keen unerring brain, which Patience fancied flashed electric search lights, comprehended that it had stumbled upon a character waging perpetual war with the pitiless Law of Circumstance, and that the issue might serve as a plot for one of the mental dramas of the day.

"Your experience and the bad blood in you, taken in connection with your bright and essentially modern mind, will make a sort of intellectual anarchist of you," he said. "I doubt if you take kindly to the domestic life. You will probably go in for the social problems, and ride some polemical hobby for eight or ten years, at the end of which time you will be inclined to look upon your sex as the soubrettes of history. Your enthusiasm may make you a faddist, but your common sense may aid you in the perception of several eternal truths which the women of to-day in their blind bolt have overlooked."

A moment later he repented his generalisations, for Patience had demanded full particulars. Nevertheless, he gave her many a graphic outline of the various phases of current history, and was the most potent educational force that she had yet encountered. She preferred him to books and admired him without reserve, trotting at his heels like a small dog. His unique and virile personality, his brilliant and imperious mind, magnetised the modern essence of which she was made. There was nothing of the old-fashioned intellectual type about him. He might have induced the coining of the word " brainy," — he certainly typed it. Although he had the white hair and the accumulated wisdom of his years, he had the eyes of youth and the fist of vigour at any age. One day when two natives looked too long upon Patience's blondinity, as she and Mr. Field were exploring a banana grove during one of their brief excursions on shore, he cracked their skulls together as if they had been two cocoanuts.

Patience laughed as the blacks dropped sullenly behind. " How funny that they should admire me," she said. " I 'm not pretty."

" Well, you 're white. Besides, there is one thing more fascinating than beauty, and that is a strong individuality. It radiates and magnetises."

" Have I all that? " Patience blushed with delight.

He laughed good-naturedly. " Yes, I 'll stake a good deal that you have. You may even be pretty some day; that is, if you ever get those freckles off."

Inherent as was her passion for nature, she enjoyed the rich beauty of the tropics the more for the companionship of a mind skilled in observation and interpretation. It was her first mental comprehension of the law of duality.

As they approached New York harbour Mr. Field said

to her: "I think I'll have to make a newspaper woman of you. When you have finished your education, don't think of settling down to any such humdrum career as that of the school-teacher. Come to me, and I'll put you through your paces. If I'm not more mistaken than I've been yet, I'll turn out a newspaper woman that will induce a mightier blast of woman's horn. Think you'd like it?"

"I'd like to be with you," said Patience, on the verge of tears. "Sha'n't I see you again till I'm eighteen?"

"No, I don't want to see or hear from you again until you've kneaded that brain of yours into some sort of shape by three years of hard study. Then I'll go to work on a good foundation. You haven't told me if you'll take a try at it."

"Of course I will. Do you think I want to be a school-teacher? I should think it would be lovely to be a newspaper woman."

"Well, it isn't exactly lovely, but it is a good training in the art of getting along without adjectives. Now look round you and I'll explain this harbour; and don't you brag any more about your San Francisco harbour."

They entered through The Narrows, between the two toy forts. A few lone sentries paced the crisp snow on the heights of Staten Island, and looked in imminent danger of tumbling down the perpendicular lawns. The little stone windows of the earthen redoubts seemed to wink confidently at each other across the water, and loomed superciliously above the forts on the water's edge. Long Island, had the repose of a giant that had stretched his limbs in sleep, unmindful

of the temporary hamlets on his swelling front. Staten
Island curved and uplifted herself coquettishly under
her glittering garb and crystal woods. Far away the
faint line of the New Jersey shore, looking like one
unbroken city on a hundred altitudes, hovered faintly
under its mist. The river at its base was a silver
ribbon between a mirage and a stupendous castle of
seven different architectures surmounted by a golden
dome — which same was New York and the dome
of a newspaper. Then a faint fairy-like bridge, delicate
as a cobweb, sprang lightly across another river to
a city of walls with windows in them — which same
was Brooklyn. Under the shadow of the arches was
a baby island fortified with what appeared to be a large
Dutch cheese out of which the mice had gnawed
their way with much regularity. The great bay, blue
as liquid sapphire, was alive with craft of every
design : rowboats scuttled away from the big outgoing
steamers ; sails, white as the snow on the heights,
bellied in the sharp wind ; yellow and red ferry boats
gave back long symmetrical curves of white smoke ;
gaunt ships with naked spars lay at rest. On Liberty
Island the big girl pointed solemnly upward as if
reminding the city on the waters of the many mansions
in the invisible stars. Snow clouds were scudding
upward from the east, but overhead there was plentiful
gold and blue.

Patience gazed through Mr. Field's glass, enraptured,
and promised not to brag. As they swung toward the
dock he laid his hand kindly on hers.

"Now don't think I'm callous," he said, "because
I part from you without any apparent regret. You are
going to be in good hands during the rest of your early

girlhood, and I could be of no assistance to you; and I am a very busy man. Let me tell you that you have made this month a good deal shorter than it would otherwise have been; and when we meet again you won't have to introduce yourself. There are my folks, and there goes the gang-plank. Good-bye, and God bless you."

II

PATIENCE leaned over the upper railing, looking at the expectant crowd on the wharf, wondering when the captain would remember her. She felt a strong inclination to run after Mr. Field. As he receded up the wharf, surrounded by his family, he turned and waved his hand to her.

"Why couldn't he have been Mr. Foord's brother or something?" she thought resentfully. "I think he might have adopted me."

As the crowd thinned she noticed two elderly women standing a few feet from the vessel, alternately inspecting the landed passengers and the decks. One was a very tall slender and graceful woman, possessed of that subtle quality called style, despite her unfashionable attire. In her dark regular face were the remains of beauty, and although nervous and anxious, it wore the seal of gentle blood. Her large black eyes expressed a curious commingling of the spiritual and the human. She was probably sixty years old. At her side was a woman some ten years younger, of stouter and less elastic figure, with a strong dark kind intelligent face and an utter disregard of dress. She carried several bundles.

"Oh, has n't she come?" cried the elder woman. "Can she have died at sea? I am sure the dear Lord would n't let anything happen to her. Dear sister, *do* you see her?"

The other woman, who was also looking everywhere except at Patience, replied in a round cheerful voice : "No, not yet, but I feel sure she is there. The captain has n't had time to bring her on shore. The Lord tells me that it is all right."

"One of those is Miss Tremont," thought Patience. "I may as well go down. They appear to be frightfully religious, but they have nice faces."

She ran down to the lower deck, then across the gang-plank.

"I'm Patience Sparhawk," she said; "are you —" The older woman uttered a little cry, caught her in her arms, and kissed her. "Oh, you dear little thing!" she exclaimed, and kissed her again. "How I've prayed the dear Lord to bring you safely, and He has, praise His holy name. Oh, I am so glad to see you. I do love children so. We'll be so happy together — you and I and Him — and, oh, I'm so glad to see you."

Patience, breathless, but much gratified, kissed her warmly.

"Don't forget me," exclaimed the other lady. She had a singularly hearty voice and a brilliant smile. Patience turned to her dutifully, and received an emphatic kiss.

"This is my dear friend, my dear sister in the Lord, Miss Beale, Patience," said Miss Tremont, flurriedly, "and she wanted to see you almost as much as I did."

"Indeed I did," said Miss Beale, breezily. "I too love little girls."

"I'm sure you're both very kind," said Patience, helplessly. She hardly knew how to meet so much effusion. But something cold and old within her seemed to warm and thaw.

"You dear little thing," continued Miss Tremont. "Are you cold? That is a very light coat you have on."

Patience was not dressed for an eastern winter, but her young blood and curiosity kept her warm.

"Here comes the captain," she said. "Oh, no, I'm all right. I like the cold."

The captain, satisfying himself that his charge was in the proper hands, offered to send her trunk to Maria-ville by express, and Patience, wedged closely between the two ladies, boarded a street car.

"You know," exclaimed Miss Tremont, " I knew the Lord would bring you to me safely in spite of the perils of the ocean. Every night and every morning I prayed : *Dear* Lord, don't let anything happen to her, — and I knew He would n't."

"Does He always do what you tell Him?" asked Patience.

"Almost everything I ask Him, — that is to say, when He thinks best. Dear Patience, if you knew how He looks out for me — and it is well He sees fit, for dear knows I have a' time taking care of myself. Why, He even takes care of my purse. I'm always leaving it round, and He always sends it back to me — from counters and trains and restaurants and everywhere. And when I start in the wrong direction He always whispers in my ear in time. Why, once I had to catch a certain train to Philadelphia, where I was to preside at a convention, and I'd taken the wrong street car, and when I jumped off and took the right one, the driver said I could n't possibly get to the ferry in time. So I just shut my eyes and prayed ; and then I told the driver that it would be all right, as I had asked the Lord to see that I got there in time. The driver laughed, and said : 'W-a-a-l, I guess the Lord 'll go back on you this time.' But I caught that ferry-boat. *He* — the Lord — made it five minutes late. And it 's always the same. He takes care of me, praised be His name."

"You must feel as if He were your husband," said Patience, too gravely to be suspected of irreverence.

"Why, He is. Does n't the Bible say — " But the car began to rattle over the badly paved streets, and the quotation was lost.

Patience looked eagerly through the windows at purlieus of indescribable ugliness ; but it was New York, a city greater than San Francisco, and she found even its youthful old age picturesque. The dense throng of people in Sixth Avenue and the immense shop windows induced expressions of rapture.

"You don't live here, do you?" she said with a sigh.

"Oh, Mariaville is much nicer than New York," replied Miss Beale, in her enthusiastic way. "I hate a great crowded city. It baffles you so when you try to do good."

"Still they do say that reform work is more systematised here, dear sister."

"Forty-second Street," shouted the conductor, and they changed cars. A few moments later they were pulling out of the Grand Central Station for Mariaville.

Miss Beale had asked the conductor to turn a seat, and Patience faced her new friends. As they left the tunnel she caught sight of a tiny bow of white ribbon each wore on her coat.

"Why do you wear that?" she asked.

"Why, we 're W. C. T. U's," replied Miss Beale.

"Wctus?"

"Temperance cranks," said Miss Tremont, smiling.

"Temperance cranks?"

"Why, have you never heard of the Woman's Christian Temperance Union?" asked Miss Beale, a chill breathing over her cordial voice. "The movement has reason to feel encouraged all through the West."

"I 've never heard of it. They don't have it in Monterey, and I 've not been much in San Francisco."

"She 's such a child," said Miss Tremont. "How could she know of it out there? But now I know she is going to be one of our very best Y's."

"Y's?" asked Patience, helplessly. She wondered if this was the "fad" Mr. Field had predicted for her, then recalled that he had alluded once to the "Temperance movement," but could not remember his explanation, if he had made any. Doubtless she had evaded a disagreeable topic. But now that it was evidently to be a part of her new life she made no attempt to stem Miss Tremont's enthusiasm.

"The Y's are the young women of the Union; we are the W's. It is our lifework, Patience, and I am sure you will become as much interested in it as we are, and be proud to wear the white ribbon. We have done so much good, and expect to do much more, with the dear Lord's help. It is slow work, but we shall conquer in the end, for He is with us."

"What do you do, — forbid people to sell liquor?"

Both ladies laughed. They were not without humour, and their experience had developed it. "No," said Miss Tremont, "we don't waste our time like that."

She gave an enthusiastic account of what the Union had accomplished. Her face glowed; her fine head was thrown back; her dark eyes sparkled. Patience thought she must have been a beautiful girl. She had a full voice with odd notes of protest and imperious demand which puzzled her young charge. One would have supposed that she was constantly imploring favours, and yet her air suggested natural hauteur, unexterminated by cultivated humility.

" I should think it was a good idea," said Patience, with perfect sincerity.

" Oh, there 's dear Sister Watt," cried Miss Tremont, and she rose precipitately, and crossing the aisle sat down beside a careworn anxious-eyed woman who also wore the white ribbon.

" Come over by me until Miss Tremont comes back," said Miss Beale, with her brilliant smile. " Tell me, don't you love her already? Oh, you have no idea how good she is. She is heart and soul in her work, and just lives for the Lord. She sometimes visits twenty poor families a week, besides her Temperance class, her sewing school, her Bible Readings, her Bible class, and all the religious societies, of which she is the most active worker. She is also the Mariaville agent for the Society for Prevention of Cruelty to Children, and trustee of the Bible Society. You should hear her pray. I have heard all the great revivalists, but I have never heard anything like Miss Tremont's prayers. How I envy you living with her ! You 'll hear her twice a day, and sometimes oftener. She has a nice house on the outskirts of Mariaville. Her father left it to her twenty years ago, and she dedicated it to the Lord at once. It is headquarters for church meetings of all

sorts.   She has a Bible reading one afternoon a week.
Any one can go, even a servant, for Miss Tremont, like
all true followers of the Lord, is humble."

Patience reflected that she had never seen any one
look less humble than Miss Beale.   In spite of her old
frock she conveyed with unmistakable if unconscious
emphasis that she possessed wealth and full knowledge
of its power.

"You look so happy," Patience said, her curiosity
regarding Miss Tremont blunted for the present.   "Are
you?"

"Happy?   Of course I am.   I've never known an
unhappy moment in my life.   When my dear parents
died, I only envied them.   And have I not perfect
health?   Is not every moment of my time occupied?—
why, I only sleep six hours out of the twenty-four.   And
Him.   Do I not work for Him, and is He not always
with me?"

"They are so funny about God," thought Patience.
"She talks as if He were her beau ; and Miss Tremont
as if He were her old man she'd been jogging along
with for forty years or so.— Do you live alone?" she
asked.

"Yes—that is, I board."

"And don't you ever feel lonesome?"

"Never.   Is not He always with me?"   Her strong
brown face was suddenly illuminated.   "Is He not my
lover?   Is He not always at my side, encouraging me
and whispering of His love, night and day?   Why,
I can almost hear His voice, feel His hand.   How
could I be lonesome even on a desert island with no
work to do?"

Patience gasped.   The extraordinary simplicity of

this woman of fifty fascinated her whom life and heredity had made so complex. But she moved restlessly, and felt an impulse to thrust out her legs and arms. She had a sensation of being swamped in religion.

" I should n't think you 'd like boarding," she said irrelevantly.

" I don't like it particularly, but it gives me more time for my work. I make myself comfortable, I can tell you, for I have my own bed with two splendid mattresses, — my landlady's are the hardest things you ever felt, — and all my own furniture and knick-knacks. And I have my own tub, and every morning even in dead of winter, I take a cold bath. And I don't wear corsets — "

" Mariaville," called the conductor.

" Oh, here we are," cried Miss Tremont. She made a wild dive for her umbrella and bag, seized Patience by the hand, and rushed up the aisle, followed leisurely by Miss Beale.

The snow was falling heavily. Patience had watched it drift and swirl over the Hudson, and should have liked to give it her undivided attention.

As they left the station they were greeted by a chorus of shrieks : "Have a sleigh? Have a sleigh? "

"What do you think, sister? " asked Miss Tremont, dubiously. " Do you think Patience can walk two miles in this snow? I don't like to spend money on luxuries that I should give to the Lord."

" Perhaps the sleigh man needs it," said Patience, who had no desire to walk two miles in a driving storm.

" We 'd better have a sleigh," said Miss Beale, decidedly. " We will each pay half."

"But why should you pay half," said Miss Tremont, in her protesting voice, "when there are three of us?"

"I will pay for myself," said Patience. "Mr. Foord gave me a twenty dollar gold piece, and I have n't spent it."

"Oh, dear child!" exclaimed Miss Tremont. "As if I 'd let you."

"Come, get in," said Miss Beale; "we 'll be snowed under, here."

And a few minutes later Patience, on the front seat, was enjoying her first sleigh-ride. She slid down under the fur robe, and winking the snow stars from her lashes, looked out eagerly upon Mariaville. The town rose from the Hudson in a succession of irregular precipitous terraces. The trees were skeletons, the houses old, but the effect was very picturesque; and the dancing crystals, the faint music of bells from far and near, the wide steep streets, delighted a mind magnetic for novelty.

They left Miss Beale before a pretty house, standing in a frozen garden, then climbed to the top of a hill, slid away to the edge of the town, and drew rein before an old-fashioned white one-winged house, which stood well back in a neglected yard behind walnut-trees and hemlocks. Beyond, closing the town, were the stark woods. Opposite was a prim little grove in which the snow stars were dancing.

"Here we are," said Miss Tremont, climbing out. "Welcome home, Patience dear." She paid the man, and hurried down the path. The door was opened by an elderly square-faced woman, who looked sharply at Patience, then smiled graciously.

" Patience, this is Ellen. She takes good care of me. Come in. Come in."

The narrow hall ran through the main building, and was unfurnished but for a table and the stair. Miss Tremont led the way into a large double room of comfortable temperature, although no fire was visible. Bright red curtains covered the windows, a neat black carpet sprinkled with flowers the floor. The chairs were stiffly arranged, but upholstered cheerfully, the tables and mantels crowded with an odd assortment of cheap and handsome ornaments. The papered walls were a mosaic of family portraits. In the back parlour were a bookcase, a piano piled high with hymn-books, and a dozen or so queer little pulpit chairs. A door opened from the front parlour into a faded but hospitable dining-room.

Patience for the first time in her life experienced the enfolding of the home atmosphere, an experience denied to many for ever and ever. She turned impulsively, and throwing her arms about Miss Tremont, kissed and hugged her.

" Somehow I feel all made over," she said apologetically, and getting very red. " But it is so nice — and you are so nice — and oh, it is all so different ! "

And Miss Tremont, enraptured, first wished that this forlorn homely little waif was her very own, then vowed that neither should ever remember that she was not, and half carried her up to the bedroom prepared for her, a white fresh little room overlooking the shelving town.

III

THE next afternoon a sewing woman came and cut
down an old-fashioned but handsome fur-lined cloak
of Miss Tremont's to Patience's diminutive needs.
When Miss Tremont returned home, after a hard day's
work, she brought with her a hood, a pair of woollen
gloves, and a pair of arctics ; and Patience felt that she
could weather a New York winter.

But Patience gave little attention to her clothes.
When she was not watching the snow she was studying
the steady stream of people who called at all hours, and
invariably talked "church" and "temperance." The
atmosphere was so charged with religion that she was
haunted by an uneasy prescience of a violent explosion
during which Miss Tremont and her friends would sail
upward, leaving her among the débris.

Her coat finished, she went in town with Miss
Tremont to Temperance Hall. The snow had ceased
to fall. The sun rode solitary on a cold blue sky, the
ground was white and hard. The bare trees glittered
in their crystal garb, icicles jewelled the eaves of the
houses. The telegraph wires, studded with pendent
spheres, looked like a vast diamond necklace of many
strings which only Nature was mighty enough to wear.
The hills were snowdrifts. The Hudson, far below,
moved sluggishly under great blocks of ice. The
Palisades were black and white. Miss Tremont and
Patience walked rapidly, their frozen breath waving
before them in fantastic shapes. It was all very delightful to Patience, who thrust her hands into her deep

pockets and would have scorned to ride. At times she danced; new blood, charged with electricity, seemed shooting through her veins. Miss Tremont's older teeth clattered occasionally. She bent forward slightly, her brow contracted over eyes which seemed ever seeking something, her long legs carrying her swiftly and with surprising grace. Patience had solved the enigma of her voice after hearing her pray, and she supposed that her eyes were on loyal watch for the miseries of the world.

After a time they descended an almost perpendicular hill to the business part of the town. Beyond a few level streets the ground rose again, wooded and thickly built upon. On the left was another hill, which, Miss Tremont informed her, was Hog Heights, the quarter of the poor.

The streets in the valley twisted and doubled like the curves of an angry python. In the centre was a square which might have been called Rome, since all ways led to it.

Temperance Hall, a building of Christian-like humility, stood on a back street flanked by many low-browed shops. On the first floor were the parlour, reading-room, and refectory, on the second a large hall, on the third bedrooms. The hall was already half full of boys and girls, kept in order by the matron, Mrs. Blair, a middle-aged woman with the expression of one who stands no nonsense.

" Now, Patience," said Miss Tremont, " you listen attentively, and next time you can take Mrs. Blair's place."

The occasion was the weekly assemblage of the Loyal Legion children, who were being educated in the ways of temperance. Miss Tremont opened with the Lord's Prayer, which she invested with all its meaning; then the children sang from a temperance hymnbook, and the lesson began. Miss Tremont read a series of questions appurtenant to the inevitable results of unholy indulgence, to which Mrs. Blair read the answers, which in turn were repeated by the children. Then they sang " Down with King Alcohol," a minister came in and made a dramatic address, and the children, some of whom were attentive and some extremely naughty, filed out.

"I only come on alternate Fridays," said Miss Tremont, as they went downstairs ; " Sister Beale takes the other. Come and see our reading-room. These are our boarders," indicating several prim old maids that sat in the front room by the window.

In the dining-room a half dozen tramps were imbibing free soup. The reading-room was empty.

`IV

BEFORE a week had passed Patience was so busy that her old life slept as heavily as a bear in winter. She passed her difficult examinations and entered the High School, selecting the three years course, which included French, German, mathematics, the sciences, literature, and rhetoric.

The recesses and evenings were spent in study, the afternoons in assisting Miss Tremont ; occasionally she snatched an hour to write to her friends in California. Besides the temperance work, she had a class in the

church sewing school, kept the books of various societies, and occasionally visited the poor on Hog
Heights. The work did not interest her, but she was
glad to satisfactorily repay Miss Tremont's hospitality.
But had she wished to protest she would have realised
its uselessness: she was carried with the tide. It
might be said that Miss Tremont was the tide. Her
enthusiasm had no reflex action, and tore through
obstacles like a mill-race. When night came she was
so weary that more than once Patience offered to put
her to bed; but the offer was declined with a curious
mixture of religious fervour and hauteur. Miss Tremont
had none of the ordinary vanity of woman, but she
resented the imputation that she could not work for
the Lord as ardently at sixty as she had at forty.

When she prayed Patience listened with bated breath.
A torrent of eloquence boiled from her lips. All the
shortcomings and needs of unregenerate Mariaville,
individual and collective, were laid down with a vehement precision which could leave the Lord little doubt
of His obligations. The Temperance Cause was rehearsed with a passion which would have thrilled the
devil. Sounding through all was a wholly unself-
conscious note of command, as when one pleads with
the pocket of an intimate friend for some worthy
cause.

Patience saw so many disreputable people at this
time that her mother's pre-eminence was extinguished.
They had a habit of commanding the hospitalities of
Miss Tremont's barn, sure of two meals and a night's
lodging. Miss Tremont insisted upon their attendance
at evening prayers, and Patience assumed the task of
persuading them to clean up. Her methods were less

gentle than Miss Tremont's: when they refused to
wash she turned the hose on them.

Projected suddenly into the dry bracing cold of an
eastern winter she quickly became robust.   Before
spring had come, her back was straight and a faint
colour was in her rounding cheeks.   If there had been
time to think about it, or any one to tell her, she would
have discovered that she was growing pretty.   But at
this time, despite the distant advances of the High
School boys, Patience found no leisure for vanity.
Sometimes she paused long enough to wonder if she
had any individuality left; if environment was not
stronger than heredity after all; if immediate impressions could not ever efface those of the past, no matter
how deeply the latter may have been etched into the
plastic mind.   But she was quite conscious that she
was happy, despite the vague restlessness and longings
of youth.   She loved Miss Tremont with all the sudden
expansion of a long repressed temperament endowed
with a tragic capacity for passionate affection.   In
Monterey the iron mould of reserve into which circumstance had forced her nature, had cramped and
warped what love she had felt for Mr. Foord and
Rosita; but in this novel atmosphere, where love
enfolded her, where everybody respected her, and
knew nothing of her past, where there was not a word
nor an occurrence to remind her of the ugly experiences of her young life, she quickly became a normal
being, living, belatedly, along the large and generous
lines of her nature.

She had no friends of her own age with whom to
discuss the problems dear to the heart of developing
woman.   The girls at the High School rarely talked

during recess, and she left hurriedly the moment the scholars were dismissed for the day. The " Y's " she persistently refused to join, as well as the young people's societies of Miss Tremont's church.

" I 'll be your helper in everything," she said to her perplexed guardian ; " but those girls bore me, and, you know, I really have n't time for them."

And Miss Tremont, despite the fact that Patience gave no sign of spiritual thaw, was the most doting of old maid parents. After the first few weeks she ceased to dig in Patience's soul for the stunted seeds of Christianity, finding that she only irritated her, and trusting to the daily sprinkling of habit and example to promote their ultimate growth.

V

WITH summer came a cessation of school, Loyal Legion, and sewing school duties ; but the Poor took no vacation and gave none. Nevertheless, Patience had far more leisure, and borrowed many books from the town library. She read much of Hugo and Balzac and Goethe, and in the new intellectual delight forgot herself more completely than in her work.

Moreover, the town was very beautiful in summer, and she spent many hours rambling along the shadowy streets whose venerable trees shut the sunlight from the narrow side ways. The gardens too were full of trees ; and the town from a distance looked like a densely wooded hillside, a riot of green, out of which housetops showed like eggs in a nest. Over some of

the steep old streets the maples met, growing denser
and denser down in the perspective, until closed by
the flash of water.

The woods on the slope of the Hudson were thick
with great trees dropping a leafy curtain before the
brilliant river, and full of isolated nooks where a girl
could read and dream, unsuspected of the chance
pedestrian.

After one long drowsy afternoon by a brook in a
hollow of the woods, Patience returned home to find a
carriage standing before the door. It was a turnout of
extreme elegance. The grey horses were thorough-
breds; a coachman in livery sat on the box; a footman
stood on the sidewalk. She looked in wonder. Miss
Tremont had no time for the fine people of Mariaville,
and they had ceased to call on her long since.
Moreover, Patience knew every carriage in the town,
and this was not of them.

She went rapidly into the house, youthfully eager for
a new experience. Miss Tremont was seated on the
sofa in the front parlour, holding the hand of a tall
handsomely gowned woman. Patience thought, as she
stood for a moment unobserved, that she had never
seen so cold a face. It was the face of a woman of
fifty, oval and almost regular. The mouth was a
straight line. The clear pale eyes looked like the
reflection of the blue atmosphere on icicles. The
skin was as smooth as a girl's, the brown hair parted
and waved, the tall figure slender and superbly carried. She was smiling and patting Miss Tremont's
hand, but there was little light in her eyes.

As Patience entered, she turned her head and
regarded her without surprise; she had evidently

heard of her. Miss Tremont's face illumined, and she held out her hand.

"This is Patience," she said triumphantly. "I haven't told you half about the dear child. Patience, this is my cousin, Mrs. Gardiner Peele."

Mrs. Gardiner Peele bent her head patronisingly, and Patience hated her violently.

"I am glad you have a companion," said the lady, coldly. "But how is it you haven't the white ribbon on her?"

Miss Tremont blushed. "Oh, I can't control Patience in all things," she said, in half angry deprecation. "She just won't wear the ribbon."

Mrs. Peele smiled upon Patience for the first time. It was a wintry light, but it bespoke approval. "I wish she could make you take it off," she said to her relative. "That dreadful, dreadful *badge*. How can you wear it? — you —"

"Now, cousin," said Miss Tremont, laughing good-naturedly, "we won't go over all that again. You know I'm a hopeless crank. All I can do is to pray for you."

"Thank you. I don't doubt I need it, although I attend church quite as regularly as you could wish."

"I know you are good," said Miss Tremont, with enthusiasm, "and of course I don't expect everybody to be as interested in Temperance as I am. But I do wish you loved the world less and the Lord more."

Mrs. Peele gave a low, well modulated laugh. "Now, Harriet, I want you to be worldly for a few minutes. I have brought you back two new gowns from Paris, and I want you, when you come to visit me next week, to wear them. I have had them trimmed with white ribbon bows so that no one will notice one more or less —"

"I'm not ashamed of my white ribbon," flashed out Miss Tremont, then relented. "You dear good Honora. Yes, I'll wear them if they're not too fashionable."

"Oh, I studied your style. And let me tell you, Harriet Tremont, that fashionable gowns are what you should be wearing. It does provoke me so to see you —"

But Miss Tremont leaned over and kissed her short. "Now what's the use of talking to an old crank like me? I'm a humble servant of my dear Lord, and I couldn't be anything else if I had a million. But you dear thing, I'm so glad to see you once more. You do look so well. Tell me all about the children."

Patience, quite forgotten, listened to the conversation with deep interest. There was a vague promise of variety in this new advent. As she watched the woman, who seemed to have brought with her something of the atmosphere of all that splendid existence of which she had longingly read, she was stirred with a certain dissatisfaction: some dormant chord was struck — as on the day she drove by Del Monte. When Mrs. Peele arose to go, she thought that not Balzac himself had ever looked upon a more elegant woman. Even Patience's untrained eye recognised that those long simple folds, those so quiet textures, were of French woof and make. And the woman's carriage was like unto that of the fictional queen. She nodded carelessly to Patience, and swept out. When Miss

Tremont returned after watching her guest drive away, Patience pounced upon her.

"*Who* is she?" she demanded. "And *why* did n't you tell me you had such a swell for a cousin?"

"Did I never tell you?" asked Miss Tremont, wonderingly. "Why, I was sure I had often talked of Honora. But I 'm so busy I suppose I forgot."

She sat down and fanned herself, smiling. "Honora Tremont is my first cousin. We used to be great friends until she married a rich man and became so dreadfully fashionable. The Lord be praised, she has always loved me; but she lives a great deal abroad, and spends her winters, when she is here, in New York. They have a beautiful place on the Hudson, Peele Manor, that has been in the family for nearly three hundred years. Mr. Peele is an eminent lawyer. I don't know him very well. He does n't talk much; I suppose he has to talk so much in Court. I 've not seen the children for a year. I always thought them pretty badly spoiled, particularly Beverly. May is n't very bright. But I always liked Hal — short for Harriet, after me — better than any of them. She is about nineteen now. May is eighteen and Beverly twenty-four.

"Then there is Honora, cousin Honora's sister Mary's child, and the tallest woman I ever saw. Her parents died when she was a little thing and left her without a dollar. Honora took her, and has treated her like her own children. Sometimes I think she is very much under her influence. I don't know why, but I never liked her. She is Beverly's age. Oh !" she burst out, "just think ! I have got to go to Peele Manor for a week. I promised. I could n't help it.

And oh, I do dread it. They are all so different, and they don't sympathise with my work. Much as I love them I'm always glad to get away. Wasn't it kind and good of her to bring me two dresses from Paris?"

Patience shrewdly interpreted the prompting of Mrs. Peele's generosity, but made no comment.

Miss Tremont drew a great sigh: "My temperance work — my poor — what will they do without me? Maria Twist gets so mad when I don't read the Bible to her twice a week. Patience, you will have to stay in Temperance Hall. I shouldn't like to think of you here alone. I do wish Honora had asked you too — "

"I wouldn't go for worlds. When do you think your dresses will come? I do so want to see a real Paris dress."

"She said they'd come to-morrow. Oh, to think of wearing stiff tight things. Well, if they are uncomfortable or too stylish I just won't wear them, that's all."

"You just will, auntie dear. You'll not look any less fine than those people, or I'll not go near Hog Heights."

Miss Tremont kissed her, grateful for the fondness displayed. "Well, well, we'll see," she said.

But the next day, when the two handsome black gowns lay on the bed of the spare room, she shook her head with flashing eyes.

"I won't wear those things," she cried. "Why, they were made for a society woman, not for an humble follower of the Lord. I should be miserable in them."

Patience, who had been hovering over the gowns, — one of silk grenadine trimmed with long loops of black and white ribbon, the other of satin with a soft knot of white ribbon on the shoulder and another at the back of the high collar, — came forward and firmly divested Miss Tremont of her alpaca. She lifted the heavy satin gown with reverent hands and slipped it over Miss Tremont's head, then hooked it with deft fingers.

"There !" she exclaimed. "You look like a swell at last. Just what you ought to look like."

Miss Tremont glanced at the mirror with a brief spasm of youthful vanity. The rich fashionable gown became her long slender figure, her unconscious pride of carriage, far better than did her old alpaca and merino frocks. But she shook her head immediately, her eyes flashing under a quick frown.

"The idea of perching a white bow like a butterfly on my shoulder and another at the back of my neck, as if I had a scar. It's an insult to the white ribbon. And this collar would choke me. I can't breathe. Take it off ! Take it off !"

"Not until I have admired you some more. You look just grand. If the collar is too high, I'll send for Mrs. Best, and we'll cut it off and sew some soft black stuff in the neck — although I just hate to. Auntie dear, don't you think you could stand it?"

Miss Tremont shook her head with decision. "I could n't. It hurts my old throat. And how could I ever bend my head to get at my soup? And these bows make me feel actually cross. If the dress can be made comfortable I'll wear it, for I've no right to disgrace Honora, nor would I hurt her feelings by scorning her gowns ; but I'll not stand any such mockery as these flaunting white things."

Patience exchanged the satin for the grenadine gown. This met with more tolerance at first, as the throat was finished with soft folds, and the white ribbon was less demonstrative.

"It floats so," said Patience, ecstatically.   "Oh, auntie, you *are* a beauty."

"I a beauty with my ugly scowling old face?   But this thing is like a ball dress, Patience — this thin stuff! I prefer the satin."

"You will wear this on the hot evenings.   All thin things are not made for the ball-room.   You need n't look at yourself like that.   I only wish I'd ever be half as pretty.   Auntie, why did n't you ever marry?"

Miss Tremont's face worked after all the years. Memories could not die in so uniform a nature.

"My youth was very sad," she said, turning away abruptly.   "I only talk about it with the dear Lord." And Patience asked no more questions.

VI

THE dressmaker was sent for, and the satin gown divested of its collar.   Miss Tremont ruthlessly clipped off the beautiful French bows and sewed a tiny one of narrow white ribbon in a conspicuous place on the left chest.   The grenadine was decorated in like manner. Patience wailed, and then laughed as she thought of Mrs. Gardiner Peele.   She wished she might be there to see that lady's face.

Miss Tremont changed her mind four times as to the possibility of leaving Mariaville for a week of sinful idleness, before she was finally assisted into the train by Patience's firm hand.   Even then she abruptly left her seat and started for the door. But the train was moving. Patience saw her resume her seat with an impatient twitch of her shoulders.

"Poor auntie," she thought, as she walked up the street; "but on the whole I think I pity Mrs. Peele more."

Her bag had been sent to Temperance Hall, and she went directly there, and to her own room. As the day was very warm, she exchanged her frock for a print wrapper, then extended herself on the bed with "'93." It was her duty to assuage the wrath of Maria Twist, but she made up her mind that for twenty-four hours she would shirk every duty on her calendar.

But she had failed to make allowance for the net of circumstance. She had not turned ten pages when she heard the sound of agitated footsteps in the hall. A moment later Mrs. Blair opened the door unceremoniously. Her usually placid face was much perturbed.

"Oh, Miss Patience," she said, "I'm in such a way. Late last night a poor man fell at the door, and I took him in as there was no policeman around. I thought he was only ill, but it seems he was drunk. He's been awake now for two hours, and is awful bad — not drunk, but suffering."

"Why don't you send for the doctor?" asked Patience, lazily.

"I have, but he's gone to New York and won't be back till night. The man says he can doctor himself — that all he wants is whisky; but of course I can't give him that. Do come over and talk to him. Miss Beale is over at White Plains, and I don't know what to do."

Patience rose reluctantly and followed the matron to

8

the side of the house reserved for men. As she went
down the hall she heard groans and sharp spasmodic
cries. Mrs. Blair opened a door, and Patience saw
an elderly man lying in the bed. His grey hair and
beard were ragged, his eyes dim and bleared, his long,
well-cut but ignoble face was greenishly pale. He was
very weak, and lay clutching at the bed clothes with
limp hairy hands. As he saw the matron his eyes lit
up with resentment.

"I did n't come here to be murdered," he ejaculated. "It's the last place I'd have come to if I'd
known what I was doing. But I tell you that if I don't
have a drink of whisky I'll be a dead man in an
hour."

"I can't give you that," said Mrs. Blair, desperately.
"And you know you only think you need it, anyhow.
We try to make men overcome their terrible weakness;
we don't encourage them."

"That's all right, but you can't reform a man when
his inside is on fire and feels as if it were dropping
out — but my God! I can't argue with you, damn
you. Give it to me."

"I'm of the opinion that he ought to have it,"
said Patience.

The man turned to her eagerly. "Bless you," he
said. "It's not the taste of it I'm craving, miss; it's
relief from this awful agony. If you give it to me, I
swear I'll try never to touch a drop again after I get
over this spree. It'll be bad enough to break off then,
but it's death now."

Mrs. Blair looked at him with pity, but shook her
head.

"I've been here seven years," she said to Patience,

"and the ladies have yet to find one fault with me. I don't dare give it to him. Besides, I don't believe in it. How can what's killing him cure him? And it's a sin. Even if the ladies excused me — which they would n't — I'd never forgive myself."

"I'll take the responsibility," said Patience. "I believe that man will die if he does n't have whisky."

The man groaned and tossed his arms. "Oh, my God!" he cried.

Mrs. Blair shuddered. "Oh, I don't know, miss. If you will take the responsibility — I can't give it to him — where could you get it?"

"At a drug store."

"They won't sell it to you — we've got a law passed, you know."

"Then I'll go to a saloon."

"Oh, my! my!" cried Mrs. Blair, "you'd never do that?"

"The man is in agony. Can't you see? I'm going this minute."

The door opened, and Miss Beale entered. She looked warm and tired, but came forward with active step, and stood beside the bed. A spasm of disgust crossed her face. "What is the matter, my man?" she asked. "I am sorry to see you here."

"Give me whisky," groaned the man.

Miss Beale turned away with twitching mouth.

"The man is dying. Nothing but whisky can save him," said Patience. "If you called a doctor he would tell you the same thing."

"What?" said Miss Beale, coldly, "do you suppose that he can have whisky in Temperance Hall? Is that what we are here for? You must be crazy."

"But you don't want him to die on your hands, do you?" exclaimed Patience, who was losing her temper.

"My God!" screeched the man, "I am in Hell."

"My good man," said Miss Beale, gently, "it is for us to save you from Hell, not to send you there."

"I'll be there in ten minutes." His voice died to an inarticulate murmur; but he writhed, and doubled, and twisted, as men may have done when fanatics tortured in the name of religion.

"Good heavens, Miss Beale," cried Patience, excitedly, "you can't set yourself up in opposition to nature. That man must have whisky. If he were younger and stronger it would n't matter so much; but can't you see he has n't strength to resist the terrible strain? The torture is killing him, eating out his life —"

"Oh, it is terrible!" exclaimed the matron. "Perhaps it is best —"

"Mrs. Blair!" Miss Beale turned upon her in consternation. Then she bent over the man.

"You can't have whisky," she said gently; "not if I thought you were really dying would I give it to you. If it is the Lord's will that you are to die here you must abide by it. I shall not permit you to further imperil your soul. Nor could that which has not the blessing of God on it be of benefit to you. Alcohol is a destroyer, both of soul and of body — not a medicine."

The man's knees suddenly shot up to his chest; but he raised his head and darted at her a glance of implacable hate.

"Damn you," he stuttered. "Murderer —" Then he extended rigid arms and clutched the bed clothes, his body twitching uncontrollably.

Miss Beale looked upon him with deep compassion.

"Poor thing," she exclaimed, "is not this enough to warn all men from that fiend?" She laid her hand on the man's head, but he shook it off with an oath.

"Whisky," he cried. "O my God! Have these women — *women !* — no pity?"

"I'm going for whisky —" said Patience.

Miss Beale stepped swiftly to the door, locked it, and slipped the key into her pocket.

"You will buy no whisky," she said sternly. "I will save you from that sin." Suddenly her face lit up. "I will pray," she said solemnly, "I will pray that this poor lost creature may recover, and lead a better life —"

"I swear I'll never touch another drop after I'm out of this if you 'll give it to me now —"

"If it be the Lord's will that you shall live you will not die," said Miss Beale. "I will pray, and in His mercy He may let you live to repent."

She fell upon her knees by the bed, and clasping her hands, prayed aloud; while the man reared and plunged and groaned and cursed, his voice and body momentarily weaker. Miss Beale's prayers were always very long and very fervid. She was not eloquent, but her deep tear-voiced earnestness was most impressive; and never more so than to-day, when she flung herself before the throne of Grace with a lost soul in her hand. A light like a halo played upon her spiritualised face, her voice became ineffably sweet. Gradually, in her ecstatic communion with, her intimate nearness to her God, she forgot the man on the bed, forgot the flesh which prisoned her soaring soul, was conscious only of the divine light pouring through her, the almost palpable touch of her lover's hand.

Suddenly Patience exclaimed brutally : " The man is dead."

Miss Beale arose with a start. She drew the sheet gently over the distorted face. " It is the Lord's will," she said.

After Patience was in her own room and had re-lieved her feelings by slamming the door, she sat for a long time staring at the pattern of the carpet and pon-dering upon the problem of Miss Beale.

" Well," she thought finally, *"she's* happy, so I suppose it 's all right. No wonder she 's satisfied with herself when she lives up to her ideals as consistently as that. I think I 'll label all the different forms of selfishness I come across. There seems to be a large variety, but all put together don't seem to be a patch to having fun with your ideals. Miss Beale would be the most wretched woman in Westchester county if she 'd given that man whisky and saved his life."

VII

THE man was buried with Christian service at Miss Beale's expense, and her serene face wore no shadow. The following day she said to Patience : " I spent nearly all of the last two nights in prayer, and I almost heard the Lord's voice as He told me I did right."

" You ought to write a novel," said Patience, drily, but the sarcasm was lost. In a moment Patience for-got Miss Beale : the postman handed her two letters, and she went up to her room to read them.

The first she opened was from Miss Tremont.

Oh my dear darling little girl, how I wish, *how* I wish I were with you and my work once more. I ought to be happy because they are all so kind, but I 'm not. I feel as if I were throwing away one of the few precious weeks I have left to give to the Lord (arrange for a prayer meeting on Wednesday, the day of my return, and we 'll have a regular feast of manna). Do you miss me? I think of you every moment. You should have seen dear Cousin Honora's face when I came down to dinner in the black satin. She did n't say anything, she just *looked* at the bow, and I felt sorry for her. But I know I am right. Hal giggled and winked at me. (I do love Hal!) Honora Mairs said so sweetly after Cousin Honora had left the room: "Dear Cousin Harriet, I think you are so brave and consistent to wear the little white bow of your cause. It is so *like* you." Was not that sweet of her? Beverly has very heavy eyebrows, and he raised them at my ribbon, and turned away his head as if it hurt his eyes. He is a very elegant young gentleman, and his mother says he is a great stickler for form, whatever that may mean. (They speak a different language here anyway. I don't under-stand half what they say. Hal talks slang all the time.) I don't like Beverly as much as I did, although he 's quite the handsomest young man I ever saw and very polite; but he smokes cigarettes all the time and big black cigars. When I told him that five hundred million dollars were spent annually on tobacco, he got up and went off in a huff. May is just a talkative child — I never heard any one talk so much in my life, — and about nothing but gowns and young men and balls and the opera. Beverly talks about horses all the time, and Hal thinks a great deal of society, although she listens to me very sweetly when I talk to her about my work. Yesterday she said: "Why, Cousin Harriet, you 're a regular steam engine. It must be jolly good fun to carry a lot of sinners to heaven on an express train." I told her it was a freight train, and it certainly is, as you know, Patience dear. She replied: "Well, if you get there all

the same, a century more or less does n't make any difference. You must be right in it with the Lord." That was
the only time I 'd heard the dear Lord's name mentioned
since I arrived, so I did n't scold her. But Patience, dear,
I hope you 'll never use slang. I 've talked to Hal about
you, and she says she 's coming to see you.

Honora does n't use slang. She is very stately and
dignified, and Cousin Honora (it 's very awkward when
you 're writing for two people to have the same name, is n't
it?) holds her up as a model for the girls. Hal and
she *fight*. I can't call it anything else, although Honora
does n't lose her temper and Hal does. Hal said to me (of
Honora) yesterday (I use her own words, although they 're
awful; but if I did n't I could n't give you the same idea of
her): "She 's a d—— hypocrite: and she wants to marry
Beverly, but she won't, — not if I have to turn matchmaker
and marry him to a variety actress. She makes me wild.
I wish she 'd elope with the priest, but she 's too confound-
edly clever." Is n't it dreadful — Honora is a Catholic.
She became converted last year. Perhaps that 's the reason I can't like her. But even the Catholic religion teaches
charity, for she said to me this morning: "Poor Hal is
really a good-hearted child, but she 's worldly and just a
little superficial."

They have n't any company this week — how kind of
Cousin Honora to ask me when they are alone! I wish you
were here to enjoy the library. It is a great big room overlooking the river, and the walls are covered with books —
three or four generations of them. Mr. Peele is intellectual, and so is Honora; but the others don't read much, except Hal, who reads dreadful-looking yellow paper books
written in the French language which she says are "corkers,"
whatever that may mean. I do wish the dear child would
read her Bible. I asked her if I gave her a copy if she 'd
promise me to read a little every day, and she said she
would, as some of the stories were as good as a French
novel. So I shall buy her one.

We sit in the library every evening   In the morning

we sit in the Tea House on the slope and Honora embroiders Catholic Church things, Cousin Honora knits (she says it's all the fashion), May *talks*, and Hal reads her yellow books and tells May to "let up." I sew for my poor, and they don't seem to mind that as much as the white ribbon. They say that they always sew for the poor in Lent. Hal says it is the "swagger thing." In the afternoon we drive, and I do think it such a waste of time to be going, going nowhere for two hours.

Well, Patience, I shall be with you on Wednesday, praise the Lord. Come to the train and meet me, and be sure to write me about *everything*. How is Polly Jones, and old Mrs. Murphy, and Belinda Greggs? Have you read to Maria Twist, and taken the broth to old Jonas Hobb? Give my love to dear sister Beale, and tell her I pray for her. With a kiss from your old auntie, God bless you,

HARRIET TREMONT.

"Dear old soul," thought Patience. "I think I know them better than she does, already. She is worth the whole selfish crowd; but I should like to know Hal. Beverly must be a chump."

VIII

THE other letter was from Rosita. Patience had not heard from her for a long while. Three months previously, Mr. Foord had written of Mrs. Thrailkill's death, and mentioned that Rosita had gone to Sacramento to visit Miss Galpin — now Mrs. Trent — until her uncle, who had returned to Kentucky, should send for her.

Oh, Patita! Patita! [the letter began], what do you think? *I am on the stage.* I had been crazy to go on ever

since *that night*. A theatrical man was in Monterey just before mamma's death, and he told me they were always wanting pretty corus girls at the Tivoli; so after the funeral I
told everybody I was going to stay with Miss Galpin until
Uncle Jim sent for me — I hated to lie, but I had to — and
I went up to San Francisco and went right to the Tivoli.
He took me because he said I was pretty and had a fresh
voice. I had to ware tights. You should have seen me.
At first I felt all the time like stooping over to cover up my
legs with my arms. But after a while I got used to it, and
one night we had to dance, and everybody said I was the
most graceful. The manager said I was a born dancer and
actress. The other day what do you think happened? A
New York manager was here and heard me sing, — I had a
little part by that time, — and he told me that if I took lessons I could be a prima donna in comic opera. He said I
not only was going to have a lovely voice, but that I had a
new style (Spanish) and would take in New York. He offered to send me to Paris for a year and then bring me out
in New York if I 'd give him my word — I 'm too young to
sign a contract — that I would n't go with any other manager.
At first my manager, who is a good old sole (I did n't tell
you that I live with him and his wife, and that their awful
good to me and stand the fellers off), would n't have it; but
after a while he gave in — said I 'd have to go the pace
sooner or later (whatever that means), and I might as well
go it in first class style. His wife, the good old sole, cried.
She said I was the first corus girl she 'd ever taken an interest in, but somehow it would be on her conscience if
I went wrong. But I 'm not going wrong. I don't
care a bit for men. There was a bald-headed old
fool who used to come and sit in the front row every
night and throw kisses to me, and one night he threw
me a bouquet with a bracelet in it. I wore the bracelet,
for it was a beauty with a big diamond in it ; but I never
looked at him or answered any of his notes, and Mr. Bell —
the manager — wrote him he 'd punch his head if he came
near the stage door. No, all I want is to act, act, act, and

sing, sing, sing, and dance, dance, dance, and have beautiful cloths and jewels and a carriage and two horses. Mr.
Soper has told me ten times since I 've met him that "virtue
in an actress pays," and he 's going to send a horrid old
woman with me to Paris, as if I 'd bother with the fools anyhow. I 'm sure I can't see what Mrs. Bell cries about if I 'm
going to be famous and make a lot of money. Anyhow, I 'm
going. I do so want to see you, Patita dear. Maybe you
can come up to the steamer and see me off. I wonder if
you have changed. I 'm not so very tall; but they all say
my figure is good. Mr. Soper says it will be divine in a year
or two, but that I may be a cow at thirty, so I 'd better not
lose any time. Good-bye. Good-bye. I want to give you
a hundred kisses. How different our lives are! Is n't
yours dreadfully stupid with that old temprance work?
And just think it was you who taught me to act first! Mr.
Soper says I must cultivate the Spanish racket for all it 's
worth, and that he expects me to be more Spanish in New
York than I was in Monterey. He is going to get an opera
written for me with the part of a Spanish girl in it so I can
wear the costume. He says if I study and do everything
he tells me I 'll make a *furore*. *Hasta luego* — Patita *mia*.
              ROSITA ELVIRA FRANCESCA THRAILKILL.

P. S. — I 'm to have a Spanish stage name, "La Rosita,"
I guess. Mr. Soper says that Thrailkill is an "anti-
climax," and would never "go down."

IX

PATIENCE read this letter with some alarm. All that she
had heard and read of the stage made her apprehen-
sive. She feared that Rosita would become fast, would
drink and smoke, and not maintain a proper reserve
with men. Then the natural independence of her cha-

racter asserted itself, and she felt pride in Rosita's courage and promptness of action. She even envied her a
little : her life would be so full of variety.

"And after all it 's fate," she thought philosophically.
"She was cut out for the stage if ever a girl was.
You might as well try to keep a bird from using its
wings, or Miss Beale and auntie from being Temperance. I wonder what my fate is. It 's not the stage,
but it 's not this, neither — not much. Should n't wonder
if I made a break for Mr. Field some day. But I
could n't leave auntie. She 's the kind that gets a hold
on you."

She did her duty by Hog Heights during Miss Tremont's brief holiday, but did it as concisely as was
practicable. She found it impossible to sympathise with
people that were content to let others support them,
giving nothing in return. Her strong independent
nature despised voluntary weakness. It was her private
opinion that these useless creatures with only the animal
instinct to live, and not an ounce of grey matter in
their skulls, encumbered the earth, and should be
quietly chloroformed.

Despite her love for Miss Tremont, she breathed
more freely in her absence. She was surfeited with
religion, and at times possessed with a very flood of
revolt and the desire to let it loose upon every church
worker in Mariaville. But affection and gratitude
restrained her.

X

MISS TREMONT returned on Wednesday morning. She stepped off the train with a bag under one arm, a bundle under the other, and both arms full of flowers.

" Oh, you darling, you darling ! " she cried as she fell upon Patience. " How it does my heart good to see you ! These are for you. Hal picked them, and sent her love. Are n't they sweet? "

" Lovely," said Patience, crushing the flowers as she hugged and kissed Miss Tremont. " Here, give me the bag."

Miss Tremont would go to Temperance Hall first, then to call upon Miss Beale, but was finally guided to her home. The trunk had preceded them. Patience unpacked the despised gowns, while listening to a passionate dissertation upon the heavy trial they had been to their owner.

" I think you had a good time all the same," she said. " You look as if you 'd had, at any rate. You 've not looked so well since I came. That sort of thing agrees with you better than tramping over Hog Heights —"

" It does not ! " cried Miss Tremont. " And I am so glad to get back to my work and my little girl."

" And the Lord," supplemented Patience.

" Oh, He was with me even there. Only He did n't feel so near." She sighed reminiscently. " But I 've brought pictures of the children to show you. Let us go down to the parlour where it 's cooler, and then we 'll stand them in a row on the mantel. They 're the first pictures I 've had of them in years." She caught a package from the tray of her trunk, in her usual abrupt fashion, and hurried downstairs, Patience at her heels.

Miss Tremont seated herself in her favourite upright chair, put on her spectacles, and opened the package. "This is Hal," she said, handing one of the photographs to Patience. "I must show you her first, for she 's my pet."

Patience examined the photograph eagerly. It was a half length of a girl with a straight tilted nose, a small mouth with a downward droop at the corners, large rather prominent eyes, and sleek hair which was in keeping with her generally well-groomed appearance. She wore a tailor frock. Her slender erect figure was beautifully poised. In one hand she carried a lorgnette. She was not pretty, but her expression was frank and graceful, and she had much distinction.

"I like her. Any one could see she was a swell. What colour hair has she?"

"Oh, a kind of brown. Her eyes are a sort of grey. Here is May. She always has her photographs coloured."

"Oh, she 's a beauty!" The girl even in photograph showed an exquisite bit of flesh and blood. The large blue eyes were young and appealing under soft fall of lash. The mouth was small and red, the nose small and straight. Chestnut hair curled about the small head and oval face. The skin was like tinted jade. It was the face of the American aftermath. She wore a ball gown revealing a slender girlish neck and a throat of tender curves.

"She is a real beauty," said Miss Tremont. "Poor

Hal says, 'she can't wear her neck because she hasn't got any.' Did you ever hear such an expression?"

"Hal looks as if she had a good figure."

Miss Tremont shook her head. "I don't approve of all Hal does — she pads. She doesn't seem to care much who knows it, for when the weather's very warm she takes them out, right before your eyes, so it isn't so bad as if she were deceitful about it. Here is Beverly."

Patience looked long at the young man's face. This face too was oval, with a high intellectual forehead, broad black brows, and very regular features. The mouth appeared to pout beneath the drooping moustache. The expression of the eyes was very sweet. It was a strong handsome face, high-bred like the others, but with a certain nobility lacking in the women.

"He is said to be the handsomest young man in Westchester County, and he's quite dark," said Miss Tremont. "What do you think of him?"

"He is rather handsome. Where is Honora?"

"She never has pictures taken. But, dear me, I must go out and see Ellen."

Patience disposed the photographs on the mantel, then, leaning on her elbows, gazed upon Beverly Peele. The Composite, Byron, the Stranger, rattled their bones unheard. She concluded that no knight of olden time could ever have been so wholly satisfactory as this young man. Romance, who had been boxed about the ears, and sent to sleep, crept to her old throne with a sly and meaning smile. Patience began at once to imagine her meeting with Beverly Peele. She would be in a runaway carriage, and he would rescue her. She would be skating and fall in a hole, and he would pull her out. He would be riding to hounds in his beautiful pink coat (which was red) and run over her.

She pictured his face with a variety of expressions. She was sure that he had the courage of a lion and the tenderness of some women. Unquestionably he had read his ancestors' entire library — "with that forehead," — and he probably had the high and mighty air of her favourite heroes of fiction. In one of her letters Miss Tremont had remarked that he loved children and animals; therefore he had a beautiful character and a kind heart. And she was glad to have heard that he also had a temper: it saved him from being a prig. Altogether, Patience, with the wisdom of sixteen and three quarters, was quite convinced that she had found her ideal, and overlooked its extreme unlikeness to the Composite, which was the only ideal she had ever created. A woman's ideal is the man she is in love with for the time being.

She went up to her room, and for the first time in her life critically examined herself in the mirror. With May Peele and one or two beauties of the High School in mind, she decided with a sigh that *she* was no beauty.

"But who knows," she thought with true insight, "what I 'd be with clothes? Who could be pretty in a calico dress? My nose is as straight as May's, anyhow, and my upper lip as short. But to be a real beauty you 've got to have blue eyes and golden or chestnut hair and a little mouth, or else black eyes and hair like Rosita's. My eyes are only grey, and my hair 's the colour of ashes, as Rosita once remarked. There 's no getting over that, although it certainly has grown a lot since I came here."

Then she remembered that Rosita had once decorated her with red ribbons and assured her that they were becoming. She ran down to the best spare room, and, divesting a tidy of its scarlet bows, pinned them upon herself before the mirror, which she discovered was more becoming than her own. The brilliant colour was undoubtedly improving — "And, my goodness!" she exclaimed suddenly, "I do believe I have n't got a freckle left. It must be the climate."

"What on earth are you doing?" said an abrupt voice from the doorway.

Patience started guiltily, and restored the bows to the tidy.

"Oh, you see," she stammered, "May is so pretty I wanted to see if I could be a little less homely." Patience was truthful by nature, but the woman does not live that will not lie under purely feminine provocation. Otherwise she would not be worthy to bear the hallowed name of woman.

"Nonsense," said Miss Tremont, crossly, "I thought you were above that kind of foolishness. You, must remember that you are as the Lord made you, and be thankful that you were not born a negro or a Chinaman."

"Oh, I am," said Patience.

XI

THEREAFTER, Patience roamed the woods munching chestnuts and dreaming of Beverly Peele. Hugo and Balzac and Goethe were neglected. Her brain wove

9

thrilling romances of its own, especially in the night to
the sound of rain. She never emerged from the woods
without a shortening of the breath; but even Hal did
not pay the promised call; nor did Beverly dash
through the streets in a pink coat, a charger clasped
between his knees.

"Well, it's fun to be in love, anyhow," she thought.
"I'll meet him some time, I know."

Much to her regret she was not permitted to go to
New York to see Rosita off. Miss Tremont had a
morbid horror of the stage, and after Patience's exhibi-
tion of vanity was convinced that "actress creatures"
would exert a pernicious influence.

And, shortly after, Patience received news which
made her forget Rosita and even Beverly Peele for a
while. Mr. Foord was dead. Patience had hoarded
his twenty dollar gold piece because he had given it to
her. She bought a black hat and frock with it, and
felt as sad as she could at that age of shifting impressions. A later mail brought word that he had left her
John Sparhawk's library, which could stay in the Custom
House until she was able to send for it, and a few hundred dollars which would remain in a savings bank until she was eighteen. He had nothing else to leave
except his books, which went to found a town library.
All but those few hundreds had been sunken in an an-
nuity. Miss Tremont was quite content to be overlooked in the girl's favour.

By the time Patience was ready to return to Beverly
Peele the new term opened, and the uncompromising
methods of the High School left no time for romance.
Once more her ambition to excel became paramount,
and she studied night and day. She had no temptation

to dissipate, for she was not popular with the young people of Mariaville. The Y's disapproved of her because she would not don the white ribbon; and the church girls, generally, felt that except when perfunctorily assisting Miss Tremont she held herself aloof, even at the frequent sociables. And they were scandalised because she did not join the church, nor the King's Daughters, nor the Christian Endeavor.

The High School scholars liked her because she was "square," and cordially admired her cleverness; but there were no recesses in the ordinary sense, and after school Miss Tremont claimed her. Even the boys "had no show," as they phrased it. Occasionally they lent her a hand on the ice; but like all Californians, she bitterly felt the cold of her second winter, and in her few leisure hours preferred the fire.

Sometimes she looked at Beverly Peele's picture with a sigh and some resentment. "But never mind," she would think philosophically, "I can fall in love with him over again next summer." When vacation came she did in a measure take up the broken threads of her romance, but they had somewhat rotted from disuse.

Rosita wrote every few weeks, reporting hard work and unbounded hope. "The *dueña*," as she called her companion, "was an old devil," and never let her go out alone, nor receive a man; but she "did n't care," she had no time for nonsense, anyhow. She was learning her part in the Spanish opera, which had been written for her, and it was "lovely."

"It must be a delightful sensation to have your future assured at seventeen," thought Patience. " Mine is as problematical as the outcome of the Tem-

perance cause. I have had one unexpected change,
and may have more. If it were not for Rosita's letters
I should almost forget those sixteen years in California.
I certainly am not the same person. I have n't lost
my temper for a year and a half, and I don't seem to
be disturbed any more by vague yearnings. Life is too
practical, I suppose."

Miss Tremont did not visit the Gardiner Peeles this
summer : they spent the season in travel. Late in the
fall Rosita returned to America. She wrote the day
before she sailed. That was the last letter Patience received from her. Later she sent a large envelope full
of clippings descriptive of her triumphal début ; thereafter nothing whatever. Patience, supposing herself
forgotten, anathematised her old friend wrathfully, but
pride forbade her to write and demand an explanation.

She noticed with spasms of terror that Miss Tremont
was failing. The rush and worry of a lifetime had
worn the blood white, and the nerve-force down like an
old wharf pile. But Miss Tremont would not admit
that she had lost an ounce of strength. She arose at
the same hour and toiled until late. When Patience
begged her to take care of herself, she became almost
querulous, and all Patience could do was to anticipate
her in every possible way. But when school reopened
she had little time for anything but study. She was
to finish in June, and the last year's course was very
difficult.

She graduated with flying colours, and Miss Tremont
was so proud and excited that she took a day's vacation. A week later Patience hinted that she thought
she should be earning her own living ; but Miss Tremont
would not even discuss the subject. She fell into a

rage every time it was broached, and Patience, who would have rebelled, had Miss Tremont been younger and stronger, submitted : she knew it would not be for long.

XII

PATIENCE was languid all summer, and lay about in the woods, when she could, reading little and thinking much. Her school books put away forever, she felt for the first time that she was a woman, but did not take as much interest in herself as she had thought she should. She speculated a good deal upon her future career as a newspaper woman, and expended two cents every morning upon the New York "Day." But she forgot to study it in the new interest it created : she had just the order of mind to succumb to the fascination of the newspaper, and she read the "Day's" report of current history with a keener pleasure than even the great records of the past had induced. She longed for a companion with whom to talk over the significant tendencies of the age, and gazed upon Beverly Peele's dome-like brow with a sigh.

Once, in the Sunday issue, she came upon a column and a half devoted to Rosita, " The Sweetheart of the Public," "The Princess Royal of Opera Bouffe." The description of the young prima donna's home life, personal characteristics, and footlight triumphs, was further embellished by a painfully *décolleté* portrait, a lace night gown, a pair of wonderfully embroidered stockings, and a rosary.

Patience read the article twice, wondering why fame

realised looked so different from the abstract quality of her imagination.

"Somehow it seems a sort of tin halo," she thought. Then her thoughts drifted back to Monterey, and recalled it with startling vividness. "Still even if I have n't forgotten it, it is like the memory of another life. Its only lasting effect has been to make me hate what is coarse and sinful; and dear auntie, even if she has n't converted me, has developed all my good.

"I wonder if Rosita has been in love, and if that is the reason she has forgotten me. But she has n't married, so perhaps it's only adulation that has driven everything else out of her head." And then with her eyes on the river, which under the heavy sky looked like a stream of wrinkling lead from which a coating of silver had worn off in places, she fell to dreaming of Beverly Peele and an ideal existence in which they travelled and read and assured each other of respectful and rarefied affection.

Early in the winter the influenza descended upon America. Mr. Peele, his wife wrote, was one of the first victims, and the entire family took him to Florida. One night, a month later, Miss Tremont returned from Hog Heights and staggered through her door.

"Oh," she moaned, as Patience rushed forward and caught her in her arms, "I feel so strangely. I have pains all over me, and the queerest feeling in my knees."

"It 's the grippe," said Patience, who had read its history in the "Day." She put Miss Tremont to bed, and sent for the doctor. The old lady was too weak to protest, and swallowed the medicines submissively.

She recovered in due course, and one day slipped out and plodded through the snow to Hog Heights. She was brought home unconscious, and that night was gasping with pneumonia.

There was no lack of nurses. Miss Beale and Mrs. Watt, who had helped to care for her during the less serious attack, returned at once, and many others called at intervals during the day and night.

Patience sat constantly by the bed, staring at the face so soon to be covered from all sight. She wanted to cry and scream, but could not. Her heart was like lead in her breast.

At one o'clock on the second night, she and Miss Beale were alone in the sick room. Mrs. Watt was walking softly up and down the hall without.

Miss Tremont was breathing irregularly, and Patience bent over her with white face. Miss Beale began to sob.

"Is it not terrible, terrible," she ejaculated, "that she should die like this, she whose deathbed should have been so beautiful, — unconscious, drugged — morphine, which is as accursed as whisky —"

"I am glad of it. It would be more horrible to see her suffer."

"I don't want to see her suffer — dear, dear Miss Tremont. But she should have died in the full knowledge that she was going to God. Oh! Oh!" she burst out afresh. "How I envy her! It's my only, only sin, but I can't help envying those who are going to heaven. I can't wait. I do so want to see the beautiful green pastures and the still waters — and oh, how I want to talk with Abraham, Isaac, and Jacob!"

Patience flung her head into her lap and burst into a fit of laughter.

XIII

An hour later she went downstairs and turned up
all the lights. Mrs. Watt had gone to the next house
to telephone for the undertakers. When she returned
she went upstairs to Miss Beale. Patience could hear
the two women praying. That was the only sound in
the terrible stillness. She paced up and down, wringing
her hands and gasping occasionally. Her sense of
desolation was appalling, although as yet she but half
realised her bereavement.

Suddenly she heard the sound of runners on the
crisp snow. They stopped before the gate. She ran
shuddering to the window. The moon flooded the
white earth. Two tall black shadows came down the
path. They trod as if on velvet. Even on the steps
and porch they made no sound. They knocked as
death may knock on a human soul, lightly, meaningly.
Patience dragged herself to the door and opened it.
The long narrow black men entered and bent their
heads solemnly. Patience raised her shaking hand,
and pointed to the floor above. The men of death
bowed again, and stole upward like black ghosts. In a
few moments they stole down again and out and away.
Patience rushed frantically through the rooms to the
kitchen, where she fell upon Ellen, dozing by the fire,
and screamed and laughed until the terrified woman
flung a pitcher of water on her, then carried her upstairs
and put her to bed.

XIV

A WEEK later Patience wandered restlessly about the lonely house. The hundreds of people that had thronged it had gone at last, even Miss Beale and Mrs. Watt.

She had cried until she had no tears left, and rebelled until reason would hear no more. Her nerves felt blunt and worn down.

Yesterday Miss Tremont's lawyer had told her that after a few unimportant bequests she was to have the income of the dead woman's small estate until she married, after which she would have nothing and the Temperance cause all. She was therefore exempt from the pettiest and severest of life's trials. Miss Tremont had also left a letter, begging her to devote herself to a life of charity and reform. But Patience had at last revolted. She realised how empty had been her part, how torrential the impulsion of Miss Tremont.

The great world outside of Mariaville pressed upon her imagination, gigantic, rainbow-hued, alluring. It beckoned with a thousand fingers, and all her complex being responded. She longed for a talent with which to add to its beauty, and thought no ill of it.

She had sat up half the night thinking, and this morning she felt doubly restless and lonely. She wanted to go away at once, but as yet she had made no plans; and plans were necessary. She was too tired to go to Mr. Field and apply for work; and she knew that her delicate appearance would not commend itself to his approval. She went to the mirror in the

best spare bedroom and regarded herself anxiously.
Her black-robed figure seemed very tall and thin, her
face white and sharp.

"Even red bows —" she began; then her memory
tossed up Rosita. "Oh," she thought, "if I could
only see her,— see some one I care a little for. I
believe I'll go — there may have been some reason — her letters may have miscarried — I must see
somebody."

She ran upstairs, put on her outing things, and
walked rapidly to the station. The sharp air electrified
her blood. The world was full of youth and hope
once more. She forgot her bereavement for the hour.
She hoped Rosita would ask her to visit her: the
popular young prima donna must have drawn many
brilliant people about her.

When she reached New York she inquired her way
to "Soper's Opera House," obtained Rosita's address,
and took the elevated train up town. She found the
great apartment house with little difficulty, and was
enraptured with its marble floors and pillars, its liveried
servants and luxurious elevator.

"I certainly had rich ancestors," she thought, "and
I am sure they were swells. I have a natural affinity
for all this sort of thing."

She was landed at the very top of the house. The
elevator boy directed her attention to a button, then
slid down and out of sight, leaving Patience with the
delightful sensation of having stepped upon a new
stratum, high and away from the vast terrestrial cellar.

A trim French maid opened the door. She stared
at Patience, and looked disinclined to admit her. But
Patience pushed the door back with determined hand.

"I wish to see La Rosita," she said in French.

"But madame is not receiving to-day."

"She will see me, I am sure. Tell her that Miss Sparhawk is here."

The woman admitted her reluctantly, and left her standing in an anteroom, passing between heavy portières. Patience followed, and entered a large drawing-room furnished with amber satin and ebony : a magnificent room, heavy with the perfume of great baskets of flowers, and filled with costly articles of decoration. The carpet was of amber velvet. Not a sound of street penetrated the heavy satin curtains.

An indefinable sensation stole over Patience's mind, a ghost whose lineaments were blurred, yet familiar. She felt an impulse to turn and run, then twitched her shoulders impatiently, and approaching other portières, parted them and glanced into the room beyond.

It was evidently a boudoir, a fragrant fairy-like thing of rose and lace.

In a deep chair, clad in a *robe de chambre* of rose-coloured silk, flowing open over a lace smock and petti-coat, lay Rosita. Her dense black hair was twisted carelessly on top of her head and confined with a jewelled dagger. One tiny foot, shod in a high-heeled slipper of rose-coloured silk, was conspicuous on a low *pouf.* The flush of youth was in her cheek, its scarlet in her mouth. The large white lids lay heavily on the languorous eyes. In one hand she held a pink cigar-ette in a jewelled holder. She spoke in a low tantalis-ing voice to a man who sat before her, leaning eagerly forward.

The maid had evidently not succeeded in gaining

her attention. Patience, conquering another impulse to run, pushed the hangings aside and entered. Rosita sprang to her feet, the blood flashing to her hair; but her eyes expanded with pleasure.

"Patita! Patita!" she stammered, then caught Patience in her arms. As both girls looked as if about to weep, the man hurriedly departed.

The girls hugged each other as of old; then Rosita divested Patience of her wraps and told the astonished maid to take them out of sight.

"Now that you are here, you shall stay," she said, "stay a long, long while. Have you had luncheon?"

"No — but I'm not — yes, I am, though, come to think of it. Get me something to eat. Rosita, how good it is to see you again! Why, why didn't you write to me?"

"O—h; I will tell you, perhaps; but you must have luncheon first. I take a late breakfast, just after rising, so it will be a few minutes before yours is ready." She rang a bell and gave an order to the maid, then pushed Patience into the deepest and softest chair in the room.

"Now," she said, smiling affectionately, "lie back and be comfortable; you look tired. Oh, Patita, I am so glad to see you. Isn't it like old times?"

With a grace which long practice had made a fine art, she sank upon one end of a divan, and back among a mass of cushions. Her white arms lay along the pillows in such careless wise as to best exhibit their perfection; her head dropped backward slightly, revealing the round throat. The attitude was so natural as to suggest that she had ceased to pose.

Patience stared at her, wondering if it could be the same Rosita. All the freshness of youth was in that beautiful face and round voluptuous form, but she looked years and years and years older than the Rosita of Monterey. Patience suddenly felt young and foolish and green. The world that had been so great and wonderful to her imagination seemed to have shrunken to a ball, to be tossed from one to the other of those white idle hands.

"What has changed you so?" she asked abruptly.

Rosita gave the low delicious laugh of which Patience had read in the New York "Day." She relit her cigarette and blew a soft cloud.

"I will tell you after luncheon. You are the only person I would never fib to. I believe those grey eyes of yours are the only honest eyes in the world. Why are you in black?"

Patience told her, and was drawn on to speak of herself and her life. Rosita shuddered once or twice, an adorable little French shudder, and cast upward her glittering hands, whose nails Patience admired even more than their jewels.

"*Dios de mi alma!*" she cried finally. "What an existence! — I cannot call it life. I should have jumped into the river. That life would drive me mad, and I do not believe that it suits you either."

She spoke with a Spanish accent, and with the affected precision of a foreigner that has carefully learned the English language. Her monotony of inflection was more effective than animation.

"No, it does n't," said Patience, "and I have no intention of pursuing it. I 'm going to be a newspaper woman."

Rosita gave forth a sound that from any other throat would have been a shriek.

"A newspaper woman! And then you will come and interview me. How droll! I shall have to become eccentric, so that I can furnish you with 'stories,' as they call them. I have been pumped dry. When the newspaper women have run out of everything else they come to me, and they love me because I am good-natured, and turn my things upside down for them. I never refuse to see them, so they have never written anything horrid about me. Oh, I can tell you I have learned a great many lessons since I left Monterey. But here is your luncheon. While you are eating it I will do something for you that I have never done for any one else off the stage : I will sing to you."

The maid placed a silver tray on a little table, and while Patience ate of creamed oysters and broiled partridge, Rosita sang as the larks of paradise may sing when angels awake with the dawn. Once Patience glanced hastily upward, half expecting to see the notes falling in a golden shower. When she expressed her admiration, Rosita's red lips smiled slowly away from the white sharp little teeth.

"Do you like it, Patita *mia* ?" she asked with bewitching graciousness. "Yes, I can sing. I have the world at my feet."

She resumed her languid attitude on the divan. "*Bueno*," she said, "now I am going to tell you all about it. People are always a little heavy after eating : I waited on purpose. But you must promise not to move until I get through. Will you?"

"Yes," said Patience, uncomfortably. "I hope it is nothing very dreadful."

" That all depends upon the way you look at things.
It will seem odd to tell it to you. You used to be the
one to do what you felt like and tell other people that
if they did not like it they could do the other thing ;
but I suppose you are W. C. T. U'd."

" No, I'm not. Go on."

" Well, I will." She paused and laughed lightly.
" Funny world. We do not usually tell this sort of
story to a woman, but you and I are different. *Bueno.*

" I went to Paris and studied hard. Yes, I am lazy
yet, but I had made up my mind to be a great, great,
great success. I had what in insane people is called
the fixed idea, and the American in me conquered the
Spanish. Everybody praised my voice. No one said.
it was the greatest voice in the world, nor even better
than two or three others over there ; but I had no dis-
couragement. I attracted a great deal of attention
from men, but the *dueña* never let them get a word
with me, and I did not care. I used to wonder at the
stories told about some of the other girls, and did not
half understand. Two sold themselves ; but why ? with
a fortune in one's throat. Others fell in love, and
talked about the temperament of the artist, but I could
not understand that nonsense either.

" *Bueno*, at the end of the time Soper came over
and bought me eight trunks full of the most beautiful
clothes you ever saw, — mostly for the stage, but lots
for the house and street. He said I was a first-class
investment, and worth the outlay. When he heard me
sing he shook all over. I ought to tell you that I had
been kept on short allowance, and had had very dowdy
clothes, which broke my heart.

" *Bueno*, we came home. On the steamer, Soper

treated me like a father, but never let me talk to a
man.   Either he or the *dueña* was at my heels all the
time.   He is a coarse-looking man, but I really liked
him because he had been so good to me, and there
was something very attractive about him.   When we
reached New York the *dueña* left us.   She said she
was going straight to Philadelphia to her home.   Soper
and I got in another cab and drove to an apartment
on Broadway.   I did not know until the next day that
it was his apartment.   That was in the evening.   The
next morning, while I was at a late breakfast, he sent
me a note, saying that he would call in an hour and have
a business talk with me.   I was practising my scales
when he came in, and he clapped his hands and offered
me a chair.   He drew one up for himself, and then
said in a perfectly business-like voice : —

" ' When I ran across you I knew that you only
needed training to become a queen of opera bouffe, and
to make a fortune for some one besides yourself.   I
also saw that you were going to become a beautiful
woman.   I made up my mind that I would own both
the woman and the ,artist.   Don't look like a little
tigress — still, I 'm glad you can look that way, — you
may be able to do Carmen yet.   Don't misunderstand
me.   I am not a villain, merely a practical man with
an eye to beauty.   I have no idea of letting you get
under the influence of any other man, — not even if
you were n't so pretty.   Let me console you by telling
you that for the sort of woman you are there is no
escape.   You were made to drive men mad, and for the
comic opera stage.   That sort of combination might as
well get down to business as early in the game as possible : it saves time.

"'Had I never discovered you, you would have drifted from company to company, gone the pace with nothing to show for it, and worn out your youth at one-night stands. I saved you from a terrible fate. You know the rest. You know what you owe me. You have developed even beyond my hopes, but — mark you this — I have not advertised you in any way. You are as unknown as on the day you left California. If you mount the high horse and say: "Sir, you are a villain. Go to, go to!" I shall merely turn you loose without your trunks. You may imagine that with your voice and beauty you could get an engagement anywhere. So you could — without advertising, without an opera, and without a theatre of your own. Every existing troupe has its own prima donna; you would have to take a second or third rate part, — and unquestionably in a travelling troupe. There is no place for you in New York but the one I propose to create. Lillian Russell practically owns the Casino, and will, unless all signs fail, for many years. She would not tolerate you on the same stage five minutes; neither would any prima donna who had any influence with her manager, — and they mostly have. Your career would be exactly what it would have been if I had not met you, — full of hardships and change and racing about the country; arriving at six in the evening, singing at eight, leave the next morning at four, get what sleep you could on the train. That's about the size of it. You'd be painting inside of a year, if not wearing plumpers. And what you're mad at now, you'd be looking upon as a matter of course then, and grateful for the admiration.

"'Moreover, no success is worth a tinker's dam that

10

ain't made in New York, — I think I wrote you that on an average of once a month. If you show that you have horse sense, and will sign a contract with me for five years, I'll make you the rage in New York inside of two months. Now it is success or failure : you can take your choice. I'll be here to-morrow at ten.' And he was gone before I could speak.

"*Bueno*, after I had gotten over being fearfully mad I sat down and thought it all over. I knew that all he said was true. I had heard too much in Paris. He had kept writing me that virtue paid in an actress to keep me straight, but I had heard the opposite . about nine hundred times. *Bueno*, I was in a trap. I had made up my mind to succeed. I had even worked for it, — and you know how much that meant with me. I made up my mind that succeed I would, no matter what the price. It is one of two things in this world, — success or failure, — and if you fail nobody cares a hang about your virtue.

"You know I never was sentimental nor romantic. Soper had made a plain business proposition in a practical way that I liked. If he had gone on like a stage lover it would have been much harder. And after all I would be no worse than a society girl who sells herself to a rich husband. So, after turning it over for twenty-four hours — or all the time I was awake — I concluded not to be a fool, but La Rosita, Queen of Opera Bouffe. When he called I merely shrugged my shoulders and said '*Bueno*.' He laughed, and said I would certainly succeed in this world ; that the beautiful woman with the cool calculating brain always got there. So — here I am. What do you think of it?"

During this recital her voice had not for one instant

broken nor hardened. She told her story in the soft sweet languid voice of Spain ; she might have been relating an idyl of which she was the Juliet and Soper the Romeo.

Patience stared at her with wide eyes and dry lips.

"And you have never regretted it?" she asked; "you don't care?"

Rosita raised her beautiful brows. "Regret? Well, no, I should say not. Have I not realised my dreams and ambition? Am I not rich and famous and happy instead of a scrambling nobody? Regret?—No—rather. What is more, I know how to save. A good many of us have learned that lesson. When I have lost voice and youth I shall be rich, — rich. We do not end in a garret, like in the old days. And I do not drink, and I rest a great deal—it will be a long time before I go off. Besides, there are the beauty doctors— Oh, no, I am not regretting. And Soper is getting tired of me, I am happy to say."

Patience rose and went into the room where the maid had carried her hat and jacket. It was a bedroom, a white nest of lace and velvet. When she returned she said : " I should like to go home and think it over. I feel queer and stunned. You have taken me so completely by surprise that I can hardly think."

Rosita coloured angrily.

"You are shocked, I suppose," she said with a sneer. "I should think—" She paused abruptly. She was still an amiable little soul.

Patience understood perfectly, and turned a shade paler. " I told you that I did not understand how I felt. In fact, I hardly ever know just how I feel about anything. I suppose it is because I have the sort of

mind that is made to analyse, and I have n't had experience enough to know how. And I never judge any one.
Why should I? Why should we judge anybody? We
are not all made alike. I could n't do what you have
done, but that is no reason why I should condemn you.
That would be absurd. If any one else had told me
this story I should only have been interested — I am so
curious about everything. But you see you are the only
girl friend I ever had, and that is what makes me feel
so strangely. Good-bye;" and she hurriedly left the
room.

XV

WHEN she reached home she forgot her horror of
death chambers, and went to Miss Tremont's room and
flung herself on the bed. She did not cry — her tears
had all been spent; but she felt something of the profound misery of the last year in Monterey. During the
intervening years she had seen little of the cloven hoof
of human nature; the occasional sin over on Hog
Heights hardly counted; creatures of the lower conditions had no high lights to make the shadows startling. But to-day the horror of old experiences rushed
over her; she was filled with a profound loathing of
life, of human nature.

So far, of love, in its higher sense — if it possessed
such a part — she had seen nothing; of sensuality, too
much. True, she had spent two weeks with Miss Galpin, during that estimable young woman's engagement;
but Miss Galpin took love as a sort of front-parlour,
evening-dress affair, and Patience had not deigned to

be interested. She had speculated somewhat over Miss Tremont's early romance, but could only conclude that it was one of those undeveloped little histories that so many old maids cherish.

She recalled all the love stories she had read. Even the masters were insipid when they attempted to portray spiritual love. It was only when they got down to the congenial substratum of passion that they wrote of love with colour and fire. Was she to believe that it did not exist, — this union of soul and mind? Her dreams receded, and refused to cohere. She wondered, with natural egoism, if any girl of her age had ever received so many shocks. She was on the threshold of life, with a mass of gross material out of which to shape her mental attitude to existing things. True, she had met only women of relative sinlessness during these last years, but their purity was uninteresting because it was that of people mentally limited, and possessed of the fad of the unintellectual. Moreover, they had their erotism, the oddest, most unreal, and harmless erotism the world has known in the last two thousand years; and after all quite incidental: her keen eyes had long since observed that the old maids were far more religious than the married women, that the girls cooled perceptibly to the great abstraction as soon as a concrete candidate was approved.

She longed passionately for Miss Tremont. All her old restlessness and doubt had returned with the flight of that ardent absorbing personality. She wished that she could have been remodelled; for, after all, the dear old lady, whatever her delusions, had been happy. But she was still Patience Sparhawk; she could only be thankful that Miss Tremont had cemented her hatred of evil.

She rose abruptly, worn out by conjectures and analysis that led nowhere, and went out into the woods.

"Oh," she said, lifting her arms, "this at least is beautiful."

The ground was hard and white and sparkling. The trees were crystal, down to the tiniest twig. They glittered iridescently under the level rays of the sun descending upon the Palisades on the far side of the Hudson. The river was grey under great floating blocks of ice. Groves of slender trees in the hollows of the Palisades looked like fine bunches of feathers. On the long slopes the white snow lay deep; above, the dark steeps were merely powdered, here and there; on the high crest the woods looked black.

She walked rapidly up and down, calmed, as of old, by the beauty of nature, but dreading the morrow and the recurring to-morrows. Suddenly through those glittering aisles pealed the rich sonorous music of the organ. The keys were under the hands of a master, and the great notes throbbed and swelled and rolled through the winter stillness in the divine harmonies of "The Messiah." Patience stood still, shaking a little. On a hill above the wood a large house had been built recently; the organ must be there.

The diamond radiance of the woods was living melody. The very trees looked to bow their crystal heads. The great waves of harmony seemed rolling down from an infinite height, down from some cathedral of light and stars.

The ugly impressions of the day vanished. The sweet intangible longing she had been used to know in Carmel tower flashed back to her. What was it? She recalled the words of the Stranger. It was long since she had thought of him. She closed her eyes and stood with him in the tower. His voice was as distinct as the notes of the organ. She felt again the tumult of her young half-comprehending mind. Was not life all a matter of ideals? Were not the bad and the good happy only if consistent to a fixed idea? Did she make of herself such a woman as the Stranger had evoked out of the great mass of small feminity, could she not be supremely happy with such a man? Where was he? Was he married? He seemed so close — it was incredible that he existed for another woman. Who more surely than she could realise the purest ideal of her imaginings, — she with her black experience and hatred of all that was coarse and evil? She closed her eyes to her womanhood no longer. It thrilled and shook her. If he would come — She trembled a little.

All men were henceforth possible lovers. Unless the Stranger appeared speedily his memory must give way to the definite. The imperious demands of a woman's nature cannot be satisfied with abstractions. The ideal which he stood for would lend a measure of itself to each engaging man with whom she exchanged greeting.

XVI

"MISS PATIENCE!" cried a strident voice.

Patience turned with a violent start. Ellen was a large blotch on the white beauty of the wood.

"There's a young lady to see you. She didn't give her name as I remember."

Patience followed the servant resentfully. The world was cold and dull again. But when she recognised the Peele coachman and footman on the handsome sleigh before the door she forgot her dreams, and went eagerly into the house.

A girl was standing before the mantel, regarding through a lorgnette a row of photographs. She turned as she heard footsteps, and came forward with a cordial smile on her plain charming face. She wore a black cloth frock and turban which made Patience feel dowdy as Rosita's magnificence had not.

"I am Hal," she said, "and you are Patience, of course. I hope you have heard as much of me as I have of you. Dear old girl, I was awfully fond of her. You look so tired — are you?"

"A little. It is so good of you to come. Yes, I've heard a very great deal of you."

"I'll sit down, thank you. Let's try this sofa. I've already tried the chairs, and they're awful. But I suppose dear old Harriet never sat down at all. I wonder if she'll be happy in heaven with nothing to do."

Patience smiled sympathetically. "She ought to be glad of a rest, but I don't believe she is."

"She thought we were all heathens — dear old soul; but I did love her. What was the trouble? We only had one short letter from Miss Beale. Do tell me all about it."

Miss Peele had an air of reposeful alertness. She leaned forward slightly, her eyes fixed on Patience's with flattering attention. She looked a youthful worldling, a captivating type to a country girl. Her voice was very sweet, and exquisitely modulated. Occasionally it went down into a minor key.

"What shall you do with yourself, now?" she asked anxiously, when Patience had finished the brief story. "I am so interested in you. I don't know why I have n't called before, except that I never find time to do the things I most care for; but I have wanted to come a dozen times, and when we returned yesterday and heard of the dear old girl's death I made up my mind to come at once. And I 'm coming often. I know we shall be such good friends. I 'm so glad she left you her money so you won't have to work. It must be so horrid to work. I 'm going to ask mamma to ask you to visit us. She 's feeling rather soft now over Cousin Harriet's death, so I 'll strike before she gets the icebergs on. She is n't pleasant then. I 'll tell her you don't wear the white ribbon yet —" She broke into a light peal of laughter. "Poor mamma! how she used to suffer. Cousin Harriet's white bow was the great cross of her life. It will go far toward reconciling her — Don't think that my parent is heartless. She merely insists upon everything belonging to her to be *sans reproche*. That 's the reason we don't always get along. What lovely hair you have — a real *blonde cendrée*. It 's all the rage in Paris. And that great coil is beautiful. Tell me, did n't you find that Temperance work a hideous bore?"

"Oh, yes, but no one could resist Miss Tremont."

"Indeed one could n't. I believe she 'd have roped me in if I 'd lived with her; but I 'm a frivolous good-for-nothing thing. You look so serious. Do you always feel that way?"

Patience smiled broadly. "Oh, no. I often feel that I would be very frivolous indeed if circumstances would permit. It must be very interesting."

"You get tired of yourself sometimes — I mean I do. Are you very religious?"

"I am not religious at all."

"Oh, how awfully jolly. I do the regulation business, but it is really tragic to carry so much religion round all the time. I wonder how Cousin Harriet and the Lord hit it off, or if they liked each other better at a distance? I corresponded once with the brother of a school friend for a year, and when I met him I could n't endure him. Those things are very trying. I am going to call you Patience. May I? And if ever you call me Miss Peele you 'll be sorry. How awfully smart you 'd look in gowns. My colouring is so commonplace. If I did n't know how to dress, and had n't been taught to carry myself with an air, I 'd be just nothing — no more and no less. But you have such a lovely nose and white skin — and that hair! You are aristocratic looking without being swagger. I 'm the other way. You can acquire the one, but you can't the other. When you have both you 'll be out of sight.

"What fun it would be," she rambled on in her bright inconsequential way, "if Bev should fall in love with you and you 'd marry him. Then I 'd have such fun dressing you, and we 'd get ahead of my cousin Honora Mairs, whom I hate, and who, I 'm afraid, will get him. Propinquity and flattery will bring down any man — they 're such peacocks. But I 'll bring him to see you. You ought to have a violet velvet frock. I 'd bet on Bev then. But, of course, you can't wear colours yet, and that dead black is wonderfully becoming. Can I bring him up in a day or two?"

"Oh, yes," said Patience, smiling as she recalled her brief periods of spiritual matrimony with Beverly Peele;

" by all means. I 'll be so glad to meet all of you. And you are certainly good to take so much interest in me."

" I am the angel of the family. Well, I must be off, or I 'll have to dine all by me lonely. None of the rest of the family uses slang: that is the reason I do. May is a grown-up baby, and never disobeyed her mamma in her life. Honora is a classic, and only swears in the privacy of her closet when her schemes fail. Mother — well, you 've seen mother. As you may imagine, she does n't use slang. Papa does n't talk at all, and Bev is a prig where decent women are concerned. So, you see, I have to let off steam somehow, and as I have n't the courage to be larky, I read French novels and use bad words."

She rose and moved toward a heavy coat that lay on a chair. " Well, Patience — what a funny lovely old-fashioned name you have — I 'm going to bring Bev to see you as a last resource. I 've tried him on a dozen other girls, but it was no go. I 'll talk you up to him meanwhile — I 'll tell him that you are one of the cold haughty indifferent sort, and yet withal a village maiden. He admires blondes, and you 're such a natural one. We 'll come up Sunday on horseback. Now be sure to make him think you don't care a hang whether he likes you or not — he 's been so run after. Is n't it too funny? I did not come here on matchmaking thoughts intent, but I do like you, and we could have such jolly good fun together. I 'll teach you how to smoke cigarettes — "

" But Miss Peele — Hal — you know — I don't want to marry your brother — I have never even seen him — much as I should like to live with you — I 'd even smoke cigarettes to please you — but really — "

" Oh, I know, of course. I can only hope for the

best, and Bev certainly is fascinating. At least he appears to be," and she smiled oddly; "but being a man's sister is much like being his valet, you know. Would you mind helping me into this coat?

"I hate these heavy fur things," she said petulantly. "Oh, thanks — they don't suit my light and airy architecture, and I can't get up any dignity in them at all. I need fluffy graceful French things. You'd look superb in velvet and furs and all that sort of thing. Well, bye-bye, — no, — *au revoir*."

She took Patience's face between her hands and lightly kissed her on either cheek.

"Don't be lonesome," she said. "I'd go frantic in this house. Can't I send you some books? I've a lot of naughty French ones — "

"No!" said Patience, abruptly, "I don't want them. Don't think I'm a prig," she added, hastily, as a look of apprehension crossed Miss Peele's face; "but I had a hideous shock to-day, and I don't want to read anything similar at present — "

"Oh, tell me about it. How could you have a shock in Mariaville?"

"I did n't. It was in New York — "

"Oh, was it real wicked? Did you have an adventure? Do tell me — Well, don't, of course, if you don't want to, only I'm so interested in you. Well, I must, must go;" and despite the furs she moved down the walk with exceeding grace. As she drove off she leaned out of the sleigh and waved her hand.

"Oh!" thought Patience, "I'm so glad she came. It was like fresh air after a corpse covered with sachet bags." And then she went to the mantel and gazed upon Beverly Peele.

XVII

WHEN Sunday came Patience dressed herself with unusual care. It did not occur to her that people in different spheres of life arose at different hours, and she expected her guests any time after eight o'clock.

Of course she must wear unrelieved black, but after prolonged regard in the becoming mirror of the best spare room, she decided that it rather enhanced her charms, now that a week's rest had banished the circles from her eyes and cleared her skin.

She had coiled her soft ashen hair loosely on the top of her head, pulling it out a little about her face — she wore no bangs. Her restless eyes were dark and clear and sparkling, her mouth pink. She carried her slender figure with a free graceful poise. The carriage of her head was almost haughty. Her hips had a generous swell. Her hands and teeth were very white.

"I certainly have a look of race," she thought, "if I'm not a beauty. I'd give a good deal to know that my ancestors really did have good blood in their veins. I don't care so much for money, but I'd like to be sure of that."

After breakfast she wandered about restlessly. She had known few moments of peace since Miss Peele's visit. The train had been fired, and her being was in a tumult. Beverly Peele, the Stranger, and the vague ideals of her earlier girlhood were inextricably mixed. The result was a being before whom she trembled with mingled rapture and terror. Her vivid imagination had evoked a distinct entity, and the love scenes that

had been enacted between the girl and this wholly satisfactory eidolon were such as have time out of mind
made life as it is seem a singularly defective composition to the wondering mind of woman.

At times she was terrified at the rich possibilities of
her nature, so little suspected. The revelation gave
her vivid comprehension of woman's tremendous power
for sacrifice and surrender, possibilities of which she
had read with much curiosity, but little sympathy. For
those women she felt a warm honour, a fierce desire to
espouse their cause. For Rosita she had only loathing
and contempt.

It was not only passion that was awake. Sentiment,
that finer child of the brain, and the sweet faint feeling
which assuredly lingers about the region of the heart,
whatever its physical cause may be, were there in full
measure to lend their potent lashings to that primeval
force which is as mighty in some women as in some
men. It is doubtful if a woman ever loves a man when
in his arms with the same exaltation of soul and passion
which she feels for that creation of her brain that he
little more than suggests, and that is only wholly hers
when the man himself is absent. Imagination in
woman is as arbitrary as desire in man, and she is
beaten down and crushed by this imperious and capricious brain-imp so many times in her life that the
wonder is she is not driven to the hopes and illusions of
religion, or to humour, long before the skin has yellowed
and the eye paled.

And when the imagination has full sway, when the
man has not been beheld, when he has been invested
' with every quality dear to the heart of the generously
endowed woman, when, indeed, all eidola blend, and

she has a confused vision of an immense and mighty force bearing down upon her which shall sweep every tradition out of existence and annihilate the material world, then assuredly man himself would do well to retire into obscurity and curse his shortcomings.

It was four o'clock, and she had been through the successive stages of hope, despair, hope, melancholia, hope, and resignation, before she heard the sharp clatter of hoofs on the road. She ran to the dining-room window, her heart thumping, and peered through the blind. They were coming! Hal sat her horse like a swaying reed, but the young man on the large chestnut rode in the agonised fashion of the day. He was of medium height, she saw, compactly and elegantly built, and the beauty of his face had defied the photographer's art.

Patience ran to the kitchen and told Ellen to answer the bell immediately, then sat down by the stove to compose herself. She was still trembling, and wished to appear cold and stately, as Hal had recommended. When Ellen returned and announced the visitors, she sprang up, patted her hair, pulled down the bodice of her gown, and then, with what dignity she could muster, went forth to meet her fate. She did wish she had a train. It was so difficult to be stately in a skirt that cleared the ground.

As she entered the parlour Mr. Peele was standing by the opposite door. His riding gear was very becoming. Patience noted swiftly that his eyes were a spotted brown and that his mouth pouted under the dark moustache.

Hal came forward with both hands extended. "We have come, you see," she said, "and we had to make a

wild break to do it — had a lot of company; but I
was bound to come. Patience, this is Beverly. He's
quite frantic to meet you. It was all I could do to
keep him away until to-day."

The young man bowed in anything but a frantic
manner, and stood gracefully until the girls were seated.
Then he took a chair and caressed his moustache,
regarding Patience attentively.

"Would you mind if Bev smoked?" asked Hal.
"He is just wild for a cigar. We had to ride so hard
to keep warm that he did n't have a chance, and he's
a slave to the weed."

Patience glanced swiftly at the door, half-expecting
to see the indignant wraith of Miss Tremont, then,
almost reluctantly, gave the required permission. Mr.
Peele promptly lit a cigar. Patience wondered if he
would ever speak. Perhaps he did not think it worth
his while. He looked very haughty.

"We had a perfectly beautiful ride," said Hal, in
her plaintive voice. "I'd rather be on a horse than
on an ocean steamer, and I do love to travel. You
look ever so much better than you did, Patience. You
must have needed a rest."

Mr. Peele removed his cigar. "Perhaps that was what
she had been *im*patiently waiting for," he remarked.

Patience stared at him. Her eyes expanded. Something seemed crumbling within her.

"Oh, Bev, you do make me so tired," said his sister.
"I tell him eighteen times a day that punning is the
lowest form of wit, but he's incorrigible. I suppose it's
in the blood, and I'm glad it broke out in him instead
of in me. It is well to be philosophical in this
life —"

" When you can't help yourself — " interrupted Mr. Peele, easily.

Patience felt it incumbent upon her to make conversation, although her thoughts were dancing a jig.

" You have a beautiful horse," she said to the young man.

His eyes lit up with enthusiasm. " Isn't she a beauty?" he exclaimed. " She's taken two prizes and won a race. She's the daughter — "

" Patience doesn't know anything about horses," interrupted Hal. "What does she care whose daughter Firefly is?"

" Oh, I'm very much interested," faltered Patience.

" Are you really?" cried Mr. Peele, with a smile so beautiful that Patience caught her breath. " I've got the rarest book in the country on horses — beautiful pictures — coloured — I'll bring it up and explain it to you. Tell you a lot of stories about famous horses."

" I shall be delighted."

" Do you ride?"

" I used to ride a pony, but I haven't been on a horse for so long I've almost forgotten what it's like."

" That's too bad. There's nothing like it. Makes you feel so good. When I have dyspepsia I just jump on Firefly, and I'm all right in less than no time. I take a canter for dyspepsia — although I can't — er — always feel at home that way. Ahem!"

Patience wanted to tear her hair. It was with an effort that she kept her face from convulsing with disgust. She caught sight of the young man's intellectual brow, and, without any premonitory consciousness, laughed aloud. Mr. Peele smiled back with the pleasure of appreciated wit, and resumed his cigar.

"Bev is n't such a fool as he looks," remarked Hal, airily. "Just have patience with him. We all have our little failings."

Patience sat as if turned to clay. She could not talk. All her natural animation had deserted her. She wished they would go and leave her alone. But Hal pulled off her riding gloves, and made herself comfortable on the sofa. As she rattled on, Patience noticed how beautiful her nails were. She turned her own hands over so that the palms lay upward.

"Never mind," said young Peele, in a low tone. "They're much prettier."

"What's that?" cried Hal. "What are you blushing about, Patience? How lovely it is to blush like that. I've forgotten how — and I'm only twenty-two. There's tragedy for you. It's not that I've had so many compliments about my beauty, nor yet about my winning ways, — which are my strong point, — but I found so much to blush about when I was first launched upon this wicked world that I exhausted my capacity. And Bev always did tell such naughty stories — " She paused abruptly. "Dear me! perhaps I've made a bad break, and prejudiced you against my brother; and I want you to be good friends so that we can have jolly times together. Perhaps you have an ideal man — a sort of Sir Galahad. I have n't sounded you yet."

"Sir Galahad is not my ideal," said Patience, with the quick scorn of the woman who is born with intuitive knowledge of man. "I could not find anything interesting in an elongated male infant."

"Oh, how lovely!" cried Hal. "Give me the man of the world every time. I tell you, you appreciate the difference when you have to entertain 'em. And the elongated infant, as you put it, never understands a woman, and she has no use for that species whatever. He does n't even want to understand her, and a woman resents that as a personal insult. The bad ones hurt sometimes, but they 're interesting ; and when you learn how to manage them it 's plain sailing enough. Mrs. Laurence Gibbs — a friend of mamma's, awfully good, goes in for charity and all that sort of thing — said the other day that at the rate women were developing and advancing, the standard of men morally would have to be raised. But I said ' Not much ! ' that the development of woman meant that women were becoming more clever, not merely bright and intellectual, and that clever women would demand cleverness and fascination in man above all else ; and that Sir Galahads were not that sort. It 's experience that makes a man interesting to us women, — they represent all we 'd like to be and don't dare. If they were like ourselves — if they did n't excite our imaginations — we would n't care a hang for them. Mrs. Gibbs was horrified, of course, and told me I did n't know what I was talking about. But I said I guessed it was the other way. I 'm not clever — not by a long sight, — and if I can't stand a prig I know a clever woman can't and won't."

"I 'm so glad I 'm not a prig," murmured Mr. Peele.

"Oh, you 're a real devil. If you were clever now, you 'd have to be shut up to protect society ; but as it is, you just go on your good looks, so you 're not as dangerous as some."

She rattled on, not giving the others a chance for more than a stray remark. Patience, listening with deep curiosity to this new philosophy, became aware of an increasing desire to turn her eyes to the man that had so bitterly disappointed her. A direct potent force seemed to emanate from him. It was her first experience of man's magnetism, but she knew that he possessed it to a remarkable degree. When he finally shot out an insignificant remark she felt, in the excuse it gave her to turn to him, a sensation of positive relief. He was leaning back in his chair, in the easy attitude of a man that has been too accustomed to luxury all his life to look uncomfortable in any circumstances. With his picturesque garb, his noble, beautiful face, his subtle air of elegance and distinction, he looked the ideal hero of girlhood's dreams. Patience wondered what Nature had been about, then recalled the many tricks of that capricious dame made famous in history, the round innocent faces of the worst boys in the Loyal Legion class, the saintly physiognomy of a Mariaville minister who had recently fallen from grace.

Peele was watching her out of his half-closed eyes, and as she met them he smiled almost affectionately. Patience averted her head quickly, angry that she had felt an impulse to respond, and fixed her attention on Hal. "Dear old Cousin Harriet," that young woman was remarking, "how I do wish that I were even sorrier than I am that she is dead. I try to think it 's because I saw so little of her; but I know it 's just because I 'm so beastly selfish. I don't care a hang for anything that does n't affect my own happiness — "

"You 're not selfish," interrupted Patience, indignantly.

"Oh, but I am," said Miss Peele, with a comical little air of disgust which sat as gracefully upon her as all her varying moods and manners. "I get up think-ing what I can get out of the day, and I go to bed glad or mad according to what the day has done for me. I don't go in for Church work like Honora — dear Honora! — nor am I always doing some pretty little thing for people like May. I suppose you think I'm an angel because I came to see you. I assured myself at great length that it was my duty — but it was plain curiosity, no more nor less; and now I like you awfully, better than any woman I ever met — and I do so want you to come and visit us, but — "

"Could n't you come and stay with me?" asked Patience, hurriedly. She had no desire to visit Mrs. Gardiner Peele. "You know you have more or less company, and I should be very quiet for a while. And oh! I should so like to have you."

"Oh, I'd love to! I'll come and stay a week. I'm so sick of the whole family, Bev included. We won't be going anywhere for three months out of respect for Cousin Harriet — mamma is very particular about those things — and I can get away as well as not. I'll come on Tuesday, — can I? Bev will come up occasionally and see how I'm getting on — won't you, Bevvy, dear?"

"I'd much rather you would not be here," said Mr. Peele, calmly.

"Oh — really — well, we're all young yet. I'm coming all the same. I suppose we must be going. We have to get home to dress for dinner, you know."

She rose, and drew on her gloves. Her brother stood up immediately and helped her into her covert coat. "Well, Patience," she said, kissing her lightly, "you'll see me on Tuesday. I'll come by train, and wire you beforehand. Mamma'll raise Cain, but I'll manage it.

It's only occasionally she's too much for me. The cold glare of those blue eyes of hers freezes my marrow at times and takes all the starch out of me. It's àwful to have been brought up under that sort of eye. When Honora marries it's the sort of eye she'll have. She cultivates the angelic at present. Have I talked you to death, Patience? So good of you to ask me to come."

Peele held out his hand, and Patience could do no less than lay hers within it. As it closed she resisted an impulse to nestle her own more closely into that warm grasp. He held her hand longer than was altogether necessary, and she felt indignantly that she had no desire to draw it away.

"That'll do for one day," said Hal, drily. "Come along, Beverly Peele. We won't get home for coffee at this rate."

When they had gone Patience threw herself on the sofa and burst into tears, then laughed suddenly. "I feel like the heroine of a tragedy," she thought. "And the tragedy is a pun !"

XVIII

HAL arrived on Tuesday afternoon. Patience for twenty-four hours after Beverly Peele's visit looked upon life through grey spectacles. She had an impression of being a solitary figure on a sandy waste, illimitable in extent. Life was ugly practical reality. It frightened her, and she cowered before it, hating the future, her blood chilled, her nerves blunt, her brain stagnant.

But by Tuesday morning, being young and buoyant, she revived, and roamed through the woods, entirely loyal to the Stranger. She made up her mind that she would find him, that he could not be married. He must have waited for her. "Oh!" she thought, "if I could not believe that something existed in this world as I have imagined it, some man good enough to love and look up to, I believe I'd jump into the river. At least I have heard Him talk. He could not be a disappointment, like that hollow bronze. If there are many men in the world like Beverly Peele I don't wonder women are in revolt. Women start out in life with big ideals of man, and if they are disappointed I suppose they unconsciously strive to make themselves what they should have found in man. But it is unnatural. It seems to me that man must be able to give woman the best she can find in life, whether he does or not. Something in civilisation has gone wrong."

"I've been so restless," she said to Hal, as the girls sat on the edge of the bed in the spare room, holding each other's hand. "If you had not been coming I'd have gone to New York before this and seen Mr. Field, the editor of the 'Day'— He promised me once he'd make a newspaper woman of me —"

"A what?" cried Hal. "What on earth do you want to be a newspaper woman for?"

"Well, I must be something. I couldn't live out of Mariaville on my income, and the few hundred dollars Mr. Foord left me, and I don't know of anything else I want to be."

"You are going to be Mrs. Beverly Peele," said Hal, definitely. "Beverly has the worst attack of my recollection. He has simply raved about you. Tell me, don't you like him?"

Patience said nothing.

Hal leaned forward and turned Patience's face about. "Don't you like him?" she asked in a disappointed tone. "Tell me. Please be frank. I hate people who are not."

"Well, I'll confess it — I was disappointed in him. You see, I'd thought about him a good deal — several years, if you want to know the truth — and I was sure he was an intellectual man —"

Hal threw back her head and gave a clear ringing laugh. "Bev intellectual! That's too funny. I don't believe he ever read anything but a newspaper and horse literature in his life. But we all think he's bright. I think it my duty to tell you that he has a fearful temper. He's always been mamma's pet, and she never would cross him, so he flies into regular tantrums when things don't go to suit him; but on the whole he's pretty good sort. Don't you think he's good-looking?"

"Oh, wonderfully," said Patience, glad to be enthusiastic.

"Well, I'm sure you'll like him when you've forgotten the ideal and got used to the real. Do please try to like him, for I'm bent on having you for a sister-in-law."

"Well, I'll try," said Patience, laughing.

"You have no idea," continued the astute Miss Peele, "how many girls have been in love with him. I've known girls that looked like marble statues — the marble statue with the snub nose; that's our swagger New York type, you know, — well, I've seen them make perfect idiots of themselves about him. But so far he's rather preferred the ladies that don't visit at Peele Manor. I've brought some cigarettes. Can I smoke?"

"You can just do anything you like."

"Thanks. Well, I think I'll begin by lying down on this soft bed. It's way ahead of the chairs and sofa in the parlour."

She exchanged her frock for a *peignoir*, and extended herself on the bed. Patience sat beside her in a rocking chair, her troubles forgotten.

"By the way," said Hal, suddenly removing her cigarette, "what was the shock you had the other day? Tell me."

"Well, I will," and Patience told the story of Rosita from beginning to end. Hal listened with deep interest.

"That's a stunner," she said, "and worth coming to Mariaville for. The little rip. She did n't tell you half. I'll bet my hopes of a tiara on that. But she does dance and sing like an angel. And so you were children together? How perfectly funny! Now tell me your history, every bit of it."

Patience hesitated, then impulsively told the story, omitting few particulars.

Miss Peele's cigarette was allowed to go out. "Well, well," she said, when Patience had finished. "Fate did play the devil with you, did n't she? I'm so glad you've told me. I'll tell the family what I like, and you keep quiet. I have the inestimable gift of selection. You poor child! I'm so glad you fell in with Cousin Harriet; and now you are going to be happy for the rest of your life. Oh, it's so good to be here in this quiet place. I'm so tired of everybody. Sometimes

I get a fearful disgust. The same old grind, year after year. If I could only fall in love; but when I do I know it 'll be with a poor man. I never did have any luck."

"Would n't you marry him?"

Hal shook her wise young head. "I don't know. You never can tell what you 'll do when you get that disease; but I do know that I 'd be miserable if I did. Money, and plenty of it, is necessary to my happiness. You see we 're not so horribly rich. Papa gives mamma and May and me two thousand dollars each a year, and his income comes mostly from his practice. We have n't anything else but a little house in town, and Peele Manor — which of course we 'll never sell — and a big farm adjoining. Bev runs that, and has the income from it — about three thousand dollars a year. When he wants more mamma gets it for him, and when he 's married of course he 'll have a lot more. Two thousand stands me in very well now, but as a married woman I want nothing under thirty thousand a year — and that 's a modest ambition enough. You can't be anybody in New York on less. Oh, dear — life is a burden."

"Your woes are not very terrible," said Patience, drily.

"Oh, you 'd think so if you were me. We suffer according to our capacities and point of view. What is comedy to one is tragedy to another. If I had to wear the same clothes for two seasons I 'd be as miserable as a defeated candidate for the Presidency. Beer makes one man drunk and champagne another. Bev, by the way, never drinks. He 's rather straight than otherwise. What 's your ideal of a man, by the way? Of course you have an ideal."

"Oh, I don't know," said Patience, vaguely. "A man with a big brain and a big heart and a big arm."

Miss Peele laughed heartily. "You are not exacting in your combinations, not in the least."

The week passed delightfully to Patience, although Hal became rather restless toward the end. She arranged Patience's hair in six different fashions, then decided that the large soft coil suited her best. Patience's nails were manicured, she was taught how to smoke cigarettes, and select extracts from French novels were read to her. Hal was an accomplished gossip, and regaled her hostess with all the whispered scandals of New York society. She was a liberal education.

Beverly did not call, nor did he write, and Hal anathematised him freely.

"But I have my ideas on the subject," she said darkly. "Just you wait."

XIX

On the evening of Hal's departure, as Patience was braiding her hair for the night, there was a sharp ring at the bell, and a few moments later Ellen came upstairs with a card inscribed "Mr. Beverly Peele." Patience felt disposed to send word that she had retired, so thoroughly had she lost interest in the young man; but reflecting that he had probably ridden ten miles on a cold night to see her, told Ellen to light all the burners in the parlour, and twisted up her hair.

As she went downstairs she saw a heavy overcoat on the hall table.

"If it had occurred to me that he had come by train," she thought, "I'd have let him go home again."

He came forward with his charming smile, looking remarkably handsome in his evening clothes.

"It was kind of you to come," she said, too unsophisticated to feel embarrassed at receiving a man at night in a house where she lived alone with a servant. "Of course you knew how lonely I must be."

"Hal is good company, is n't she?" he asked, holding her hand and staring hard at her. "But I should think she 'd miss you more than you 'd miss her."

Patience withdrew her hand abruptly. Her face wore its accustomed cold gravity, contradicted by the eager eyes of youth. "Won't you sit down? I hope Hal has missed me, but she has hardly had time to tell you so."

"Has n't she? She has had several hours, and I suppose you know by this time how fast she can talk. She 's awfully bright, don't you think so?"

"Indeed she is."

"She is n't a beauty like May, nor intellectual like Honora, but you can't have everything — that is, everybody can't."

"Does any one?" asked Patience, indifferently.

"Hal says you are the cleverest woman she has ever met, — and — "

"I 'm afraid Hal is carried away by the enthusiasms of the moment," said Patience, as he paused. She was highly gratified, nevertheless.

" — you are the prettiest woman I ever saw," he continued, as if she had not spoken.

" Oh, nonsense ! " exclaimed Patience, angrily, but the colour flew to her face.

" I mean it," and indisputably his eyes spoke admiration. " I 've thought of no one else since I was here. I have n't come before, because there 's nothing in calling on your sister, and that 's what it would have amounted to. But, you see, I 'm here the very night she left."

" You are very flattering." Patience was beginning to feel vaguely uncomfortable. She realised that the lore gathered from novels was valueless in a practical emergency, and longed for the experience of Hal. " I understand that you are considered fascinating, and I suppose most women do like to be flattered."

" I never paid a woman a compliment before in my life," he said, unblushingly. " You don't look a bit like any woman I ever saw. Hal says you look like a ' white star on a dark night,' and that 's about the size of it. You have such lovely hair and skin. I 've always rather admired plump women, but your slenderness suits you — "

" Oh, please talk about something else ! I am not used to such stuff, and I don't like it. Suppose you talk about yourself." (She had read that man could ever be beguiled by this bait.) " Are you as fond of travel as Hal is ? "

" I never travel," he said shortly. " When I find a comfortable place I stay in it. Westchester County suits me down to the ground."

" You mean to say that you can travel and don't? that you don't care at all to see the beautiful things in Europe ? "

" Oh, my mother always brings home a lot of pho-

tographs and things, and that's all I want of it. I
never could understand why Americans are so restless.
I'm sick of the very sound of Europe, anyway."

"Are you fond of New York? "

" New York is the centre of the earth, and full of
pretty — interesting things, dontcherknow? I've had
some gay times there, I can tell you. But I've
settled down now, and prefer Westchester County to
any place on earth. I'd rather be behind or on
a horse than anything else."

" Don't you care for society? "

" I hate it. One winter was enough for me. Wild
horses would n't drag me into a ball-room again. Of
course when the house is full of company in summer
I like that well enough. I play billiards with the men
and spoon — flirt with the girls and the pretty married
women ; but I 'm just as contented when they 've all
cleared out."

" Do you mean to say that you stay in the country
by yourself all winter? What do you do? Read? "

" N–o–o–o. I don't care much about books. We
have a big farm and I run it, and I skate and drive
and ride and smoke — Oh, there's plenty to do.
Occasionally I go to town and have a little fun."

" What do you call fun if you don't like society,
— the theatre? "

" The theatre ! " he laughed. " I never sat out
a play in my life. Oh, I don't know you well enough
to tell you everything yet. Sometime, I 'll tell you
a lot of funny things."

" Perhaps you enjoy the newspapers in winter," said
Patience, hastily.

" Oh, I read even the advertisements. The papers

are all the reading any man wants. There are two or three good sensational stories every day."

"I don't read those," said Patience, disgustedly. This idol appeared to be clay straight up to his hair. "I like to read the big news and Mr. Field's editorials."

"Oh, you need educating. I read those too — not Field; he's too much for me. But I didn't come here to talk about newspapers — "

"Won't you smoke a cigar?"

"No, thanks. I smoked all the way down, and in the cab too, for that matter — "

"Are the horses standing out there in the cold? Wouldn't you like to tell him to take them to the barn?"

"I suppose he can look after his own horses. They're nothing but old hacks, anyhow." He leaned forward abruptly and took her hand, pressing it closely. "Oh!" he said. "I've been wild to see you again."

Patience attempted to jerk her hand away, acutely conscious of a desire to return his clasp. She did the worst thing possible, but the only thing that could be expected: she lost her head. "I don't like you to do that," she exclaimed. "Let me go! What do you mean, anyhow?"

"That you are the loveliest woman I ever saw. I have been wild about you — " He had taken her other hand, and his face was close to hers. He had lowered his lids slightly.

"And you think that because I am alone here you can say what you like?" she cried passionately. "You would not dare act like this with one of your mother's guests!"

"Oh, would n't I?" He laughed disagreeably. " But what is the use of being a goose — "

Patience sprang to her feet, overturning her chair: but she only succeeded in pulling him to his feet also; he would not release her hands.

"I wish you would leave the house," she said, stamping her foot. "If you don't let me go, I 'll call Ellen."

"Oh, don't make a goose of yourself. And I 'm not afraid of a servant. I 'm not going to murder you — nor anything else. Only, — do you drive all men wild like this? "

"I don't know anything about men," almost sobbed Patience, "and I don't want to. Will you go?"

"No, I won't." He released her hands suddenly; and, as she made a spring for the door, flung his arms about her. She ducked her head and fought him, but he kissed her cheeks and brow and hair. His lips burnt her delicate skin, his powerful embrace seemed absorbing her. She was filled with fury and loathing, but the blood pounded in her ears, and the very air seemed humming. The man's magnetism was purely animal, but it was a tremendous force.

"You are a brute, a beast!" she sobbed. "Let me go! Let me go!"

"I won't," he muttered. He too had lost his head. "I 'll not leave you." He strove to reach her mouth. She managed to disengage her right arm, and clinching her hand hit him a smart blow in the face. He laughed, and caught her hand, holding it out at arm's length.

"Ellen!" she cried. As she lifted her head to call he was quick to see his advantage. His mouth closed suddenly on hers.

The room swam round her. She ceased to struggle.

Her feet had touched that nether world where the electrical forces of the universe appear to be generated, and its wonder — not the man — conquered her. She shook horribly. She felt a tumultuous impulse to spring upon her ideals and beat them in the face.

Heavy footfalls sounded in the kitchen hall.

"There is Ellen !" she gasped, wrenching herself free. The man stamped his foot. He looked hideous.

" Go !" said Patience. "Go, just as fast as you can, and don't you ever come here again. If you do, it won't do you any good, for you 'll not see me."

And she ran upstairs and locked her door loudly.

XX

For some time she walked rapidly up and down, pressing her hands to her hot face. Chaos was in her. She could not think. She only felt that she wanted to die, and preferred the river. She poured water into a basin and plunged her face into it again and again. The water had the chill of midwinter, and sent the blood from her brain; but she felt no cleaner. Still, her brain was no longer racing like a screw out of water, and she sat down to think. It was her trend of mind to face all questions with the least possible delay, and she looked at herself squarely.

"So," she thought, " I am the daughter of Madge Sparhawk, after all. The horror of that night left me as I was made. Three years with the best woman the sun ever shone on only put the real me to sleep for a time. All my ideals were the vagaries of my imagination, a sort of unwritten book, of the nature of those that geniuses write, who spend their leisure hours in debauchery. I am no better than Rosita. I have not even the excuse of love — if I had — if it had been Him — I might perhaps — perhaps — look upon passion as a natural thing. Certainly it is not disagreeable," and she laughed unpleasantly. "But I despised this man. He has not the brain of a calf nor the principle of a savage, and yet it is he that made me forget every ideal I ever cherished. If I met Him now, I would not insult him with the gift of myself. . . .

"If Beverly Peele came in here now I verily believe that I should kiss him again. What — what is human nature made of? I have the blood of refined and enlightened ancestors in my veins — I know that. I have seen nothing of sexual sin that did not make me abhor it. Barring my mother, I had the best of influences in Monterey, and I knew the difference. I have — or had — a natural tendency toward all that was refined and uplifting. I was even sure I had a soul. My brain is better, and better furnished, than that of the average woman of my age. And yet, at the first touch, I crumble like an old corpse exposed to air. I am simply a body with a mental annex, and the one appears to be independent of the other.

"Is the world all vile?" she continued, resuming her restless walk. "This man attacked me as if he had no anticipation of a rebuff. And yet I am the friend of his sister, the adopted daughter of his mother's cousin, and, he has every reason to think, of irreproachable life. If the world — his mother's world — were not full of such women as he imagined me to be — he would never have taken so much for granted. He acted as if he thought me a fool, and I appear to be remarkably green. I am certainly learning. Oh — the brute ! the brute !" And she flung herself on the bed and burst into violent weeping, which lasted until she was so exhausted that she fell asleep without disrobing.

XXI

THE next morning her head ached violently. She started for the woods, but turned back. They held her lost ideals. She sat all day by the window, looking at the Hudson, listless, and mentally nauseated.

During the afternoon a special messenger brought a note of abject apology from Beverly Peele. She burnt it half read and told the man there was no answer. There is only one thing a woman scorns more than a man's insult, and that is his apology.

The next day he called, but was refused admission by the sturdy Ellen. Patience spent the day on Hog Heights. On the following day he called again, with the same result. The next day Hal came.

"What is the row between you and Bev?" she exclaimed, before she had seated herself. "He says you've taken a dislike to him, and is in the most beastly temper about it. I never saw him so cut up. He's sent me here to patch it up and give you this letter. Do tell me what is the matter?"

"Well, I'll tell you," said Patience, grimly. "The idea of his sending his sister to patch it up !" And she gave an account of Mr. Peele's performance, woman-like omitting her own momentary forbearance.

Hal listened with an amused smile. "So Bev made a bad break," she remarked when Patience had concluded. "I'm not surprised, for he's pretty hot-headed, and head over ears in love. You mustn't take life so tragically. I've had several weird experiences myself, although I'm not the kind that men lose their head about as a rule; only given the hour and the occasion, some men will lose their head about any woman. Perhaps I should have said New York men. They are a rare and lovely species. They admire God because he made himself of their gender and knew what he was about when he invented woman. I was out on a sleighing party one moonlight night last winter, and on the back seat with a man I'd never seen out of a ball-room before. The way that man's legs and arms flew round that sleigh made my hair curl. You see, a lot of us are fast, but then plenty of us are not. The trouble is that the men can't discriminate, as we look pretty much alike on the outside. They're not a very clever lot — our society men — and they don't learn much until they've been taught. Then when they are forced to believe in your virtue they feel rather sorry for you, and later on are apt to propose — if you have any money. Bev would propose to you if you were living in a tent and clad in a gunny sack. He would have preferred things the other way — it's so much less trouble — but as he can't, he won't stop at any such trifling nuisance as matrimony. Oh, men are a lovely lot ! Still, the world would be a pretty stupid place without them. You'll learn to manage them in time, and then they'll only amuse you. They are not really so bad at heart — they've been badly educated. I know four married women of the type we call ' friskies,' whom my mother would shudder at the thought of excluding from her visiting list, and whom I 'd bet my new Paquin trunk, several men I know have had affairs with. So what can you expect of a man ? "

" Is the world rotten ? " asked Patience, in disgust.

" It 's just about half and half. I know as many good women as bad. Half the women in society are good wives and devoted mothers. The other half, girls and married women, old and young, are no better than your Rosita. Sometimes their motives are no higher. Usually, though, it 's craving for excitement. I don't blame those much myself. The most fascinating woman I know is larky. She as much as told me so. Some of the confessions I 've had from married women would make you gasp. Well — let 's quit the subject. Promise me you 'll forgive Bev."

" I shall not. I hate him. I shall never look at him again if I can help it."

" Oh, dear, dear, you are young ! And I do so want you for a sister. May is such a fool, and I do hate Honora."

" You would n't have me loathe myself for the sake of being your sister, I suppose ? "

" Of course I would n't have you marry Bev if you could n't like him ; but I believe you really do, only things have n't turned out as you planned in that innocent little skull of yours. Bev is a good fellow, as men go. You 'll get used to him and his kind in the course of time; and then you 'll enjoy life in a calm practical way."

" Is there no other way ? " asked Patience, bitterly.

" Not in my experience. And if you stay here in your woods you 'll get tired of your ideals after a while.

You can't live on ideals — the human constitution is n't made that way. If it was there 'd be no such thing as society. We 'd live in caves and bay the moon. So you 'd better come into the world, Patience dear, and accept it as it is, and drain it for all it 's worth."

"Oh, hush! You are too good to talk like that."

"Good? — what is good? I am the result of my surroundings — a little better than some, a little worse than others. So was Cousin Harriet. So is La Rosita. I 'm not cynical. I merely see life — my section of it — exactly as it is. If you become a newspaper woman you 'll probably receive a succession of shocks. As nearly as I can make out they 're about like us — half and half. I became quite chummy with a news- paper woman, once, crossing the Atlantic. She was awfully pretty, and, as nearly as one woman can judge of another, perfectly proper. She related some wild and weird experiences she had had with men. Yours would probably be wilder and weirder, as you appear to be possessed of an unholy fascination; and in a year or two you 'll be a beauty. All you want is a little more figure and style — or rather clothes."

"Well, if I 'm to have wild and weird experiences I prefer to have them with men of brains, not with a lot of empty-headed society men."

"Don't generalise too freely, my dear. There are newspaper men and newspaper men, — according to this girl I 've just told you of. Some are brainy, some are merely bright; some are gentlemen, most are common beyond words. And, as she said — after you 've worked with man in his shirt sleeves, you don't have many illusions about the animal left."

"I have not one, and I lost them in an hour. Your

brother is supposed to be a gentleman with a long array of ancestors, and he acted like a wild Indian."

"My dear, he merely lost his head. That was a compliment to you, and you should not be too hard on a man in those circumstances. He won't do it again, I'm sure of that. He has some control. I warned him before he came not to pun, and he says he didn't, not once. Now, tell me one thing — Don't you like him just a little?"

"No," said Patience; but she flushed to her hair, and Hal, with her uncanny wisdom, said no more.

XXII

THE next day Patience went to the woods for the first time since Beverly Peele's onslaught. A natural reaction had lifted her spirits out of the slough, and she turned to nature, as ever. She could never be the same again, she thought with a sigh; and once more she must readjust herself. She wondered if any girl had ever done so much readjusting in an equal number of years.

. The woods were no longer a scene of enchantment. The ice had melted. The trees were grey and naked again. The ground was slush, and nasty to walk upon.

"But the spring must come in time," she thought; "and then perhaps I'll feel new too — but not the same, for like the spring I shall have other seasons behind me.

"But — perhaps — who knows? — I may be the better for knowing myself. I was in a fool's paradise

before.   Perhaps I was in danger of becoming an
egoist, and imagining myself made of finer fibre than
other women.   Great writers show that the same brute
is in all of us, and I can believe it.   Some work it off
in religion, but the majority don't.   There seems to be
some tremendous magnetic force in the Universe that
makes the human race nine-tenths Love — for want of
a better name.   Circumstances and ancestors deter-
mine the direction of it.   It seems too bad that Civilisation has not done more for us than to give us the
analytical mind which understands and rebels, and no
more, at the inheritance of the savage.   But now that
I know myself, perhaps I can go forward more surely
on the path to the higher altitudes of life.   I should
like to be as good as auntie, and worldly-wise beside.

"I suppose my horrid experience with this man will
make me more exacting with all men.   I think I could
not blunder into matrimony, as some women do.   I feel
as if I never wanted to see another man, but that
impression will pass — all impressions appear to pass.
I may even want to meet Him after a time, and perhaps
he will forgive.   Should n't be surprised if he 'd want
a good deal of forgiveness himself.   Meanwhile I can
work, and learn all I can of what life means, anyway.
I 'll go to Mr. Field — "

The soft ground echoed no footfalls, but Patience
suddenly became aware that some one was approaching her.   She turned, and saw Beverly Peele.

BOOK III

BOOK III

I

"I DO hope you 'll make a hit, Patience," said Hal, regarding her critically. "The public, even the little public of a garden party, is a thing you can't bet on, but you certainly are stunning. If ever papa loses his fortune, in the curious American way, I shall follow the ever seductive example of the English aristocracy and go in for dressmaking. That frock is a triumph of art, if I do say it myself."

Patience revolved slowly before the Psyche mirror which stood between two open windows in one corner of Hal's pretty terra-cotta bedroom. She too was· pleased with the airy concoction of violet and white. On a chair lay a picture hat, another bird of the same feather. Hal placed it on Patience's head, a little back, and the violet velvet of the interior made a very effective frame for the soft ashen hair and white skin.

"You certainly carry yourself well," continued Hal, "and before long you will acquire an air. Always keep in mind that *that* is the most important thing in life — our life — to acquire. But you look like a lily, a purple and white forest lily."

"I have n't the faintest idea what to talk to fashionable people about."

"Don't be too clever — don't frighten the men and antagonise the women. You see, you 're not known at all, so people won't begin by being afraid of you — as they would if they knew all that went on in that pretty skull of yours. Just be Mrs. Beverly Peele. Nobody would ever suspect Bev of marrying a clever woman. You can't do the artless and infantile, like May : your face is too strong; but you can be unsophisticated, and that always goes."

"I 'm not unsophisticated ! "

"Oh, don't look like that. All the light seems to go out of your skin. I mean give everybody the impression that you have everything to learn, and that each, individually, can teach it all. It 's awfully fetching. That is what has made May's success. Of course you would n't be another May, if you could ; but you want to begin at the beginning — don't you know? You must let society feel that it gives you everything, tells you everything. Then it will love you. But if it suspects that you are alien — the least little bit — then there will be the devil to pay. Of course a few of the best sort would like you, but I 'm set on your making a hit."

"I 'm afraid I 'll never take," said Patience, with a sigh, " but I am wild to see Vanity Fair, all the same. It must be great fun — all that brilliancy and life. But somehow I don't feel in tune with the people I have met, so far."

"Oh, that 's natural. You are not acclimatised yet, so to speak. Society is a distinctly foreign country to those that have not been brought up in it. Just sit down on the edge of that chair and rest while I take a look at myself."

"White is certainly my day colour," she continued,

revolving in her turn before the mirror. "It is wonderful how it clears the skin, especially with a touch of blue near the face. Pink would make me as yellow as October, and green would suggest thirty-five. Your grey matter will be spared the wear and tear of The Study of Colour, but if I had n't reduced it to a fine art, I'd have had to turn literary or something when May came out."

"You look just like a fairy! I never saw anything so dainty."

"Oh, of course; I'm so little and light that I have to work the fairy racket for all it's worth. It's a heavenly day, is n't it? The country's got its best spring clothes on, sure enough."

The girls leaned out of each of the windows in turn, scrutinising the grounds. In front and on both sides of the house the land rolled away in great irregular waves. Woods were in the sudden hollows, on the lofty knolls; between, shelving expanses of green, bare but for an occasional oak or elm. Beside the driveway was a long narrow avenue of elms, down which two might pace shoulder to shoulder, and no more. In a deep hollow on the right was the orchard, a riot of pink and white. The immediate grounds were small and trim, and fragrant with the flowers of civilisation; out on the hills beyond the wild-flowers and tall grass, the locust and hawthorn, had their way. Behind all flowed the Hudson under the green Palisades, its surface gay with sail and steamboat.

A dancing booth had been erected on one of the lawns, and the musicians were already assembling under the silken curtains.

"It looks very well," said Hal, "and you could n't

have a more perfect day for your *début*. Not that I care much for garden parties; the fresh air makes me sleepy, and there's no concentration, as it were — as there is in a ball-room, don't you know? But mamma decreed that the world should make your acquaintance out of doors, and that is the end of it. I wonder if you'll manage to induce Bev to go to town for the winter."

"I hope so! It will be horribly dull to stay here all winter, with all of you away."

"That's an edifying sentiment for a bride of three months. However, I agree with you. I'd go mad shut up in a country house in winter with the most fascinating man that ever breathed. And the dickens of it is, mamma always takes his part, whether he's wrong or right. She'll preach wifely duty to you until you'd live on a desert island to get rid of her."

"I've heard her," said Patience, gloomily.

"I wondered if that was what she was at in the library yesterday. When mamma has her chin well up and her lower lip well out I can tell at long range that she's embracing the cause of virtue. But she tackled you rather early in the game, considering you have n't made any notable break as yet."

"I would n't go driving with Beverly yesterday, — the sun makes my head ache, — and I'd also begged him to take me to the theatre to see Rosita, and he would n't."

"Oh, you'll never get Bev to the theatre. We'll go by ourselves to a matinée. However, it's better than being a newspaper woman on several dollars a week — come now, own up?"

"I enjoyed Florida and New Orleans and Canada immensely."

" That was a tremendous concession for Bev to make — he detests travelling. He certainly is in love ; but I imagine he expects you to live on that same concession for some time to come — thinks it 's your turn to do the self-sacrificing act. Such is man. Anyhow, I 'm glad it 's all turned out so comfortably, and that you are here, and that all is settled — "

" I want to ask you something. I could n't get it out of Beverly. Did your mother make a very violent objection to his marrying me? Of course I am a social nobody, and she must have made great plans for her only son. She did n't say anything when she came to call ; but, you see, she did n't call until three days before the wedding, and Beverly's and your excuses were not very good."

" Oh, of course she raised Cain," said Miss Peele, easily ; " that was to be expected. But papa put his foot down and said he was glad to have Beverly marry a clever woman : it might be the making of him. And *I* just fought ! Of course I 'd told papa that you were as high bred as any woman in America, and that you 'd look a swell in less than no time. That weighed heavy with him, for, in his opinion, God may have made himself first, but he made the Peeles next, and no mistake. And Bev ! He went into the most awful tantrums you ever saw. I think that was what brought mamma round — she was afraid he 'd burst a blood-vessel. When she wrote and asked Miss Beale to live with you I knew the day was won. And now that you are Mrs. Beverly Peele she 'll respect you accordingly, although you 'll have some lively tussles. But make her think you adore Bev, and you 'll pull through. Suppose we go down now. Tra-la-la ! I wish it were over."

II

THE girls descended the twisted stair into the wide hall. All the doors and windows were open, and the soft air blew through the great house, lifting the lace and silken curtains.

A girl, looking like a large butterfly, in her yellow frock, was fluttering about the hall amidst the palms and the huge vases of flowers. Her skin was of matchless tints, her large blue eyes as guileless as those of an infant.

"Oh! Oh!" she cried, as Hal and Patience reached the first landing, "how perfectly sweet! Hal, is my frock all right in the back? My things never fit quite as well as yours do. Is n't Patience too fetching for words? I wish I was just white like that. How perfectly funny that we should be giving a garden party for Bev's wife! Who would have thought it last year? Is n't it odd how things do happen? And has n't Honora been perfectly lovely about it? I always knew she did n't care. I wonder if any decent men will come up! It's so hard — Hal, *does* my frock wrinkle in the back?"

"Oh, no, no," drawled Hal, without looking at her. She glanced at the tall clock in an angle. "They'll be here in ten minutes, now — Oh—h—h!"

A portière was pushed aside, and a girl entered the hall from a dark background of books and heavy curtains. She was far above the ordinary height of woman, and extremely slender. Golden hair clustered about a long face, pale rather than white. The large azure eyes had the extraordinary clarity of childhood, and an expression of perfect purity. The nose was long, the mouth thin, but well curved and very red. She wore a clinging gown of white crêpe and a large knot of blue wild-flowers at her belt. She moved slowly forward, managing her long limbs with much dexterity, but could hardly be called graceful. Patience thought her the most beautiful woman she had ever seen, and murmured her admiration to Hal, who snorted in a gentle, ladylike way.

"They will be here in a moment, I suppose," said Honora, wearily. "I think I shall not go out. I'll stay in the drawing-room and entertain the older people. Some one must attend to them, and I really prefer the house."

"You are always so amiable," said Hal, drily, "and you certainly won't get freckled."

"It is true that I don't like freckles," said Honora, calmly, "and I do like the older people. Even you, when you have a few white hairs, may become more or less interesting. Patience, dear, you look very lovely. You must let me kiss you." She bent her cool lips to the brow of the bride, swaying over her. Her voice could not be described by any adjective devoid of the letter L. It was liquid, silvery, cold, light.

"She certainly is a stunning-looking woman," said Hal, as Honora passed into the drawing-room, "but she's a whole rattlesnake, and no mistake. I've never seen her strike real hard yet; she merely spits occasionally, and always in that amiable way. You can imagine how subtle she is, and what a dangerous force such self-control is. I shall never understand how she failed to get Bev."

"Perhaps, as May suggests, she did n't want him."

"Oh, did n't she! Just wait! you 'll hear from her yet. There 's the whistle. The train 'll be here in three minutes. Let us group ourselves gracefully under Peele the First."

They went into the large white drawing-room, whose old-fashioned woodwork was as it had been nearly three hundred years ago, even to the heavy shutters over the small-paned windows. The ceiling was fretted with floral designs, executed in *papier maché,* surrounding a *bas relief* of " our well beloved Whyte Peele," who had received the grant of these many acres from James the First. All the woodwork was painted white, and carved. The furniture, modern, but of colonial design, was up-holstered in pale pink and blue.

Beyond a side hall was a long dining-room panelled to the ceiling in oak, and hung on all sides with dead and living Peeles. The carved oaken table was spread with the light unsubstantial feast of the modern time. Adjoining the dining-room were two small reception-rooms looking upon the terrace at the back of the rambling old house. In the middle of this hall, under the carved twisted stair, was a round enclosure whose door opened upon a well, from whence a secret passage led to the river.

Mrs. Peele swept across the hall from the dining-room, and raising her lorgnette, considered Patience.

"You look very well," she said, coldly. "Don't get nervous, please; it is the one thing for which people have no toleration. Where is Beverly?"

"He has gone for a drive. You know he does not like entertainments." Patience's nerves were muttering, and her mother-in-law's admonition was not of the nature of balm.

Mrs. Peele raised her brows. "It is odd that a bride should have so little influence over her husband," she remarked ; and Patience was now in that equable frame of mind which carries one through the severe ordeals of life.

How she did live through that ordeal of introduction to some five hundred people she never knew. Fortunately, all but the neighbours arrived on the special train which had been sent for them, and there was little for her to do but smile and bend her head as Mrs. Peele named her new daughter-in-law to her guests.

And whatever might be that exalted dame's private opinion of her son's choice, whatever methods she might employ in untrammelled domestic hours to make her disapproval felt, to the world she assumed her habitual air of being supremely content with all that pertained to the house of Peele. Had Patience been the daughter of a belted earl she could not have been presented to New York with a haughtier pride, a calmer assumption that New York must embrace with gratitude and enthusiasm this opportunity to meet the daughter-in-law of the Gardiner Peeles.

Her manner gave Patience confidence after a time. Her own pride had already conquered diffidence ; and trying as the long ordeal was, she thrilled a little at the sudden realisation of half-formed ambitions. There was no taint of the snob in her ; some echo-voice of other generations lifted itself out of the inherited impressions which had moulded her brain cells, and protested against its descendant ranking below the first of the land.

Many of the guests were politely indifferent to the honour provided for them ; the girls stared at her in a

manner calculated to upset any *débutante's* equilibrium ;
but the gracious kindness of others and the languid
admiration of the men kept her in poise.

The neighbours arrived shortly after the train, and it
was an hour before the greater part of the company
had dispersed over the grounds, and Patience could sit
down. Mrs. Peele remained in the drawing-room with
some eight or ten people, and as Hal and May had
both disappeared, Patience stayed with her mother-in-
law, not knowing where to go.

She thought the girls very forbidding with their pert
noses and keen eyes, although she admired their lumi-
nous skin and splendid grooming, striking even in the
airy attire of spring. The older women looked as if
they would patronise her did Mrs. Peele withdraw her
protecting wing, and one man, passing the window,
inserted a monocle and regarded her deliberately.
Suddenly Patience experienced a sensation of profound
loneliness. No force in life is surer of touch than the
subtle play of spirit on spirit, and Patience read that
these people did not like her and never would, that
they recognised the alien who would regard their world
spectacularly, never acquire their comic seriousness.

" Are you fond of golf, Mrs. Peele ? " asked one girl,
languidly.

" I never have played golf."

The girl raised her brows. " Really ! Are you fond
of tennis ? "

" I have never played tennis." Patience repressed
a smile as the girl looked frankly shocked. Still the
guest was evidently determined to be amiable.

" I hope you don't think it frivolous ? "

" Oh, no, I should like to learn all those things very
much."

"Well, Miss Peele can teach you. She is awfully clever at all those things. Don't you think Miss Mairs looks like Mary Anderson?"

" Mary Anderson?"

"Yes, the actress, you know."

" I have never seen her."

The girl was visibly embarrassed. Another, who looked as if harbouring a grin in her straight little mouth, came to the rescue.

"Oh, I do think Mr. Peele is so good-looking," she exclaimed, with a fine show of animation. "We all think you are to be congratulated."

Patience smiled at the frank rudeness of this remark, and said nothing.

"You know Amy Murray was wild about him. She's not here to-day, I notice. We did think it too bad that he would n't go out. Some of the girls have met him here, but I never have. They say he is awfully fascinating."

" Oh, yes, he is fascinating," said Patience.

"What have you been doing with yourself if you have never learned to golf nor play tennis?" asked another girl, insolently. She was a tall girl, with a wooden face, a tight mouth, and an "air."

" Oh, I read, mostly," said Patience, with an extremely bored air.

The mother of the third girl turned swiftly and smiled at the bride, a humorous smile in which there was some pity. Patience had observed her before. She was a tall woman with a slender figure of extreme elegance. Her dark bright face was little older than her daughter's. Her ease of manner was so great that it was almost self-conscious.

"Oh, say!" she exclaimed, "don't think we 're all like that. The girls don't have much time to read — that's true — but after they settle down they do, really. Hal reads French novels — the little reprobate! — We read French novels too, but a lot else besides. Oh, really! Outsiders — the people that only know society through the newspapers, don't you know? — misjudge us terribly, really. Some of the brightest women of the world are in New York society — why shouldn't they be? And if the girls don't study it's their own fault; they certainly have every opportunity under the sun. I was made to study. My father was old-fashioned, and had no nonsense about him. I always say I was educated beyond my brains, but I'd rather have it that way than the other. Now, I assure you I read everything. I have a standing order on the other side with an English and a French book-seller, to send me every book the minute it attracts attention — "

"Oh, you 're real intellectual, you are," drawled Hal's mocking voice.

The lady turned with a start and a little flush.

"Oh, Hal!" she cried gaily, "how you do take the starch out of one."

"You 've got enough to stock a laundry, so you needn't worry. I 've come to rescue my fair sister-in-law before you talk her to death. Come, Patience."

Patience arose with alacrity, and followed her out of the house.

"Don't you like her?" she asked.

"Oh, immensely. She's as bright as a woman can be who has so little time to think about it. She's a tall and majestic pillar of Society, you know, and she carries it — the intellect, not the pillar — round like a chip on her shoulder. That makes me weary at times. I've heard her talk for an hour without stopping. The only thing that makes me forgive her is her slang. We have a match occasionally."

" Her daughter does n't look as if she used slang."

" Oh, she does n't. She 's no earthly use whatever. Are you enjoying yourself? "

" Not particularly. But it 's a lovely scene."

The lawns, and knolls, and woods were kaleidoscopic with fashionettes in gay attire, shifting continually. There were not men enough to mar the brilliant effect. The music of birds soared above the chatter of girls, the sound of wood and brass. The river flashed away into the distance, a silver girdle about Earth's green gown.

"Yes, very pret," said Hal. " But come, I 'm going to introduce you to my latest."

" You did n't tell me that you had a latest."

" I 've only met him a few times — he 's from Boston. I expect I forgot about him."

They were walking over the lawns toward the Tea House, a long low rustic building which stood on the edge of the slope. A hubbub of voices floated through the windows, peals of laughter, affected shrieks.

" A lot of my intimates are there," said Hal. " I 've managed to get them together. May is doing the hostess act with her accustomed grace and charm, and I 'm taking a half hour off."

They went round to the front of the house and entered. It was an airy structure of polished maple. Little tables, each with a delicate tea-service, were scattered about with artistic irregularity; round the wall ran a divan, luxurious, but not too low for whale-

boned forms. On this the girls were stiffly lounging.
The men were more at their ease. All were smoking,
the girls daintily, but firmly.

"Hal! Hal! sweet Queen Hal!" cried one of the
young men, rising to his feet. "I've been keeping
this place — directly in the middle — for you. See, it
shall be a throne." He piled three cushions atop, and
with exaggerated homage led her forward amidst the
ejaculatory applause of the others.

"Isn't Norry too witty?" said one girl to Patience, as
she made room for her, "and so original! Whoever
else would have thought of such a thing? — although
Hal ought to be a queen, don't you think so? We
just rave about her. Do you smoke? try my kind."

Patience, thankful that at last she could do something like these people, accepted the cigarette. During
her three months' trip she had not smoked, as Beverly
thought it shocking.

"Mr. Wynne," cried Hal, suddenly, "come over
here and talk to my sister-in-law. Patience, this is
the young man from Boston, famous as the only New
Englander whose ancestors did not come over on the
'May Flower.'"

A man with a smooth serious face rose from his
cushions and came forward.

"Awfully good-looking," murmured the girl who had
proffered the cigarette, "and wonderfully smart, considering he's not a New Yorker. It's too bad he's so
beastly poor, for he's terribly *épris* with Hal."

The young man, who had paused a moment to speak
with Hal, inserted himself as best he could between
Patience and her new acquaintance.

"I am glad you are here," murmured the bride.

"You do not look quite at home, and I am not, either."

He smiled with instant sympathy. "Oh, I don't care very much for society, and I don't like to see women smoke. It's an absurd prejudice to have in these progressive days, but I can't help it."

"You mean you don't like to see Miss Peele smoke," said Patience, mischievously.

He flushed, then laughed. "Well, perhaps that is it. They are all charming, these girls, but there is something about Miss Peele that distinguishes her. Did you ever notice it?"

"Oh, yes. She is herself, and these others are twelve for a dozen."

"That is it." He glanced about at the girls in their bright gowns, which clung to their tiny waists and hips, their narrow chests and modest busts, with the wrinkleless perfection that has made the modern milliner the god he is. Their polished skin and brilliant shallow eyes, their elegant sexless forms, their haughty poise and supercilious air, laid aside among themselves but always in reserve, their consciousness of caste, were the several parts of a unique and homogeneous effect, which, Patience confided to Mr. Wynne, must mark out the New York girl in whatever wilds she trod.

"Oh, it does," he said. "The New York girl is *sui generis*, and so thoroughly artificial a product that it seems incredible she can exist through another generation. I will venture to predict that the species will be extinct in three, and that American women of a larger and more human type will gradually be drawn into New York, and found a new race, so to speak. Why, it seems to me that the children of these women must be pigmies — imagine one of those girls being the mother of a man. It is well that New York is not America."

Involuntarily Patience's eyes wandered to Hal. Her waist was as small, her figure as unwomanly as the others.

"It is true," said Wynne, answering her thought; "but she is so charming that one is quite willing she should do nothing further for the human race."

Patience burst into a light laugh.

"What 's the matter?" asked Wynne.

"It suddenly struck me — the almost comical difference between these girls and the ' Y's,' and the ' King's Daughters.' It does not seem possible that such types can exist within ten miles of each other. I should explain that I have passed the last three years in a country town."

"It is odd how religion holds its own in those small places. It is opera, theatre, balls, Browning societies, everything to those people shut out of the manifold distractions of cities. Religion seems to be the one excitement of the restricted life. Human nature demands some sort of emotional outlet — "

"What on earth are you two talking about?" cried the girl on the other side. "Will you have another cigarette, Mrs. Beverly? — that is what we shall all call you, you know. Mr. Wynne, please talk to me a while. Is n't this Tea House too sweet?"

"It is more, — it is angelic," said Wynne, gravely.

"Oh! you 're guying!" Even her voice pouted. "Oh! please shake those ashes off my gown — quick! — thanks. Oh, your eyes are grey. I thought they were brown. I 'm afraid of grey eyes, are n't you, Mrs.

Beverly — Oh, dear! your eyes are grey too. What ever shall I do?" and she cast up her hands. Even her sleek hair seemed to quiver.

" It is the misfortune of the American race to run to grey eyes," said Wynne. " Habit should have steeled you by this time —"

" Oh, he made a pun! he made a pun!" cried the girl.

" I did not! — I beg pardon, but I never did such a thing in my life," cried Wynne, indignantly; and Patience felt suddenly depressed, although she too had found a friend in habit.

Hal rose while the girl was lisping mock apologies.

" I 've got to go," she said. " Is n't it hateful? But I must go and do my duty. Patience, you must come too. Why are you blocking the doorway, Mr. Wynne?"

"I am going with you."

" Really? Well, bye-bye ; " and the three went off, followed by a gentle chorus of regrets.

" Patience, my dear," said Hal, " there is a group of people over there looking hideously bored. You go and cheer them up, while I do my duty by those austere and venerable dames who are staring through their lorgnettes at the dining-room windows — "

" Oh, Hal, I can't! Don't send me to those people alone. What can I say to them?"

" Patience, my dear, this is a world of woe. One day you will be châtelaine of this place and be giving garden-parties on your own account, so you 'd better take the kindergarten course, and be thankful for the chance. Go on."

Patience walked unwillingly over to a group of four

women seated under a drooping oak. She had forgotten the names of nine tenths of the guests, but she recognised Mrs. Laurence Gibbs, a plain rather dowdy little woman with sad face and abstracted gaze. Beside her on the rustic seat was a woman who gave a dominant impression of teeth : they fairly flashed in the shadows. In a chair sat a woman of remarkable prettiness. She would have been a beauty had her features been larger, so regular were they, so sweet her expression, so soft her colouring of pink and white and brown, so tall and full her figure. In another chair was a young woman of no beauty but much distinction. Her prematurely white hair was curled and tied at the base of her head with a black ribbon, realising an eighteenth century effect. Her face was dark and brilliant. She sat forward, her slim figure full of suppressed energy. She had been talking with much animation, but as Patience approached she paused abruptly. The pretty woman burst into a merry laugh.

"Mrs. Lafarge was just remarking what hideous bores garden parties are," she said audaciously.

"Oh, you need n't mind me," said Patience, sitting down on the grass, as there was no other seat. "I quite agree with you."

"Oh, that 's awfully good of you, Mrs. Peele," said Mrs. Lafarge, "and awfully mean of you, Mary Gallatin. Of course this is one of the loveliest places on the Hudson, and I love to come here; but there are not enough men. That 's the whole trouble."

"That always seems to be the cry with you American women," said she of the teeth. "You have no resources. You should be independent of men. They seem to be of you."

"Perhaps you are driven to resources in Russia," said Mrs. Gallatin, sweetly, "but your observation is faulty. We are spoiled over here, and that is the reason we grumble occasionally."

"You see we have n't a large leisure class, as you have," said Mrs. Gibbs, hastily.

"I really think the reason men avoid garden parties is that they are afraid they might be betrayed into sentiment," broke in Mrs. Lafarge. "They do protect themselves so fiercely. How did you ever make Tom Gallatin propose, Mary dear? He had the most ideal bachelor apartment in New York, and entrenched himself as in a fortress."

"Oh, one or two fall by the wayside every year, you know, and this time Gally happened to stumble over me. Poor Gally, he told me yesterday that he had n't seen me to speak to for a month. The idea of the lower classes grumbling. I should like to know who works as hard as we do. How do you manage to do the society and the charity, both?" she asked of Mrs. Gibbs. "Does Mr. Gibbs ever see *you?*"

"I never neglect my husband," said Mrs. Gibbs, sternly. "When I must neglect anything it is society. I came to-day because I longed for a glimpse of the country, and I have not been able to go to Woody Cliffs yet — the poverty is so terrible this year. I wish you would come with me sometime and see for yourself —"

"God forbid! I never could stand the smells. I give my pastor so much a year, and I really think that 's doing one's share. Of course if you like it, it 's another thing."

"Like it!" cried the Russian. "You speak as if it

were her pastime. I cannot express how gratifying it
is to me to meet a serious woman occasionally in New
York society."

" I had a lovely time in Petersbourg," murmured Mrs.
Gallatin. " I never met an offensive Russian inside of
the country. Poor America ! "

" I don't understand," said the foreigner, stiffly.

"Oh, I am sure you understand English — you
express yourself so clearly. We all weep over America
occasionally, you know. It is a sort of dumping ground
for foreigners, — who sit at our feet, and abuse us."

" One is at liberty to abuse insolence," said the Russian, with suppressed wrath, "and the women of New
York are the most insolent I have ever met."

" Oh, not among ourselves — not really. We think
it insolent in outsiders to elbow their way in — "

" Mary ! Mary ! " cried Mrs. Gibbs. " I hear that
you spent some years with Miss Harriet Tremont," she
continued, addressing Patience. " She passed her
entire life in charitable work, did she not ? "

" Oh, she did, and she enjoyed it too. Don't you ? "
Mrs. Gallatin laughed softly.

" Enjoy it ? " said Mrs. Gibbs. " I never have looked
at it in that way. I think it my duty to aid my miserable fellow beings, and I am thankful that I am able to
aid them."

" Odd, the fads different people have," murmured
Mrs. Gallatin. " Now mine is Russians. What is yours,
Leontine ? "

"Oh, Mary, you deserve to be shaken," exclaimed
Mrs. Lafarge, as the Russian sprang to her feet and
stalked away.

" I can't help it. She 's a boor, and I wish she 'd go

back and live with a Cossack. Foreigners are all very well on their native heath, but as soon as they are transplanted to this side and treated with common decency they become intolerable. They grovel at our feet, swell because we receive them, and sneer at us behind our backs."

"I think you have a way of irritating them, my dear," said Mrs. Gibbs. "You are a very naughty girl. Won't you sit up here by me, Mrs. Peele? I am afraid the ground is damp. I shall ask you some time to explain to me Miss Tremont's methods. I often feel sadly at sea."

"Oh, dear!" said Patience, "I doubt if I know them. I just followed her blindly. I may as well confess it — I did n't take a very great interest in the work."

"Oh, how lovely!" cried Mrs. Gallatin.

"I am sorry that I have made a mistake," said Mrs. Gibbs, stiffly.

"Oh, well — you know — there is such a thing as getting too much of anything — "

"Is there?" Mrs. Gibbs rose, and shook out her skirts with an absent air. "I think I will go over and talk to Mrs. Peele;" and she walked away with an awkward gait, her head bent forward. She certainly did not have an "air."

"Dear! dear!" exclaimed Mrs. Gallatin. "Just think! you have lost the interest of Mrs. Laurence Gibbs. She might have invited you to her exciting musicales or her cast-iron dinners."

"Oh, don't abuse her," said Mrs. Lafarge. "She is a harmless little soul, and does what she thinks is right."

"She is happier too," said Patience, her thoughts in

Mariaville. "It is odd, but they always are. I think it's because they've unconsciously cultivated the supremest and most inspired form of egoism, and naturally they get a tremendous amount of joy out of it — "

"Hear! Hear!" cried Mrs. Gallatin. "She analyses!"

"My dear, you mustn't do that out loud," said Mrs. Lafarge. "You'll be a terrible failure if you do."

"That would be a pity, because you are so pretty," said Mrs. Gallatin, smiling. "I've been staring at you whenever I've had the chance, and you don't know how many charming things I've heard said of you this afternoon."

"Oh, have you really?" asked Patience, warming instantly, as much to the kindly sympathy as to the agreeable words.

"Indeed I have. That violet against your hair and skin makes a perfect picture of you. *N'est-ce pas,* Leontine?"

"It certainly does."

"I think you are both very kind," said Patience, with a young impulse to be frank. "I feel so out of it all. You see this is my first experience of this sort of thing, and some of those girls have made me feel like a barbarian."

"They'd be glad of your freshness, not only of looks but of mind," said Mary Gallatin. "I should think it would be a blessed relief to have some other sort of interest but just this," and she swept out her arm disdainfully. "That's the reason I go, go, all the time. I don't dare think. When you have no talent, and are not intellectual, and not frantic about your husband, what are you to do? There's no other resource, in spite of that

Russian prig. I 'd give a good deal to be beginning it all again at eighteen."

" There is no spice in life without violent contrasts," said Mrs. Lafarge. " That 's the real reason why so many of our good young friends are larky. The trouble with this world is that although there is variety enough in it, each variety travels in a different orbit. The social scheme is all wrong, somehow."

" True ! True ! " said Mrs. Gallatin, plaintively. " But I see they are about to eat. The open air always makes me hungry. That is variety enough for the present."

As they crossed the lawn she laid her arm about Patience's waist. " Bev does n't like society," she said, " and I'm afraid you 're not in any danger of satiety; but don't think out loud when you are in it. Leontine never does, do you, Leontine? And she is clever too. It must be delightful to be clever. Heigh-ho ! Well, you must be sure to come to see me anyhow. I feel positive we shall be friends. Come some morning at eleven. That is just after I have had my tub and am back in bed again. I love to see my friends then. Oh, dear, we must scatter. There are not two seats together anywhere. Bye-bye."

III

" THANK God they 're gone." Hal divested herself of her tight smart frock, got into a lawn gown, lit a cigarette, and extended herself on the divan in her bedroom. " Well, Patience, how did you like it? "

" I don't think I made the hit you expected."

"N-o-o-o, you did n't exactly create a *furore;* but I don't know that any one could do that with so much oxygen round : makes peoples so drowsy, don't you know?   But you were admired awfully.   And then you are an unconventional beauty, and that always takes longer.   Now, May made a howling sensation, but people are tired of her already.   That type does n't wear. My plain phiz wears much better, because there was never any chance of reaction with me.   Oh, dear, here comes Bev."   ·

A knock, and in response to Hal's languid invitation, Beverly entered.   He was in evening clothes, and as handsome as ever ; but he looked rather sulky.

"You might have met me when I got home," he said to his wife.   "I have n't seen you since luncheon."

"Tragic ! " exclaimed Hal.

"I was so tired I just drifted in here and fell in a heap," said Patience, apologetically.   "My skull feels empty, and aches inside and out."

"Then you don't like society?" said Mr. Peele, eagerly.

"Oh, very much indeed !   I think it is delightful, delightful !   Only the first time is rather trying, you know.   I met some charming people, and want to meet them again."

Peele grunted, and lit his cigar.   His eyes devoured his wife's fair face.   Patience looked at Hal.

"My mother says you carried yourself very well," remarked Mr. Peele, gracefully ; "that after the first you were quite at your ease.   That was one reason I went away : I was so afraid you 'd break down, or something."

Patience flushed angrily, but made no reply.   She

had learned that even a slight dispute would move her husband to a violent outbreak.

" She looked more to the manor born than half the guests," said Hal, " and if you took her out next winter she 'd become the rage — "

" I don't wish my wife to be the rage ! And she is going to stay here. If she loves me as much as I love her she 'll be as contented with my society as I am with hers."

" As if any woman ever loved a man as much as he loved her," remarked Miss Peele. " I am sure Patience is no such idiot."

" What? " cried Beverly. Patience rose hastily.

" I think I 'll go and brush my hair," she said, moving to the door; but he sprang to his feet and stood in front of her.

" Tell me ! " he cried, his voice shaking. " Don't you love me as much as I love you? "

" Oh, Beverly," she said, impatiently, " how can you get into such tempers about nothing? You have asked me if I loved you about nine thousand times since we were married. How am I to know how much you love me? Have you a plummet and line about you? "

" You are dodging the question. And you have never asked me if I loved you — not once — "

Patience slipped past him and ran down the hall to her room. Before she could close the door he was beside her. He caught her in his arms and kissed her violently.

" I shall always be mad about you," he said. " And I believe you are growing cold. You have not been the same lately. Sometimes I think that you shrink from me as you did at first. Tell me what I have

done. I 'd sell my soul to keep you. If you are tired
of me, I 'll kill myself — "

She disengaged herself. " Listen," she said ; " I 've
tried to explain — but you don't seem to understand —
that I did n't want to fall in love with you — not in that
way. That should not come first. Then when I found
myself made of common clay, I said that I would forget
that I had ever been Patience Sparhawk, and begin life
again as Mrs. Beverly Peele. Novelty helped me ; and
when one is travelling, one's ego appears to be dis-
solved into the changing scene — one is simply a sensitised plate. But now I am beginning to feel like
Patience Sparhawk again, and it frightens me a little."

Beverly, to whom the larger part of these remarks
were pure Greek, blanched to the lips.

" Then you regret it," he stammered.

" I did n't say that. I only mean that I seem to
spend life readjusting myself; and that now I seem to
be all at sea again."

" You don't love me any longer ! Oh, God ! " and
he flung himself on the floor, and burying his face in a
chair, groaned aloud.

Patience was disgusted, but his suffering, primary as
it was, touched her. Moreover, her broad vein of philosophy was active once more. She was by no means
prepared to leave him — the tide was ebbing very slowly.
She sat down on the chair, and lifted his face to her
lap. " There," she said, " I am sorry I spoke. You
don't seem to understand me. If you did, though, this
scene could never have occurred. But I love you —
of course — and I do not regret it. So get up and
bathe your eyes. It is after seven o'clock."

He kissed her hands, his face glowing again. The

words were all sufficient to him. "Then if you love me you will see how happy I 'll make you," he exclaimed. "I 'll never leave you a minute I can help; but if you stop loving me I 'll make life hell for you."

"I thought you said you 'd kill yourself."

"Well, I would, but I 'd get square with you first."

"Well, suppose you go into your own room now, and let me dress for dinner."

IV

THE summer passed agreeably enough. Circumstances prevented Beverly bestowing an undue amount of his society on his wife, and until a woman is wholly tired of a man she retains her self respect. Moreover, Patience chose to believe herself in love with him: "it had been in her original estimate of herself that she had been at fault." She persuaded herself that she loved him as much as she could love any man, and she did her pathetic best to shed some glimmer of spiritual light into a man who might have been compounded in a laboratory, so little soul was in him. But despite the clay which was hers, she loved it a great deal for a time in loving it at all, for that was her nature.

She went to several other garden-parties, and found them more amusing than her own, although the young men that frequented them were quite uninteresting: even Beverly scintillated by contrast, for he, at least, had a temper; these more civilised youths appeared to have no emotions whatever.

Peele Manor was full of company all summer. Patience found the married men more entertaining than the younger ones, although they usually made love to her; but after she had outgrown her surprise and dis-approval of their direct and business-like methods, it amused her to fence with them. They had more self-control than Beverly Peele, and were a trifle more skil-ful, but their general attitude was, as she expressed it to Hal: "There's no time to lose, dontcherknow! Life is short, and New York's a busy place. What the deuce is there to wait for? Sentiment? Oh, sentiment be hanged! It takes too much time."

Hal was an accomplished hostess, and allowed her guests little time to make love or to yawn. There were constant riding and driving and yachting parties, pic-nics and tennis and golf. In the evening they danced, romped, or had impromptu "Varieties."

Patience was fascinated with the life, although she still had the sense of being an alien, and moments of terrible loneliness. But she was too much of a girl not to take a girl's delight in the dash and glitter and pic-turesqueness of society. She was not popular, although she quickly outgrew any external points of difference; but the essential difference was felt and resented.

On the whole there was concord between herself and her mother-in-law. Mr. Peele she barely knew. His family saw little of him. He had not attended the wed-ding. When Patience had arrived at Peele Manor after her trip, he had kissed her formally, and remarked that he hoped she "would make something of Beverly."

He was an undersized man with scant iron grey hair whose tint seemed to have invaded his complexion. His lips were folded on each other so closely, that Patience watched them curiously at table: when eating they merely moved apart as if regulated by a spring; their expression never changed. His eyes were dark and rather dull, his nose straight and fine, his hands small and very white. He was not an eloquent man at the bar; he owed his immense success to his mastery of the law, to a devilish subtlety, and to his skill at playing upon the weak points of human nature. No man could so adroitly upset an " objection," no man so terrify a witness. It was said of him that he played upon a jury with the consummate art of a great musician for his instrument. He rarely lost a case.

His voice was very soft, his manners exquisite. He was never known to lose his temper. His cold aristocratic face looked the sarcophagus of buried passions.

He deeply resented his children's failure to inherit his brain, but in his inordinate pride of birth, forgave them, for they bore the name of Peele. Hal was his favourite, for she, at least, was bright.

May admired her sister-in-law "to death," as she phrased it, and bored her with attentions. Patience preferred Honora, who puzzled and repelled her, but assuredly could not be called superficial, although her claims to intellectuality were based upon her preference for George Eliot and George Meredith to the lighter order of fiction, and upon her knowledge of the history of the Catholic Church.

One day, as Patience was crossing the lawn in front of the house, May called to her from the hall, beckoning excitedly. She and Hal and Honora were standing by a table on which was a saucer half full of what appeared to be dead leaves. As Patience entered, May lifted the saucer to her sister-in-law's nostrils.

"Why? What?" asked Patience, then paused.

"Oh, — what a faint, delicious, far-away perfume," she said after a moment. "What is it?"

May dropped the saucer and clapped her hands. Hal laughed as if much gratified. Honora's eyes wandered to the landscape with an absent and introspective regard.

"What is it?" asked Patience again.

"Why, it's dried strawberry leaves," said May. "Don't you know that they say in the South that you can't perceive their perfume unless every drop of blood in your veins is blue? The common people can't smell it at all."

Patience blushed and moved her head disdainfully, but she thrilled with pleasure.

"Won't you come up and see my room?" said Honora, softly. "You've never called on me yet, and I think I have a very pretty room."

"Oh, I'll be delighted," said Patience, who was half consciously avoiding Beverly: Peele Manor was without guests for a few hours.

"Now you must tell me if you like my room as much as you do me," said Honora, who looked more like an angel than ever, in a white mull frock and blue sash. Her manner to Patience was evenly affectionate, with an undercurrent of subtle sadness and reproach.

As she opened the door of her room, Patience exclaimed with admiration. The ceiling was blue, frescoed with golden stars, the walls with celestial visions. A blue carpet strewn with lilies covered the floor, fluttering curtains of blue silk and white muslin, the old windows. From the dome of the brass bedstead mull curtains hung like clouds. A faint odour of incense mixed with the sweet perfumes of summer.

"Is it not beautiful?" said Honora, in a rapt voice. "It makes me think of heaven. Does it not you? It was dear Aunt Honora's last Christmas gift to me. It was so sweet of her, for of course I am only the poor cousin."

Patience looked at her, wondering, as she had often done, whether the girl were a fool, or deeper than any one of her limited experience. Honora rarely talked, but she had reduced listening to a fine art, and was a favourite in society. Whether she had nothing to say, or whether she had divined that her poverty would make eloquence unpardonable, Patience had not determined. One thing was patent, however: she managed her aunt, and her wants were never ignored.

"Now," she said softly, "I am going to show you something that I don't show to every one — but you are dear Beverly's wife." She folded a screen and revealed an altar covered with cloth of silver, antique candlesticks, and heavy silver cross.

"My faith which sustains me in all the trials of life," whispered Honora, crossing herself. "Ah, if I could have made dear Beverly a convert. Once he seemed balancing — but he slipped away. I have tried to win Hal and May to the true faith too; but we were always so much more to each other — Beverly and I, — playmates from childhood. I think I know him better than anybody in the world."

Patience felt an interloper, a thief and an alien, but out of her new schooling answered carelessly: "Oh, he is awfully fond of you, but I don't think he is inclined to be religious. This room is too sanctified to speak above a whisper in. Come to my room and talk to me awhile."

218 Patience Sparhawk and Her Times

Honora opened a door by the head of her bed, and they passed through a large lavatory, then through Beverly's room to that of the bride, a square room whose windows framed patches of Hudson and Palisade, and daintily furnished in lilac and white. A photograph of Miss Tremont hung between the windows. On one side were shelves containing John Sparhawk's library.

Beverly arose from a deep chair, where he had been smoking and glowering upon the Hudson. Patience caught Honora firmly by the waist and pushed her into the most comfortable chair in the room, then with much skill engaged her in a discussion with Beverly upon the subject of music, the one subject besides horse which interested him.

V

In August the girls went to Newport, and Patience became very tired of her mother-in-law. May returned engaged to a wealthy Cuban, who had been dancing attendance on her blondinitude for some months past, and Mrs. Peele became so amiable that she forgot to lecture her daughter-in-law or irritate her with the large vigilance of her polaric eyes. The girls left again for Lenox and Tuxedo. On the first of January the family moved to their town house for the winter.

Patience was alone with her husband.

During the first three days of this new connubial solitude it snowed heavily. Beverly could not ride nor drive, and wandered restlessly between the stable and the library, where his wife sat before the blazing logs.

There were some two thousand volumes at Peele

Manor. Patience had had no time to read since her marriage, but on the morning of the family's departure she made for the library, partly in self defence, partly with pleasurable anticipation. She hoped that Beverly would succumb to the charms of the stable, where there were many congenial spirits and a comfortable parlour; but she had barely discovered Heine's prose and had read but ten pages of the "Reisebilder," when the door opened, and he came in. She merely nodded, and went on reading. She was barely conscious of his presence, for Heine is a magician, and she was already under his spell.

"Well, you might shut up your book and talk to me," said Beverly, pettishly, flinging himself into a chair opposite her. "This is a nice way to treat a fellow on a stormy day."

"Oh, you read too," murmured Patience.

"No, I will not. I want to talk to you."

Patience closed the book over her finger and looked at him impatiently. Then an idea occurred to her, and she spoke with her usual impulsiveness.

"Look, Beverly," she said, "you and I have to spend many months alone together, and if we are to make a success of matrimony we must be companions, and to be companions we must have similar tastes. Now I'll make a bargain with you: I'll try to like horses if you'll try to like books. On pleasant days I'll ride and drive with you, and when it storms we'll read together here in the library. I am sure you will like it after a time. If you find it tiresome to read to yourself I'll read aloud. I don't mind, and then we can talk it over."

"All right," said Beverly. "Anything you say. What's that you're reading now?"

" Heine's prose. He is wonderful — such a style and such sardonic wit, and such exquisite thoughts. I'll begin all over again. Now light a cigar and make yourself comfortable."

For a half hour she read aloud, and then Mr. Peele remarked,—

" Hang it ! The skating is spoiled for a week."

" Oh, Beverly, you have n't been listening."

" Well, I don't like it very much. He skips around so. Besides, I always did hate Germans. Give me America every time."

" Well, read something American then," said Patience, crossly.

" You find something and read it to me. I like to hear your voice, even if I can't keep my mind on it. Wait a while though. I guess I 'll go and see how the stable is getting on."

He bent down to kiss his wife, but she was once more absorbed, and did not see him. He snatched the book from her with an oath and flung it across the room. She sprang to her feet with flashing eyes, pushed him aside with no gentle hand, and ran after the book.

" You sha'n't read that book ! " he cried. " The idea of forgetting your husband for a book — *a book!* You are a lovely wife ! You are a disgrace to the name ! You would rather read than kiss your husband ! I 'll lock this room up, damned if I don't."

" I 'll go and live with Miss Beale and do Temperance work," sobbed Patience. " I won't live with you."

" Oh, you won't — what? What did I marry you for? My God ! What did I marry you for? My life

is hell, for I'm no fool. I know you don't love me.
You married me for my money."

"I wish I had," she exclaimed passionately, then
controlled herself. "I hope we are not going to
squabble in the usual commonplace way. I shall not,
at any rate. If you lose your temper, you can have the
quarrel all to yourself. I shall not pay any attention
to you. Now go out to the stable and cool off, and
when you come back I'll read something else to
you."

"Do you love me?"

"Oh, yes — yes."

And Beverly disappeared, slamming the door behind
him.

"I wonder if any one on earth has such a temper,"
she thought. "And people believe that vulgarity and
lack of control are confined to the lower classes! What
is the matter with civilisation anyhow? I can only
explain my own remarkable aberration in this way:
youthful love is a compound of curiosity, a surplus of
vitality, and inherited sentimentalism. It is likely to
arrive just after the gamut of children's diseases has run
its course. Of course the disease is merely a complacent state of the system until the germ arrives, which
same is the first attractive and masterful man. All
diseases run their course, however. I could not be
more insensible to Beverly Peele's dead ancestors out
in the vault than I am to him. No woman is capable
of loving at nineteen. She is nothing but an overgrown
child, a chaos of emotions and imagination. There
ought to be a law passed that no woman could marry
until she was twenty-eight. Then, perhaps a few of us
would feel less like — Well, there is nothing to do but

make the best of it, regard life as a highly seasoned comedy, in which one is little more than a spectator, after all — and at present I have Heine."

Beverly did not return for an hour. When he did she rose at once, and running her eye along the shelves, selected a volume of Webster's Speeches.

"You like politics," she said; "and all of us should read the great works of our great men. I'll read the famous Seventh of March Speech."

And she did, Beverly listening with considerable attention. When she had finished he remarked enthusiastically,—

"Do you know what that speech has made me make up my mind to do? I'm going to run for the Senate, and make speeches like that myself."

Patience merely stared at him. She wondered if he were really something more than a fool; if there was a sort of post-graduate course.

"What makes you look at me like that? Don't you think I can?"

"Well — " She hardly knew what to say.

"Well! Is that the way you encourage a fellow? You are a nice wife. Here my father has been at me all my life to do something, and just as soon as I make up my mind, my wife laughs at me."

"I did n't laugh at you."

"Well, it's all the same. If I never do anything, it'll be your fault."

"Go to the Senate just as fast as ever you can get there. And you might as well spend the rest of the day studying Webster; but suppose you read to yourself for a while: my throat is tired."

"I don't like to read to myself."

"Well, anyhow, I hear Lawson coming. Luncheon is ready."

The table in the dining-room had been divested of its leaves, and the young couple sat only a few feet apart. The room had once been a banqueting-hall. It was very large and dark. The white light filtered meagrely through the small panes. The wind moaned through the naked elms.

"The country is awfully dull in winter," remarked Patience. "I wish we were in town."

"That's a beautiful speech to make to a husband. I don't mind so long as you are here."

"Of course I am deeply flattered," and she smiled upon him. There seemed nothing else to do.

"Damn it!" cried Beverly, "this steak is as thin as a plate and burnt to a cinder. Patience, I do wish you'd give some of your attention to housekeeping and less to books. It is your place to see that things are properly cooked, now that Honora is gone."

"Oh, dear. I don't know anything about cooking, or housekeeping, either."

"Well, then, I'd be much obliged if you'd learn as quickly as possible. Take this steak out," he said to the maid, "and bring some cold beef or ham. Damn it! I might have known that when Honora went away I'd have nothing fit to eat, with this new cook."

But Patience refused to continue the conversation, and when the ham and beef came he ate of them with such relish that his good-nature returned as speedily as it had departed.

During the afternoon the scene of the morning was repeated with variations, and the same might be said of the two following days. Then came an interval of sleighing and skating. Then rain turned the snow to slush, and once again Beverly exhibited the characteristics of a caged tiger.

"I shall have nervous prostration before the winter is over," thought Patience, who was still determined to take the situation humorously, still refused to face her former self. "I do wish the family would come back, mother-in-law and all."

Occasionally, despite Beverly's indignant protests, she went to town for the day, and shopped or paid calls with Hal. On one occasion they went to see Rosita. That "beautiful young prima donna of ever increasing popularity" wore black gauze over gold-coloured tights, and acted and sang and danced and allured with consummate art. The opera house was two-thirds crowded with men, although there was the usual matinée contingent of girls and young married women.

"Well," thought Patience, "she's way ahead of me, for she's made a success of herself, at least, and is not bothered with scruples and regrets."

The winter dragged along as slowly as if time had lamed the old man, then fallen asleep. The relations between Patience and Beverly became very strained. His frequent tempers were alternated by sulks. He was genuinely unhappy, for limited as he was, mentally and spiritually, he was very human; and in his primitive way he loved his wife.

Patience's resolution to go through life as a cynical humourist, deaf and blind to the great wants of her nature, died hard, but it died at last. Monotony accentuated fact, and the time came when pretence failed her, and she visibly shrank from his lightest caress. The tide of horror and loathing had risen slowly, but definitely. He threatened to kill her, to commit suicide, to get a divorce; but his threats did not disturb her. He was too weak to kill himself, too proud to make himself ridiculous in the divorce courts, and too much in love to put her beyond his reach. What sustained her was the hope that his passion would die a natural death, and that they would then go their diverse ways as other married people did, — that had come to seem to her the most blessed meaning of the holy state of matrimony. Then she could enjoy her books, and he would permit her to spend the winters in New York, or in travel.

Beverly's affections, however, showed no sign of dissolution.

VI

ONE afternoon in March, Patience, glancing out of the library window, saw Hal coming up the lawn from the path that led down the slope to the station. She suppressed a war-whoop with which she and Rosita had been used to awake the echoes of the Californian hills, opened the window, and vaulted out.

"Well," cried Miss Peele, as Patience ran toward her, "you do look glad to see me, sure enough. Bev can't be very exciting, for you don't look as if it were me particularly — just somebody. Oh, matrimony! matrimony! I envy the women that have solved the problem in some other way — the journalists and artists, and authors and actresses, and even the suffragists, God rest them. Hello, there's Bev. He looks as if he were about to cry. What have you been doing to him?"

"I left him writing an order for some new kind of horse-feed," said Patience, indifferently. Her husband stood at the window, staring gloomily at the beaming faces. When the girls entered the room he had gone.

"He looks as if he had just been let out of the dark room. Do you beat him? What do you suppose my mother will say?"

"Oh, I suppose he's bored too. You see it's nearly three months now. I tried to make him read, but after the third day he went to sleep."

Hal drew a low chair to the fire, close to the one Patience occupied. She laughed merrily.

"Fancy your trying to make Bev intellectual! That would be a good subject for a one-act farce. Well, I've come up here to tell you something, and to talk it over. I, too, am contemplating matrimony."

"Oh, don't!" cried Patience.

"I believe that is usually the advice of married people, but the world goes on marrying itself just the same. But my problem is much more complicated than the average, for there are two men in the question."

"Two? You don't mean to say you don't know your own mind?"

"That is exactly the fact in the case. You remember Reginald Wynne? Well, Patience, I do like that man. I never liked any man one tenth as much. I might say he's the only serious man I've ever met, the only one, to put it in another way, that I ever could take seriously as a man. He has brains — he's a lawyer, you know, and they say very fine things of him — and he is so kind, and *strong*. When I am with him I don't feel frivolous and worldly and one of a dozen. If I have any better nature and any apology

for a brain, they are on top then. He is the last sort
of man I ever thought I 'd fall in love with, but it takes
us some years to become acquainted with ourselves,
does n't it? I do respect him so, and it is such a novel
sensation. He even makes me read. Fancy! And
I 've even promised him that I won't read any more
French novels, excepting those he selects, nor smoke
cigarettes. So, you see, I am in love.

"But, Patience," she continued with tragic emphasis,
"he has n't a red — and I know I 'd be miserable,
poor. When papa saw which way the wind was blowing,
he took me into the library and told me that although he
made fifty thousand dollars a year, we spent nearly all
of it, and that he should not have much to leave besides
his life insurance — one hundred thousand — which of
course would go to mamma. It is a matter of honour
never to sell this place, and the revenue from the farm
— which is to go to Beverly — would keep it up in a
small way. The town house is to be May's and mine;
but what will that amount to? May and I have always
pretty well understood that if we want to keep on having the things that habit has made a necessity to us,
we must marry rich men! Oh, dear! Oh, dear!"

"Well, the other man?"

"He has appeared on the scene lately. He is not
the usual alternative by any means, for he is very attractive in his way. He has the manners of the man of
the world, a *fin de siècle* brain, and the devil in his eye.
He is rather good-looking and tremendously good form.
And, my dear, he has three cold millions. Think what
I should be with three millions! Fancy me in Boston on
three or four hundred dollars a month. Oh, Patience,
what shall I do?" And Hal, the most undemonstra-

tive of women, laid her head on Patience's knee and sobbed bitterly.

" I had to come to see you, Patience," she continued after a moment. " I have no one else; I could never have said a word of this to mamma or May. And I like you better than any one in the world except Reginald Wynne. And you seem to understand things. Do tell me what to do."

" Do this: Be true to your ideals. If love means, and has always meant more to you than anything else in the world, marry Reginald Wynne. If money and power and luxury are the very essentials of happiness to you, marry the other man. No temporary aberration can permanently divert one's paramount want from its natural course. As soon as the novelty has gone, the ego swings back to its old point of view as surely as water does that has been temporarily dammed. There is only one thing that persists, and that is the ideal, — that habit of mind which is bred of heredity and environment, even where care or consciousness is lacking. It is as relentless and pitiless as the law of cause and effect. I believe it would outlive a very leprosy of the soul. And it makes no difference whether that ideal be great or small, high or low, its hold is precisely the same, for it is individuality itself. Rosita is happy because she has realised her ideal. Miss Tremont was happy because she lived up to hers. Miss Beale was supremely satisfied with herself when she let a man die whom she might have saved by smirching her ideals. The religionists are happy generally, not through communion with the presiding deity, as they imagine, but because they have arbitrarily created a sort of spiritual Blackstone whom they delight to obey.

The author is happy when he toils, even without hope of reward. Martyrs have known ecstasy — But one could go on for a week. Don't marry Wynne if you feel that you would be unhappy in poverty after the first few months; and if you feel that great wealth without love would be misery, don't marry the other."

"Oh, I could like Latimer Burr well enough," said Hal, staring gloomily at the fire; "and after a time I suppose I 'd forget. You see, I have been in love so short a time that the wrench would be a good deal less violent than the wrench from luxury — I 'd soon get over it, I expect. But I do like him — I never thought I could feel like this."

Patience fondled the sleek head, but she was not in a mood to feel in sympathy with love. The only thing that to her seemed of paramount importance was to fix a clear eye on the future.

"You see," she said, "the present is ever with us, and the past recedes farther and farther. If the rich man can give you what you most want, time will make you forget the very sensation of love. If you marry Wynne and the love goes, you will have equal difficulty to recall it, and nothing to compensate in the present."

"I 'm not afraid that it would go; but I know that I should be thoroughly miserable poor, and make him miserable too. I do love it all so — all that money means — why, one can't even be well groomed without money. It has gone to make up nine-tenths of my composition; the other tenth is only a bit of miserable wax. But I love this new feeling, and I never believed that anything could be so sweet. Oh, dear; I 'll have to dry up. Here comes Bev."

"Remember this," said Patience, "and let it console you: however you feel or are torn, you'll do one thing only, — follow along the line of least resistance."

Beverly entered and kissed his sister affectionately. Her back was to the light, and he did not notice her swollen eyes.

"Well, you are looking hilarious," she remarked in her usual flippant tones. "Has Tammany gone lame, or Mrs. Langtry refused to take her five bars?"

"My wife does n't love me!" Beverly had brooded upon his wrongs for two months. Hal's words were as a match to a mine.

"Oh!" exclaimed Patience, springing to her feet, "don't let us have a scene for Hal's benefit. Do cultivate a little good taste, if good sense is too far beyond you."

Her words were not soothing, and Beverly exploded in one of his most violent passions. He tore up and down the room, banging his fist alternately on the table, the mantel, and the books, and once he hit the panel of a door so heavy a blow that it sprang. Patience sat down and turned her back. Hal endeavoured to stop him; but he had found a listener, and would discharge his mind of its accumulated virus. He told the tale of the winter in spasmodic gusts, hung and fringed with oaths. Finally he flung himself out of the room, shouting all the way across the hall.

For a moment there was an intense and meaning silence between the two women; then Hal stood up and laid her palms to her head.

"Patience!" she said, "Patience! this is awful. What have I done? Oh, does it really mean anything?

I have seen Bev go into tempers all my life — but — Tell me, please — does this really mean anything — "

"Whether it does or does not it need not worry you beyond warning you against mistakes on your own account. I married with my eyes open, and I can take care of myself. Don't marry your rich man unless you like him well enough to pretend to like him a good deal more. If you do, you'll end by loathing him and yourself — and what is more, he'll know it."

"Oh, no, I don't think I am as intense as you are — but what do you suppose makes Beverly such a wild animal? We are none of us like that, and never have been, as far as I know, although some of the old boys were pretty gay, not to say lawless. But for two or three generations we seem to have been a fairly well-conducted lot. Beverly is almost a freak."

Patience crossed the room, and lifting down a volume of Darwin's "Descent of Man" read from the chapter on Civilised Nations : —

"'With mankind some of the worst dispositions which occasionally, without any assignable cause, make their appearance in families, may perhaps be reversions to a savage state from which we are not removed by very many generations.'"

VII

Two weeks later Patience received a letter from Hal which induced no surprise.

The die is cast [it read]. Reginald Wynne has gone back to Boston, and I am going to marry Latimer Burr. On the first of April we sail for Europe — mamma and May and I — to get our things.

Don't imagine that I am doing the novel-heroine act, and sprinkling my pillow o' nights. I did feel terribly, and I 'll never love any other man; but the thing is done, and done for the best, and that is the end of it. What you said about following along the line of least resistance is as sure as love and fate and a good many other things; for what Latimer Burr can give me I want more than what Reginald Wynne can give me, and it drew me like a magnet. And the other thing you said is equally true, — that the only joy in life is to pursue your ideals to the bitter end. Mine are not lofty, but they are *me*, and that is all there is to it. I shall not weep it out, because I 've no beauty to lose, and weeping does no earthly good, anyway. If it would give Wynne Burr's fortune I 'd drown New York.

We 'll be back on the first of June. We 're only going over to order things. I wish you joy of Honora. It 's too bad Bev is so much in love with you, or you might switch him off on to her. Oh, Patience, dear, you don't know how much I 've thought about you. It hurts me *hard* to think that you are unhappy. I feel as guilty as a murderer, but really I thought you 'd get along. So many women had been in love with Bev, I thought you would be, too. I don't think it had ever occurred to me that women sometimes had a soul. If I had known as much then as I do now I 'd have done all I could to keep you apart, for Beverly Peele certainly has not the attenuated ghost of a soul.

But Patience, dear, do stand it out. Don't, *don't* get a divorce. Remember that all over the world women are as miserable as you are, and as I might be if I would let myself go. Now, at least, you have compensations; and when I am married I 'll do everything I can to make life gay and pleasant for you; but don't make a horrid vulgar newspaper scandal and leave yourself without resources. This world is a pretty good place after all when you are on top, but it must be hell underneath.

Lovingly   HAL.

VIII

The day Mrs. Peele and her daughters sailed for France Mr. Peele and his niece returned to the Manor. Honora kissed Patience on either cheek.

"Oh, I am so glad to come back to my lovely room, and to see you, Patience dear," she said wearily. "We have had such a gay winter, and I am so tired. Dear me, how fresh and sweet you look in that white frock. I just long to get into thin things."

When Mr. Peele came up in the evening he narrowed his lids as he kissed Patience, and regarded her critically. "Well, how does Beverly wear in a three months' *tête-a-tête?*" he asked. "Gad! I should n't care to try it."

"Oh," she said flushing, "we did n't talk much. He had the farm and the horses to attend to, you know, and I had the library. Oh, I am so glad you have that library."

He laughed aloud, with the harsh notes of a voice unused to such music.

"I see you have had a Paul and Virginia time, as Hal would say. I 'm sorry you 've put your foot in it, for even you can't make anything of him; but make the best of it. Don't leave him — Hal has told me something, you see. It was best that she should. There must be no scandal. If he makes too great a nuisance of himself come to me; and if he cuts off your allowance at any time just let me know, and I 'll see that you have all the money you want. He does n't own the farm. I like you. You 're a clever woman. If you 'd been my daughter I 'd have been proud of you.''

And whether he really found pleasure in his daughter-in-law's society, or whether he merely thought it politic to lighten her burden, from that time until the return of the family he devoted his evenings to her. He was deeply read, and Patience, after years of mental loneliness, was grateful for his companionship, although personally he antagonised her. He was a mentality without heart or soul, and she knew that he would sacrifice her as readily as he accepted her if it better suited his purpose.

She clung to Honora during the day and read aloud to her in the Tea House, while that devoted young Catholic embroidered for the village church or sewed for the poor of her beloved priest. Father O'Donovan, a young man with a healthy serious face and a clear eye, frequently joined them. Every morning the girls rode or sailed. Beverly frequently made one of the party, and Patience and Honora exercised all their tact to keep him in good humour. In the evening he played duets with his cousin. Her touch was as light and hollow as an avalanche of icicles from the roof, he pounded the piano as if it were a prize fighter's chest.

One evening Patience did not go downstairs until a few moments before dinner was announced. As she entered the library she saw that a stranger stood at the window with Mr. Peele. The priest was present, and she shook hands with him before going over to greet the stranger and her father-in-law. While she was agreeing with him that Honora in her white robe and blue sash looked exactly like an angel, the man at the window turned, and she recognised Mr. Field. She ran forward and held out her hand.

"Oh! Oh!" she cried. "I'm so glad to see you again. I've wanted and wanted to."

He took her hand, smiling, but regarded her with the keen gaze she so well remembered.

"Bless my soul," he said, "but you have changed. It is not too much to say that you have improved. Even the freckles have gone, I see. I thought I was to make a newspaper woman of you. I felt rather cross when you married. But this life certainly agrees with you. You look quite the *grande dame* — quite — ah! Good evening, sir," as Beverly entered and was presented. Mr. Field darted a glance from one to the other, his mouth twitching sardonically.

He sat at Patience's right during dinner, and they talked constantly. Beverly was sulky, and said nothing. Mr. Peele rarely talked at table, even to Patience. Honora and the priest conversed in a solemn undertone. It is doubtful if two courses had been served before the terrible old man understood the situation.

"There's tragedy brewing here," he thought, grimly. "That fellow has the temper of a fiend in the skull of a fool, and this girl is not the compound I take her to be if she lives a lie very long for the sake of champagne and truffles. I'd give a good deal to foresee the outcome. Unless I'm all wrong there'll be a two column story on the first page of the 'Day' some fine morning. Well, she'll have its support, right or wrong. She's a brick, and he's the sort of fellow a man always wants to kick. — What is that?" he asked of the priest, who had begun a story that suddenly appealed to Mr. Field's editorial instinct.

" A physician over at Mount Vernon, who stands very high in his profession, has been accused of poisoning his wife. She died in great agony, and her mother insisted upon a post-mortem. Her stomach was full of strychnine. He maintains that she threatened to commit suicide repeatedly, and that he is innocent; but opinion is against him, and people seem to think that the jury will convict him. I knew both, and I feel positive of his innocence."

" Undoubtedly he is innocent," said Mr. Field. "No physician of ordinary cleverness would bungle like that. Strychnine! absurd! Why, there are poisons known to all physicians and chemists which absolutely defy analysis. I don't doubt that more than one doctor has put his wife out of the way, and the world none the wiser."

" Is that true?" said Patience, eagerly, leaning forward. Her curious mind leapt at any new fact. "What are they like?"

" That I can't say. That is a little secret known to the fraternity only, although I don't doubt they give their friends the benefit of their knowledge occasionally. Indubitably a large proportion of murderers are never discovered — unless they discover themselves, like the guilty pair in ' Thérèse Raquin.' "

" Oh, they belonged to the cruder order of civilisation," said Patience, lightly. " I am sure that if I committed a murder, I should not be bothered by conscience if I had felt myself justified in committing it. It seems to me that if the development of the intellect means anything it means the casting out of inherited prejudices. Of course I don't believe in murder," she continued, carried away as ever by the pleasure of abstract reasoning, "but if a man of the world and of brains, after due deliberation, makes way with a person who is fatal to his happiness or his career, then I think he must have sufficient development of mental muscle to scorn remorse. The highest intelligences are anarchistic."

"Undoubtedly there are those that have reached that point of civilisation," said Mr. Field, "but for my part, I have not. Although I keep abreast of this extraordinary generation, my roots are planted pretty far down in the old one. But assuredly if I did feel the disposition to murder, and succumbed, I'd cover up my tracks."

"Do these poisons give pain? Are they mineral or vegetable?"

As Mr. Field was about to answer, a peculiar expression crossed his face, and Patience, following his eyes, looked at Beverly. Her husband was staring at her with his heavy brows together, the corners of his mouth drawn down in an ugly sneer. To her horror and disgust she felt the blood fly to her hair. At the same time she became conscious that Mr. Peele, the priest, and Honora were exchanging glances of surprise. Beverly gave an abrupt unpleasant laugh, and pushing his chair violently back, left the room. Patience glanced appealingly about, then dropped her glance to her plate. She felt as if the floor were dissolving beneath her feet.

IX

A week later, after a pleasant morning in the Tea
House with Honora and Father O'Donovan, she left
it to go to the library. As she turned the corner of the
house she saw Beverly standing close to one of the
windows.

"What are you doing there?" she asked in surprise.

His brows were lowered and his skin looked black, as
it always did when his angry passions were risen.

"I've been watching you and that priest," he said
savagely, following her as she retreated hastily out of
earshot of the people in the Tea House. "I saw you
exchanging glances with him! Now I know why you
want to know so much about poisons —"

"Are you insane?" she cried. "What on earth are
you talking about?"

"No, I'm not insane — by God! You're in love with
that priest, and I know it. But I'm on the watch —"

"Oh, — you — you —" stammered Patience. She
could not speak. Her face was crimson with anger and
disgust. In her husband's eyes she was an image of
guilt. He burst into a sneering laugh.

"You think I'm a fool, I suppose, because I don't
know anything about books. But a woman said once
that I had the instincts of the devil, and I've no idea
of —"

Patience found her tongue. "You poor fool," she
said. "It was ridiculous of me to pay any attention
whatever to you; but I am not used to being insulted,

even by you. And remember that I am not used to any display of imagination in you. As for *love* — " the scorn with which she uttered the word made even him wince — " do not worry. You have made me loathe the thing. I could not fall in love with a god. Don't have the least fear that I shall be unfaithful to you., I could n't ! "

, She walked away, leaving Beverly trembling and speechless. When she reached her room she locked the doors and sobbed wildly.

" Oh, what shall I do? What shall I do?" she thought. " I can't stand it any longer. I believe I really would kill him if I stayed. I feel as if my nature were in ruins. I hate myself! I loathe myself! I 'll leave this very day ! "

But she had said the same thing many times. Why does a woman hesitate long before she leaves the man who has made life shocking to her? Indolence, abhorrence of scandal, shame to confess that she has made a failure of her life, above all, lack of private fortune and the uncertainty of self-support. For whatever the so-called advanced woman may preach, woman has in her the instinct of dependence on man, transmitted through the ages, and a sexual horror of the arena. Patience let the days slip by, hoping, as women will, that the problem would solve itself, that Beverly Peele would die, or become indifferent, or that she would drift naturally into some other sphere.

X

Mrs. Peele and the girls returned with the June roses ; the house was filled with guests at once. The Cuban had gone to his islands for the summer, and May chose to wear the willow and occasionally to weep upon Patience's unsympathetic shoulder ; but as frequently she consoled herself with the transient flirtation. Hal, apparently, was her old gay self. She did not mention Wynne's name, and Patience was equally reticent.

"I should be the last to remind any woman of what she wished to forget," she thought. "And love — what does it amount to anyhow? If He came I believe I should hate him, because once I felt something like passion for him too."

She had looked forward with some curiosity to meeting Latimer Burr. He also had been in Paris. He followed his lady home on the next steamer, and immediately upon his return came to Peele Manor. Patience did not meet him until dinner. She sat beside him, and at once became acutely aware that he was a man of superlative physical magnetism. She proscribed him accordingly — magnetism was a repellent force at this stage of her development. She was rather surprised that she could feel it again, so completely had Beverly's evaporated.

Burr was a tall heavily built man about forty years old. He carried himself and wore his clothes as only a New York man can. His face was florid and well modelled, his mouth and half closed eyes sensual. But his voice and manners were charming. He appeared to be deeply in love with Hal, and his voice became a caress when he spoke to her. Patience did not like his type, but she forgave him individually because he was fond of Hal and appeared to possess brains.

She fell into conversation with him, and his manner would have led her to believe that while she spoke neither Hal nor any other woman existed. To this Patience gave little attention : she had met that manner before ; it was pleasant, and she missed it when lacking ; but she had practised it too often herself to feel more than its passing fascination. His eyes, however, were more insistently eloquent than his manner, and their eloquence was of the order that induced discomposure.

Patience at times looked very lovely, and she was at her best to-night. Her white skin was almost transparent, and the wine had touched her cheeks with pink. The sadness of her spirit had softened her eyes. Her gown of peacock blue gauze fitted her round elastic figure very firmly, and her bare throat and neck and arms were statuesque. She had by no means the young married woman look, but she had some time since acquired an "air," much to Hal's satisfaction. To all appearances she was a girl, but her figure was womanly. Although about five feet six, and built on a more generous plan than the average New York woman, she walked with all their spring and lightness of foot. Her round waist looked smaller than it was ; she never laced. Lately she had discovered that she "had an arm," as Hal would have phrased it, and the discovery had given her such satisfaction that she had forgotten her troubles for the hour, and sent for a dressmaker to take the sleeves out of her evening gowns.

16

Mr. Burr also discovered it, and murmured his approval as caressingly as were he addressing his prospective bride.

"The milk-white woman!" he ejaculated softly. "The milk-white woman!"

"Can't you get any farther?" asked Patience. "If you were a poet now, that would make a good first line for a rhapsody — to Hal, for instance."

He laughed indulgently. "How awfully bright you are. I am afraid of you." But he did not look in the least afraid. "You are to be my sister, you know. We must become friends at once."

"And flattery is the quickest and surest way of establishing the fraternal relation? Well, you are quite right; but just look at my hair for a change, will you?" (She felt as if her skin must be covered with red spots.) "Or my profile. They are also good points."

"They are exquisite. I have rarely seen a woman so beautiful."

"Dear! Dear! How relieved you must be to feel that you can keep your hand in without straying too far from Peele Manor. And there is also Honora."

"I don't admire Miss Mairs. She is too tall, and her nose is too long."

"Poor dear Honora! But how well you understand women! What tact! I like you so much better than I did before."

He laughed again in his indulgent way. "You must n't guy me. It is your fault if I pay you too many compliments. You are a very fascinating woman."

"You are wonderfully entertaining. What must you be when you are in love! What do you and Hal talk about?"

" Is n't Hal a dear little girl? I do love her. I never loved a woman so much in my life — never proposed before. She is so bright. She keeps me amused all the time. I always said I 'd never marry a woman that did n't amuse me, and I 've kept my word. It is n't so much what she says, don't you know, as the way she says it. Dear little girl ! "

On this subject they could agree, and Patience kept him to it as long as possible.

After dinner Burr went with Mr. Peele into the library. Patience, passing through the room, found them talking earnestly upon the great question of the day, — the financial future of the country. She paused a moment, then sat down. To her surprise she found that Burr was master of his subject, and possessed of a gift of words which fell little short of eloquence.

The argument lasted an hour, during which Patience sat with her elbows on the table, her chin on her folded hands, her eager eyes glancing from one to the other. Occasionally she smiled responsively as Burr made some felicitous phrase. When the discussion was over, Mr. Peele left the room. Burr arose at once and seated himself beside her.

" I never talked so well," he said. " You inspired me ; " and he took her hand in the matter-of-fact manner she knew so well.

" You talked quite as well before you saw me — "

" I knew you were there — "

" Kindly let me have my hand. I have only two — "

" Nonsense ! Let me hold your hand. I want to ! I am going to — Why are you — "

" Have n't you Hal's hand ? "

" Oh, my God ! You don't expect me to go through

life holding one woman's hand? Hal is the most fascinating woman in the world, and I love her — but I want you to let me love you, too."

"It is quite immaterial to me whether you love me or not; and, I think, if you want plain English, that you are a scoundrel."

"Oh, come, come. You — *you* — must know more of the world than to talk like that. Why am I a scoundrel?" He looked much amused.

"You are engaged to one woman and are making love to another."

"Well, what of that so long as she does n't know it? I shall be the most uxorious and indulgent of husbands — but faithful — that is not to be expected."

"You must have great confidence in me. Suppose I describe this scene and conversation to Hal?"

"You will not, — not out of regard for me, but because you love Hal — dear little girl! And you are one of the few women devoid of the cat instincts. That long-legged girl, now, has a whole tiger inside of her, but you have only the faults of the big woman. I hope you have their weaknesses."

"Well, you shall never know if I have. Please let go my hand."

He flung it from him. "Oh, well," he said, haughtily, "I hoped we should be friends, but if you will have it otherwise, so be it;" and he stalked out, and devoted himself to Hal for the rest of the evening.

XI

"Funny world," thought Patience. She shrugged her beautiful young shoulders cynically, and went forth to do her duty by the guests. As she passed out of the front door to join some one of the scattered groups on the lawns, she heard a voice which made her pause and tap her forehead with her finger. It was a rich deep voice, with a vibration in it, and a light suggestion of brogue. She turned to the drawing-room, whence it came. A man in riding clothes was talking to Mrs. Peele, who was listening with a bend of the head that meant much to Patience's trained eye. The man had an athletic nervous figure, suggestive of great virility and suppressed force, although it was carried with a fine repose. The thick black hair on his large finely shaped head glinted here and there with silver. His profile was aquiline, delicately cut and very strong, his mouth, under the slight moustache, neither full nor thin, and both mobile and firm, the lips beautifully cut. The eyes, deeply set, were not large, and were of an indefinite blue grey, but piercing, restless, kind, and humourous. There were lines about them, and a deep line on one side of his mouth. His lean face had a touch of red on its olive. He might have been anywhere between thirty-five and forty.

Patience recognised him and trembled a little, but with excitement, not passion. She had understood herself for once when she had said that in her present conditions she was incapable of love. Beverly Peele would have to go down among the memories before his wife could shake her spirit free, and turn with swept brain and clear eyes to even a conception of the love whose possibilities dwelt within her.

But she was fully alive to the picturesqueness of meeting this man once more, and suddenly became possessed of the spirit of adventure. There must be some sort of sequel to that old romance.

She withdrew to the shadow of a tree, where she could watch the drawing-room through the window. Burr entered, slapped the visitor on the back, and bore him away to the dining-room, presumably to have a drink. When they returned, Mr. Peele was in the room. He shook hands with the stranger more heartily than was his wont. In a few moments he crossed over to the library, and Patience, seeing that her early hero would be held in conversation for some time to come, followed her father-in-law and asked casually who the visitor was.

"Oh, that's Bourke, Garan Bourke, the legal idol," sarcastically, "of Westchester County. In truth he's a brilliant lawyer enough, and one of the rising men at the New York bar, although he will go off his head occasionally and take criminal cases. I don't forgive him that, if he *is* always successful. However, we all have our little fads. I suppose he can't resist showing his power over a jury. I heard an enthusiastic youngster assert the other day that Bourke whips up a jury's grey matter into one large palpitating batter, then moulds it with the tips of his fingers while the jury sits with mouth open and spinal marrow paralysed. Personally, I like him well enough, and rather hoped he and Hal would fancy each other. But he doesn't seem to be a marrying man. You'd better go over and meet him. He'll just suit you."

Patience returned to her post. Burr had disappeared, Bourke was talking to half a dozen women. In a few moments he rose to go. Patience went hastily across the lawns to the narrow avenue of elms by the driveway. No two were billing and cooing in its shadows, and Beverly was in bed with a nervous headache.

The moon was large and very brilliant. One could have read a newspaper as facilely as by the light of an electric pear. As Bourke rode to the main avenue a woman came toward him. He had time to think her very beautiful and of exceeding grace before she surprised him by laying her hand on his horse's neck.

"Well?" she said, looking up and smiling as he reined in.

"Well?" he stammered, lifting his hat.

"I am too heavy to ride before you now."

He stared at her perplexedly, but made no reply.

"Still if I were up a tree — literally, you know — and a band of terrible demons were shouting at a man beside a corpse — "

"What?" he said. "Not you? — not you? That homely fascinating little girl — no, it cannot be possible — "

"Oh, yes," lifting her chin, coquettishly. "I have improved, and grown, you see. I was more than delighted when I saw you through the window. It was rather absurd, but I disliked the idea of going in to meet you conventionally — "

He laid his hand strongly on hers, and she treated him with a passivity denied to Latimer Burr.

"I am going to tie up my horse and talk to you a while, may I?" America and the law had not crowded all the romance out of his Irish brain, and he was keenly

alive to the adventure. He had forgotten her name
long since, and it did not occur to him that this lovely
impulsive girl was the property of another man ; but
although he had lived too long, nor yet long enough,
to lose his heart to the first flash of magnetism from
a pretty woman, yet his blood was thrilled by the commingling of spirituality and deviltry in the face of this
high-bred girl who cared to give the flavour of romance
to their acquaintance. He saw that she was clever, and
he had no intention of making a fool of himself; but
he was quite willing to follow whither she cared to lead.
And it was night and the moon was high ; the leaves
sang in a crystal sea ; a creek murmured somewhere ;
the frogs chanted their monotonous recitative to the
hushed melodies and discords of the night world ; the
deep throbbing of steamboats came from the river.

He tied his horse to a tree, and they entered the
avenue.

"You told me that it was a small world, and that
we should probably meet again," she said ; " and I never
doubted that we should."

"Oh, I never did either," he exclaimed. He was
racking his brains to recall the conversation which had
passed between them a half dozen years ago, and for
the life of him could not remember a word ; but he
was a man of resource.

"I am glad that it is at night," he continued, " even
if the scene is not so charming as Carmel Valley from
that old tower. How beautiful the ocean looked from
there, and what a jolly ride we had in the pine
woods !"

She understood perfectly, and grinned in the dark.

"Ah ! I remember I gave you some advice," he ex-

claimed with suspicious abruptness. "I thought afterward that it was great presumption on my part."

"I wonder if you had an ideal of your own in mind
when you spoke?"

"An ideal?" He cursed his memory and floun-
dered hopelessly. Even his Irish wit for once deserted
him.

"Oh, I hoped you had not forgotten it. Why, I
have made a little 'Night Thoughts' of what you said,
and it has been one of the strongest forces in my development. Shall I repeat it to you?"

"Oh, please." He was blushing with pleasure, but
sore perplexed.

And she repeated his comments and advice, word
for word.

"Is it possible that you remember all that? I am
deeply flattered." And he was, in fact.

"What more natural than that I should remember?
I was a lonely little waif, full of dreams and vague
ideals, and with much that was terrible in my actual
life. I had never talked with a young man before —
a man of seventy was my only experience of your sex,
barring boys, that don't count. And you swooped
down into my life in the most picturesque manner
possible, and talked as no one in my little world was
capable of talking. So, you see, it is not so remarkable
that I retain a vivid impression of you and your words.
I was frightfully in love with you."

"Oh — were you? Were you?" He was very much
at sea. It was true that she had paid him the most
subtle tribute one mind can pay to another, but her
very audacity would go to prove that she was a brilliant
coquette. He had a keen sense of the ridiculous, and

he was still a little afraid of her. He took refuge on the broad impersonal shore of flirtation, where the boat is ever dancing on the waves.

"If you felt obliged to use the past tense you might have left that last unsaid."

"Oh, there are a thousand years between fifteen and twenty-one. I am quite another person, as you see."

"You are merely an extraordinary child developed; and you have carried your memory along with you."

"Oh, yes, the memory is there, and the tablets are pretty full; but never mind me. I want to know if your ideals are as strong now as I am sure they were then — if any one in this world manages to hold onto his ideals when circumstances don't happen to coddle them."

"Oh, I don't know," he said. "I'm afraid I haven't thought much about them since that night. I doubt if I'd given too much thought to them before. Deep in every man's brain is an ideal of some sort, I imagine, but it is seldom he sits down and analyses it out. He knows when he's missed it and locked the gates behind him, and perhaps, occasionally, he knows when he's found it — or something approximating it. We are all the victims of that terrible thing called Imagination, which, I sometimes think, is the sudden incursion of a satirical Deity. I have not married — why, I can hardly say. Perhaps because there has been some vague idea that if I waited long enough I might meet the one woman; but partly, also, because I have had no very great desire to marry. I keep bachelor's hall over on the Sound, and the life is very jolly and free of small domestic details. There are so many women that give you almost everything you want—or at least four or five will make up a very good whole—that I have never yet faced the tremendous proposition of going through life expecting one woman to give me everything my nature and mind demand. But there are such women, I imagine," he added abruptly, trying to see her face in one of the occasional splashes of moonlight.

"A very clever woman—Mrs. Lafarge; perhaps you know her—said to me the other day, that many men and women of strong affinity took a good deal of spirituality with them into marriage, but soon forgot all about it—matrimony is so full of reiterant details, and everything becomes so matter of course. Do you think that is true?"

"I am afraid it is. The imagination wears blunt. The Deity is sending his electricity elsewhere—to those still prowling about the shores of the unknown. Perhaps if one could keep the danger in mind—if one were unusually clever—I don't know. I fancy civilisation will get to that point after a while. Unquestionably the companionship of man and woman, when no essentials are lacking, is the one supremely satisfying thing in life. If we loved each other, for instance—on such a night—it seems to me that we are in tune—"

"But we don't love each other, as it happens, and we met about three quarters of an hour ago. We'll probably hate each other by daylight."

"Oh, I hope not," he said, accepting the ice-water. "But tell me what your ideals were. I hope they have proved more stable than mine."

"Oh, mine were a sort of yearning for some unseen force in nature; I suppose the large general force from which love is a projection. Every mortal, except the purely material, the Beverly Peele type, for instance, has an affinity with something in the invisible world, an uplifting of the soul. Christianity satisfies the great mass, hence its extraordinary hold. Do you suppose the real link between the soul of man and the soul of nature will ever be established?"

He laughed a little, piqued, but amused. "You are very clever," he said, "and this is just the hour and these are just the circumstances for impersonal abstractions. Well — perhaps the link will be established when we have lived down this civilisation and entered upon another which has had drilled out of it all the elements which plant in human nature the instincts of cupidity and sordidness and envy and political corruption, and all that goes to make us the aliens from nature that we are. About all that keeps us in touch with her now are our large vices. There is some tremendous spiritual force in the Universe which projects itself into us, making man and nature correlative. What wonder that man — particularly an imaginative and intelligent child — should be affected and played upon by this Mystery? What wonder that the heathens have gods, and the civilised a symbol called the Lord God? — a concrete something which they can worship, and upon which unburden the load of spirituality which becomes oppressive to matter? It is for the same reason that women fall in love and marry earlier than men, who have so many safety-valves. On the other hand, men who have a great deal of emotional imagination and who can neither love nor accept religion take refuge in excess. It is all a matter of temperament. Cold-blooded people — those that have received a meagre share of this great vital force pervading the Universe, which throws a continent into convulsions or a human being into ecstasy — such, for instance, are religious only because their ancestors were, — their brain is pointed that way. Their blood has nothing to do with it, as is the more general case — for Christianity is pre-eminently sensuous."

"What do you suppose will take its place? The world is bound to become wholly civilised in time; but still human nature will demand some sort of religion (which is another word for ideality), some sort of lodestar."

"A superlative refinement, I think; a perfected æstheticism which shall by no means eradicate the strong primal impulses; which shall, in fact, create conditions of higher happiness than now exist. Do we not enjoy all arts the more as they approach perfection? Does not a nude appeal with more subtle strength to the senses the more exquisite its beauty, the more entire its freedom from coarseness? When people strive to place human nature on a level with what is highest in art and in nature itself, the true religion will have been discovered. So far, man himself is infinitely below what man has achieved. It is hard to believe that genius is the result of any possible combination of heredity. It would seem that it must, like its other part, imagination, be the direct and more permanent indwelling of the supreme creative force — as if the creator would lighten his burden occasionally, and shakes off rings which float down to torment favoured brains."

"I always knew that I should love to hear you talk," murmured Patience.

His hand closed over hers. He drew it through his

arm and held it against his heart, which was beating irregularly.

"And I have n't talked so much nor such stuff to a woman since God made me. I believe that I could talk to you through twenty years. You have said enough to-night to make me hope that our minds have been running along the same general lines. Tell me — honestly — no coquetry — has what I said that night had the slightest effect in your development?"

She told the tale of the day in the crystal woods, giving a sufficiently comprehensive sketch of the events which had led up to it to make her the more keenly interesting to the man whose brain was beginning to whirl a little.

"If you had come at that moment," she concluded, "I would have gone with you to the end of the earth. I have a pretty strong personality, but there was a good deal of wax in me then, and if you could have gotten it between your hands I think that what you moulded would have closely resembled your ideal — the impression you had already made had so strongly coloured and trained my imagination. But," she continued hastily, and glancing anxiously to the far distant end of the avenue, "you see my life changed immediately after that, and I went into the world and became hard and bitter and cynical. I have no ideals left, and I do not want any — I have seen too much — "

"Hush!" he said passionately, "I do not believe a word of it. Why, that was not two years ago, and you are still a young girl. Have you loved any one else?" he asked abruptly, his voice less steady.

"No!"

He was too excited to note the meaning of her emphasis. He was only conscious that he was very close to a beautiful woman who allured him in all ways as no one woman had ever done before.

"You are full of a girl's cynicism," he said; "you have seen just enough to make you think you know the world — to accept the superficial for the real. You — you yourself are an ideal. All you need is to know yourself, and I am going to undertake the task of teaching you — do you hear? If I fail — if I have made a mistake — if it is only the night and your beauty that have gone to my head — well and good; but I shall have the satisfaction of having tried — of knowing — "

"No, no! No, no!" she said. "You must not come here again. I do not want to see you again — "

"Nonsense! You have some sentimental foolish idea in your head, — or perhaps you are engaged to some man who can give you great wealth and position. I shall not regard that, either. If I feel to you by daylight as I do now, I'll have you — do you understand?"

Patience opened her lips to tell him the truth, then cynically made up her mind to let matters take their course. At the same time she was bitterly resentful that she should feel as she did, not as she had once dreamed of feeling for this man.

"Very well," she said, "I shall be here for a while."

"And I shall see you in the course of a day or two. I'm going now. Good-night." He let her arm slip from under his, but held her hand closely. "And even if it so happened that I never did see you again, I should thank you for the glimpse you have given me of a woman I hardly dared dream existed."

When he had gone she anathematised fate for a moment, then went back to her guests.

XII

LATIMER BURR was evidently a man upon whom rebuff sat lightly. The next morning he came suddenly upon Patience in a dark corner, and tried to kiss her. Whenever the opportunity offered he held her hand, and once, to her infinite disgust, he planted his foot squarely on hers under the dinner table. A few hours later they happened to be alone in one of the small reception-rooms.

" Look here," exclaimed Patience, wrathfully, "will you let me alone? "

" No, I won't," he said good-naturedly. " Jove ! but you are a beauty ! "

She wore a gown of white mull and lace, trimmed with large knots of dark-blue velvet. She had been talking all the evening with Mr. Peele, Mr. Field, and Burr, and was somewhat excited. Her lips were very pink, her eyes very bright and dark. She held her head with a young triumph in beauty and the intellectual tribute of clever men.

" Hal would be delighted. She has always wanted me to become the fashion."

"You never will be that, for there are not enough brainy men in society to appreciate you. If all were like myself, you would be wearied with the din of admiration — "

"There's nothing like having a good opinion of oneself."

"Why not? I don't set up to be an intellectual man — intellectual men are out of date ; but I'm a brainy man, and I'd like to know how I'm to help being aware of the fact. I certainly don't claim to be pretty, so you can't say I'm actually wallowing in conceit."

Patience was forced to laugh. "Oh, you'd do very well if you'd exercise as much sense in regard to women as you do to affairs. Just answer me one question, will you? Are you so amazingly fascinating that women have the habit of succumbing at the end of the second interview?"

"I never set up to be an ass."

"But your manner is quite assured. You seem very much surprised that I don't tumble into your arms and say 'Thank you.' Oh, you New York men are so funny!"

"Well, answer me one question — you don't love your husband, do you?"

"No, I don't."

"Do you like me?"

"I would if you wouldn't make such an idiot of yourself. You certainly are very agreeable to talk to."

He came closer, his lids falling. The fine repose of his manner was a trifle ruffled. "Do you love anybody else?" he asked.

"I do not."

"Then let me love you."

"I shall not."

"Then if you don't love your husband and you like me and will not let me love you, you must have a lover."

Patience burst into brief hilarity.

" Is that the logic of your kind? "

" A beautiful woman that does not love her husband always loves another man."

" Or is willing to be loved by the first man that happens to have no other affair on hand."

" You have said that you like me."

" I did n't say I loved you ! "

" I 'd make you ! "

"Oh ! " with a deep contempt he was incapable of understanding, "you could n't. But tell me another thing ; I 'm very curious. Has it never occurred to you that a woman must be wooed, that it is somewhat necessary to arouse sentiment and feeling in her before she is willing to advance one step? Why, you and your kind demand her off-hand in a way that is positively funny. What has become of all the old traditions? "

" Oh, bother," he said. " Life is too short to waste time on old-fashioned nonsense. If a man wants a woman he says so, and if she 's sensible and likes him she meets him half way. Men and women of the world know what they want."

"That is all there is to love then? It no longer means anything else whatever? "

" Oh — you are all wrong. If you were not a spiritual woman I would n't cross the room to win you. One can buy the other sort. It is your spirituality, your intellectuality, that fascinates me as much as your beauty."

"What do you know about spirituality?" she said contemptuously. " I don't like to hear you speak the word. You desecrate it."

He flushed purple. " There are few things I don't

understand — and a good deal better than you do, perhaps."

" You have a clever man's perception, that is all. Association with all sorts of women has taught you the difference between them. But what could you give a spiritual woman? Nothing. You have not a shrunken kernel of soul. The sensual envelope is too thick; your brain too crowded with the thousand and one petty experiences of material life. You are as ingenuous as all fast men, for the women you have spent your life running after make no demands upon subtlety — "

" Take care," he said angrily; " you are going too far. I tell you I have as much soul as any man living."

" Perhaps. I doubt if any man has much. Men give women nothing, as far as I can see. If we want companionship there seems nothing to do but to de- · scend to your level and grovel with you."

" I would never make you grovel. I would reverence — "

" Oh, rot ! " she cried, stamping her foot. " What a fool — and worse — the average woman must be. You have no idea how ingenuously you are giving away the women of society. And soul ! The idea of a man who pretends to love the woman he is engaged to and is making love to another, and that her sister-in-law and most intimate friend, claiming to have a soul ! Have you no sense of humour? I say nothing about honour, as I wish to be understood, if possible ; but you are clever enough to see the ridiculous in most things — Please don't walk over me. There is plenty of room. And the windows are open, you know — "

" Yes, and I am here," cried a furious voice, and Beverly sprang into the room.

Patience stepped back with a faint exclamation.
Burr turned white. Beverly was shaking with rage.
His face was almost black; there were white flecks on
his nostrils.

"I kept quiet," he articulated, "to hear every word.
You dog!" to Burr. "I may be pretty bad, but I'd
never do what you have done. And as for you," he
shook his fist at his wife, "you were only leading
him on. If I could only have held myself in another
moment I'd have seen you in his arms. Get out
of this house," he roared, "both of you. You'll
never marry my sister. I'm going to tell her this
minute —"

Burr sprang forward and caught him by the collar;
but Beverly was not a coward. He turned, flinging
out his fist, and the two men grappled. Patience
closed the door and glanced out of the window. No
one was near. Voices floated up from the cliffs. Burr
was the more powerful man of the two, and in a
moment had flung Beverly, panting, into a chair.

"Keep him here," said Patience, rapidly, and she
left the room.

"Man is certainly still a savage, a brute," she
thought. "What is the matter with civilisation?"

As she crossed the lawn, she met one of the servants.

"Go and find Miss Hal, and ask her to come here,"
she said. A few moments later her sister-in-law hurried up from the cliffs.

"What is it?" she called cheerily. "Has Bev had
an apoplectic fit?"

"Beverly has been making a greater fool of himself
than usual," said Patience, as the girls met, "and
I want to see you before he does. I was standing in

one of the reception-rooms talking to Mr. Burr after Mr. Field and Mr. Peele had gone out, and he had on all his manner and was telling me how beautiful I was, in his usual after dinner style, when Beverly leaped through the window like the wronged husband in the melodrama and accused us of making love. He threatened to come and tell you, and he and Mr. Burr wrestled like two prize-fighters. If Beverly were put on the witness stand he 'd be obliged to admit that Mr. Burr had not so much as touched my hand. I suppose you will believe me?"

Hal gave her light laugh. "Certainly, my dear, certainly; although if I were a man I should fall in love with you myself. I would n't bet on Latimer, but I would on you — so don't worry your little head. Do you suppose I expect a man with that mouth and those eyes to be faithful to me? Still, I must say that I should have given him credit for more decency than to make love to my sister-in-law — "

" He did n't! I swear he did n't."

"Oh, of course not! Nor will he make love to every pretty woman he finds himself alone with for five minutes. He can't help it, poor thing. Let us go and talk to the gentlemen."

As they entered the little room she exclaimed airily, " Been making a fool of yourself again, Bev? No, don't speak. Patience has told me all about it. I have every confidence in her and Latimer. Better go and take a spin with Tammany. Latimer, you really must mend your manners. They 're too good. From a distance a stranger would really think you were making love when you are swearing at the heat. Now, come down to the Tea House. Good-night, Bevvy dear."

And she went off between her lover and her sister-in-law, leaving her brother to swear forth his righteous indignation.

That night Patience opened the door of her husband's room for the first time. Beverly, who had just entered, was so astonished that the wrath he had carefully nourished fell like quicksilver under a cool wave, and he stared at her without speaking.

"I wish to tell you," said his wife, "that you were entirely justified in being angry to-night. I could have suppressed Burr by a word, but I chose to lead him on to gratify my curiosity. Hal wishes to marry him, and I am determined that she shall. If I had admitted the truth to her or permitted you to enlighten her, her self-respect would have forced her to break the engagement. That would have been absurd, for the match is exactly what she wants, and she is not marrying with illusions. But you have been treated inconsiderately, and I apologise for my share in it. Will you forgive me?"

"Of course I'll forgive you," said Beverly, eagerly. "I wasn't angry with you, anyhow — only with that scoundrel. But I never believed you'd do this. Do you care for me a little?"

Patience averted her face that she might not see the expression on his. Despite her loathing of him she gave him a certain measure of pity. With all the preponderance of the savage in him and the limitations of his intelligence he had his own capacity for suffering, and to-night he stood before her crushed under the sudden reaction, his eyes full of the dumb appeal of shrinking brutes.

"If we are going to live peacefully don't let us

discuss that subject," she said gently. " We have both missed it, and I sometimes think that you are more to be pitied than I am. However, I shall not flirt — I promise you that. Good-night."

That was the last of Mr. Burr's illegal love-making at Peele Manor. He had had a fright and a lesson, and he forgot neither.

XIII

" GARAN BOURKE is coming to dinner to-night," said Hal, the next day. " It's the hardest thing in the world to get him; he never goes anywhere; but he half promised mamma, when he called the other night, that he'd come some day this week, and he wrote yesterday, saying he'd dine with us to-day. I want you to meet him. He is awfully clever, and when he talks I want to close my eyes and listen to his voice. If the dear girls ever get the vote and do jury duty, all he'll have to do will be to quote law. He needn't take the trouble to sum up. His voice will do the business every time."

Patience, in a French gown of black chiffon, was very beautiful that night. She did not go down to dinner until every one was seated. Bourke sat next to Mrs. Peele. Her own chair was near the end of the opposite side of the long table. For a time she did not look at Bourke. When she did she met his eyes; and knew by their expression that some one had told him she was the wife of Beverly Peele.

After dinner he went with Mr. Peele and Burr into

the library. Patience was about to follow a party of young people down to the bluff, when Mr. Field drew her arm firmly through his.

" You are not going to desert your court? " he said· " Why, you don't suppose I come up here to talk to Peele, do you? If you go out with those boys I 'll never come here again."   And he led her into the library.

It was nearly twelve o'clock when she found herself alone with Bourke. The others had gone out, one by one. She had made no attempt to follow them. She sat with defiant eyes and inward trepidation. Bourke regarded her with narrowed eyes and twitching nostrils.

"So you are married? " he said at last.

"Yes."

" And you deliberately made a fool of me? "

"No — no — I did nothing deliberately that night — no — I acted on impulse. And all that I said was quite true. Of course I should have told you — "

" But it would have spoiled your comedy."

"No — no — don't think that. I see that I was dishonest — I am not making excuses — I never thought you 'd become really interested — "

" I am not breaking my heart. Don't let that worry you. The mere fact of your dishonesty is quite enough to break the spell — for you are not the woman I imagined you to be. I was merely worshipping an ideal for the hour. Do you love your husband? "

" No."

" Then you are a harlot," he said, deliberately. " It only needed that."   He rose to his feet and looked contemptuously at her scarlet face. " At all events it was an amusing episode," he said. " Good-night."

XIV

IT was a matter of comment before the summer was over, both among the guests at Peele Manor and the neighbours, that Mr. and Mrs. Beverly Peele had come to the parting of the ways.   As the young man's infatuation was as notable as his wife's indifference, he received the larger share of sympathy.   The married men championed Patience and expressed it in their time-honoured fashion ; and although they worried her she looked forward with terror to the winter: she would willingly have taken them all to board and trusted to their wives to keep them in order.

Beverly had confided his woes long since to his mother.   She declined to discuss the subject with her daughter-in-law, but treated her with a chill severity. Fortunately they were gay that summer, and Patience had much to do.   Hal and May were absorbed in preparations for their wedding, and the duties of hostess fell largely on her shoulders.

Late in the fall there was a double wedding under the medallion of Peele the First.   Immediately thereafter May went to Cuba ; and Hal to Europe, to pay a series of visits.   Mrs. Peele continued to entertain, and was obliged to confess that her daughter-in-law was very useful, and in deportment above reproach.   Outwardly Patience looked almost as cold a woman of the world as herself, and gave no evidence of the storms brewing within ; but one day she hung out a signal. Mrs. Peele announced that she should go to town on

the first of December. Patience followed her into her
bedroom and closed the door.

"May I speak to you a moment alone?" she asked.

"Certainly," said Mrs. Peele, frigidly. "Will you
sit down?"

She herself took an upright chair, and suggested,
Patience thought, a judge on his bench.

"I want to go to town with you this winter."

"I should be happy to have my dear son with me,
and I will not deny that you are a great help to me;
but Beverly is as strongly opposed as ever to city life.
I asked him myself to go down for the winter, but he
refused. He is one of Nature's own children, and loves
the country."

"He certainly is very close to Nature in several of
her moods. But I wish to go whether he does or
not."

"You would leave your husband?" Mrs. Peele
spoke with meditative scorn.

"It will be better for both of us not to be shut
up here together for another winter. I — I will not
answer for the consequences."

"Is that a threat?"

"You can take it as you choose."

"Do you not love my son?"

"No, I do not."

"And you are not ashamed to make such an
admission?"

"Would you prefer to have me lie about it?"

"It is your duty to love your husband."

"That proposition is rather too absurd for argument,
don't you think so? Will you persuade Beverly to let
me go with you to town?"

"I shall not. You should be glad, overjoyed, to have such a husband. You should feel grateful," she added, unburdening her spite in the vulgarity which streaks high and low, " that he loved you well enough to overlook your lack of family and fortune — "

But Patience had left the room.

That evening she went to her father-in-law and stated her case. She spoke calmly, although she was bitter and sore and worried. "I cannot stay here with Beverly this winter," she continued. "I need not explain any farther. Mrs. Peele will not consent to my going to town with her. But could n't I live abroad? I could do so on very little. I should care nothing for society if I could live my life by myself. I should be quite contented with books and freedom. But I cannot stay here with Beverly alone again."

Mr. Peele shook his head. "It would n't do. I understand; but it would only result in scandal, and I don't like scandal. We have never gone to pieces, like so many great New York families. Our women have been proud and conservative, and have not used their position to cloak their amours. I have perfect confidence in you, of course ; but if you went to Europe and left Beverly raging here, people would say that you had gone to meet another man. Moreover, it would do no good. Beverly would follow you. And he will give you no cause for divorce : he has the cunning peculiar to the person of ugly disposition and limited mentality. No, try to stand it. Remember that all the humours of human nature have their limit. Beverly will become indifferent in time. Then he will let you come to us. I intend to take a rest in a year or two and go abroad, and I shall be glad to have you with us. I do not mind

telling you that you are the brightest young woman I
have ever known — and Mr. Field has said the same
thing."

But Patience was not in a mood to bend her neck to
flattery. She shook her head gloomily.

" If I have any brain, cannot you see that I suffer the
more? Mr. Peele, I cannot stay here with Beverly !
Do you know that sometimes I have felt that I could
kill him? I am afraid of myself."

" Hush ! Hush ! Don't say such things. You excit-
able young women are altogether too extravagant in
your way of expressing yourselves. Words carry a great
deal farther than you have any idea of — take an old
lawyer's word for it. Now try to stand it. In fact,
you must stand it. I 'll do all I can. I 'll leave a
standing order with Brentano to send you all the new
books, and I 'll insist upon your coming up every week
or so to have some amusement. But for God's sake
make no scandal."

XV

ON the first of December Patience and Beverly were
alone once more. The weather was fine, and Beverly
temporarily absorbed in breaking in a colt on his private
track. Patience spent the first day wandering about
the woods, tormented by her thoughts. She remembered with passionate regret the old crystal woods
where she had been a girl of dreams and ideals. Her
ideals were in ruins. The hero of her dreams had told
her a hideous truth that had made her hate him and
more abundantly despise herself. She longed ardently

to get away to a mountain top, a hundred miles from civilisation. Nature had been her friend in the old Californian days, and the green or white beauty of her second environment had satisfied her in that peaceful intermediate time. But Westchester County, although exquisitely pretty, lacked grandeur and the suggestion of colossal throes in remote ages with which every stone in California is eloquent. That was what she wanted now. But there was no prospect of getting away. Did she have enthusiasm enough left to leave summarily she had little money. She was very extravagant, and left the larger part of her quarterly allowance with New York shops and milliners and dressmakers; but she knew that the end was approaching, and listlessly awaited it.

Heavy with rebellious disgust she returned to the house and went mechanically to the library. For a while she did not read; she felt no impulse to do so. But after a time she took down a book in desperation, a volume of a new edition de luxe of "Childe Harold." She had not read it during her brief Byronic fever, and had not opened the poet since. Gradually she forgot self. She began with the third canto, and when she had finished the fourth she discovered that her spirits were lighter, a weight had risen from her brain. She had always regarded "notes" as an evidence of the amateur reader, but to-day she scrawled on a fly-leaf of Mr. Peele's new morocco edition : —

"As the Christian goes to his God for help, the intellectual, in hours of depression and disgust and doubt go to the great Creators of Literature, those master minds that lift our own temporarily above the terrible enigma of the commonplace, and possess us to the extinction of

personal meditation. Are not these genii as worthy of dei-
fication by the higher civilisation as was Jesus Christ — their
brother — by the great illogical suffering mass of mankind?
'Faith shall make ye whole,' said Christ; 'come unto me,
all ye that are heavy laden.' 'Develop your brain, and I
will give you self-oblivion, philosophy, and a soul of many
windows,' say the great masters of thought and style, the
stupendous creative imaginations."

Beverly came home in high good humour; his colt
had showed his blood, and nearly pulled him out of the
break-cart. Patience endeavoured to appear interested, and he was so pleased that the atmosphere during dinner was quite domestic. Afterward he went to
sleep on a sofa by the library fire, and his wife read.

A week passed more placidly than Patience had expected. Beverly was evidently under stress to make
himself agreeable. His wife suspected that he had had
a long and meaning conference with his father. In
truth he was desperately afraid that she would leave
him. Patience did not know whether she hated him
most when he was amiable or violent; but she hated
herself more than she hated him.

"I think I'll go to town and see Rosita," she
thought one morning as she awakened. "It seems to
me that she is the fittest companion I could find."

At the breakfast-table she appeared in a tailor frock
and turban, and informed Beverly that she was going to
town to pay some visits. Beverly looked at her for a
moment with black face, then dropped his eyes without
comment. He recalled his father's advice.

"What train shall you come home in?" he asked
after a moment. "I'll go down to the station to meet
you."

"I cannot say. I shall be back to dinner."

"Are n't you going to kiss me good-bye?" he asked
sullenly, when she was about to open the front door.
She hesitated a moment, then raised her face, closing
her eyes, lest he should see the impulse to strike him.
He saw the hesitation and turned away with an oath,
then ran after her, flung his arms about her and kissed
her. She walked down to the station with burning
face, rubbing her mouth and cheeks violently, careless
of the wide-eyed regard of two gardeners.

XVI

WHEN she arrived at Rosita's the maid admitted her
without protest, not recognising in this elegant young
woman the countrified girl of two years before. She
left Patience in the dark drawing-room, but returned in
a moment and announced that Madame would see Mrs.
Peele at once. Patience followed the woman through
the boudoir and bedroom to the bath-room, a classic
apartment of pink tiles. The tub was merely one corner of the room walled off with tiles; and in it, covered
from throat to foot with a sheet, her head on a silken
strap, lay Rosita. By her side sat a girl in a fashionable ulster and large hat, a note-book and pencil on
her lap. Rosita looked like a dark-haired Aphrodite,
and was as fresh as a rose. A maid had just dried one
pink and white hand, and she held it out to Patience.

"Patita! Patita! Patita!" she said with her sweet
drawl and accent, and without a trace of resentment in
her soft heavy eyes. "Where, where have you been all

these years? Miss Merrien, this is my oldest and
dearest friend, Mrs. Beverly Peele [she pronounced the
name with visible pride]. Patita, this is Miss Merrien
of the 'Day.' She is interviewing me."

Patience flushed as she bent her head to the young
woman, who regarded her with conspicuous amazement,
and whose nostrils quivered a little, as if she scented a
"story." She was a pretty girl with a dark rather worn
face, a frank eye, and a nervous manner.

"Patita, sit down there just for a moment while I
look at you. Then we will go into the other room.
I could not wait to see you. *Dios de mi alma*, but you
have changed, Patita *mia*. Who would ever have
thought that you would be such a beauty and such a
swell. Gray cloth and chinchilla! Just think, Miss
Merrien, we used to wear sunbonnets and copper-toed
boots, and drove an old blind horse that would not go
off a walk."

"May I put that down?" asked the girl, eagerly.

"Oh, please don't," exclaimed Patience. Miss Merrien's face fell. Then she smiled, and said good-
naturedly, "All right, I won't."

"And now Patita is a swell," pursued Rosita,
as if no interruption had occurred, "and I am a
famous *prima donna*. Such is life. Patita, do you
know that I have two hundred thousand dollars invested?"

"Really?"

"*Si, señorita!* Oh, my price has gone up, Patita
mia," and she laughed her low delicious laugh.

Miss Merrien smiled. "A man shot himself for that
laugh the other day — I suppose you read about it,"
she said.

"No, I did not. I have read the newspapers irregularly of late — the 'stories,' at least."

"It is true," said Rosita, complacently. "Oh, Patita, life is so lovely. To think that we both had such great destinies! *Pobre* Manuela, and Panchita, and all the rest! *Bueno*, go into the bedroom, both of you, and I will be there in ten minutes."

Patience and Miss Merrien seated themselves in the white bower of velvet and lace.

"Please do not put me into your story," said Patience, hastily. "It would not do — you see my husband would not like it — but we are old friends, and I wanted to see her."

Miss Merrien nodded intelligently. With the suspicion of her craft she leaped to the conclusion that the fashionable young woman came to her disreputable friend for an occasional lark.

"Oh, I promise you. If you had n't asked me I should though. It would make a fine story."

"Tell me," said Patience abruptly, "do you like being a newspaper woman? Is it very hard work?"

"Yes, it 's hard work," Miss Merrien answered in some surprise; "but then it is the most fascinating, I do believe, in the whole world. I have a family and a home out West, and I could go back and be comfortable if I wanted to; but I would n't give up this life, with all its grind and uncertainty, for that dead and alive existence. I only go out there once a year to rest. I came on here for an experiment, to see a little of the world. I had a dreadful time catching on; once I thought I'd starve, for I was bound I would n't write home for money; but I hung on and got there. And I 'm here to stay."

18

"Oh, is it really so pleasant? Sometimes I wish I were a newspaper woman."

"You? You? I never saw anybody that looked less like one."

"I am very strong. I am naturally pale, that is all."

"Oh, your skin is lovely : it's that warm dead white. I was n't thinking of that. But you look like the princess that felt the pea under sixteen mattresses."

"One adapts one's self easily to luxury. I have only had it two years. I do like it certainly. Nevertheless, I'd like to be a newspaper woman. You look tired ; are you?"

"Yes, I am, Mrs. Peele. It's hard work, if it is fascinating ; for instance, I've chased about this entire week for stories that have n't panned out for a cent. I have n't made ten dollars. I came up here as a last resource. La Rosita is always good-natured, and I hoped she'd have a story for me. But all I've got is a crank that's following her about threatening to kill her if she does n't marry him, and that's such a chestnut. If I could only fake something I know she'd let it go, but my imagination's worn to a thread — "

The portière was pushed aside, and Rosita entered. She wore a glistening night-robe of silk and lace and ribbon under a yellow plush bath gown. Her dense black hair fell to her knees. She slid into bed and ordered her maid to admit the manicure. An old woman, looking like a witch and clad in shabby black, came in and took a chair beside the bed. The maid brought a crystal bowl and warm water, and a golden manicure set, and Rosita held forth her incomparable arm with its little Spanish hand. She lay with indolent grace among the large pillows.

"You certainly are a beauty," exclaimed Miss Merrien, enthusiastically.

Rosita smiled with much pleasure. "I love to hear a woman say that, and I shall make good copy for many years yet. I shall not fade like most Spanish women. Oh, I have learned many secrets."

"I wish you hadn't told them to me, and then I should still have them to write about. They made a great story."

"*Dios! Dios!*" said Rosita, plaintively, "I wish we could think of something. I hate to send you away with nothing at all. I love to be written about. Patita, can't you think of something?"

"Now, Mrs. Peele," said Miss Merrien, "let us see if you are a good fakir. That is one of the first essentials of being a successful newspaper woman."

"Oh, dear! Is it? If I could fake I'd make books. I'd like that even better. Rosita, did you ever tell the newspapers about that time I coached you for your first appearance on any stage, and the great hit you made?"

"What is that?" asked Miss Merrien, sharply.

"I never thought of it. Patita, you tell the story."

This Patience did, while Miss Merrien wrote rapidly in shorthand, pausing occasionally to exclaim with rapture.

"Oh, my good angel sent me here this morning," she said when Patience had finished. "I won't mention your name, of course, but you won't mind my saying that you are one of the Four Hundred."

"I don't suppose there is any objection. I am such an obscure member of it that no one will suspect me. Only don't give any details."

"Oh, I won't, indeed I won't." She slipped her book into her muff and rose to go. "You don't know how much obliged I am. I'll do as much for you some day. If ever you want to be written up, let me know."

"I never should want to be in the newspapers."

"Oh, there's no telling. You have n't had a taste of it yet. Well, good-morning," and she went out.

Patience leaned back in her luxurious chair, and watched the old woman polish the pretty nails. Rosita babbled, and Patience watched her face closely. Its colouring was as fresh, its contours as perfect as ever, but there was a faint touch of hardness somewhere, and the eyes held more secrets than they had two years ago. They were the eyes of the wanton. For a moment Patience forgot her surroundings. Her mind flew back to the old days, to the rickety buggy with the two contented innocent little girls, then, by a natural deflection, to her tower and her dreams. She longed passionately for the old Mission, and wondered if Solomon were still alive. Then she thought of Bourke, and came back to the present with a shudder. The woman had gone.

"What is the matter?" asked Rosita. "Is it true — what the men say — that you are not happy with your husband?"

"I hate him," said Patience.

"Why don't you get a divorce?"

"I have no grounds."

"No grounds? Fancy a wife having no grounds!"

"I have not the slightest doubt of his faith."

"Send him to me."

"Oh, Rosita! How can you be so coarse?"

"No-o-o-o! You are my old friend. I would do anything for you. Think it over, Patita *mia*."

"I do not need to think it over. I would never do so vile a thing as that. Have you no refinement left?"

"What earthly use would I have for refinement? Patita, you are such a baby, and you always had ideals and things. Have you got them yet?"

"No," said Patience, rising abruptly. "I haven't. Good-bye."

"Good-bye, Patita dear," said Rosita, with unruffled good humour, "and if ever you are in trouble come here and I will take you in. I would even lend you money, and if you knew me you would know how much I loved you to do that. There is not another person living I would give a five cent piece to."

When Patience reached the sidewalk she filled her lungs with fresh air, then looked at her watch. It was only a half after twelve, and she decided to call on Mary Gallatin. She had never yet paid that charming young fashionette the promised morning call, although she had attended one or two of her afternoon receptions.

She told the coachman to drive to the house in Fifty-seventh Street, then threw herself back on the seat and laughed, a long unpleasant laugh. She tapped first one foot and then the other, with increasing nervousness.

"What fools we mortals be to cry for the unattainable," she said, addressing the little mirror opposite. "Probably that young newspaper woman envies me bitterly. So, doubtless, do many others. Why on earth am I longing for what I'll never find, instead of making the best of a bad bargain and the most of my position? I think I'll find my way out of the difficulty with the average woman's solution : I'll take a lover."

The carriage stopped before a house with the breadth

of stoop which in New York means plentiful wealth. She waited in the drawing-room while the cautious butler went up to see if his mistress would receive this stranger. He returned in a moment and conducted her up to a door at the front of the house. Patience entered a large room whose light was so subdued that for a moment she could see only vaguely outlined forms.

"Oh, Mrs. Beverly, how dear of you," cried a sweet voice, and Patience groped her way round the angle of a large bed and saw Mrs. Gallatin sitting against a mass of pillows. "I'm so glad you came this morning. I'm feeling so blue. I've twisted my foot, you know, and my friends are so kind to me. Mr. Rutger, give Mrs. Peele a chair. Mrs. Beverly, you know Mr. Rutger and Mr. Maitland and Mr. Owen, do you not? There is Leontine."

The three young men, who had risen as she entered, bowed and resumed their seats. Mrs. Lafarge threw her a kiss from the depths of a chair by the fire.

Patience sat down and glanced about her while Mrs. Lafarge finished an anecdote she had been telling. Her eyes became accustomed to the light, and in a moment she saw things quite distinctly. The large room was furnished in Empire style, the walls and windows and the great mahogany and brass bedstead covered with crimson satin damask. There were only a few pieces of heavy furniture, in the room, but like the bed they were magnificent. Each brass carving told a different story.

Mrs. Gallatin, smiling, exquisite, wore a cambric gown, less elaborate than Rosita's but more dainty. Her shining hair was drawn modishly to the top of her head and confined with a pink porcelain comb, carved into semblance of wild roses. A pink silk shawl slipped from her shoulders. Another wild rose was at her throat. On her hands she wore rubies only.

The story Mrs. Lafarge told was slightly naughty, and all laughed heartily at its conclusion. Patience had heard too many naughty stories in the last two years to be shocked; but when one of the young men began another he was promptly hissed down.

"You are not going to tell that before Mrs. Beverly," said Mary Gallatin. "She is quite too frightfully proper. But we're awfully fond of her all the same," and she patted Patience's hand while her lovely young face contracted in a charming scowl. Patience wondered if she had a lover — Mr. Gallatin was a dapper little man — and if that was why she looked so happy. She glanced speculatively at the men, and wondered if she could fall in love with one of them. But they were very ordinary New York youths of fashion, high of shoulder, slow of speech, large of epiglottis, vacuous of expression. She shook her head unconsciously.

"Why, what on earth are you thinking about?" cried Mrs. Gallatin, with her silvery laugh. "That wasn't a shake of disapproval, was it?"

"Oh, no, no!" said Patience, hastily. "Something occurred to me, and I forgot I was not alone. You see, I am so much alone that I've even gotten into the habit of thinking out loud." She felt that she was a restraint — the suppressed young man had relapsed into moody silence — and, as soon as she reasonably could, rose to go. Mrs. Gallatin kissed her warmly and Mrs. Lafarge came forward and kissed her also; but Patience detected a faint note of relief in their voices, and went downstairs feeling more depressed than ever. "'There seems to be no place for me," she thought. "I must be out of tune with everything."

She went to her father-in-law's house in Eleventh Street and found Mrs. Peele and Honora gowned for expected luncheon guests. The former apologised coldly for not being able to ask her to join them, but "there was only room in the dining-room for eight." Honora rippled regret, and Patience felt that she should disgrace herself with tears if she did not get out of the house. She went directly to the station, intending to return home, but as the train approached Peele Manor she turned her back squarely on the old house and decided to go on to Mariaville and see Miss Beale. She remembered with satisfaction that she knew at least one wholesome thoroughly sincere woman, however misguided.

When she reached the station she concluded to walk to the house. She felt nervous and excited. Her cheeks burned and her temples ached a little. She had taken no nourishment that day but a cup of coffee and a roll, and her head felt light. It was now two o'clock.

When she had gone a little more than half way she lifted her eyes and saw Miss Beale coming toward her with beaming face, one hand ready to wave.

"Why, Patience!" she cried, as they met. "I'm so glad to see you. I'm just going to kiss you if it is on the street. I can't say I thought you'd forgotten me, for you've sent me money for my poor every time I begged for it; but I did think you'd never come to see me."

Patience had no excuse to offer, so wisely attempted none, but returned Miss Beale's embrace heartily. The older woman's face was brilliant with pleasure.

"Dear me, how pretty you have grown! What a colour! I'm so glad to see you looking so well. How happy dear Miss Tremont would be to see you now. She was always afraid you would be delicate. But we can't wish her back, can we, Patience?"

"There's no use wishing anything undone. Where are you going?"

"Where I am going to take you. Now, don't ask any questions, but just come along."

Patience, hoping that the destination was a fair where she could get luncheon, followed submissively, and evaded Miss Beale's personal inquiries as best she could.

"How does the Temperance Cause get on?" she asked at length.

"Oh, just the same! Just the same!" said Miss Beale, with a cheerful sigh. "One makes slow progress in this wicked world; all we can do is to trust in the Lord and do our humble best. Mariaville has three new saloons, and the father of one of my scholars beat him nearly to death the other day for coming to the Loyal Legion class; but we'll win in the end."

"Meanwhile are you as much interested as ever?" asked Patience, curiously.

"Oh, my!" Miss Beale gave an almost hilarious laugh. "Well, I should think so. How could I ever lose interest in the Lord's work? Why, I never even get discouraged."

"It has occurred to me, sometimes — since I have been away and met all sorts of people — that if you really were Temperance you might have more chance of success."

"If we were what?"

"Temperance in the actual meaning of the word. You're not, you know; you're teetotalists. That is the reason you antagonise so many thousands of men who might be glad to help you with their vote otherwise. The average gentleman — and there are thousands upon thousands of him — never gets drunk, and enjoys his wine at dinner and even his whiskey and water. He does n't see any reason why he should n't have it, and there is n't any. It adds to the pleasures of life. Those are the people that really represent Temperance, and naturally they have no sympathy with a movement that they consider narrow-minded and an unwarrantable intrusion."

Miss Beale shook her head vigorously. "It is a sin to touch it!" she exclaimed, "and sooner or later they will all be drunkards, every one of them. The blessing of God is not on alcohol, and it should be banished from the face of the earth."

Patience was in a perverse and almost ugly mood. "Tell me," she said, "how do you reconcile your animosity to alcohol with the story of Christ's turning the water into wine at the wedding feast?"

"It was n't wine," said Miss Beale, triumphantly; "it was grape juice. Wine takes days to ferment, so the water could n't possibly have become wine all in a minute."

Patience burst into laughter. "But, Miss Beale, it was a miracle anyhow, was n't it? If he could perform a miracle at all it would have been as easy to make wine out of water as grape juice."

Miss Beale shook her head emphatically and set her lips. "I *know* that the Lord never would have offered wine to anybody; but grape juice is delightful, and he

probably knew it, and they called it wine. That is all
there is to it."

"Oh," exclaimed Patience, forgetting the Temperance question, as Miss Beale turned into a path and
walked toward the side entrance of the First Presbyterian Church, "are we going here?"

"Yes, this is just where we are going. There is a
special meeting of the Y's and Christian Endeavourers
of Mariaville and White Plains and two or three other
places. Ah! I've caught you now, you naughty
girl."

Patience turned away her face and frowned heavily.
All her old dislike of religion, almost forgotten during
the past two years, surged up above the impulsion of
her fermenting spirit. She felt the old impatience, the
old intolerance.

"Do you want me to go in there?" she asked. "I
came to see you."

"Oh, you're not going to get out of it," cried Miss
Beale, gayly. "And I know you better than you know
yourself. I know you always wanted to give yourself
to the Lord, only you are too proud."

Patience stared at her, wondering if she had so far
forgotten herself as to indulge in a little joke at the
expense of her idols; but Miss Beale was looking at
her with kind, earnest eyes. Patience laughed, and
shrugged her shoulders.

"Well, I'll go in to please you; but I hope it won't
be too long, for I'm horribly hungry."

"Dear, dear! Why didn't you come a little earlier?
But it won't be more than two hours, and then I'll have
a hot luncheon prepared for you."

She led Patience through the large church parlour

and straight up to a table, lifting a chair as she passed the front row of seats.

"I don't want to sit here," whispered Patience, hurriedly ; but Miss Beale pushed her into the chair, and seated herself beside her, at the back of the table.

"I am going to preside, and you are the guest of honour," she said. "Young ladies," she continued, smiling at the rows of bright and serious faces, "I am sure you will all be glad to see Patience again. I know she is glad to see you."

Patience arose and bowed awkwardly, then sat down and tapped the floor with her foot. The young women looked surprised and pleased. One and all smiled encouragingly, sure that she had been converted at last. Many of the faces were bright with youth and even mischief; others were careworn and aging. Not one of them but looked happy.

Patience under her calm exterior began to seethe and mutter once more. Once she almost laughed aloud as she thought of the effect upon these simpleminded girls if the hell within her were suddenly made manifest.

The meeting opened at once. Miss Beale offered a prayer, in which she implored that they all might love the Lord the more. Hymns were sung, the Bible read, and reports by the various secretaries and treasurers. Then one serious and not unintelligent-looking woman of thirty read a platitudinous paper beginning : "Some one has said, ' The time will come when it will be the proudest boast of every man and woman to say " I am an American." ' I say that the time will come when it will be the proudest boast of every man and woman to say, ' I am a Christian.' "

All regarded the reader with eyes of affection and approval. Each word Patience, in her abnormal state of mind, took as a personal insult to Intellect. She felt furiously resentful that in this Nineteenth Century with its educational facilities, its libraries full of the achievements of great masters of thought, there should be so low a standard of intellectuality in the middle classes. Even the fashionable women, frivolous as they were, were brighter, and keener to pierce outworn traditions. They might not be thinkers, but they had a species of lightning in their brain which rent superstition and gave them flashlight glimpses of life in its true proportions.

The girls began to give experiences. One had just joined the Y's, and she related with tears the story of her struggle between the World and the Church, and her thankfulness that at last she had been permitted to decide in favour of the Lord. Patience remembered her as the vapid daughter of rather wealthy parents who in her own day had been devoted to society and young men. She was very faded. Many of the girls wept in sympathy, and Miss Beale mopped her eyes several times.

An extremely pretty girl stood up, a girl with black hair and pale blue eyes and rich pink colour. Patience regarded her satirically, thinking what a beauty she would be if properly gowned. Miss Beale, noting her interest, patted her hand and smiled.

" I just want to say," began the girl, with deep earnestness, " that every day of my life I have greater confidence that the Lord loves me and hears what I ask Him. You know that I write the reports of the Y. W. C. T. U., and of course I have to get them printed for nothing. So when I sit down to write them I just ask the Lord to tell me what to say and how to say it, and all the way to the office I keep asking Him to tell me what to say to the editor so that he will print it and help our great cause along. And, girls, he prints it every time, and only yesterday he said to me : 'I like your stuff because it's direct and to the point, no gush, no rhetoric — it's plain horse sense.' Now, girls, you need not think I say that to compliment myself. I just say it to prove that the Lord writes those newspaper articles, not I."

Patience put her handkerchief to her face and shook convulsively. She bit her lips to keep from laughing aloud ; she wanted to scream.

Suddenly she became conscious of a deep murmur. Supposing it to be of disapproval, she straightened her mouth and dropped her handkerchief; but her face was scarlet, her eyes full of tears. The girls were leaning forward, regarding her earnestly. Miss Beale leaned over and placed her arm about her.

"Speak," she said softly. " Don't be afraid."

"What on earth are you thinking about?" gasped Patience.

"Tell us what is in your heart," said Miss Beale, in a tremulous voice.

And, "Tell us ! Tell us !" came from the girls.

"You don't know what you are saying," said Patience, freeing herself angrily. "Let me go." She was trembling with excitement. Her head felt very light. The blood was pounding in her ears. She started to her feet, meaning to rush to the door ; but Miss Beale was too quick for her. She caught her firmly by the waist and led her to the middle of the space at the head of the room.

" I know she will speak," said Miss Beale. " Patience, we all feel our awful responsibility. If you speak out now, you will be saved. If your timidity overcomes you, you may go hence and never hear His knock again."

" Speak ! Speak ! " came with solemn emphasis from the Y's.

" Oh, well, I'll speak," cried Patience. " And suppose you hear me out. It will be only polite, since you have forced me to speak. You have always misunderstood me. I am by no means indifferent to the God you worship. I have the most exalted respect and admiration for this tremendous creative force behind the Universe, a respect so great that I should never presume to address him as you do in your funny little egoism. Do you realise that this magnificent Being of whose essence you have not the most approximate idea, is the Creator, not only of this but of countless other worlds and systems, and furthermore of the psychic and physical laws that govern them and of the extraordinary mystery of which we are a part, and which has its most subtle expression in the Space surrounding us? And yet you, atoms, pigmies, tiny individual manifestations of a great correlative force called human nature, you presume to address this stupendous Being, and stand up and kneel down and talk to It, to imagine that It listens to your insignificant wants, — that It writes newspaper articles ! Is it Christianity that has destroyed the sense of humour in its disciples?

" In each of you is a shaft from the great dominating Force — that is quite true, and it is for you to develop that force — character — and rely upon it, not upon a spiritual lover, as weak women do upon some unfor-

tunate man. What good does all this religious sentimentality do you? Your brains are rotting. You have
nothing to talk about to intelligent men. No wonder
the men of small towns get away as soon as they can,
and seek the intelligent women of lower strata. Men
are naturally brighter than women, and girls of your
sort deliberately make yourselves as limited and colourless as you can. Go, make yourselves companions for
men, if you would make the world better, if you must
improve the human race. Study the subjects that
interest them, that fill their life ; study politics and the
great questions of the day, that you may lead them to
the higher ethical plane on which nature has placed
you. Quit this erotic sentimentalising over an abstract
being to whom you must be the profoundest joke of his
civilisation — "

" Hush ! " shrieked Miss Beale. For some moments
Patience had been obliged to raise her voice above the
angry mutterings of her audience. One or two were
sobbing hysterically. Miss Beale's cry was the signal
for the explosion of pent-up excitement.

" Go ! Go ! " cried the girls. " Go out of this
church ! Blasphemer ! Shame ! Shame ! "

Patience looked out undaunted upon the sea of
flushed angry faces, which a few moments before had
been all peace and love. She shrugged her shoulders,
bowed to Miss Beale, who was staring at her with horrified eyes in a livid face, and walked toward the door.
The girls pressed her forward, lest she should speak
again.

" We have a right as churchwomen to hate you,"
cried one, " for we are told to hate the devil, and you
are he incarnate."

Patience refused to accelerate her steps, but reached the door in a moment. As she was about to pass out a joyous face was uplifted to hers. It belonged to a girl still sitting. Her lap was piled with loose sheets of paper. There was an excited smirch of lead on her cheek. Even as she raised her head and spoke she continued writing. "That was a corker," she whispered, "the biggest story I've had in weeks." It was Miss Merrien.

XVII

PATIENCE was an early riser, and had usually read the "Day" through before Beverly lounged downstairs, sleepy and cross and masculine. On the morning after her day of varied experience she took the newspaper into the library and read the first page leisurely, as was her habit. The news of the world still interested her profoundly. Then she read the editorials, and, later, glanced idly at the headlines of the "stories." The following arrested her startled eye :

AN EARTHQUAKE IN MARIAVILLE !
THE GOOD PEOPLE ARE OUTRAGED !
A SENSATION BY THE BEAUTIFUL AND BRILLIANT
MRS. BEVERLY PEELE !

The story covered two thirds of a column. Patience read it three times in succession without stopping to comment. It was graphically told, much exaggerated, and as carefully climaxed as dramatic fiction. And it was interesting reading. Patience decided that if it had not been about herself she should have given

19

it more than passing attention. Her beauty and grace
and elegance, her grand air, were described with enthusiasm. Every possible point of contrast was made to
the serious and unfashionable Y's.

At first Patience was horrified. She wondered what
Mr. and Mrs. Peele would say. Beverly's comments
were not within the limitations of doubt.

"I'm in for it," she thought. Then she smiled.
She felt the same thrill she had experienced when the
men looked askance at her after her assault upon her
mother. The Ego ever lifts its head at the first caress,
and quickly becomes as insatiable as a child for sweets.
Patience glanced at the article to note how many times
her name — in small capitals — sprang forth to meet
her eyes. She imagined Bourke reading it, and Mrs.
Gallatin, and Mrs. Lafarge, and many others, and wondered if strangers would find it interesting; then,
suddenly, she threw back her head and laughed aloud.

"What fools we mortals be!" she thought. "And
the President of the United States has dozens of paragraphs written about him every day. And actors and
writers are paragraphed *ad nauseam*. If a woman is
run over in the street she has a column, and if she goes
to a hotel and commits suicide, she has two, and is a
raving beauty. Rosita is persecuted for stories. The
Ego ought to have its ears boxed every morning, as
some old-fashioned people switch their children. Well,
here comes Beverly."

Her husband entered, and for the first time in many
months she sprang to her feet and gave him a little
peck on his cheek. He was so surprised that he
forgot to pick up the newspaper, and followed her at
once into the dining-room. During the meal she

talked of his horses and his farm, and even offered to take a drive with him. He was going to White Plains to look at some blooded stock which was to be sold at auction, and promptly invited her to accompany him; but her diplomacy had its limits, and she declined. However, he went from the table in high good humour. When she left him in the library, a few moments later, he was arranging the scattered sheets of the " Day," without his accustomed comments upon " the infernal manner in which a woman always left a newspaper."

Patience went up to her room and wrote a note of apology to Miss Beale. She was half way through a long letter to Hal when she heard Beverly bounding up the stair three steps at a time.

"The cyclone struck Peele Manor at 10.25," she said, looking at the clock. " Sections of the fair — "

Beverly burst in without ceremony.

" What the hell does this mean?" he cried, brandishing the newspaper. His dilating nostrils were livid. The rest of his face was almost black.

" Beverly, you will certainly have apoplexy or burst a blood vessel," said his wife, solicitously. " Think of those that love you and preserve yourself — "

" Those that love me be damned! The idea of my wife — *my wife* — being the heroine of a vulgar newspaper story! Her name out in a headline! Mrs. Beverly Peele! My God!"

" God was the cause of the whole trouble," said Patience, flippantly. " I thought the young women were entirely too intimate with him. The spectacle conjured of The Almighty with his sleeves rolled up grinding out copy at five dollars per column was too much for me. I have the most profound admiration and respect for the Deity, and felt called upon to defend him — the others seemed so unconscious of insult — "

"This is no subject for a joke," cried Beverly, who had sworn steadily through these remarks. "I don't care a hang if you had a reason or not for making a public speech — Christ! — it's enough that you made it, that your name's in the paper — my wife's name! What will my father and mother say?"

"They will not swear. A few of the Peeles are decently well bred."

"No one ever gave them cause to swear before. You've turned this family upside down since you came into it. You've been the ruin of my life. I wish to God I'd never seen you."

"I sincerely wish you had n't. What had you intended to make of your life that I have interfered with?"

"If I'd married a woman who loved me I'd have been a better man."

"I wonder how many weak men have said that since the world began! You were twenty-six when I married you, and I cannot see that there has been any change in kind since, although there certainly is in degree. If you had married the ordinary little domestic woman, you would have been happier, but you would not have been better, for you possess neither soul nor intelligence. But I am perfectly willing to give you a chance for happiness. Give me my freedom, and look about you for a doll — "

"Do you mean to say that you want a divorce?"

"I think you know just how much I do."

"Well, you won't get it — by God! Do you under-

stand that? You 've no cause, and you 'll not get
any."

"There should be a law made for women who — who
— well, like myself."

Her husband was incapable of understanding her.
"Well, you just remember that," he said. "You don't
get a divorce, and you keep out of the newspapers, or
you 'll be sorry," and he slammed the door and strode
away.

A quarter of an hour after Patience heard the wheels
of his cart. At the same time the train stopped below
the slope. A few moments later she saw Miss Merrien
come up the walk. The maid brought up the visitor's
card, and with it a note from Mr. Field.

DEAR MRS. BEVERLY [it read], — Forgive me — but you
are a woman of destiny, or I have n't studied people sixty
years for nothing. I chose to be the first — the scent of
the old war-horse for news, you know. Peele will be
furious, but I can't bother about a trifle like that. Just give
this young woman an interview, and oblige your old
friend

J. E. F.

Patience started to go downstairs, then turned
to the mirror and regarded herself attentively. She
looked very pretty, remarkably so, as she always did
when the pink was in her cheeks; but her morning
gown was plain and not particularly becoming. She
changed it, after some deliberation, for a house-robe
of pearl grey silk with a front of pale pink chiffon
hanging straight from a collar of cut steel. The maid
had brought her some pink roses from the greenhouse;
she fastened one in the coil of her soft pale hair.

Then she smiled at her reflection, shook out her train, and rustled softly down the stair.

Miss Merrien exclaimed with feminine enthusiasm as she entered the library.

"Oh, you are the loveliest woman to write about," she said. "I do a lot of society work, and I am so tired of describing the conventional beauty. And that gown! I'm going to describe every bit of it. Did it come from Paris?"

"Yes," said Patience, amused at her immediate success. "My mother-in-law brought it to me last summer — but perhaps you had better not mention Mrs. Peele in your story."

"Well, I won't, of course, if you don't want me to. I have written the story about La Rosita for the Sunday 'Day,' and I did not hint at your identity. It made a good story, but not as good as the one about you. Mr. Field wrote me a note this morning, complimenting me, and told me to come up here and interview you. I hope you don't mind very much."

"I have n't the faintest idea whether I do or not. How do you do it?"

"Well, you see, I'll just ask you questions and you answer them, and I'll put it all down in shorthand, and then when I go to the office I'll thresh it into shape. You can be sure that I won't say anything that is n't pleasant, for I really never admired any one half so much."

"Very well, you interview me, and then I'll interview you. I have some questions to ask also."

"I'll tell you anything you like. This story, by the way, is to be in the Sunday issue on the Woman's Page. Now we'll begin. Were you always an unbeliever? Tell me exactly what are your religious opinions."

"Oh, dear me! You are not going to write a serious analysis of me?"

"Yes, but I 'll give it the light touch so that it won't bore anybody. It is to be called 'A Society Woman Who Thinks,' and will be read with interest all over America."

"But I am not a society woman."

"Well, you 're a swell, and that 's the same thing, for this purpose anyhow. The Gardiner Peeles are out of sight, and I have heard lots of times how beautifully you entertain in summer and how charmingly you gown yourself. Tell me first — what do you think of this everlasting woman question? I hate the very echo of the thing, but we 'll have to touch on it."

"Oh, I have n't given much thought to it, except as a phase of current history. One thing is positive, I think: we must adjust our individual lives without reference to any of the problems of the moment, — Womanism, Socialism, the Ethical Question, the Marriage Question, and all the others that are everlasting raging. He that would be happy must deal with the great primal facts of life — and these facts will endure until human nature is no more. Moreover, however much she may reason, nothing can eradicate the strongest instinct in woman — that she can find happiness only through some man."

"Good," said Miss Merrien. "I 'd have thought the same thing if I 'd ever had time. Now tell me if you have any religion at all."

"I suppose I should be called an anarchist. Don't be alarmed: I mean the philosophical or spiritual anarchist, not these poor maniarchists that are merely an objectionable variety of lunatics. The religious situation is this, I think : Jesus Christ does not satisfy the intellectual needs of the Nineteenth Century. And yet, indisputably, the religionists are happier than the multiplying scores that could no more continue in the old delusion than they could worship idols or torture the flesh. Civilisation needs a new prophet, and he must be an anarchist, — one who will teach the government of self by self, the government of man's nature by will, which in its turn is subservient to the far seeing brain. Human nature is anarchic in its essence. The child never was born that was brought to bend to authority without effort. We are still children, or we should not need laws and governments."

"Wait till I get that down."

"Of course these are only individual opinions. I don't claim any value for them, and should never have thought of airing them if you hadn't asked me. For my part I'm glad I live in this imperfect chaotic age. When we can all do exactly as we please and won't even remember how to want to do anything wrong — Awful ! "

"But you said the advanced thinkers needed this new religion to make them happy."

"Their happiness will consist in the tremendous effort to reach the difficult goal. That will take centuries, just as the spiritualised socialism of Jesus Christ has taken twenty centuries, and only imperfectly possessed one third of the globe. When anarchy is a cold hard fact — well, I suspect the anarchists will suddenly discover that *ennui* is in their vitals, and will gently yawn each other to death. Then the tadpoles will begin over again; or perhaps there will then be mental and moral developments that we in our present limitations cannot conceive. Have n't you had enough?"

"No, no. I've a dozen questions more."

Miss Merrien, like all good newspaper reporters, was an amateur lawyer and a harmless hypnotist. In an hour she had extracted Patience's views of society, books, dress, public questions, and the actors in the great national theatre, the Capitol at Washington.

"Oh, this is magnificent," she announced, when the pages had been folded. "Now can I look at the house?"

"We will have luncheon first. No, don't protest. I am delighted. Mr. Peele is away for the day, otherwise I fear you would not have had this interview."

"Oh, you don't believe in the submission of wives, then?"

"I've never thought much about it," said Patience, indifferently. "There is too much fuss made about it all. When a man commands his wife to do a thing she does not care to do, and when a woman does what she knows will displease her husband, it is time for them to separate."

"Oh, that is too simple. It would n't do to reduce the woman question to a rule of three. What would all the reformers do? And the poor polemical novelists! Oh, these are the famous portraits, I suppose?"

"You can look at them if the luncheon is bad," said Patience, as they took their seats at table. "I'm not a very good housekeeper, although I actually did take some lessons of Miss Mairs. And sometimes I forget to order luncheon. I did to-day."

But the luncheon proved to be a very good one, and Miss Merrien did it justice, while Patience explained the portraits. Afterward she showed her guest over the lower part of the house. Then they went back to the library, and Patience had her interview.

"Tell me exactly how does a woman begin on a newspaper?" she asked.

"Oh, different ones have different experiences," said Miss Merrien, vaguely. "Sometimes you have letters, and are put on as a fashion or society reporter, or to get interviews with famous women, or to go and ask prominent people their opinion on a certain subject — for a symposium, you know; like 'What Would You do if You Knew that the World was to End in Three Days?' or, 'Is Society Society?' I have written dozens of symposiums. Sometimes you do free-lance work, just pick up what you can and trust to luck to catch on. But of course you must have the nose for news. I was at a matinée one day and sat in front of two society women. Between the acts they talked about a prominent woman of their set who was getting a divorce from her husband so quietly that no newspaper had suspected it. They also joked about the fact that her lawyer was an old lover. I knew this was a tip, and a big one. I wrote all the names on my cuff, and before the matinée was over I was down at the 'Day' and had turned in my tip to the City editor. He sent a reporter to the lawyer to bluff him into admitting the truth. The next day we had a big story, and after that the editor gave me work regularly."

"How much do you make a week?"

"Sometimes forty, sometimes not twenty; but I average pretty well and get along. Still, when you have to lay by for sickness and vacations, and put about one half on your back it does n't amount to much. You see, a newspaper woman must dress well, must make a big bluff. If she does n't look successful she won't be, to say nothing of the fact that she could n't get inside a smart house if she looked shabby. And then she 's got to eat good nourishing food, or she never could stand the work. Of course there 's got to be economy somewhere, so I live in a hall bedroom and make my own coffee in the morning. Still, I don't complain, for I do like the work. If I had to go back home I 'd ruin the happiness of the entire family."

"What do you look forward to? — I mean what ultimate? You don't want to be a reporter always, I suppose. Everybody is striving for some top notch."

" Oh, maybe I 'll become Sunday editor, or I might fall in with somebody that wanted to start a woman's newspaper, or magazine — you never can tell. There are n't many good berths for women. Of course there are a good many very bright newspaper women, and it 's a toss up who goes to the top."

" You don't seem to take matrimony into consideration."

" Oh, I don't deny I get so tired sometimes that I 'd be only too glad to have a man take care of me. I guess we all look forward to that, more or less. I think I 'd always work, but not so hard. It would make all the difference in the world if you knew some one else was paying the bills. And then, you see, we go to pieces in eight or ten years. A man is good for hard newspaper work until he 's forty, but we women are made to be taken care of, and that 's a fact. We take turns having nervous prostration. I have n't had it yet, but I 'm looking cheerfully forward to it."

"Now I want to tell you," said Patience, "that I am going to be a newspaper woman."

"Oh, nonsense, Mrs. Peele! Excuse me, but you belong here. Your rôle is that of the châtelaine in exquisite French gowns and an air half of languor, half of pride. You were not made for work."

"That is very pretty, but I suspect you don't want to lose me for copy."

"Well, I don't deny it. I wish you 'd keep the ball rolling, and give me a story a month."

"I 'm afraid I 've given you my last. In a week or two I shall be a châtelaine in a pink and grey gown no longer, but a humble applicant for work in Mr. Field's office."

"Is it possible that you mean it?"

"Do I look as if I were joking?"

"You don't look unhappy — Pardon me — but — but — does he beat you?"

"Oh, no," said Patience, laughing outright, "he does n't beat me. I have better grounds for desertion than that. Do you think you would do me a favour? I shall have to slip away. He would never let me go with a trunk. I am going to ask you to let me send you a box of things every few days. That will excite no comment among the servants, as we are always sending clothes to the poor. May I?"

"Of course you may. I 'll do everything I can to help you. But — I can't imagine you out of this environment. Don't you hate to give it up, — all this luxury, this ease, this atmosphere?"

"Yes, I like it all. I 'm a sybarite, fast enough.

But I 've weighed it all in the balance, and Peele Manor stays up. I have a hundred dollars or so, and that will last me for a time. I 'll give it to you to take care of for me. I never was wealthy, but I have no idea of economy. I don't think I should like a hall room though. Are the others so very expensive?"

"They are if you have a good address, and that 's very important. And you want to be in a house with a handsome parlour."

"I have no friends, — none that will come to see me."

" Oh, you 'll make friends. You 're an awfully sweet woman. I can't bear to think — Well, there 's no use saying any more about it. I expect you 're the sort that knows your own mind. I should like to keep on seeing you a great lady, but if you can't be a happy one I suppose you are right. Well, I 'll stand by you through thick and thin, and I 'll show you the ropes. Now I must get back to the office and work up my story. Here 's my address. There 's a spare room on the floor above mine. If you 're in dead earnest I 'd better take it right away; then I can unpack your things and hang them up. But — but — do you really mean it?"

"Of course I do."

" You know Mr. Field personally, don't you?"

"Very well, indeed; and he told me when I was sixteen that he should make a newspaper woman of me."

" Oh, well, then, you 'll have a lot of push, and your road won't be as hard as some — not by a long short. About six out of every ten newspaper women either go to the wall or to the bad. It is a mixture of knack and pluck as much as brains that carries the favoured minority through. You have brains and pluck, and you 'll have push, so you ought to get there. About the knack of course I can't tell. Good-bye."

XVIII

THE evening mail brought from Mrs. Peele to her son a note which he read with a rumbling accompaniment, then tossed to Patience.

"Do you intend to permit your wife to disgrace your family?" it read. "If I had my way that abominable paper, the 'Day,' should never enter this house — nor any other paper that dealt in personalities. I literally writhe every time I see my name — your father's honoured name — in the society columns. You may, then, perhaps, imagine my feelings when your father handed me the 'Day' this morning with his finger on that outrageous column. He was speechless with wrath, and will personally call Mr. Field to account. I am in bed with a violent headache, in consequence, and dictating this letter to Honora. But although I deeply feel for you, my beloved son, I must *insist* that you assert your authority with your wrong-headed wife and command her to refrain from disgracing this family. I don't wish to reproach you, but I cannot help saying that it is *always* a dangerous experiment to marry beneath one. This girl is not one of us, she never can be; for, not to mention that we know nothing whatever of her family, she comes from that dreadful savage *new* Western country. In spite of the fact that she has been clever enough to superficially adapt herself to our ways, I always knew that she would break out somewhere — I always said so to Honora. But I don't wish to add to your own sorrow. I know how you, with all your proud Peele reserve, must feel. Only, my son, use your authority in the future."

Patience finished this letter with a disagreeable lowering of the brows. She made no comment, however, but opened a book and refused to converse with her husband.

On Sunday morning she found three columns on the Woman's Page of the "Day" devoted to her beauty, her intellect, her gowns, and her opinions. It was embellished with a photograph of Peele Manor and a sketch of herself, which Miss Merrien had evidently made from memory. When Beverly came down she handed the newspaper to him at once, to read the story with the raw temper of early morning. She hoped that Mrs. Peele would read it in similar conditions.

After he had gone through the headlines he let the newspaper fall to the floor, and stared at her with a face so livid that for a moment she felt as if looking upon the risen dead. Then gradually it blackened, only the nostrils remaining white.

"So you deliberately defy me?" he articulated.

"Yes," she said, watching him narrowly. She thought that he might strike her.

"You did it on purpose to drive me crazy?"

"I had no object whatever, except that it pleased me to be interviewed. Understand at once that I shall do exactly as I please in all things. This is not the country for petty household tyrants. I don't doubt there are many men in this world whom I should be glad to treat with deference and respect if I happened to be married to one of them; but with men like you

304 Patience Sparhawk and Her Times

there is only one course to take. I have asked you
to let me live abroad. If you consent to this, it may
save you a great deal of trouble in the future; for, I
repeat, I shall in all things do exactly as I choose."

"We'll see whether you will or not," he roared.
"You'll do as I say, or I'll lock you up."

"Oh, you will not lock me up. You are way
behind your times, Beverly. There is no law in
the United States to compel me to obey you."

"I'll stop your allowance. You'll never get another
cent from me."

"That has nothing whatever to do with it. Now, I
ask you for the last time, Will you let me travel?"

"No!" he shouted, and he rushed from the room.

BOOK IV

20

BOOK IV

I

MISS MERRIEN lived in West Forty-fourth Street, near
Broadway. Ten days after her visit to Peele Manor
Patience rang the door-bell of the house that was to be
her new home, one of a long impersonal row.

The maid that answered her ring handed her a note
from Miss Merrien, and conducted her up to a hall
room on the third floor. Patience closed the door,
and looked about her with the sensation of the shipwrecked. For a moment she was strongly tempted to
flee back to Peele Manor. The room was about eight
feet square, and furnished with a folding-bed, which
was likewise a bureau, and with a washstand, a table,
and two chairs. The furniture and carpet were new,
and there were pretty blue and white curtains on the
window. Nevertheless the tiny room with its modern
contrivances was the symbol of poverty and struggle
and an entirely new existence. Her second impulse
was to sit down on a chair and cry; but she set her
teeth, and read Miss Merrien's note instead.

I am so sorry not to be able to meet you [it read];
but I am a slave, you know. Before I was out of bed
this morning I received an assignment to go to a woman's
club meeting at eleven. But I'll get back in time to go

down to the shop with you. Don't get blue — if you can help it. Remember that every woman feels the same way when she first makes the break for self-support; and that your chances are better than those of most. There's a little restaurant round the corner — the maid will show you — where you can get your luncheon. *Au revoir.* I'm so glad the sun is out.

Anna Chetwynde Merrien.

P. S. Your clothes are in the closet in the hall. The key is in the washstand drawer.

Patience felt in better cheer after reading Miss Merrien's kindly greeting, but the day dragged along very heavily. She went out and bought all the newspapers, and studied them attentively for hints; but they did not tell her inexperience anything, and after a time she let them fall to the floor and sat staring at the blank windows opposite. For the first time doubts assailed her. She had been so full of young confidence, and pride in her brains and health and courage, that she had not regarded the issue of her struggle with the world in the light of a problem; but face to face with the practical details, she felt short of breath and weak in the knees.

At two o'clock Miss Merrien came in, looking very tired. There were black scoops under her eyes, and the lines about her mouth were strongly accentuated. But she smiled brightly as Patience rose to greet her.

"Well, you are here," she said. "I changed my mind fifty times about your coming, but on the whole I thought you would. Fortunately I have nothing on hand for this afternoon. I'll rest, and then go down with you to the shop. Oh, I am so tired, my dear. Can I lie down on your bed awhile?"

"I shall be delighted to learn how to open it," said Patience, who was wondering if her fair face was to become scooped and lined.

Miss Merrien deftly manipulated the bed, loosened her frock, and flung herself full length.

"I spent all day yesterday and half the night tramping over Brooklyn hunting up facts in the case of that girl who was found dead in a tenement-house bed in a grand ball gown. A great story that, but it has done me up. Tell me — how do you feel?"

"Oh, I'm glad I'm here, but I wish it was six months from now."

"Of course you do. That's the way we all feel. But you'll soon swing into place, and be too busy to think. I do wish you could get work in the office, so that you could keep regular hours and meals, and not lose your good looks; but there's no berth of that sort. I tell you it is a sad day when a girl under twenty-five sees the lines coming. The Revolting Sisterhood say that the next century is to be ours; but I doubt it. Men lighten our burdens a little now, but I'm afraid they'll hate us if we worry and supplant them any further. Well, I'm going to take a nap. Wake me promptly at 3.10."

She closed her eyes and fell asleep immediately. The lines grew fainter as she slept, and the hair fell softly about her face. Patience reflected gratefully that three months of absolute leisure and peace of mind would give back to the girl all her freshness and rounded contours. At ten minutes past three she awakened her. Miss Merrien sat up with a sigh.

"I feel better, though. Cultivate those cat-naps. They refresh you wonderfully. Now, we'll go."

II

THEY went down town on the Elevated, leaving it at
Park Row.   Patience was so much interested in the
great irregular mass of buildings surrounding City Hall
Square, at the dense throngs packing the crooked side
streets, at the fakirs with their nonsensical wares, at the
bewildering array of gilt newspaper names on the rows
and stories of polished windows, that she forgot her
errand for the moment, and was nearly run over.

"Yes, this is the heart of New York, sure enough,"
assented Miss Merrien.   "All those big buildings over
there are on the famous Newspaper Row.   Brooklyn
Bridge is just behind.   This is the Post Office on the
right, and that flat building in the square is the City
Hall.   I tell you when you get down here, the rest
of New York, including all the smart folk, seems pretty
insignificant."

"Oh," exclaimed Patience, with a sudden sinking of
the heart, "there is the ' Day ' building."

"That is our shop.   Now, brace up."

Patience needed the admonition.   She forgot City
Hall Park.   All her doubts returned, with others in
their wake.   She knew something of the snobbery of
the world.   As Mrs. Beverly Peele she had been an
object of respectful interest to Mr. Field.   What would
she be as an applicant for work?   True, he had been
kind to her when she was a small nobody, but that
might have been merely a caprice.

They climbed up two narrow stairs in an ugly old
building, and entered a large gas-lit room full of desks.

Many young men were writing or moving about; several were in their shirt sleeves.

"This is the City room," said Miss Merrien, "and these are the reporters. Those men in that little room there are the editors and editorial writers. Mr. Field's room is just beyond. Now send your card in by this boy. The Chief's harder to see than the President of the United States, but I guess he'll see you."

Patience gave the boy her card, and at the end of half an hour, during which she was much stared at by some of the men and totally ignored by others, the boy returned and conducted her to Mr. Field's office.

It was a typical editor's den of the old-fashioned type. A big desk covered with papers, a revolving chair, and one other chair completed the furniture. A large cat was walking about, switching its tail. The floor was bare. The light straggled down between the tall buildings surrounding, and entered through small windows. It was Mr. Field's pride to have the greatest newspaper and the most unpretentious " shop " in the United States.

He rose as Patience entered, his eyes twinkling.

"Well," he said, as he handed her the extra chair, "there's a mighty row on, isn't there? Peele has been here, and now we do not speak as we pass by. But we hadn't had a good woman sensation for a month. I tried to explain that to Peele, but it didn't seem to impress him. I suppose you've come to beg for mercy."

"No — I haven't come for that."

"Why, what is the matter? I never saw you look the least bit rattled before. You are always the young queen with a court of us old fellows at your feet. But tell me ; you know there 's nothing I would n't do for you."

Patience drew a long breath of relief.

" Oh, you make it easier — I 've been horribly frightened. But I 'll get to the point — I suppose you 're very busy down here. Can I have ten minutes ? "

He laughed. "We are usually what you might call busy in this office, but you may have twenty minutes. Take your time."

" Well, it 's this : I 've left Peele Manor for good and all, and I want to be a newspaper woman."

Mr. Field's shaggy white brows rushed up his forehead. His black eyes expanded.

"My God ! What did you make such a break as that for ? "

"There are many reasons. I can't give them all. But all the same I 've left, and I 'm not going back."

"Well, your reasons must be good, for you had a delightful position, and you became it. Are you sure you are not acting rashly ?"

" I 've thought and thought and thought about it. I can't understand why I did n't leave before. I suppose my ideas and intentions did n't crystallise until I met Miss Merrien. She has been very kind. I sent my clothes to her by degrees ; she engaged a room for me in her house ; we are going to cook together ; and I have given her what money I have to take care of."

"Well, well, you have acted deliberately. I don't know that I am so much surprised, after all, and I 'll say nothing to persuade you to go back. I respect your courage and independence, and I 'll do all I can. I have n't the slightest idea what you can do, but we 'll find out." He leaned forward and patted her hand. Patience had one moment of painful misgiving, but again she had misjudged him. "If you get discouraged, just remember that the old man at the helm is your friend and won't let you go under."

"I'm sure you're awfully good," said Patience, tears of contrition and gratitude in her eyes. "I knew you would."

Mr. Field touched a bell. A boy entered.

"If Mr. Steele is still in the office ask him to step here," said the chief.

"Steele is the editor of the Evening 'Day,'" he explained, "and has a remarkable faculty for discovering other people's abilities."

Patience expected to see a man of middle years and business-like demeanour. She stared in amazement as a young man under thirty entered and was presented. He was closely built, but held himself carelessly. His smooth rather square face was very pale, and despite the irregularity of feature, bore an odd resemblance to the Greek fauns. The mouth was large and full, the eyes large, dark blue, and very cold. His fashionable attire accentuated the antiquity of his face and head.

"Mr. Steele," said Mr. Field, "this is Mrs. Beverly Peele, of whom you have heard so much lately. She has made up her mind to support herself. When she was a little girl I told her that I should one day make a newspaper woman of her, and she has come to hold me to my word — much to my satisfaction. I put her in your hands, and feel confident you will make a success of her."

Patience expected to see a look of blank surprise cross the young editor's face, but she did not know the

modern newspaper youth. Mr. Steele could not have
displayed less emotion had the new-comer been a young
woman with letters from Posy County, Illinois. He
merely bowed to her, then to his chief. Patience rose
at once.

"I won't keep you," she said to Mr. Field. "I 'll
only thank you again, and promise to work as hard as
Miss Merrien."

"I have n't the slightest doubt of your success.
Always remember that," said Mr. Field. Patience saw
Mr. Steele's eyebrow give a slight involuntary jerk;
but it was immediately controlled, and he bowed her
through the door.

"We had better go upstairs to the evening room,"
he said. "There is no one there at present."

Patience followed him up a precipitous stairway into
a walled-off section of the composing-room.

"Sit down," he said politely, but Patience for the
first time in her life felt terrified and humble. This
young man, of whom she had never heard before, had
the air of a superior being, omnipotent in her destiny.
His manner conveyed that he was not one whit im-
pressed by the fact that she had stepped down from the
Sacred Reservation, took not the faintest interest in
her as a pretty woman. She was merely a young
person particularly recommended by his chief, and as
such it was his duty to give her consideration.

He took a chair opposite her own, and she felt as if
those classic guileless eyes were exploring her innermost
brain.

"What can you do?" he asked coldly.

"Oh, nothing," she said desperately, "absolutely
nothing. I suppose you feel like remarking that the
'Day' is not a kindergarten."

"Well, it certainly is not. Nevertheless, as Mr. Field thinks that you have ability, and wishes you to write for his paper, I, of course, shall do all I can to abet him. I shall begin by giving you a few words of advice. Have you a good memory; or should you prefer to write them down?"

He spoke very slowly, as if he had a deep respect for the value of words.

"I have read a great deal," said Patience, proudly, "and my memory is very good indeed."

There was a faint twitching of one corner of Mr. Steele's mouth, but he continued in the same business-like tone : —

"Read the 'Day' through carefully, morning and evening. Observe the style in which facts are presented, and the general tone and atmosphere of the paper. Cultivate that general style, not your own. Remember that you are not on this newspaper to make an individual reputation, but to become, if possible, a unit of a harmonious whole, and to give the public the best news in the style to which this newspaper has accustomed it. When you are sent on an assignment remember that you are to gather facts — facts. Keep your eyes open, and cultivate the faculty of observation for all it is worth. When you have gathered these facts put them into as picturesque a shape as you choose — or as you can. But no rhetoric, no rhapsodies, no flights, no theories. If the facts admit of being treated humorously, treat them in that way, by all means, — that is, if you can imitate a man's humour, not a woman's flippancy. A good many women can. And never forget that it must not be your humour but the inherent humour of the subject. Be concise. When you feel disposed to say a thing in ten

words say it in five. That is all I can think of at
present. Be here at eight o'clock to-morrow, and I will
give you an assignment."

He rose, and Patience felt herself dismissed. She
sat for a minute looking at him with angry eyes. Not
even in the early days of her married life had she been
so patronised as by this unknown young man. She felt
as if he had plucked her individuality out with his thumb
and finger and contemptuously tossed it aside.

"Is anything the matter?" he asked indifferently,
although one corner of his mouth twitched again.

"No!" Patience sprang to her feet and ran down
the stair, at the imminent risk of breaking her neck.
Miss Merrien was waiting for her.

"Why, what on earth is the matter?" she exclaimed.

"Oh, let us get out into the air! Come, and then
I'll tell you."

But they were not able to converse until seated in the
Elevated Train. Then Patience exclaimed with an
accent of cutting sarcasm, —

"Who, *who* is Mr. Steele?"

Miss Merrien smiled broadly. "Oh, I see. Did he
patronise you? You must get used to editors. Remember they are monarchs in a small way, and love their
power — the more because their dominion is confined
within four walls. But Morgan Steele is one of the
kindest men in the office. I'd rather work for him
than for any one. He puts on an extra amount of side
on account of his youth, but the reporters all adore him.
He won't keep an incompetent man two days, and
during those two days the man's life is a burden; but
he is always doing good turns to the boys he likes.
When you know him you'll like him."

"I think him an insolent young cub, and if I did n't hate to bother Mr. Field I'd refuse to write for him. What on earth is a youngster like that in such a responsible position for?"

"Oh, my dear, this is the young man's epoch. Just cast your eyes over the United States and even England, and think of the men under thirty that are editors and authors and special writers and famous artists and leaders of enterprises. They are burnt out at forty, but they begin to play a brilliant part in their early twenties. I heard a man say the other day of another man who is only twenty-six and supposed to be ambitious: 'Well, he'd better hump himself. He's no chicken.' A man feels a failure nowadays if he has n't distinguished himself before thirty."

"They are certainly distinguished for conceit."

"Oh, when you get used to newspaper men you'll like them better than any men you've known. What is objectionable is counteracted by their brains and their intimate and wonderfully varied knowledge of life. A newspaper man who is at the same time a gentleman, is charming. It is true they have no respect for anybody nor anything. They believe in no woman's virtue and no man's honesty — under stress. Their kindness — like Morgan Steele's — is half cynical, and they look upon life as a thing to be lived out in twenty years — and then dry rot or suicide. But no men know so well how to enjoy life, know so thoroughly its resources, or have all their senses so keenly developed, particularly the sense of humour, which keeps them from making fools of themselves. No man can feel so strongly for a day, and that after all is the philosophy of life. All this makes them very interesting, although, I must confess, I should hate to marry one. It seems to be a point of honour among them to be unfaithful to their wives; however, I imagine, the real reason is that no one woman has sufficient variety in her to satisfy a man who sees life from so many points of view daily that he becomes a creature of seven heads and seven hearts and seven ideals. Now, tell me all about your interviews with Mr. Field and Morgan Steele."

Patience told the tale, and Miss Merrien raised her eyebrows at its conclusion. " Well, you need not lie awake nights trembling for the future. You are in for push and no mistake. If the Chief has taken you under his wing in that fashion you can be sure that Morgan Steele will work you for all that is in you, whether he wants to or not." Suddenly she laughed, and leaning over looked quizzically at Patience. " You vain girl," she said, " you are piqued because Morgan Steele did not succumb as other men — including Mr. Field — have done to your beauty and charm. But I 'll tell you this, by way of consolation : it is a point of etiquette — or prudence — among editors never to pay the most commonplace attentions to, or manifest the slightest interest in the women of the office. It would not only lead to endless complications, but would impair the lordlings' dignity : in other words, they would be guyed. So cheer up. You have n't gone off since this morning. I see three men staring at you in true Elevated style."

Patience laughed. " Well, I will admit that I have no respect whatever for a man that is unappreciative of the charms of woman. I 'd like to give Mr. Steele a lesson, but I won't. I would n't condescend. I 'll be as business-like as he is. He knew why I was angry to-day, I am afraid, but he won't see me angry again. Why is Mr. Field so much nicer?" ·

" Oh, he owns the paper."

III

PATIENCE'S indignation had worn itself out by bedtime. When Miss Merrien left her for the night she locked her door and spread her arms out with an exultant sense of freedom. She seemed to feel the ugly weight of the past two years fall from her, and to hear it go clattering down the quiet streets. Her sense of humour and the liveliness of her mind had saved her from morbidity at any time, although she had not escaped cynicism. She now felt that she could turn her back squarely on the past, that she was not a woman whose mistakes and dark experiences would corrode the brain and spirit, ruining present and future. She could not make the same mistake again ; and it was better to have made it in early youth when the etchery of experience eats the copper of the ego more lightly. The future seemed to her to be full of infinite possibilities. She could be her own fastidious dreaming idealising self again. New friends dotted the dusk like stars. She felt ten years away from the man to whom she had nodded a careless good-bye that morning. A vague pleasurable loneliness assailed her, the instinct of plurality. Then she laughed suddenly and went to bed.

The next morning, at eight o'clock, after a cup of black coffee to stiffen her nerves, she presented herself in the evening room of the "Day." Two men and a woman were writing at little tables. Mr. Steele in his shirt sleeves was at his desk, reading copy. She sat down, priding herself that her face was as impassive as his own. In a few moments he called her to his desk.

"You have read in the newspapers, I suppose, of this crusade of Dr. Broadhead, the fashionable Presbyterian clergyman, against the voting of Immigrants?" he asked.

"Of course."

"Well, he is doing his best to get the women of New York to help him, and is holding his first meeting this morning in Cooper Union — eleven-thirty. One of our best men will go to report the addresses, but I want you to go and sit in the audience, and observe how many fashionable women are there, what they wear, and what degree of interest they appear to take in the proceedings. Above all, I want you to keep your eyes and ears open for any significant fact which may or may not appear. It usually does. That is all. — Well, what do you want?" This to the office boy.

Patience went slowly downstairs, feeling as if she had been sent out to discover the North Pole with a chart and a row-boat. When she reached Cooper Union, two hours later, and found herself for the moment an integer of one of the many phases of current history, she forgot the agonising travail of the "news sense," and became so deeply interested that she observed the many familiar faces abstractedly, and, later, "faked" their costumes.

She hurried to her room before the meeting was over and wrote her "story." It concluded thus : —

" Some four hundred women were present, at half-past eleven in the morning ; the hour indicating that they were women of leisure, which in its turn presupposes the large measure of education and refinement, and a general superiority over the toiling millions. They were very enthusiastic. When Dr. Broadhead entered the applause was deafening. They interrupted him every few minutes. When he sat down, and Mr. Lionel Chambers came forward he, too, was warmly welcomed, for his popularity is well established. He smiled, and began something like this : —

" ' Ladies : Dr. Broadhead has left me little to say. I being somewhat versed in politics, however, in other words, in hard fighting with the enemy, he believes that I may be able to give you a little useful advice.' (Applause and cries of 'Yes ! Yes !') 'Now, ladies, there are several points upon which I must ask your attention.' (No man ever had more serious attention.) ' I will check them off in detail. First of all, ladies, my advice to you is to — ' (every ear went forward) — ' is — to — pray.'

" He paused. There was an intense and disgusted silence, with the exception of one or two muttered exclamations of impatience. *There were just four hundred women in the city of New York who were beyond that sort of thing.* He saw his mistake at once, blundered on confusedly, recovered himself, and gave them much sound, practical advice which they received with every mark of gratitude."

She hastened down to the office, her eyes shining with the proud delight of authorship. Steele looked busier than any one she had ever seen, but he asked sharply :

"Got anything?"

"Yes."

"Let me see it.   Skip the descriptive part."

She handed him the latter part of her story, and he ran his eye hastily over it.   A gleam shot from his eyes, but he compressed his lips.

"That's not bad — but I don't know that I dare print it.   The religious hypocrisy of this country beats that of England, strange as it may appear.   However, I'll think it over.   Come down to-morrow morning."

The article was printed, and the result was a shower of protesting letters from clergymen and religious women.   Patience was sent to interview a number of representative women, of various spheres of life, on the subject, and found herself fairly launched.   She hardly had time to realise whether she liked the work or not, but when she was not too tired, concluded that she did.   As this phase wore off, she developed considerable enthusiasm, and felt her bump of curiosity enlarge.

She practically forgot the past, except to wonder occasionally that she heard nothing from the Peeles. Upon her arrival in New York, on the morning of her departure from Peele Manor, she had mailed a note to Beverly, which merely announced that she had left him, never to return.   He was the sort of a man to put the matter in the hands of a detective, but so far — and the weeks were growing into a month — he had given no sign of any kind.   She cared little for the cause of his silence, however; she was too thankful for the fact. Occasionally Steele gave her a brief word of praise, and she was more delighted than she had ever been at the admiration of man.

IV

PATIENCE sprang out of bed, full of the mere joy of living. She felt as happy as a wild creature of the woods, and for no reason whatever. She longed for Rosita's voice that she might carol, and wondered if it were possible that she had ever thought herself the most miserable of women. The small room would not hold her, and she went out and took a long walk in the sharp white air; it was Sunday, and she was not obliged to go to the office.

When she returned, the servant told her that a gentleman awaited her in the parlour. She turned cold, but went defiantly in. The visitor was Mr. Field, and the revulsion of feeling was so great, and her exuberance of spirits so undiminished, that she ran forward, threw her arms about his neck, and kissed him.

"I am so happy I must kiss some one," she said, "and after all you are the right person, for it is owing to you that I am happy."

" Well ! well ! " he said laughing, " I am delighted ; and also relieved that you did not take it into your head to do that down at the office. I 've just dropped in to ask after your health and to say good-bye. How do you stand it ? "

" Oh, I am well. I never felt so well. I get tired, but I sleep it off. I made twenty-five dollars last week, and I celebrated the occasion by coming home in a cab. Oh, I can tell you I feel all made over, and Peele Manor seems prehistoric."

"You always did live at a galloping rate mentally.
You are doing first rate — not but what you'll do better
a year from now.   There 's pulse in your stuff.   Keep
your enthusiasm as long as you can.   Nothing takes its
place.   Here 's something for you."

A messenger boy had entered with a note.

" For me ? "

" For Mrs. Beverly Peele."

"Oh, dear ! " she exclaimed, " it has come.   This
is from Mr. Peele.   Do let me read it — I can't wait."

She tore the envelope open and read hastily : —

DEAR PATIENCE, — On the night of the day of your
departure from Peele Manor, my son came up to us in a
distracted condition.   He had also contracted the grippe.
The combination of disorders produced delirium and serious
illness.   For that reason and others we have not endeavoured to communicate with you.   In fact, I only ascertained yesterday that you were working for Mr. Field,
who I consider has further betrayed my friendship in
associating himself with you in your insubordination.

Of course you are at liberty to act as you choose.   The
laws of this country are wretchedly inadequate regarding
the authority of the husband.   But one thing I insist upon:
that you call upon us and make a definite statement of
what you purpose to do.   If you have repented and wish
to return to us, we will overlook this wretched mistake.   If
you intend definitely to leave your husband and to follow
the disgraceful life of a reporter on a sensational newspaper,
you owe it to us to come here in person and define your
position.   The family with which you have allied yourself,
my dear young woman, is not one to be dismissed with
a note of three lines.

I particularly request that you call at three o'clock this
afternoon.

Yours truly

GARDINER PEELE.

Patience handed the note to Mr. Field, who read it with much interest.

"Go by all means," he said; "otherwise they will annoy you with petty persecutions, and Beverly will haunt the 'Day.' Keep up all your pluck, and remember that this is a free country, and that they can compel you to do nothing you do not wish to do. You are mistress of the situation, and can call upon me for proof that you are supporting yourself adequately."

"Oh, I don't want to go. I never want to look at one of them again. I'd just managed to forget them all."

"But you must go. It would look cowardly if you did n't; and, when you come to think of it, you certainly do owe them some sort of explanation. Poor Peele! he must have actually suffered at being treated in such cavalier fashion."

"Oh, well, I'll go! I'll go! But I wish I'd never seen them."

"You don't look at all pretty with that face, and I shall run. By the way, I came to tell you that I start for Paris to-morrow to join my wife, who has been on the other side for some months. Otherwise she would have called before this. Steele will take care of you."

V

WHEN Patience went up to her room she slammed the door, closed the window violently, then sat down and beat a tattoo on the floor with her heels. Her spirits were still high, but cyclonic. She would willingly have smashed things, and felt no disposition to sing.

Nevertheless she rang the bell of the house in Eleventh Street at three o'clock. The butler bowed solemnly, and announced that the family awaited her in the library. Patience, piqued that they were assured of her coming, was half inclined to turn back, then shrugged her shoulders, walked down the hall, and through the dining-room to the library in the annex.

The afternoon sun irradiated the cheerful room, but Beverly, with sunken eyes and pallid face, sat huddled by the fire. He sprang to his feet as Patience entered, then turned away with a scowl and sank back in his chair. His mother sat opposite. She merely bent her head to Patience, then turned her solicitous eyes to her son's face. Honora came forward and kissed her sweetly. Mr. Peele did not shake hands with her, but offered her a chair by the long table. Patience took it, and experienced a desire to laugh immoderately. They had the air of a Court of Inquiry, and appeared to regard her as a delinquent at the bar.

Mr. Peele sat in his revolving chair, tipped a little back. He had crossed his legs and leaned his elbows on the arms of the chair, pressing his finger tips lightly together.

"Now," he said coldly, "we are ready to hear you."

"I have nothing in particular to say. I gave you fair warning, and you refused to listen, or to let me go abroad and so avoid publicity. I therefore took the matter in my own hands and went."

"You ignore your duty to your husband; your marriage vows?"

"There is only one law for a woman to acknowledge, and that is her self respect."

"The husband that loves you is entitled to no consideration?"

"Not when he exercises none himself. I refuse to admit that any human being has the right to control me unless I voluntarily submit myself to that control."

"Are you aware that you are uttering the principles of anarchy?"

"Well, the true anarchists of this world are not the bomb throwers. When a man and woman are properly married there is no question of authority or disobedience; but a woman is a common harlot who lives with a man that makes her curse the whole scheme of creation."

Honora lifted a screen and hid her face. Beverly muttered inaudible remarks. Mrs. Peele lifted her eyebrows and curled her mouth. Mr. Peele moved his head slowly back and forth.

"I shall not attempt to contradict any of your remarkable theories," he said. "It is apparent that you are imbued with all the pernicious thought of the time. I am thankful that it is not my destiny to live among the next generation of women. Will you kindly tell me how you should have acted in this matter if you had had children?"

"Oh, I don't know! I have thought of that. No woman should have a child until she has been married three years. By that time she would know whether or not she had made a mistake."

"And what shall you do if you are unable to support yourself?"

"Starve. No one has a right to live that the world has no use for, that can give the world nothing. Man's chief end is not bread and butter. If I can give the world anything it will be glad to give me a living in return. If I am a failure I'll walk out of existence as quietly as I altered my life. But I have n't the slightest doubt of my ability to take care of myself."

Mr. Peele pressed his lips together. The old man and the young woman regarded each other steadily, the one with malevolence in his eye, the other with defiance in hers. In that moment Mr. Peele hated her, and she knew it. She had made him feel old and a component part of the decaying order of things, while she represented the insolent confidence of youth in the future.

"Women make too much fuss," continued Patience. "If they don't like their life why don't they alter it quietly, without taking it to the lecture platform or the polemical novel? If they don't like the way man governs why don't they educate their sons differently? They can do anything with the plastic mind. I am sure it could be proved that most corrupt politicians and bad husbands had weak or careless mothers. If the men of a country are bad you can be sure the women are worse —"

Beverly sprang to his feet, overturning his chair. "Damn it!" he cried. "You can talk all you like, but you are mine and I'll have you."

Patience turned and fixed her angry eyes on his face. "Oh, no, you will not. Your father will tell you that I am quite free."

Mr. Peele gave a short dry laugh. "She has the best of it," he said. "You cannot compel her to return to you, and she has the air of one who has tasted of the independence of making money — "

"Then I 'll dog her steps. I 'll make life hell for her — "

"You will do nothing of the sort, sir. Much as I disapprove of this young woman's course, she has in me an unwilling abettor. I shall not have my domestic affairs made food for the newspapers and their hordes of vulgar readers. Field would take up her cause and hound me to my grave. You will keep quiet, and in the course of time get a divorce of which no one will be the wiser until you marry again. If the gossip does not get into the papers it will not rise above a murmur. If you add to my annoyance I shall turn you out of Peele Manor and cut you off without a cent. You will not pretend that you can support yourself."

Patience rose. " If you have nothing more to ask I shall go," she said. " Beverly can bring his suit as soon as he chooses. It will go by default."

Beverly flung off his mother's restraining arm and rushed forward. "You shall not go !" he cried.

"Don't touch me !" cried Patience ; but before she could reach the door Beverly had caught her in his arms. Excitement gave him strength. He held her with hard muscles and kissed her many times.

The ugly temper she had kept under control broke loose. She lifted her hand and struck him violently on the mouth. Her face too was convulsed, but with another passion. She felt as if the past month had been annihilated.

" Will you let me go ? " she gasped. " Oh, how I hate you !" Then as he kissed her again, " I could kill you ! I could kill you ! " She flung herself free, and shaking with passion faced the scandalised family.

"You had better keep him out of the way," she said. "Do you know that once I nearly killed my own mother?"

VI

PATIENCE slept little that night. Her head ached violently. When she presented herself at the office Steele sent her to report a morning lecture. It was dull, and she fell asleep. When she returned to the office Steele happened to be alone.

"I have no report," she said. "I fell asleep. That is all I have to say."

For a few seconds he stared at her, then turned on his heel. In a moment he came back. "The next time you do that," he said, "hunt up the reporter of some other newspaper and get points from him. First-class reporters always stand in together. Here's a good story badly written that has come up from Honduras. Take it home and revamp it, and let me have it to-morrow."

"You are awfully good. I thought you would tell me to go, and I certainly deserve to."

"You certainly do, but we won't discuss the matter further."

That was an unhappy week for Patience, and she lost faith in her star. A great foreign actress, whom she was sent to interview, haughtily refused to be seen, and the next morning capriciously sent for a reporter of the "Eye," the hated rival of the "Day." She was put on the trail of a fashionable scandal and failed to gather any facts. She was sent to interview a strange old woman, supposed to have a history, who lived on a canal boat, and became so interested in the creature that she forgot all about the "Day," and did not appear at Mr. Steele's desk for three days. When she did he looked sternly at her guilty face, although the corners of his mouth twitched.

" I'm delighted to see you have not forsaken us," he said sarcastically. " May I ask if the canal boat woman quite slipped your memory? "

"N-o-o. I have been there ever since."

" Indeed? " His ears visibly twitched. " That alters the case. Did you get the story out of her? "

Patience looked at him steadily for a moment, then dropped her eyes.

" There is nothing to tell," she answered.

Steele sprang to his feet.

"Come out here," he said. He led her into a corner of the composing-room, and they sat down on a bench.

" Now tell me," he said peremptorily. " What have you heard? You have news in your eye. I see it."

" I have nothing to tell."

" Suppose you tell the truth. You have the story, and you won't give it up. Why not? "

"Well — you see — she confided in me — she said I was the only woman who had given her a decent word in twenty years; and if I told the story she would be in jail to-morrow night. Do you think I 'd be so low as to tell it? "

" Sentimentality, my dear young woman, is fatal to a

newspaper reporter. Suppose the entire staff should go silly; where would the 'Day' be?"

"It might possibly be a good deal more admirable than it is now."

"We won't go into a discussion of theory *v.* practice. I want that story."

"You won't get it."

"Indeed." He looked at her with cold angry eyes. "The trouble is that you have not been made to feel what the discipline of a newspaper office is — "

Patience leaned forward and smiled up audaciously into his face. "You would do exactly the same thing yourself," she said; "so don't scold any more. I admit that you frighten me half to death, but all the same I know that you would never send a poor old woman to prison — not to be made editor-in-chief."

He reddened, and looked anything but pleased at the compliment. "Do you know that you have just said that I am a jay newspaper man?" he asked.

But Patience only continued to smile, and in a moment he smiled back at her, then, with an impatient exclamation, left her and returned to his desk.

VII

Two months later Steele asked her to come to the office at six o'clock, an hour at which the evening room was empty, and suggested that she should give up reporting, and start a column of paragraphs.

"I should like it better, of course," said Patience, after he had fully explained the requirements of the

new department. "I was going to tell you that I *would
not* go to that Morgue again."

"Oh, you would n't? Well, you stood it rather
longer than I thought you would."

"And I 'm tired of interviewing insolent conceited
people. Oh, by the way, I should thank you for all
these nice things you 've just said to me."

He dropped his business-like manner suddenly.
"How do you stand it?" he asked. Then in reply to
her look of surprise : " Oh, you know, the Chief, when
he went away, told me to look out for you."

Patience immediately became the charming woman
accustomed to the homage of man. Steele's pre-eminence was gone from that moment.

"I am remarkably well, thank you, considering how
you have bullied me — and I can tell you that I
did not fancy at all being ordered about by such an
infant."

"Oh ! Thanks ! But when a man 's too polite he
does n't get anything done for him — not in this business. And is it a crime to be an editor before you
are thirty ? "

" Oh, you have reason to be proud of yourself."

"You mean that I have the big head. Well, that
is the disease of the age, you know. It would never
do for a newspaper man to get a reputation for eccen-
tricity. You 'll have it yourself inside of six months if
these paragraphs are a success."

" Never ! I scorn to be so unoriginal."

" Well, we 'll encourage your sentiments, and keep
you as the office curio ; but I did n't really bully you,
did I ? "

" Oh, I 'll admit that you were kinder than I deserved,

once in a while : when I fell asleep at the lecture, for instance."

He laughed heartily. "That was the richest joke. There was absolutely nothing to say to you. If you only stood at the end of a long perspective of this business and could fully appreciate the humour of that situation ! An experienced reporter, if he could n't have lied out of it, or borrowed news, would never have shown up. You looked like a naughty child expecting to have its ears boxed."

"Oh, yes, Miss Merrien guyed me for a whole week ; I know all about that now. And now that you 've come down off your pedestal I 'll thank you for all your patience and good training. If I 've learned to write I owe it to your blue pencil ; and I don't need to be told by Miss Merrien that you 've saved me from a great deal of hard work."

He smiled charmingly. There were times when he looked like an old man with the mask of youth ; to-day he looked a mere boy. "Oh, any one would do as much for you, even if the Chief had n't given orders. You are an unusual woman, you know. You proved that — but, of course, I have no right to speak to you of that." He stood up suddenly and held out his hand. "Well, be good to yourself," he said. "If you feel yourself breaking, take a rest."

"I wonder," she thought, as she went downstairs, "if that young man knows he betrayed the fact that he has been thinking a good deal about me ? He certainly is an interesting youth, and I should like to know him better."

Patience did not find her paragraphs as easy as she expected. It was one thing to work on a given idea, and another to supply idea and execution both ; but after a time her sharpened brain grew more magnetic and life fuller of ideas than of lay figures. The men in the office frequently gave her tips, and one clever young reporter, who worshipped her from afar, fell into the daily habit of presenting her with a slip of suggestions.

Her choicest paragraphs were usually edited by Steele's ruthless hand, and now and again she was moved to wrath. Upon such occasions Mr. Steele merely smiled, and she was forced to smile in return or retire with the sulks.

VIII

PATIENCE was writing busily in her little bedroom. The March winds were howling down the street. Her door opened, and a very elegant young woman entered.

" Hal ! " cried Patience.

" You dear bad girl ! "

They kissed a half dozen times, then sat down and looked at each other. Hal had quite the young married woman air, and held herself with a mien of conscious importance, entirely removed from conceit : she was *grande dame*, and the late object of attentions from smart folks abroad.

" Well, how are you? " asked Patience. " Oh, but I am glad to see you. Tell me all about yourself. When did you get back? "

" Day before yesterday. I 've returned with thirty-two trunks, the loveliest jewels you ever saw, and quite a slave of a husband. I must say I never thought Latimer would keep up such a prolonged bluff, but he fills the rôle as if he 'd been husbanding all his life. Oh, no. Don't look at me like that. I 've forgotten it, and I 've no regrets. *Mon Dieu!* To think that I might be in Boston on four hundred a month! I shall be a leader, my dear. You can do as much with a hundred and fifty thousand a year as you can with a million, for you can only spend just so much money anyhow. All that the big millionaires get out of their wealth is notoriety. Nobody 'd remember about them if it was n't for the newspapers. But you bad bad girl! What have you been and gone and done? Why did n't you wait for me? I would have rescued you."

"Oh, you could n't, Hal dear. I did n't want to be rescued for a day or a month. I 've run away for good and all."

"But, Patience, what an alternative! Do you mean to say you live in this cubby-hole?"

"I 'm mighty happy in this cubby-hole, I can tell you; happier than I ever was at Peele Manor."

"That certainly was the mistake of my life. However, you 've solved the problem more promptly than most women do. The celerity with which you untied that knot when you set about it moved me to admiration. By the way, do you know that Bev is ill?"

"Is he? What is the matter?"

"I don't know exactly, — one of those organic afflictions that men are always getting. How uninteresting men are when their interior decorations get out of gear. And they always will talk about them. Latimer is ever groaning with his liver; but no wonder. I 've had to eat so much rich stuff to keep him from feeling lonesome that I 've actually grown fat. Well, we don't know what is the matter with Bev, yet. The doctor says it 's a result of the influenza. He has some pain, and makes an awful fuss, like all men."

" Where are you going to stay, now ? "

" I am at the Holland, but will spend the summer at the Manor and the fall at Newport. Our house on the Avenue — opposite the park, you know — will be finished by winter. That house will be a jewel. I got the most beautiful things abroad for it. Then you will come and live with me."

Patience shook her head.

" It would n't do, and you will see it. I belong to another sphere now ; but I can see you sometimes."

" Well, put up that stuff, and come to the Holland and dine with me. You can finish up to-night. I have yards and yards to talk to you about. I 'll never give you up, — remember that."

IX

WHEN the hot days and nights of summer came Patience did not find routine and the hunt as fasci-nating sport as when the electric thrill of cooler seasons was in the air. Her paragraphs acquired some reputa-tion, and her mind grew tense in the effort to keep them up to a high standard, and to prepare at least one surprise a day. She grew thin and nervous, and began to wonder what life and herself would be like five years hence. Mr. Field and Steele helped her as much as they dared, and she managed to make about fifty dollars a week : her success gave Mr. Field the excuse to pay her special rates. It never occurred to her to give up, and she assured Hal that she would have nervous prostration four times a year before she would return to Peele Manor.

There were times when she passionately longed for the isolation of a mountain top. Nature had been part of her very individuality for all the years of her life until this last, and a forested mountain top alone was the antithesis of Park Row. [She sometimes had a whimsical idea that her grey matter was becoming slowly modelled into a semblance of that famous precinct.] She loved it loyally; but the isolation of high altitudes sent their magnetism to another side of her nature. She was getting farther and farther away from herself in the jealous absorption of her work, — the skurrying practical details of her life. She felt that she could no longer forecast what she should do under given circumstances, that something in her was slowly changing. What the result would be she could not predict; and she craved solitude and the opportunity to study herself out.

In August Mrs. Field took her to her house in the Berkshire hills. Although she had no solitude there, she returned much refreshed, and did good work all winter. Steele she never saw outside of the office, but he managed to treat her with a certain knightliness, and she lay awake, occasionally, thinking about him. Hard work and the practical side of life had disposed of a good deal of her romance, but she was still given to vagaries. Steele's modernity fascinated her. No other epoch but this extraordinary last quarter of the nineteenth century could have produced him.

She was a great favourite in the office. Again a

thaw had succeeded a second glacier period, induced
by entire change of environment, and she liked' nearly
everybody she knew, and became a most genial and
expansive young woman. She often laughed at herself,
and concluded that she would never strike the proper
balance until she fell in love (if she ever did), when
the large and restless currents of her nature would unite
and find their proper destination. She had no "weird
experiences." Her abounding feminity appealed to
the chivalry of the gentlemen among whom she was
thrown, and she was clever enough not to flirt with
them, to treat them impartially as good comrades.
The second-class men detested her, and were not con-
ciliated : the underbred newspaper man touches a lower
notch of vulgarity than any person of similar social
degree the world over.

One morning she awoke about four o'clock, — that
is, her mind awoke ; her body was still too full of sleep
to move to the right or left. It was one of her favourite
sensations, and she lay for a time meditating upon the
various pleasures, great and small, which are part of
man's inheritance.
Suddenly she became conscious that it was raining.
She had moved into a back room on the second floor.
Beside one window was a tin roof upon which the rain
poured with heavy reiterance. In the back yard was
a large ailanthus tree which lifted itself past her windows to the floor above. A light wind rustled it.
The rain pattered monotonously upon its wide leaves,
producing a certain sweet volume of sound.
It was long since she had listened to rain in the
night. It was associated in her mind with the vague

sweet dreams of girlhood and with her life in Carmel Valley. She had loved to wander through the pine woods when the winter rains were beating through the uplifted arms, swirling and splashing in the dark fragrant depths. It said something to her then, she hardly knew what, nor when it roared upon the roof of the old farmhouse, or flung itself through the windows of Carmel tower, as she and Solomon huddled close to the wall.

But when it had beaten upon the roof of her little room in Miss Tremont's house it had sung the loneliness of youth into her soul, murmured of the great joy to which every woman looks forward as her birthright. Hard worked and absorbed as she may have been during the day, if the rain awoke her in the night, it was to dreams of love and of nothing else, and of the time when she should no longer be alone.

This morning she listened to the rain for a time, then moved suddenly to her side, her eyes opening more widely in the dark. The rain said nothing to her. She listened to it without a thrill, with no longing, with no loneliness of soul, and no vague tremor of passion.

Nothing in her unhappy experience had so forcibly brought home to her the changes which her inner self had undergone in the last few years. Life was a hard clear-cut fact; she could no longer dream. Imagination had taken itself out of her and gone elsewhere, into some brain whose dear privilege it was to have a long future and a brief past.

The tears scalded her eyes. She cursed Beverly Peele. She wished she had remained in Monterey. There, at least, she would never have married any one, for there was no one to marry.

"Even if my life had been a success," she thought,

"if Beverly Peele had been less objectionable, or had died, and I had had the world at my feet, it would be too high a price to pay. Not even to care that one is alone when the rain is sweeping about with that hollow song! To think and dream of nothing beyond the moment! To have accepted life with cynical philosophy, and feel no desire to shake the Universe with a great passion! To be beyond the spell of the rain is to be a thousand years old, and a thousand centuries away from the cosmic sense. I wish I were dead."

And there were other moods. Sometimes the devil which is an integral part of all strong natures — of woman's as well as of man's, and no matter what her creed — awoke and clamoured. There were four or five men in the office whom she liked well enough when absent, and in whom the lightning of her glance would have changed friendship to passion. Why she resisted the temptation which so fiercely assailed her at times she never knew. Conventions did not exist for her impatient mind excepting in so far as they made life more comfortable; she had in full measure youth's power to know and to give joy, and she owed no one loyalty. And at this time she imaged no future: she had lost faith in ideals. It was only at brief intervals that there came a sudden passionate desire — almost a flash of prophetic insight — for the one man who must exist for her among the millions of men. And this, if anything, took the place of her lost ideals and conquered the primal impulses of her nature. Or was it a mere matter of destiny? Woman is a strange and complex instrument. She is as she was made, and it is not well to condemn her even after elaborate analysis.

X

ONE morning in May, Hal came in before Patience was out of bed. She sat down on a chair and tapped the floor with her foot.

"I come charged with a message, a special mission, as it were," she said. "I hardly know where to begin."

"Well?"

"Don't look at me like that, or I'll never have the courage to go on. Bev is desperately ill, — not in bed, but he has the most frightful pains: his disease, which has been threatening for a year, has developed. It may or may not be fatal. The doctor says it certainly will be unless he has peace of mind, and he is fretting after you like a big baby. The grippe seems to have broken the back of his temper, and he is simply a great calf bleating for its parent. It would be ridiculous if it were not serious. You'd better come back to us, Patience."

"I won't."

"I knew you would say exactly that; but when you think it over you will come. Remember that the doctor practically says that you can either save or prolong his life. Mamma is simply distracted. You know she adores Bev, and she broke down completely last night and told me to come and beg you to return. You know what that means: you'll have nothing to fear from her."

"Oh, I can't go back! I can't! I think I should die if I went back."

"We don't die so easily, my dear. Now, I'll go and let you think it over," and the diplomate kissed Patience and retired.

Patience endeavoured to put the matter out of her mind, but it harassed her through her day's duties, and her work was bad. Steele told her as much the next afternoon when she came into the office late, intending to write there instead of at home. Her room was haunted by Beverly's pallid face and sunken eyes.

"Oh, well," she said, flinging herself down before a table, "perhaps it's the last, so it doesn't matter."

"Why? What do you mean? You do look pale. Are you ill?"

Patience hesitated a moment, then told him of the complication. He listened, without comment, looking down upon the skurrying throngs.

"I suppose I must go," she said in conclusion. "Anyway I feel that I shall go, whether I want to or not."

He came over to the table and regarded her with his preternatural seriousness.

"Yes," he said, "you will go. It will be like you."

"Oh, I am no angel. It's not that — please! It's — don't you know there are some good acts you can't help? Not only do traditions and conventions drive you into them, but your own selfishness — I haven't the courage to be lashed by my conscience. If I could give that morphine, do you think I'd go?"

He smiled. "Do you analyse everything like that? However, I choose to keep to my illusions. I think that you have magnificent theories, but act very much like other people. Can I go up and see you sometimes? I may have a chance to know you, now."

She put up her hand and took his impulsively. "Yes, come," she said. "That is the only thing that will make life supportable."

XI

SHE went home and wrote the following letter to Beverly Peele : —

" I will return to Peele Manor and remain while you are seriously ill, under the following conditions: (1) That you pay me what you would be obliged to pay a trained nurse; (2) That you will treat me on that basis absolutely. My feeling toward you has undergone no change. I am not your wife. But as your physician holds me responsible for your life, I will be your nurse on the terms stated above."

The next day she received this telegram : —

Come. Terms agreed to.

BEVERLY PEELE.

She was received by the various members of the household with infinite tact. Mrs. Peele's cold blue eyes sheltered an angry spark, but she behaved to her errant daughter-in-law exactly as if matrimonial vacations were orthodox and inevitable. Honora kissed her sweetly, and asked her if the roses were not beautiful. When Mr. Peele came home he said, "Ah, good-evening." Beverly, who had evidently been coached, did not offer to kiss her, but immediately explained every detail of his disease. Hal and her husband were in the North Carolina mountains.

Beverly was not a good actor, and his eyes followed his wife with kaleidoscopic expression. She frequently encountered hungry admiration and angry resentment; and if he had made up his mind to abide by her decree he as clearly evidenced that he considered her his salaried property: he demanded her constant attendance. He looked so wan and hopeless that Patience was moved to pity, and even to tenderness, and devoted herself to his care.

For the first two weeks she felt hourly as if she must pack her trunk and flit back to the "Day." She longed for a very glimpse of the grimy men in the composing-room, and felt that the sight of Morgan Steele in his shirt sleeves would give more spiritual satisfaction than the green and grey of the Palisades.

The life at Peele Manor seemed doubly flat after her emancipation. At the breakfast table, Mrs. Peele and Honora discussed their small interests. At luncheon, Beverly — who arose late — gave the details of his night. At dinner there was little conversation of any sort. The mornings, and the afternoons from four to six — when Beverly drove with his mother and Honora — were Patience's own. Although discontented, she was by no means unhappy: she was out of bondage forever. If Beverly grew better she could return to the "Day" after a reasonable time had elapsed.

She spent most of her leisure rambling over the hills in idle reverie or meditating upon her checkered life. She gave a good deal of thought to the many phases of life which had flashed before her startled eyes in the last year, but was too young not to be more interested in herself than in problems, however momentous. Still,

346 Patience Sparhawk and Her Times

she did not feel much more intimate with herself than she had felt in Park Row.

She frequently wondered with some pique and much disapproval that she heard nothing from Morgan Steele. The few glimpses she had caught of the nature behind the mask tempted her to idealise him, and she finally succumbed. One night she awoke to the fact that she had been walking the stars with him, discussing the mysteries of the Universe. She pictured the smile with which he would regard the workings of her imagination, were they revealed to him, and recalled his business-like demeanour, his shirt sleeves, his Park Row vocabulary, and his impatient scorn of "damned slush."

It happened to be midnight when these later thoughts arrived, and she laughed aloud.

"What are you laughing at?" demanded a querulous voice from the next room.

"Nothing."

"Nothing? Do you suppose I'm an idiot? Tell me what you were laughing at."

"Go to sleep, go to sleep."

"I can't go to sleep. You lie there and laugh while I lie here and suffer."

"Why did n't you say you were suffering? Do you want the morphine?"

"No, I don't."

An hour later Patience was roused from her first heavy sleep.

"Patience! Patience! Oh, my God! My God! My God!"

Patience stumbled out of bed and into her dressing-gown and slippers, shaking her head vigorously to dispel the vapours in her brain.

" Yes, yes ! " she said. " I 'm coming. Do please don't make such a fuss. You 'll wake up everybody — "

" Not make a fuss ! Oh, I wish you had it for a minute — "

Patience ran into the lavatory and turned up the gas. The night was very warm, and the door leading into Honora's room stood wide. The light fell full on her face. Patience saw that her eyes were open.

" I hope Beverly did n't wake you up," she said. "He does make such a noise."

" I was awake. I never sleep well in warm weather. I don't envy you, though."

" Oh, I don't mind if only I don't make a terrible mistake some night and give him an overdose. He takes particular pains to wait until I am in my first sleep and then I hardly know what I am doing. There ! this is the third time I have dropped the wretched stuff. What is the good of drop bottles, anyway ? "

" Why don't you use the hypodermic ? "

" I can't. It would make me ill to puncture people. And this does him as much good." She set the bottle down impatiently, drew a basin full of cold water, dashed it over her face, then dropped the dose and took it to Beverly.

" Stay with me," he commanded. " You know it does n't take effect at once, and I feel better if I hold your hand." She sat down beside him and nodded sleepily until the morphine did its work.

XII

THE next afternoon, a few moments after Beverly had gone for his drive, Morgan Steele's card was brought up to Patience.   She had imagined that this first call would induce a mild thrill of nerve, but she merely remarked to the butler: " Tell him I will be down in a moment," walked to the long mirror in the corner, and shook out her violet and white organdie skirts.   Her long hair was braided and tied with a lavender ribbon.

" I look very well," she thought, and went downstairs.

Steele awaited her in the drawing-room, and, as she entered, was standing with his head thrown back, regarding the medallion of Whyte Peele.   She noted anew how well he dressed and carried his clothes. He looked quite at home in the drawing-room of Peele Manor.   Her first remark followed in natural sequence, —

" How odd not to see you in your shirt sleeves."

He turned with a start and a sudden warmth in his face.

" Oh, well, I hope you'll never see me that way again.   How charming you look in that frock and with your hair in that braid !   *I* always imagine *you* in prim tailor things, with your hair tucked out of sight under a stiff turban.   This is lovely.   You look like a little girl. Those awful dress reformers should see you."

" It's a comfort to think that the She-males cannot exterminate the artistic sense.   Let us go into the library."

"Is there a large comfortable chair there? These are impressive but unpleasant. Perhaps you would not suspect it, but I love a comfortable chair and a cigar better than anything in life."

"One thing I do suspect — that we shall have to become acquainted all over again. You are not exactly like a fallen angel outside of the office, but you certainly have not patronised me for five minutes."

"Oh, you can take your revenge now and patronise me. Hang the shop! I don't want to think about it."

In the library he critically inspected every chair, selected one that pleased him, and drawing it to the open window sank into it with a deep sigh of content. Patience gave him permission to smoke, and a moment later he looked so happy that she laughed aloud.

"You may laugh," he said plaintively, "but you have less imagination than I thought if you don't understand what this is to a man after Park Row. After an hour of that water and your muslin frock, I shall go back as refreshed as if my brain had taken a cold bath."

"I'd fly back to the office this minute if I could. I've felt like a bottle of over-charged champagne for two weeks."

"You have the enthusiasm of youth. When you are my age — sixty-five — you will be thankful for the *dolce far niente* of a colonial manor. This sort of life suits you — you are a born châtelaine. You have lost your tired expression, and are actually stouter. Besides, I want to come up here to see you."

"Will you come often?"

"As often as you will let me. I am free every afternoon, you know, and if I followed my tactless inclination I'd come seven times a week. However, don't look alarmed; I'm only coming once a week — " He sat up suddenly, his eyes sparkling. " By Jove !" he exclaimed. " What a beauty !"

Patience followed his eyes, which were directed ardently upon a sail-boat skimming up the river.

" Are you fond of sailing?" she asked.

" Am I? I could live in a boat. I'd rather be in a boat than — than even talking to you."

" Well, you shall be inside of a boat in five minutes," she said good-naturedly. " Wait until I get my hat and gloves !"

" Being only the nurse," she said, as they walked down the wooded slope to the boathouse, " I don't know that I have any right to take liberties, but I will, all the same. I feel that it is an act of charity."

" It certainly is, and you really are an angel. — She's a good boat," he said approvingly, a few moments later, as he unreefed the sail.

Patience arranged the cushions and made herself comfortable, and they shot up the river in a stiff breeze. She watched Steele curiously. He looked as happy as a schoolboy. His hat was on the back of his head, his eyes shone. Once as he threw back his head and laughed, he bore an extraordinary resemblance to the Laughing Faun.

" I've lived in a boat for a whole summer," he said, " and never seen a woman nor wanted to, nor a man neither, for that matter. There are three months in the year when I want nothing better in life than this." His large cool eyes moved slowly to hers. " Still," he added, " I do believe it's an improvement to have you here. What fun if we had a little yacht and could sail like this all summer! I think we'd hit it off, don't you? We should n't either of us talk too much."

Patience laughed. It was impossible to coquet with Steele. He took no notice of it. "I should be afraid you'd tip me over if you got tired of me."

"I should n't get tired of you," he said seriously. "I never met a woman I liked half as much. You're lovely to look at, and your mind is so interesting to study. Guess I'd better come about."

They sailed for two hours. The wind fell, and they talked in a desultory fashion. They discovered that they had the same literary gods, and occasionally Steele waxed enthusiastic. He had read more than most men of forty; nor was there anything youthful about the fixity of his opinions.

"Oh, dear!" said Patience, suddenly, "why did we never meet before? I like you better than any one I ever knew. I've been hunting all my life for a mental companion."

"So have I," he said, smiling at her in his half cynical way, "and now I've found you I don't propose to let you go; not even next winter."

He confided to her that he had written a good deal, although he had published nothing. Patience wondered where he had found time to accomplish so much.

"I'm going to bring up some of my stuff and read it to you," he said. "You can take that as a compliment if you like, for I've only shown it to one other person — a man."

"Now, I know why you like me! You are going to study me."

"Well, it's partly that," he replied coolly. "You are

a new type — to me at any rate, and I shall probably know a good deal more after I have known you a year or so than I do now. Who is that? What an amiable-looking person!"

Patience followed his glance. Beverly stood at the foot of the slope, with distorted face.

"Oh, dear," she said, "that is Mr. Peele. I am afraid he is going to be disagreeable. Of course I am not obliged to stay — but in a way I am."

Steele ran the boat into the dock, handed her out, and reefed the sail before he spoke. Then he turned and looked at her squarely.

"Would you rather I did not come?" he asked.

"No! No! I want you to come. I'll think it over and write you — or — I wonder if you are horrid like most men and would misunderstand me if I asked you always to come on a certain day and meet me in that wood up there, instead of going to the house?"

"Look here," he said in his old business-like tone, "just let me set your mind at rest. I haven't the slightest intention of making love to you. In the first place I am just now tired and sick of that sort of thing — a state a man does get into occasionally, although a woman will never believe it. In the second place I like to think of you as *sui generis;* a woman on a pedestal. It is very refreshing. A week from to-day I'll be in that wood, and I'll stay there from four to six whether you come or not. There comes my train."

"You must flag it. Hurry. I'll expect you Thursday."

XIII

"Who is that man?" thundered Beverly, as she crossed the track behind the train.

Patience raised her eyebrows. "What have you to do with my visitors?"

"You sha'n't receive men, and you sha'n't sail in my boat."

"Of course the boat is yours. I shall not use it again."

"You are my nurse."

"Your nurse is always ready to be dismissed," and she walked up the slope, taking no further notice of him.

Hal returned the following week; and, as Beverly improved steadily, the house was filled with company once more. Whenever Patience hinted that she was no longer required, Beverly immediately went to bed and rent the air; but as a matter of fact his attacks were growing less and less frequent.

Patience, in the circumstances, was not impatient to return to work until the hot weather was over. Her position was very pleasant, Hal was ever her loyal friend, and she saw Morgan Steele once a week.

The wood was a wild place on a slope of the bluff some distance above the house. Its underbrush made it unpopular with the guests of Peele Manor. Steele left the train at the regular station a mile up the road and walked back without encounter. In the heart of the dark cool little wood Patience swung two hammocks and filled them with pillows. Steele lay full length in his and looked comfortable and happy, a cigar ever between his lips. Patience, in hers, sat in as dignified an attitude as she could assume.

"Does it make you feel romantic?" he said one day, looking at her quizzically.

"What do you mean?" she asked, flushing a little.

"Oh, I think you have a queer romantic sentimental streak through your modernity — or had. I 've been wondering if there was any of it left."

"I never told you."

"No, but you suggest it. Tell me: did n't you once have ideals and that sort of thing?"

"I don't see how you can even guess it, for I have none now."

"Oh, yes, you have. You won't when you 're thirty, but you have all sorts of kiddish notions stored away yet in that brain of yours." He had seen Peele a few days before in the train, and knew the history of their courtship quite as well as if she had related it to him, but he was curious to know what she had been before. He drew her on until she told him the story of the tower and the owl.

That little picture pleased his artistic sense, but when she described her girlish ideals and dreams he threw back his head and laughed loud and long.

"What would I have done with you if I had met you then?" he said, looking with intense amusement at her half angry face. "I should have run, I expect. You are a thousand times more interesting now."

"Not to myself."

"Of course not, because you are less of an egoist, and draw a larger measure of your individuality from your environment. But you are real now, where before you were unreal — you were a sort of waxwork with numerous dents. The two extremes in this world are nature and civilisation. Children belong by right to nature, and she holds on to them as long as possible. When civilisation gets hold of them she proceeds to pick out with a pair of tweezers all but the primal passions; and the result is the only human variety capable of enjoying life."

" Don't you believe in ideals? " asked Patience, rather wistfully.

" Of course not," he said contemptuously. " Life is what it is, and you can't alter it. And as we are only just so big and have only just so many years in which to get over a limited surface of this mighty complication called Life, all we can do is to keep our eyes open, and pick out here and there what appeals to our taste most strongly, swallowing the disagreeable majority as philosophically as possible. When you know the world — and yourself — you can't have ideals, and the sooner you quit wasting time thinking about them the sooner you begin to enjoy life. And remember that we live but from day to day — we may be a cold cadaver tomorrow. Life is a game of chance. To set up ideals is as purposeless as to waste this life preparing for an impossible next. Omar expressed it better than I can when he said : —

> " 'To-morrow? Why, to-morrow I myself may be
> With yesterday's seven thousand years.' "

"You have certain ideals though," said Patience. " You are intellectually ambitious; and you say that you never run after a merely pretty face, and never wasted time on any sort of woman unless she had brains; and the men at the office say that you are scrupulously square in money matters. So that I can't see that you are altogether without ideals."

"Those are mere matters of taste and worldly sense. I aim for nothing that is impossible. When I think I want a thing I set about to accomplish it. If I find that it is impossible I quit without further loss of time. You don't suppose I have an ideal woman, do you? How can any man that knows women? — although he may often succumb to a happy combination. When I was exactly twelve my Sunday School teacher forestalled any inclination I might have developed to idealise woman. I met her once after I was grown, by the way, and it did me good to tell her what I thought of her. That is where you women have the advantage of us. It is so long before you know man at all that after you do it is hard work making him over as he is. The woman never lived that understood man by intuition. That is the reason a woman so seldom has any fascination but that of mere youth until she's pretty well on to thirty. You, of course, have had an exceptional experience, but you are a good deal of a kid yet."

XIV

MORGAN STEELE was a type of the precocious young United States newspaper man which only this end of the century has evolved: Preternaturally wise in the way of the world and the nature of woman; with young blood and cold judgment; wary, deliberate, calculating; full of kind impulses; generous with his money, yet careful of it; ready to make cold-blooded use of a man to-day and offer him a free lodging to-morrow; possessed of more self-control than the Club man of forty; without sentimentality, yet with a certain limited power of loving; having a thorough appreciation of the finer as of the coarser shades of woman; incapable of a blind supreme rush of feeling, through the habit of eternal analysis; placidly and philosophically content with the present, and fully expecting to be laid away in the past at forty; *blasé*, yet full of boyish delight in outdoor sport; having faith in no woman, yet treating the lowest with a cynical kindness and consideration which was part of his philosophy.

One night he faced the question of his relationship to Patience with his usual deliberation.

He lay on a divan in his bachelor quarters: a long room with bedroom and bath attached. The walls of the living-room were covered with red paper, the doors and windows hung with Smyrna cloth. A rug half covered the stained floor. Between the windows was a large desk covered with papers. A long table was strewn thick with magazines. Small bookcases were filled with the works of Omar, Whitman, Emerson, Hugo, Heine, Dumas, Maupassant, Bourget, Pater, Dobson, Herrick, Ibsen, Zola, Landor, Rabelais, Stevenson, Kipling. On the mantel there was a number of photographs and a notable absence of legs. The walls were covered with artists' sketches.

"The summer will pass harmlessly enough," he thought. "I only see her once a week, and her husband is likely to be hidden in the brush; but when she returns to town in the winter I shall find myself calling

on her every night.   I'm not stuck on matrimony, but
I certainly should like her for a companion in a little
house or double apartment where there would be
plenty of elbow room and some chance of keeping up
the illusions.   I think it would be some years before I
should tire of her, and I think I could love her a good
deal.   Why in thunder does n't the man die?   She's
too good for anything else.   It would be a terrible pity
— the details smirch so.   A novelist would remark at
this point, 'And yet he never thought of sparing her.'
No, my dear fictionist, we don't, nor if she loved me
would she thank me for sparing her.   And yet it
would be a pity.   She is like some delicate wild-flower
that has been transplanted.   I should like to offer her
the best one can, instead of practically remarking:
'My dear, this brain racket is worked out for the
present.   We 'll return to it later, or not at all.'

"It is often a clever thing for those that love and
cannot marry to part when the shock comes: they
coddle the misery and have a glorious time suffering.
But that would not do for us.   We live in the thick
and rush of life, and have no time to sit down with
memories, hardly time enough to realise an ache.   We
must have our day in fact or not at all; and afterward,
thank God, there is again no time for memories.   Well,
this is only the eighth of July.   By winter that intolerable nuisance may be in the family vault."

XV

PEOPLE remarked that summer that Patience looked unusually well. At times her eyes had a certain liquid softness, at others they sparkled wickedly. Her colour was beautiful and her manner and conversation full of animation.

It was on a hot August afternoon that Patience and Steele, in the green shades of their wood, suddenly met each other's eyes and burst out laughing.

" We are in love," said Patience.

" Well — yes — I suppose we are."

" I feel very light-minded over this unexpected *dénouement.* I had imagined all sorts of dramatic climaxes; but the unexpected always will happen in this life — more 's the pity."

" Did you expect we should not fall in love ? "

" I did not think about it at all for a time — just drifted. But as the situation is so serious it is as well to take it humourously. What are we going to do about it ? "

He had removed his cigar, and was regarding her with his contemplative stare. " I have thanked your complicated ancestors more than once for your large variety of moods. I am glad and sorry that you have spoken : sorry, because this was very pleasant ; glad that the discussion of ways and means should take place here instead of in town. I shall be brutally frank. How long is your husband likely to live ? "

" He may live for twenty years. I heard the doctors — they have a consultation every once in a while — tell

Mrs. Peele so the other day. He is much better. On the other hand, he might take a turn for the worse any day."

"Then you must persuade him to give you a divorce."

"Oh, dear, I am afraid that is out of the question. I've thought of it; but — you don't know him."

"You are a clever woman: now look up your resources. Enlist the family on your side. Tell them that you are about to leave, never to return, and that you are on the road to become a famous newspaper woman; that if they will persuade your husband to give you a divorce you will drop their name; otherwise that it will be dinned in their ears for the next twenty years. Tell them that we intend to let you sign hereafter. That ought to fetch them, as they appear to look upon the newspaper business with shuddering horror. And persuade them that Beverly needs a good domestic little wife who would gladden his declining years."

"I'm sorry I feel in this mood," said Patience, abruptly. "I should far rather it had been the other way — the usual way. I suppose I am possessed with what Poe calls The Imp of the Perverse."

"My dear girl, I need not remind you that it is just as well and a good deal better. You need a shaking to wake you up, though. You imagine that you are awake already, but you are not — not by a long sight. You have buried your nature five fathoms deep. Well, time is up. I must be off. Think over what I have said. Good-bye."

XVI

ON the following Thursday morning Patience walked slowly over to where Beverly sat under a tree on one of the lawns, reading a newspaper. She had made up her mind to adopt Steele's advice, but had deferred the evil moment as long as possible.

" Beverly," she said abruptly, sitting down in front of him, " I want to speak to you."

He laid down the newspaper and regarded her with eager admiration. She had carefully selected the most unbecoming frock she possessed, a sickly green, and twisted her hair in a fashion to distort the fine lines of her head. Nevertheless, she looked as fresh as the morning, and her eyes sparkled with excitement.

"What is it?" he asked. "Oh, why — why — "

" Never mind ! I am going to have a business talk with you, and please don't get excited. If you do, you 'll be sure to have a pain, you know."

"Well, what is it? It does n't do a fellow any good to keep him in suspense."

" On the first of November I am going away — "

" You are not ! "

"And I shall not come back — not in any circumstances. You have proved that your attacks are more or less under your own control. A sojourn at some foreign baths will probably cure you. I have given you all of my life that I intend to give you. I know that self-sacrifice is the ideal of happiness of some women, but it is not mine. When I leave here on the first of

November it will be forever. There is no inducement, material nor sentimental, that will bring me back. Do you understand that much clearly?"

He burst into a volley of oaths, and beat his knees with his fists. Patience continued as soon as she could be heard: —

"Now, it can do you no possible good to retain a legal hold on me, nor can you care to hear of your name becoming familiar in Park Row. Give me my freedom, and I will take my own name — "

"You 'll get no divorce," he roared, "now nor ever. Do you understand that? I 'll brace up and live until I 'm ninety — by God I will! I 'll go abroad and live at a water cure. You 'll never be the wife of any other man. Do you understand that?"

"Oh, Beverly," she said, breaking suddenly, "don't be cruel, — don't! What good can it do you? Give me my freedom."

He grasped her wrists. His eyes were full of rage and malevolence. "Do you want to marry some one else?" he asked. "Some damned newspaper man, I suppose."

Patience stood up and shook him off. "If ever I do marry another man," she said cuttingly, "you may be sure he will have brains this time, and that he will also be a gentleman. The most vulgar persons I have ever known have been socially the most highly placed."

As she moved away he sprang after her and caught her arm. "Now look here," he said hoarsely, "you 'll neither marry, nor will you have a lover, unless you want all New York to know it. The moment you leave this place a detective goes after you. You 'll do nothing that I don't know. I may not have brains, but I'll get the best of you all the same."

Patience flung him off and went straight to Mrs. Peele. Her mother-in-law watched her with narrowed eyes until she had finished, then remarked unexpectedly: "I shall do my best to make my son divorce you. If you intend to leave us I prefer that the rupture should be complete. As you suggest, I have no desire to see the name of Peele signed to newspaper articles. Moreover, I believe I can persuade my son to marry again,— a woman of his own station, who will not desecrate the name of wife; and who," with sudden violence, "will give this house an heir." She paused a moment to recover herself, then continued more calmly: "I have talked the matter over with my husband, and he agrees with me. Of course, you will expect no alimony."

"I don't want alimony. I make more with my pen than Beverly ever allowed me."

The red came into Mrs. Peele's face. "My son was quite as generous as was to be expected. Moreover, he had the right to demand that his wife should not come to him empty handed. I shall speak to Beverly."

An hour later Patience met Mrs. Peele in the side hall. The older woman looked flushed and excited. "I have had a most terrible interview with Beverly," she exclaimed. "I can do nothing with him. You little fool, why didn't you swear that you did not want to marry another man? Heaven knows I should prefer to have you take another name as soon as possible; but you have ruined your chances by letting Beverly suspect the truth."

Patience sank upon a chair, and sat for a long while

staring straight before her. She felt the incarnation of rage and hate. Her lovely face was set and repellent. She came to herself with a start, and wondered if she had ever had any womanly impulses.

She had never wanted anything in her life as much as she wanted to marry Morgan Steele. His very unlikeness to all her old ideals fascinated her, and she was convinced that she was profoundly in love. She could hardly imagine what life with him would be like, and was the more curious to ascertain; and the obstacles enraged her impatient spirit.

The butler left the dining-room to announce luncheon.

"Send mine up to my room," she said. As she reached the first landing of the stair she turned to him suddenly. "Tell John to go to New York this afternoon, and have Mr. Beverly's morphine bottle filled. He took the last last night and he may need it again before I go down myself. Don't fail to tell him. The bottle is in the lavatory."

That afternoon she met Steele at the edge of the wood.

"I could not keep still," she said. "My brain feels on fire."

He drew her hand through his arm and held it tenderly. "What is it?" he asked. "Did you speak, and was it disagreeable?"

"I'll tell you in a minute. Just now it is enough to feel you here."

"I can only stay an hour. I should not have come at all, but I could not stay away."

When they reached the hammocks Patience flung herself into hers and told the story of the morning with dramatic indignation. Then, insensibly, she drifted into the story of her married life, and described her intense hatred and loathing of her husband.

"It was all my own fault," she said in conclusion. "I married him with my eyes open; but all the same I hate him. Sometimes I felt, and feel yet, fairly murderous. I seem to have a terrible nature — does it make you hate me?"

He laughed. "No, I don't hate you, and you know it quite as well as I do. You have wonderful possibilities — but I can't quite make up my mind that I am the man — "

"Oh, yes, you are. I could love you as much as I hate Beverly Peele."

"Well, if you think so it amounts to the same thing, for a while at least. I shall come again in a few days. I'll write you. If your husband cannot be induced to change his mind I'll talk to you about a paper that has been offered to me in Texas; but if you prefer it the other way, I'll leave you alone without a word."

"Oh, I don't know! There are some words I hate, — the words free-love and adultery. I don't want to be exploited in the newspapers, and I don't want to be insulted by my landlord. After all, expediency is the source of all morality. My life with you would be a thousand times better than it was with Beverly Peele; but I suspect that we can't violate certain moral laws that heredity has made part of our brain fibre, without ultimate regret, even when we keep the world in ignorance. I suffered horribly once, although I had not defied the conventions. But I think we must have everything, or the large share of herself that Nature has given each of us rebels, — in other words, the ideal is not complete."

"When you are very much in love," he said dryly, "you won't analyse."

Contrary to her habit, she remained in the wood for some time after he left her. Suddenly she was aroused from her reverie by a peculiar heavy sound, as of a man crawling. She listened intently, her hair stiffening : the house was a quarter of a mile away. The sound continued steadily. She sprang to her feet and fled from the wood. As she ran up the hill beyond, she glanced fearfully over her shoulder. A man shot from the lower edge of the wood and ran toward the stables.

XVII

AN hour after midnight Patience ran into Honora's room and shook her violently.

"Honora ! Honora !" she cried, "something is the matter with Beverly. I can't wake him up."

.Honora stretched herself languidly. Her eyelids fluttered a moment, then lifted. She said sleepily :

"What is it, Patience ?"

"Beverly ! Go to him — quick — while I wake up Mr. and Mrs. Peele, and send for the doctor. He dropped his own morphine to-night, and he must have taken too much."

A few moments later there was an alarmed group of people at Beverly Peele's bedside, and the butler could be heard at the telephone demanding the doctor.

Mr. Peele was in his pyjamas, and Patience struggled with an importunate desire to tell him that his hair stood on end. Mrs. Peele's back hair was in a scant braid; the front locks were on pins. Her skin looked pallid and old. Honora, as usual, looked like a vision from heaven. Hal and her husband were in Newport, and there were no guests at Peele Manor.

"Are you sure," asked Mr. Peele, as precisely as if his hair was parted in the middle and plastered on each side, "that anything is the matter? Does not the morphine always put him to sleep?"

"Not at once. You see he takes it internally, and it's twenty minutes or half an hour before it takes effect. During that time he always groans, for he never takes it until the last minute. I heard him get up and return to bed; and then I knew something must be the matter because he was so quiet — "

"How could you let him drop it himself?" exclaimed Mrs. Peele, passionately. "How could you? What are you here for?"

"I offered to drop it for him, but he would n't let me. I did n't insist, as he always put it off — and we had had a quarrel — "

"My poor son!"

"Well, something's got to be done," said Mr. Peele. "I don't like the way he's beginning to breathe. There are one or two things we can do until the doctor comes."

He raised Beverly's arms above the head, brought them down and pressed them into the chest, repeating the act twenty or thirty times. Beverly meanwhile was breathing stertorously.

"Can't I do something?" cried his mother, distractedly.

"I think we had better walk him," said Mr. Peele, whose mouth was tightening. "Call Hickman."

The butler was waiting in the hall, and came at once. He helped Mr. Peele to lift the young man from the bed. The stalwart figure hung limply between them: he was as collapsed as the new dead. Mr. Peele and Hickman walked him up and down the long line of rooms, shaking him vigorously from time to time; but they would have produced as much effect upon the bolster. Mrs. Peele had sunk into a chair. She sat with compressed lips, and dilating eyes fixed upon Patience. Honora knelt beside her, patting her hand. After a time she arose, liberated Mrs. Peele's hair from its braid and steels, and arranged it with deft hands, fetching some of her own amber pins.

Patience sat on the edge of the bed. She was beginning to feel hopelessly sleepy. The day's excitement had sapped her nerves. It was now nearly two o'clock, and she had not slept. Beverly had been ill the night before and given her little rest. She felt bitterly ashamed of herself; but every few moments she was obliged to cover her face with her handkerchief to conceal a yawn. Once or twice her head dropped suddenly.

The last time she sat up with a gasp. Mrs. Peele groaned. The two men had entered with their burden. Beverly's face was blue, and he breathed infrequently.

"His body is bathed in a cold perspiration," said Mr. Peele. "Will that doctor never come?"

"O my God!" murmured Mrs. Peele.

Patience left the bed and sat on the sill of the window. The night was very hot and still. A shuddering horror took possession of her. A palpable presence seemed skimming the dark gulf under the window. She sat with distended eyes, half expecting to see a long arm reach past her and pluck the soul from the unconscious man on the bed. She closed her eyes and put her fingers in her ears. When she removed them she drew a long breath.

"The doctor is coming," she said. "I hear the wheels."

"Did you make him understand what was the matter?" asked Mr. Peele of the butler.

"Yes, sir. He said he would bring everything necessary."

When the doctor came in he bent over the sick man and lifted his eyelids.

"It is morphine poisoning, sure enough," he said. "Have some black coffee made. I shall use the electricity meanwhile. Better telegraph to New York. I don't like this case, and don't want it alone."

Patience watched them mechanically for an hour, then slipped into her own room and into her bed. Nature had conquered her. Another moment, and she would have fallen to the floor in sleep.

Four hours later she was awakened by a vigorous shaking of her shoulder.

She sat upright and glanced about wildly. "What is it? What is the matter?" she cried. "I had such a horrible dream. I thought Beverly was drowning me — holding me down under the water — "

"Your husband is dead," said the doctor. "Do you wish to go to him?"

Patience shrank under the bedclothes, pulling them about her head. After the doctor had gone she ran over to a spare room, opened all the windows to admit light, then went to bed and slept until late in the day.

BOOK V

BOOK V

I

THE editor-in-chief of the New York "Eye" sat in the large revolving-chair in his private room, dictating to a typewriter answers to the great pile of letters on the desk before him. He opened one letter after another with expert swiftness, glanced over it, gave it a few lines of response, or tossed it, half read, into a wastebasket. But although his heed to duty was alert, his brow was contracted, and he was carrying on a double train ot thought. The subconsciousness was not pleasant.

Arnold Sturges was one of the most remarkable men in New York. Not thirty-three, he had been editor-in-chief of one of the great newspapers of the United States for a year and a half. He had elected journalism as the safety-valve for a superabundant nervous energy and a means to gratify ambition and love of power. Although possessed of a little fortune he had begun his career on the city staff. As a reporter he had worked as hard as if twenty-five dollars a week stood between him and starvation. He had risen rapidly from one editorship to another, and still no half naked man down in the printing-rooms worked more lustily. His rushing career was by no means due to work alone, nor yet to his superlative cleverness: it was said of him that he could smell news a week off, and not only ahead but backward; by which was meant that he knew the subtle and valuable relation that old news occasionally holds to that of the moment. Naturally, he had made many brilliant and memorable coups.

When friends had blocked his way he had thrust them aside as lightly as he seemed to spurn less material obstacles. Body and brain he was the dauntless servant of the "Eye;" its personality was his; his very nerves were tuned to its sensational policy. He lived for it, and would have died for it. He hardly regarded himself as an individual, although his fine intellect, his bold executive ability, his splendid suggestions, had been large factors in the success of the paper.

Cold, cruel, charming, calculating, enthusiastic, audacious, unscrupulous, fearless, relentless, brilliant, executive, had he been a factor in the French Revolution his name would have become infamously immortal. As it was, he was supreme in the field he had deliberately chosen ten years before, immediately after graduating from Harvard with such honours that the faculty had sent for and severally congratulated him upon his future.

He lived with a soubrette with whom he spent his evenings, playing *parchisi*.

To-day he was in a serious quandary. Three days before he had paid fifteen hundred dollars for a scandalous story relative to one of the most fashionable families in Westchester County, — a story which bore truth on the face of it, but which he had not yet published, as it was necessary to go through the form of verification. The family meanwhile had heard of the sale, and brought tremendous pressure to bear upon him to suppress the story: the owner of the "Eye" was travelling in

Europe. Lawyers had called and harangued. A woman had gone to his apartment and wept at his feet. A man had flourished a pistol. For tears and threats he cared nothing, but it had occurred to him when too late that the owner of the "Eye" purposed to build in Westchester County and had aspirations to the Country Club. Despite the fact that the story would make the sensation of the day, the owner might be moved to fury. On the other hand, he had paid fifteen hundred dollars for the facts, and must justify himself. It was the first time in his career that he had made a serious mistake, and he was in a cold rage.

The man would have given pleasure to a physiognomist; he was a type so marked, so essentially modern, that an amateur could not have misplaced him, as one easily could so commonplace a type as Beverly Peele. His forehead was full and wide, his grey eyes piercing, restless, hard as ice. The nose was finely cut, the mouth licentious, the face thin and sallow. At each extremity of the jaw was an abnormal development of muscle. His small thin figure was as lithe as a panther, and so crowded with pure nerve force that it seemed to shed electricity. His attire was fashionable and elegant. In flannel shirt and overalls he would still have looked a product of the higher civilisation.

The door opened. He wheeled about with a frown, then smiled pleasantly.

"Oh, it's you, Van," he said. "I'll be through in a minute. Sit down."

The man that had entered bore so striking a resemblance to Sturges that the two men might have been twins. He was, in fact, three years younger than his brother. Yet there were some points of difference. Van

Cortlandt Sturges' mouth was a straight line, his hair
was many shades lighter, almost flaxen, and he was
several inches taller. But the expression of the upper
part of the two faces was identical. He, too, had left
Harvard with high honours, and ambition devoured him.
Although only thirty he was District Attorney of Westchester County. But as yet his fame had not gone
beyond its borders, although within them his dry
incisive bitter eloquence had carried many juries.
Criminals in their cells thought on him with terror. He
had sent several men to the chair, but no man that had
been defended by Garan Bourke. People said of him
lightly that he would not go out of his way to be President of the United States until he had thrashed Bourke
on his own ground.

"I 'd like ten minutes as soon as possible," he said.
"I have an important communication to make."

"I 'll hear it now."   To the typewriter : "You can
go.   Don't return until I ring, and tell Tom to stand
in front of the door and admit no one. — Well, what
is it ? "

"Have you made up your mind to publish that Westchester County scandal ? "

"How do you know anything about that ? "

"They sent for me yesterday and besought me to
use my influence with you. I am engaged to the
woman's sister."

"The devil you are ! This is bad — bad. But I
can't do anything. I paid fifteen hundred dollars for
that story."

"I know you did. If I could give you a better,
would you let that go ? "

"Would n't I ? It 's a white elephant. I thought

you did n't know me so little as to come here with
sentiment. Fire away."

"Of course you remember the Gardiner Peeles,
although you never go anywhere. You went to one or
two children's parties there when you were a kid.
Well, Beverly Peele died suddenly night before last,
supposedly of an overdose of morphine administered
by himself. Now, old Lewis, the family physician, is a
great friend of mine, and likely to be communicative in
his cups. Last night he dined with me, and after he
was pretty well loaded told me a remarkable yarn. It
seems that Mrs. Beverly had not been on good terms
with her husband since the early days of their marriage,
and had threatened to leave him from time to time.
He treated her well, and was desperately in love with
her. She, as far as is known, had nothing against him
but personal dislike. She is said to have frequently
expressed hatred of him in violent terms. Well, winter
before last she left him, came to New York, and went to
work on the ' Day.' The Peeles did everything to
induce her to return, but she only consented to go
back temporarily this summer to nurse her husband,
who had been attacked with a chronic but not immediately fatal complaint. Meanwhile it seems she had
fallen in love with some one, and she met him every
Thursday in a wood. Jim, a stable boy, who had been
brought up on the place and was devoted to Beverly
Peele, watched her, but said nothing to his master, as
he was cautiously waiting for some proof of criminality.
On the afternoon of Peele's death there was a tremendous scene between the lovers: young Mrs. Peele telling a furious story of her husband's refusal to give her
divorce, of his threat to have her watched, to expose

her if she took a lover, and to live until ninety if
he had to go abroad and live at a foreign spa. She
reiterated that she hated him, and had frequently had
the impulse to murder him. The lover invited her to
go to Texas, and she demurred, as she disliked scandal.
Jim told this story to Lewis when driving him home
from the death-bed, — his own horse had cast a shoe,
— and the doctor advised him to keep quiet.

"The night after the interview between the lovers — or
rather the following morning — Peele died of an overdose of morphine. She says he took it himself; but it
is a remarkable fact that never before — not in a single
instance — had he dropped the morphine himself. He
had had a nurse from the first, and when the pain was
on he shook like a leaf. And yet she asserts that she
did not drop it that particular night, and adds — by
way of explanation — that they had had a violent quarrel and he had refused to let her wait on him. While
he was dying and the others were working over him,
she behaved in the most heartless manner, — deliberately went to bed in the next room and went to sleep.
When Lewis awakened her, however, and told her that
Peele was dead, she displayed symptoms of abject
terror, and tore across the hall and locked herself in
another room. Now, what do you think of it?"

Sturges' eyes were glittering like smoked diamonds.
"My God!" he cried. "That's a grand story! a
corker! I'll have Bart Tripp, the best detective reporter in New York, up there inside of two hours.
Between whiskey and gold he'll get every fact out of
the servants they've got. It's worth two of the other.
A young, beautiful, swagger woman accused of murdering her husband, and that husband a Peele of Peele

Manor! The 'Eye' will be read in the very bowels of the earth."

" And I shall conduct the case for the prosecution."

" The 'Eye' will let people know it. Don't worry about that. Does Lewis remember that he told you? "

" Not a word."

II

On the following Sunday Patience arose early. Beverly had been in the family vault down in the hollow for a week. She had wished to leave immediately after the funeral, but had remained at the insistence of Hal, who had returned at once, and was doubly depressed by her brother's death and the gloomy house. Mrs. Peele had gone to bed with a violent attack of neuralgia some days ago, and had not risen since. Honora was in constant attendance. Mr. Peele never opened his lips except to ask for what he wanted. Burr, as a matter of course, spent the days in New York or at a private club house in the neighbourhood.

Patience had moved into a room adjoining Hal's. She kept the light burning all night.

" I 'll be all right when I get back to New York," she said, " but I have a horror of death. I can't help it."

"Who has n't? " asked Hal. " I wish I were a man — or could be as selfish as one."

On this Sunday morning Patience rose after a restless night, and went downstairs as soon as she was dressed. The " Day " and the " Eye " — Burr's favorite newspaper — lay on a table in the hall. She carried them into the library and turned them over listlessly, then remembered that a great Westchester County scandal had been promised for the Sunday "Eye" by the issue of the day before, and that Hal and Burr were on the alert, suspecting that they half knew the story already.

She opened the "Eye" and glanced at the headlines of the first page. In the place of honour, the extreme left hand column, she found her story:

WAS IT MURDER?

AN OLD MANOR HOUSE IN WESTCHESTER COUNTY MAY
HAVE BEEN THE THEATRE OF A GREAT CRIME!
A YOUNG WIFE SUSPECTED OF THE FOUL DEED!

Patience read ten lines. Then she stumbled to her feet, spilling the papers to the floor. Her skin felt cold and wet, her knees trembled, her hands moved spasmodically. Something within her seemed disintegrating.

She got to the door and up to her room. Aside from the horror which sat in each nerve centre and jabbered, she was conscious of but one idea: she must fly. She flung off her robe and put on the black frock she had bought out of deference to the family's grief. She scratched herself and thrust the buttons into the wrong holes, but she could call no one to her assistance. She was thankful it was so early; she could get away without encountering any of the family. She was about to put on her black bonnet when her muddled consciousness emitted another flash and bade her disguise herself; detectives would have orders to search for a woman in weeds. She tore off the mourning frock, dropping it to the floor, and got herself into a grey one, then pinned on a grey hat trimmed with pink flowers.

She thrust a few things into a bag, and ran down the stair. She reached the station in time to flag the 8.30 train for New York. Some one else boarded the same train, but she did not see him.

Having accomplished her flight, her thoughts travelled to the objective point. Inevitably her woman's instinct turned to the man whose duty it was to protect her. She convinced herself femininely that if she could reach him all would be well; he not only loved her, but he was so amazingly clever.

At the station in New York she walked deliberately to a cab and gave the man Morgan Steele's address. She looked neither to the right nor to the left, consequently did not see that the man who had boarded the train at Peele Manor stood at her elbow when she gave the order, and followed her immediately.

When the cab reached the house in which Morgan Steele lived, she dismissed it and ran up the steps. She rang again and again, pacing the narrow stoop in an agony of fear and impatience. At the end of ten minutes an irritable half dressed Frenchman came shuffling down the stairs. There were no curtains on the door, and the man's expression struck new terror to her heart.

"What is it?" he asked surlily, as he opened the door.

"I — I — must see Mr. Steele."

"Mr. Steele is asleep. He does not receive visitors at this hour."

"I must see him." Her cheeks were flaming under the man's scrutiny. "Here," she opened her purse and gave him a bill, then pushed him aside and ran upstairs. She remembered that Steele had told her

that his rooms were on the second floor, front. The
halls were as dark as midnight. She had to feel with
her hands for a door. There was one at the end
facing the hall. She knocked so loudly that Steele
sprang out of bed.

"What is it?" he cried.

"It is I. Open the door — quick!"

Steele made no reply until he opened a door at the
side of the hall. He had tied himself into a bath
robe.

"Good heavens!" he said, "why have you come
here? Are you mad?"

"Oh, I think I am. Lock the door — quick. Oh,
have n't you heard? Did n't you know about it before?
The 'Day' is right next door to the 'Eye.' Why
did n't you warn me?"

"What on earth are you talking about? What has
happened? Do sit down and calm yourself."

"The 'Eye' is out with a big story that I murdered
Beverly Peele. That is what is the matter."

"What? Oh, you poor child! The damned ras-
cals! But you should n't have come here. Don't you
know that the 'Eye' will watch every move you make?
It takes the clever woman to do the wrong thing, every
time!"

He went to the window and peered out, then clenched
his teeth, and raising his arm brought it down violently.

"They can't put me in prison, can they?"

He pressed his finger to a bell. "I must read what
they have to say. They are very wary, and never
would have printed such a story unless they had had a
good deal of circumstantial evidence. But they will
need a terrible lot to convict you. Don't worry."

"Oh, how can you be so cool?"

"Some one has to be cool, my dear girl. If you cannot think I must think for you." A man has not much sentiment at that hour of the morning; still, Steele had sympathy in his nature, and was profoundly disturbed.

The servant came up with the newspapers, and Steele ordered coffee and rolls from the restaurant below. He threw himself into a chair, opened the "Eye," and read the story through deliberately, word for word, while Patience walked nervously up and down the room. When he had finished he laid the newspaper on the table.

"It's a damned bad case," he said.

"You don't believe I did it, do you?"

He looked at her for a moment with his peculiarly searching gaze. "No," he said, "you didn't do it. You'd be even more interesting if you had. But that's not the question. We've got to make others believe you didn't do it. The first thing for you to do is to go directly back to Peele Manor. Tell them you came up to see Miss Merrien and to engage rooms. Anything you like — only go back there and wait. If you are arrested, it must be from there, and there must be no suggestion of fear on your part — you must brace up and carry it off."

The waiter entered with the coffee and rolls, and Steele made her drink and eat.

"It is 9.45," he said. "You can catch a train that goes between ten and eleven."

When Patience had finished she drew on her gloves. "I'll go," she said, "and I'll try to do as you say. I've made a fool of myself, but I won't again — I promise. I can be as cold as stone, you know. That's the New England part of me. And so long as I know that you care I sha'n't break down — in public at least."

"Oh, I care fast enough — poor little woman. Here, leave that bag, for heaven's sake. You must n't go back with that."

III

WHEN Patience arrived at Peele Manor she knew before she reached the house that her story had been read and told. The gardener turned on his heel as she passed him and walked hastily away. A new stable boy stared at her until she thought his eyes would fly from their sockets.

As she entered the front door, Hal ran forward and threw her arms about her.

"Oh, Patience! Patience!" she sobbed hysterically. "That brutal paper! How could they do such a thing? Have they no heart nor soul?"

"You don't believe it then?" said Patience, gratefully.

"Of course I don't believe it — believe such a thing of *you!* Oh, I'm so glad you've come back. They were all sure you'd run away; but I knew you had n't. It is only the guilty that hide — But why on earth did you put on that grey frock?"

"Oh, I don't know. How can one know what one's doing — What does your father say?"

The girls were in one of the small reception-rooms. Hal removed Patience's hat and gloves.

"Oh, this has been the most terrible day of my life," she said evasively. "But you must be prudent, Patience dear. You must wear black — What is it?"

A servant had entered the room.

"Mr. Peele would like to see Mrs. Beverly in the library!"

Patience rose and shook herself a little, as if she would shake her nerves into place. Hal's face flushed, and she turned away.

As Patience crossed the hall she met Latimer Burr. He held out his hand and pressed hers warmly.

"This is terrible, Patience," he said; "but remember that Hal and I are always your friends. If the worst comes to the worst I'll send you my attorney. Remember that, and don't engage any one else, for he's one of the ablest criminal lawyers in the country."

"Oh, you are good!" she said. She smiled even through the grateful tears which sprang to her eyes. Burr had grown a visible inch. His chest and lips were slightly extended.

Mr. Peele sat in a large chair, his elbows on the arms, his finger-tips lightly pressed together. As Patience stood before him she felt as if transfixed by two steel lances.

"You murdered my son."

"I did not." Her courage came back to her under the overt attack.

"You murdered my son. The evidence is conclusive to me as a lawyer — and to my knowledge of you. My error was that I regarded your threats as feminine ravings. I wish you to leave my house at once — within the hour. I shall not have you arrested, but if you are I shall appear against you; and I have some

25

evidence, as you will admit. You have dishonoured an ancient house," he continued with cold passion, "and you have left it without an heir. Its name, after nearly three hundred years in this country alone, must die with me. If you had borne a son I should move heaven and earth to get you out of the country, but now I hope to heaven you 'll go to the chair."

Patience shuddered and chilled, but she answered: "You despised your son, and you should be thankful that he left no second edition of himself."

"He was my son, and the last of his name. Now, kindly leave this house."

Patience went up to her room and began to pack her trunk. Hal followed, and when she heard what her father had said cried bitterly. She helped Patience to pack, assisted her into the black clothes, then walked to the station with her and stood conspicuously on the platform, waving her hand as the train moved off.

IV

PATIENCE went directly to her old quarters in Forty-Fourth Street. She told the cabman not to lift her trunk down until she ascertained if there was a vacant room in the house. The bell was answered by a maid that had been there in her time. The girl stifled a scream and fled. Patience shut the door behind her with a hand that trembled again, and went slowly upstairs to Miss Merrien's room. A solemn voice answered her knock. When she opened the door Miss

Merrien sprang up and came forward. Her face was drawn, her eyes were red.

"Oh, Mrs. Peele!" she cried.

"Do you believe it? If you do, I'll go at once."

"Of course I don't believe it! How can you ask me? Sit down. How good of you to come here. Tell me — are you terribly frightened?"

"No, I don't think I am now. Why should I be? If I am so unlucky as to have been tossed up in the news hat of the 'Eye,' I cannot help it; and I suppose this is only the beginning. If I have to go to jail I have to, and that is the end of it; but they cannot possibly convict me, for I am innocent."

"Oh, you always were the bravest woman I ever knew. It is like you — Come."

The door opened, and the landlady entered and closed it carefully behind her. She was a tall thin elderly woman with a refined face stamped with commercial unquiet. Her grey hair was piled high. Her voice was low, and well modulated. She looked at Patience out of faded blue eyes in which there was a faint sparkle of resentment.

"I see that you have a trunk on your cab, Mrs. Peele," she said, "I am very sorry that I have no room."

"I had no intention of asking you for a room," said Patience, haughtily. "I merely came to call on Miss Merrien; and as I have only a few moments to spare, I should be obliged if you would leave us alone."

The landlady retired in disorder, and Miss Merrien exhausted her vocabulary of invective.

"What is the use?" said Patience. "She is right. In the struggle for bread and butter it must be self first,

last, and always.   If it were known — as it would be —
that I had been arrested from her house every other
lodger would leave.   Well, I must go roof-hunting."
She laughed suddenly.   "If I do go to jail I suppose
you'll come to interview me.   I hope so.   Good-bye."

Miss Merrien, although not a demonstrative girl,
kissed her affectionately.   "The 'Day' will defend you
for all it's worth — you know that.   And I need n't say
anything about myself."

Patience told her cabman to drive to the Holland
House, but when he stopped there she did not get out.
Reflection had convinced her that no hotel in New
York would take her in.   She dared not give a false
name lest her motive should be misconstrued.   She
put her head out of the window and gave the man
Rosita's address.

"There is no other way," she thought.   "I cannot
live in a cab.   Mrs. Field would take me in, but I
have no right to make such a test of friendship as
that."

Rosita received her with open arms.   She was looking very beautiful in flowing nainsook and lace, and ex-
haled a new and delicious perfume.

"Patita! Patita *mia!*" she purred.   "*Pobrecita!*
Who would have thought that this would happen to my
lili."   (Her accent was more pronounced than ever.)

"Can I stay with you until they arrest me, or this
blows over?"

"You shall stay with me forever.   'Are we not bound
by the ties of childhood?'   That is a line in my new
opera.   Is n't it funny?   Ay, Patita, I am so sorry."
And she sent down for the trunk and removed Patience's hat.

V

THE next morning Patience was awakened by Rosita's ecstatic voice. She opened her eyes to see her hostess standing at the bedside, the "Eye" in her hand, her face radiant.

"Patita!" she cried. "Read it — there is a whole column about you and me."

Patience sat up in bed. "Is that why you were so glad to have me come here?" she asked.

"Patita! Do not look at me like that. Oh, if I could only look that way when I am stage mad! — but they always say I look like an angry baby. Of course, that was not the reason, Patita *mia;* but it is heavenly to be written about; do not you think so? And, of course, every new story about me — and such a sensation as this — means a perfect rush — "

"Give me the paper, please."

She read the column while Rosita pattered back to her room and ate her dainty breakfast. Every move she had made on the day before was chronicled. On another page an editorial commented on the facts of her having visited a young man's apartment, and finally taken refuge with the notorious Spanish woman.

She dressed herself hastily in her black garments, and locked and strapped her trunk. "I'll go straight down and give myself up," she thought. "It's what I ought to have done yesterday. It's eleven o'clock. I wish it were nine. Come."

"Two gentlemen to see madame," said the maid.

"What — who — what do they look like?"

" Like policemen, and yet not, madame."

Patience gasped. Her knees gave way. Again she experienced that horrible feeling of disintegration. Her untasted breakfast stood on a table by the bed. She hastily drank a cup of black coffee, then walked steadily to the drawing-room.

" You have come for me?" she asked of the men.

" Yes, ma'am."

" Where am I to go?"

" To the jail at White Plains, Westchester County. You are arrested on charge of murder;" and he displayed the warrant.

Patience touched the bell button. " Take my trunk downstairs to the cab," she said to the butler. Then she stepped to the portières and said good-bye to Rosita.

" She's a cool one," said one man to the other. " She done it."

They went down in the elevator. As they left it, one of the men preceded her, the other followed close. Both entered the cab with her. She felt that they were regarding her with the frank curiosity of their kind, and kept her eyes fixed on the street with an expressionless stare. On the train they gave her a seat to herself, each taking the outside of another, one before and one behind. The passengers did not suspect the meaning of the party. She saw no one she knew. It was not the line that passed Peele Manor. For small mercies she was duly thankful. She guessed, however, that a meagre wiry black-eyed young man on the opposite side of the aisle, a man with a mean sharp common face, was Bart Tripp. He stared at her until she thought she should scream aloud, or, what would be almost as fatal, relax the proud calm of her face. It was with a sigh of profound relief that she stepped from the train at White Plains.

"We won't meet no one," said one of the detectives, as they entered the hack. "The sheriff's got ready for you, I guess; he was wired yesterday; but we took good care not to say what train we was coming on, so there would n't be no crowd. Feeling's pretty high against you, I guess."

As they drove through the ugly little town, Patience wondered why it was called White Plains. She had never seen a more undulating country. One or two of the environing hills were almost perpendicular. She also noticed with the minute observance of persons approaching crises, that the court house was a big handsome building of grey stone, and decided that she liked its architecture. The extension behind, one of the keepers told her, was the jail.

She was escorted before a police justice, who read the charge and explained such privileges as the law allowed her; then to the sheriff's office, where she was registered. A crowd of men were in the office. They watched her with deep but respectful attention, as she answered the many questions put to her, but she managed to maintain her impassive demeanour. There was a buzz of excitement by this time all through the court house, and a little of it began to communicate itself to her. The few that are sustained through life's trials by public interest are immeasurably fortunate. Before the sheriff — who could not have treated her with more consideration were she a dethroned queen — had finished, word had gone up into the court room, and a sudden trampling on the back stair indicated that the case in hand had lost its interest.

"That's all," said the sheriff, hurriedly. "Guess you'd better get along. — Tarbox," he called.

A short stout man with a ruddy kind face came forward, offered Patience his arm, pushed his way through the crowd of men in the hall, and led her out of a back door and down a long yard beside the jail. At the end of the building he inserted a key in a lock.

"Go right up, ma'am," he said politely, and she ascended a narrow flight of stairs. At its head he unlocked another door, and again they ascended, again a door was unlocked. Then Patience stepped into a long low clean well-lighted room. In the middle of its length was a stove over which a kettle boiled. On a bench sat four women. At each end and on one side were low grated windows. On the other side were a number of grated doors.

The man led Patience to the upper end of the room and swung open the door of the corner cell. It was a large cell, and had it not been for the low window with its iron bars would have been in no wise different from any room of simple comfort. A red carpet covered the floor. The bed in the corner was fresh and spotless. The rest of the furniture was new and convenient. There were even a large rocker and a student's lamp. Over the door a curtain had been hung.

"Why!" exclaimed Patience, "are all prison cells like this?"

"No, ma'am, they're not; but you see when we have a lady — which is n't often — we do what we can to make her feel at home. We can't afford to forget that this is the swell county of New York, you know. And of course you're the finest person we've ever had. You'll be treated well here, — you need n't worry about that. I 'll order one of them girls outside to wait on you."

"You are very good." For the first time tears threatened.

"Well, I 'll try to be to you, ma'am. I 'm John Tarbox, deputy sheriff, jailor, warden, and all the rest of it. I shall look after you. I 'll call twice a day, and anything you want you 'll get. If any of them hussies out there get to fighting just sing out the window, and I 'll lock them up."

"You won't lock me in?"

"Oh, no — there 's no need for that. This cell 's no stronger than the whole place. Well, make yourself comfortable. I 'll send over to the hotel to get a lunch for you. You must be hungry. Keep a stiff upper lip."

Patience, when she was alone, drew a long breath and looked about her. The cheerful room, the unexpected kindness of the sheriffs, had raised her spirits. She took off her hat and tossed it on the bed.

"I may as well take the situation humourously," she thought. "It helps more than anything else in life, I 've discovered. This can't last forever, and they can't convict me. The serious people of this world have always struck me as being the most farcical. So here goes my ninth or tenth lesson in philosophy. Such is life."

After luncheon Mag, the improvised maid, unpacked the trunk and shook out the pretty garments with many expressions of rapture. Patience gave her a red frock, and the girl was her slave thenceforth.

The afternoon hours revolved like a clogged wheel in a muddy stream. Excitement and novelty kept horror at bay, but she knew that it lurked, biding its time.

When night came she lit the lamp and tried to read a magazine that Tarbox had brought her; but it fell from her hands again and again. Her ears acted independently of her will. She had never known so terrible a stillness. The women had gone to bed at half past seven. No voice came from the distant street. The silence of eternity seemed to have descended upon those massive walls.

She was in jail!

She sprang to her feet, shuddering; then set her teeth and knelt by the window.

The heat waves of August hid the stars. Beyond the jail-yard was a mass of buildings, but no light in any window. Now and again a tramp came forth from his quarters on the ground floor and strolled about the yard, smoking his pipe; but he made no sound, and in his grey dilapidation looked like a parodied ghost. One of the women cursed loudly in her sleep, then collapsed into silence. An engine whistle shrieked, hilarious with freedom, but the rattle of the train was too distant to carry to straining ears.

She clutched the bars and shook them, then crouched, trembling and gasping. She dropped forward, resting her face on her arms. Her fine courage retreated, and mocked her. She had no wish to recall it. She longed passionately for the strong arm and the strong soul of a man. The independence and self-reliance which Circumstance had implanted, seemed to fade out of her; she was woman symbolised. No shipwrecked mariner was ever so desolate; for nothing in all life is so tragic as a woman forced to stand and do battle alone.

It was only when she arose, shivering and exhausted, and groped her way to bed, that it occurred to her that in those appalling moments she had not thought of Morgan Steele.

VI

IN the morning she awoke with a start and a chill, and sprang out of bed, governed by an impulse to fling her-self against the bars. But sleep had refreshed her, and she sat down and reasoned herself into courage and hope once more. The tussle with the world develops the iron in a woman's blood, and Patience's experi-ences of the last year and a half stood her in good stead now. When the girl came in to arrange her room and Tarbox brought her breakfast, the common-place details completed her poise. The morning mail brought her letters from Steele and Hal.

DEAR GIRL [Steele's ran], — You are blue and fright-ened and lonesome. I wish I were there to cheer you up. But the first day will be the worst. Remember that liberty is not far off. They cannot convict you. I shall see you a few hours after you get this.

M. S.

Oh, Patience dear [Hal had written], it has come! I wish I could tell you how terribly I feel. But cheer up, old girl. It will come out all right — I know it will. Latimer is hustling me out of the country so I cannot appear as a witness — he says I would do you more harm than good. But he will stay and see you through. His attorney will call on you at once. I send you a box to cheer you up a little. Do write to me, and always remember that I am your sister   HAL.

The box arrived an hour later. It contained her silver toilet-set, and all the paraphernalia of a well-groomed and pretty woman, a bottle of cologne, a box of candy, eight French novels, a large box of handsome writing paper, and a bolt of black satin ribbon. Patience arranged the toilet-set on the bureau, halved the candy with the women, then sat down with a volume of Bourget. When Tarbox came up an hour later with a card she was still reading, and quite herself.

" Well," he said, " I'm glad, I am, to see you so contented and so cool," he added, mopping his brow. " This gent is below. He says he's one of the lawyers in the case. I hoped you'd have Bourke. He's the smartest man in Westchester County ! Shall I tell him to come up, or would you like to see him down in the sheriff's office ? Anything to please you."

" Oh, here, by all means, if he does n't mind the stairs."

Tarbox gazed at her admiringly. " Well, ma'am," he ejaculated, " you are cool, but I for one believe it 's the coolness of innocence. You never did murder ! " and he walked hastily away as if ashamed of his enthusiasm.

The lawyer's card bore the name of Eugene A. Simms. He came up at once, a short thick-set man of thirty, with a square shrewd dogged face, a low brow, a snub nose, and black brilliant hard eyes. He came in with a bustling aggressive business-like air, scanning Patience as if he expected to find all the points of the case written upon her. Patience conceived an immediate and violent dislike to him.

" Will you sit down ? " she said stiffly. " You are Mr. Burr's lawyer, I believe."

" Oh, no. That 's Bourke. He has charge of the

case. I'm getting it up. I shall attend the coroner's inquest and get the case in shape for Mr. Bourke to conduct."

The blood rose to Patience's hair and receded to her heart, which changed its time; but she asked no questions.

Simms leaned forward and fixed her with his unpleasant eyes. "Be perfectly frank with me," he said, abruptly. "It's best. We can't work in the dark. We'll pull you through; that's what we are here for."

"You take it for granted that I am guilty, I suppose?"

"I'm bound to say that all the revealed facts point that way. But of course that makes no difference to us. In fact, the harder a case is the better Bourke likes it —"

"Does Mr. Bourke believe that I am guilty?"

"I haven't discussed it with him. He merely called me in, put the facts in my hands, and told me to go to work. I haven't seen him since."

"I will be perfectly frank with you," said Patience, who had recovered herself. "I did not murder Mr. Peele. I am not wholly an idiot. If I had wished to poison him do you suppose I would have selected the drug I was known to administer?"

"You might have done it in a moment of passion. You had had a quarrel with him that night."

"So much the more reason why I would not make such a fatal mistake. It is quite true that when in a passion I frequently expressed the wish to kill him. I will also tell you that one night when dropping the morphine I was seized with an uncontrollable impulse to give him a double dose. I dropped twenty-six drops. But fortunately it takes some time to do that, and meanwhile the impulse weakened, and I anathematised myself as a fool. No man nor woman of respectable brains ever made a mistake like that."

" What is your own theory?"

" I hardly believe that he committed suicide. I think that he was wild with pain, and did not count the drops. He was probably half blind. On the other hand, he was capable of anything when in a rage."

Mr. Simms scraped the floor with his boot-heels and beat a tattoo on his knee with his fingers. " Very well," he said at last. " We take your word, of course. Now tell me as nearly as you can, every circumstance of that night, and give me a general idea of your relations with him and your reasons for leaving him. It is going to be one of the biggest fights this State has ever seen, and we want all the help you can give us."

After he had gone Patience fell into a rage. Why had not Bourke come himself instead of sending his underling? If he hesitated to meet her after the abominable words he had used that second night at Peele Manor why had he undertaken her case at all? Her pride revolted at the thought of being defended by him, of owing her life to him. Once she was at the point of writing him a haughty note declining to accept his services; but Latimer Burr's kindness deserved a more gracious acknowledgment. Again, she took up her pen to inform him that unless he apologised he must understand that she could have no relations with him; but her lively fear of making herself ridiculous came to the rescue, and she threw the pen aside. She resumed her novel, but it had lost its flavour. Bourke's face was on every page. The interview in the elm walk wrote itself between the French lines; and the subsequent conversation in the library danced in letters of red. She hated Bourke the more bitterly because he had once been something more to her than any other man had been. She worked herself into such a bad humour that she almost snubbed Miss Merrien and a "Day" artist who came to interview and sketch her; and when Morgan Steele arrived, late in the afternoon, she was as perverse and unreasonable as if the widowed châtelaine of Peele Manor with the world at her feet. He understood her mood perfectly, although not the cause of it, and guyed her into good humour and her native sense of the ridiculous.

"Oh, I do like you," she said. "You understand me so. Any other man would go off in a huff. And I won't always be like this. I suppose I am nervous and upset and all the rest of it. Who wouldn't be? And you know I am tremendously fond of you."

"I know you are," he said dryly. "As you will have ample time for reflection and meditation in the next few months, you will find out just how fond. But I am more glad than I can say to find you in this mood. It is as healthy as irritability in illness. I am even willing to be sacrificed."

Patience put out her hand and patted his soft hair with a spasm of genuine affection. "You are the dearest boy in the world," she said, "and I do love you. For all your uncanny wisdom and cold-blooded philosophy you are just a big lovable good-natured boy."

"Just the kind of fellow a woman would like to have for a brother, in short."

"No! No! I think it will be the most charming thing in the world to be married to you. You are such a compound. You will interest me forever. Most people are such bores after a little."

"If you had n't started out in life with ideas upside-down, you would really love me in loving me no more than you do now. But ideals and the fixed idea have got to be·worked out to the bitter end, as you are fond of remarking. In reality, happiness means a comfortable state of affairs between a man and a woman with plenty of brains, philosophy, and passion, who are wholly congenial in these three matters, and have chucked their illusions overboard. However, we won't discuss the matter any further at present. How do you like being the sensation of the day?"

"Am I?"

"Are you? Every newspaper in town had a big story this morning, and of course the news has gone all over the country. Nothing else is to be heard in the trains or in Park Row. Oh, you will have plenty to sustain you. Lots of women would give their heads to be in your place."

He dined with her and remained until eight o'clock. After he had gone, Patience sat for some time lost in a pleasurable reverie. He always left her in a good humour, and she unquestionably loved him. Few women could help loving Morgan Steele. She sighed once as she reflected that love was not the tremendous passion she had once imagined it to be; in all her dreams she had never pictured it as a restful and tranquillising element; but she conceded that Steele's philosophy was correct.

And if he did not inspire her with a mightier passion it was her fault, not his. Miss Merrien had told her of one brilliant newspaper woman who had made a wilful idiot of herself on his behalf, and of a popular and gifted actress who at one time had taken to haunting the "Day" office, much to the enjoyment of his fellow editors and to his own futile wrath.

"No," she thought, "I made a mistake once, and the shock was so great that it either benumbed or stunted me; or else the imaginary me was killed and the real developed. And after such a marriage I doubt if there are depths or heights left in one's nature."

Then her mind drifted to her predicament, and she wondered that the workings of fear had so wholly ceased. "I suppose it is because that man is going to defend me," she said, ruthlessly, at last. "They say he could save a man that had been caught driving a knife into another man's heart with a hammer; so it is quite natural that I should feel safe."

VII

THE next day a box of books and periodicals arrived from Steele. Rosita thoughtfully subscribed to a clipping bureau, and sent Patience daily a heavy package of "stories," editorials, and telegrams of which she was the heroine. Patience became so bewildered over the contradictory descriptions of her personal appearance, the various versions of her marital drama, the hundred and one theories for the murder and defence, the ingenious analyses of her character, and the conflicting information regarding her girlhood, that she wondered sometimes if a person could come forth from the hands of so many creators and retain any original birthmarks.

26

The "Eye" telegraphed to its correspondent in San Francisco to investigate her childhood, and the correspondent evidently interviewed all her old enemies. Her mother's happy career was detailed with glee, and her own "sulky, moody, eccentric, murderous propensities" were brilliantly epitomised. The story was entitled "She Tried To Murder Her Mother," and the "Eye's" perfervid joy at this discovery throbbed in an editorial.

The story was copied the length and breadth of the United States; but it is only fair to add that Mr. Field's eloquent leaders in her defence were as widely quoted.

Miss Beale came to see her at once, and after a few tears and an emphatic warning that "this terrible ordeal was the logical punishment of her blasphemy of and disrespect to the Lord," announced her intention to sit by her during the trial, and let the jury see what a president of the W. C. T. U. thought of a prisoner whose life was in their hands. Patience told her that she loved her, and indeed was deeply grateful.

She spent her mornings reading the newspapers and attending to her correspondence. Tarbox always paid her a short call, and usually discoursed of Garan Bourke, whom he admired extravagantly. For a half hour before luncheon she permitted her fellow prisoners to sit before her in a wondering semi-circle while she manicured her nails and drew vivid word-pictures of the superior comforts incident upon the resignation of alcohol. With the exception of Mag they were weatherbeaten creatures, with hollow eyes and weak pathetic mouths. They admired Patience superlatively. She was touched by their devotion, and occasionally read them the funny stories in the illustrated weeklies. They listened with open mouth and voiceless laughter, which, however, expressed itself vocally when the stories were told in Irish or German dialect. Patience gave them the papers, and they pasted the pictures on the walls of the corridor. Never before had the female ward of the White Plains Jail presented so festive an appearance. When the W. C. T. U. ladies came to sing to the prisoners they were inclined to be horrified; but Patience assured them that love of art, however manifested, was a hopeful sign.

She was very comfortable. She had saved a thousand dollars, — to be exact, Miss Merrien had saved them for her, — and she could command all the small' luxuries of prison life. The ugly walls of her cell had been draped with red cloth, and a low bookcase was rapidly filling with the literature of the moment. She would never have consented to save those thousand dollars had not Miss Merrien represented that by judicious economy she could manage to spend every third year abroad. They did her good service now; she could accept great favours, but not small ones. Graceful tributes were to be expected by every charming woman; but if she had been dependent upon friends for the small comforts of her daily life she would have gone without them.

The W's and Y's of Mariaville forgave her, and brought her flowers, tracts, and spiritual admonitions. She received the former with gratitude and the latter with grace. Miss Merrien came as often as her duties permitted, and so did all the other newspaper women she had ever known or heard of. She was interviewed for nearly every newspaper in the Union, and in most cases treated with sensational kindness. Many strangers and a few old friends called.

Steele came regularly once a week. He dared not come oftener. The "lover in the case" was still a mystery, and it was as well that he should remain so. Five other newspaper men lived in his house; therefore Patience's visit had told Bart Tripp nothing beyond the fact that she had indubitably called on a young man at his apartments at a quarter past nine in the morning.

But despite the fact that much of her time was occupied Patience grew very restless and nervous, after the novelty wore off. She spent hours pacing up and down the corridor, and every evening after dark Tarbox took her out in the jail-yard for a walk; but she had been used to long walks and hours in the open air all her life, and no woman ever lived less suited to routine and restraint of any sort. Fear did not return, although the coroner's jury had pronounced her guilty and she had been indicted by the Grand Jury.

VIII

WHEN the dark days of winter came little light struggled through the low grating, and she was obliged to keep her lamp burning most of the time. Steele sent her one with a rose-coloured shade which shed a cheerful light but hurt her eyes. When the storms began visitors came infrequently. Moreover, as public interest cannot be kept at concert pitch for any length of time, there was less and less about her in the newspapers. Steele, who understood the intimate relationship between public interest and the resignation of a prisoner, assured her that when her trial came off in March she would once more be the popular news of the day.

At first the monotony of the long silent winter days was intolerable. But gradually, by such short degrees, that she hardly realised the change taking place within, her, she grew to love her solitude and to be grateful for it. For the first time since she had left Monterey her hours were absolutely her own. She had longed for the solitude of a forested mountain top. From her prison window she could see the naked tops of a clump of trees above the buildings opposite, and even her obedient imagination could not expand them to primeval heights; but at least she had solitude and not a petty detail to annoy her.

She sometimes wondered if it mattered where one spent the few years of this unsatisfactory life. Nothing was of permanent satisfaction. Strongly as she had been infatuated with newspaper work the interest would have lasted only just so long. She found her modernity slipping from her, herself relapsing into the dreaming child of the tower with vague desire for something her varied experience of the world had not helped her to find. Inevitably she came to know herself and the large demands of her nature, and as inevitably she said to Morgan Steele one day, —

" I think you have known all along that it was a mistake."

" Yes," he said, " I have known it."

" You have everything — everything, — good looks and distinction, brains and modernity, magnetism of a queer cold sort, knowledge of women and kindness of heart — I cannot understand. But the spark, the response, the exaltation is not there, — the splendid rush of emotion. I love you, but not in the way that makes matrimony marriage."

He looked at her with his peculiar smile, an expansion of one corner of his mouth which gave him something of the expression of a satyr. "You were badly in need of a companion, and you found one in me. You wanted to be understood, and I understood you. You wanted sympathy, and I sympathised with you; but I am not the man, and I have never for one moment deluded myself."

"Then why would you have allowed me to drift into matrimony with you? — as I should have done if I had not come here."

"Because the experiment would have been no more dangerous than most matrimonial experiments. And it would have been very delightful for a time."

"I should have loved you a good deal," she said musingly, "and habit is a tremendous force. And I should never have permitted myself to recognise a mistake again — if the decisive step had been taken. Tell me — " she added abruptly, "do you believe that if I had married you that you would always have loved me?"

"I certainly should never have been so unwise as to promise to, for that is something no man can foretell. The chances are that I should not. All phases of feeling are temporary, — all emotions, all desires, all fulfilment. Life itself is temporary."

"Should you have been true to me?"

"O–h–h, how in thunder can a man answer a question like that? That is something he never knows till the time comes. If he is sensible he wastes no time making resolutions, and if he is honest he makes no promises."

"You do not love me," she exclaimed triumphantly.

"I am merely more honest, perhaps more analytical than most men, — that is all. The man who swears he will love forever the woman that pleases him most is simply talking from the depths of ignorance straight up through his hat. No man knows anything — what he will do or feel to-morrow. He knows nothing of himself until his time comes to die, and then he knows blamed little."

Patience shook her head. "I don't know. You may be right in the analysis, but I think you lose a good deal. Love may be a species of insanity, but the man whose brain is crystal is not to be envied by the man whose brain can scorch reason and thought at times. You may save yourself heartbreak, but you miss heaven. If you are a type of the future, woman will change too. Man has been at woman's feet throughout the centuries. You and your kind will place her on an exact level with yourselves and teach her that love means a comfortable coupling of personalities. Something primitive has gone out of you. You have every ingredient in your make-up except love. Liking and passion don't make love. When it fades out of man altogether chivalry and homage will go with it. You would do a great deal for me, but you are incapable of any splendid self-sacrifice. You are entirely selfish, although in the most charming way."

"You are quite right," he said smiling, "I have not much love in me ; just enough to make life a comfortable and pleasant sojourn, but not enough to induce a regret were I obliged to toss it over to-morrow — "

" Nor to make it a life of bitter misery did I leave it."

" No — to be perfectly frank I should not be bitterly miserable. I should regret — but I should work and readjust myself. I have never yet given a glance to the past. I give few to the future. No man gets more out of the present — "

" I won't be loved like that," said Patience, passionately.

He leaned forward and took her hand, patting it gently. " You have depths and heights in your nature which I fully appreciate but which I could never stir nor satisfy," he said. "Some man will. It won't be all that you expect — you have too much imagination — but you will have your day. With your nature that is inevitable. I am sorry to give you up. You are the most delightful woman I shall ever know. And if you had married me things would probably have gone along satisfactorily enough. I should have kept your mind occupied and talked to you about yourself — those are the secrets of success in matrimony."

" Marriage with you would be like playing at matrimony. I want a home and husband and children. I have seen enough to know that unless one is a fanatic like Miss Tremont or Miss Beale, or the temporary result of a new and forced civilisation like Hal, or a mercenary wanton like Rosita — in short, if one is woman *par excellence*, and most of us, clever or otherwise, even gifted, usually are, nothing else is worth the toil and perplexity of being alive. But you mustn't leave me," she added hurriedly ; " I can't stand it here if you don't come to see me."

" I shall come exactly as I have done. Why not?

Our love-making has barely progressed beyond friend-ship : we shall hardly recognise any change. I should feel lost if I could not have a talk with you once in a while. I intend to have that for the rest of my life. It isn't usually the man that proposes the brother racket, but I merely define the basis upon which we have really stood all along."

After he had gone Patience drew a long sigh of relief. The first terrible mistake of her life was buried with Beverly Peele. A second had been averted. Something seemed rebuilding within her: the unde-flected continuation of the little girl in the tower. For the first time she understood herself as absolutely as mortal can ; and she paid a tribute to the zigzag of life which had helped her to that final understanding.

IX

On the third of February she received a letter, the handwriting of whose address made her change colour : she had seen it once on Mrs. Peele's desk. It was the first communication of any sort that she had received from the man who was to defend her life. She opened the letter with angry curiosity.

MY DEAR MRS. PEELE, [it read], —You will pardon me I am sure for not having called before this when I tell you that I have had a rush of civil cases which have hardly given me time for sleep and have kept me constantly in New York. And of course you have understood that there was really nothing I could do until my able confederate,

Mr. Simms, had gathered in and digested all the facts in the case. Now, however, I am free, and the time has come when I shall be obliged to see you twice a week until the first of March. I have worked the harder in order to be at liberty to devote myself wholly to your case. Need I add how absolute that devotion will be, my dear Mrs. Peele, or how entirely every resource I possess shall be at your service?

At two o'clock on Monday I shall be in the sheriff's private office with Mr. Simms and my assistant, Mr. Lansing. Will you kindly meet us there?

With highest regard, I am, dear Mrs. Peele,

Yours faithfully,

GARAN BOURKE.

Patience read this carefully worded epistle twice, then laughed and shrugged her shoulders.

"I am glad he has declared himself," she thought. "Of course I should have ignored the past, but it is a relief to think that there will be no awkwardness."

X

ON Monday at two o'clock Tarbox came up to her cell to escort her down to the sheriff's office.

"Bourke's there, and I never saw him looking better," he said, rubbing his hands. "Oh, he'll pull you through. Don't you worry."

Patience was very nervous, but her years of self-repression and her experience at Peele Manor had forged a key with which she could at times lock nerve and muscle into subjection. As she entered the sheriff's office she smiled upon Mr. Bourke as graciously as any young and beautiful woman would be expected to smile upon a great lawyer enlisted in her service.

Bourke came forward with the same ballast, although the red was in his face.

"It was better for you to come down here," he said. "There could be no privacy in your cell, and we must have absolute privacy for these meetings. Of course you know that we are going to rehearse you. Mrs. Peele, this is my assistant, Mr. Lansing." He indicated a good-looking well-dressed young fellow, with boyish blue eyes and a tilted nose. She liked him at once and gave him her hand. Mr. Simms had risen as she entered, and they had nodded distantly.

"Take this chair, Mrs. Peele," continued Bourke. "Yes. This is the first of many rehearsals. We shall keep them up until the trial. You will imagine yourself on the witness stand. Mr. Simms, whom, fortunately, you don't like, is the district attorney, Lansing is the judge, I am the counsel for the defence. I shall make the direct examination, and then Mr. Simms will cross-examine you with all the subtlety, the venom, and the irritating minutiæ of a district attorney determined to make himself immortal. I think we have outlined with reasonable completeness all that will or can be asked you, so that you can hardly be taken off your guard : you must be prepared to give direct answers without suspicious promptness, and avoid saying anything that could be misconstrued."

"Must I go on the stand?" asked Patience, fearfully. "I thought one was not obliged to, and I shall be so nervous."

Bourke shook his head emphatically. "The judge might reiterate a hundred times to the jury that your failure to go on the witness stand should not be counted against you, and still it would count — more than anything. It is something a jury never overlooks. These rehearsals are to keep you from being nervous, as much as anything else."

" Do you believe I am innocent?" asked Patience, giving way to an uncontrollable impulse.

" I do — both personally and professionally."

Simms laughed. " Bourke is so enthusiastic," he said, " that if he had made up his professional mind that you were innocent, the personal would follow suit."

" No, but I do," said Bourke, laughing, and looking at Patience with eyes which for the moment were more kind than keen. " Now, here goes."

When the two hours' rehearsal were over she was very pale. " I did not know the case could look so black," she said.

" It is a black case," said Simms.

" Do you really take so much interest?" she asked Bourke, curiously. " You make me feel as if the issue were yours and not mine. Or is that only your professional pride ? "

" Bourke is the most ambitious man at the New York bar," said Simms.

" And the most human," added Lansing.

Patience smiled at the young man and turned to Bourke, whose eyes were twinkling. " I take a very deep personal interest in your case," he said gallantly.

" Bourke is an Irishman," said Simms, with sarcasm.

" We 'll excuse you," said Bourke. " You know you have business with Sturges," and Simms gathered up his papers and retired, followed by Lansing. As the door closed Bourke's face changed. He became serious at once.

"Mrs. Peele," he said, "it would be foolish and unkind to conceal from you the fact that you are in a very grave position. I have never known a more damaging chain of circumstantial evidence. The only jury we can possibly get together, the only men in Westchester County who will know nothing about the case, will be farmers and small tradespeople. These men are narrow minded, unworldly, religious, bigoted people who will look with horror upon a woman accused of murder; who will be surlily prejudiced against you because you did not love your husband, and because you left him; and above all they are likely to think you should be executed if for no other reason than because,"
— He hesitated. The blood came into his face. "Tell me, is it true? I don't believe it. I can't believe it — "

"That I had a lover? No, I did not have a lover. If that spy reports exactly what he heard, he must himself prove that I did not. I liked — I do like — a man, a former editor of mine, immensely. At that time I believed myself in love with him; but I was as mistaken as I suppose all impulsive and mentally lonely people are once or oftener in their lifetimes. Although he visits me now we have come to a complete understanding. I shall not marry him."

Bourke looked at the floor for a moment. "Yes," he said finally. "Yes. That is a great point, of course. Well — as a rule I can do anything I like with a jury in Westchester County; I know and have known for twenty years almost every man within forty miles; but we shall have to go out into the highways and byways

for talesmen: your case has attracted almost universal attention. It is just possible, therefore, that the
jury may convict you — Don't be frightened — Don't
look like that — please ! — If that happens I shall take
the case to the General Term, and failing that, to the
Court of Appeals. One way or another I shall get
you off — I pledge you my life on that," he added
vehemently. "Will you put your faith in me and keep
up?"

"I am sure no woman could help it," said Patience,
smiling graciously.

That night, somewhat to her amusement, she thought
on Bourke with a certain sweet tremor until she fell
asleep. She did not yet love him, but he satisfied her
imagination; and he was the first man that ever had.

XI

PATIENCE was rehearsed eight or ten times, Mr. Simms
cross-examining by a different method upon each occasion, racking his brain for new points with which to
confound her. She began to feel quite at ease on the
witness stand, and equal to the coming tilt with the
district attorney. Aside from a natural nervousness
she felt no fear of the approaching crisis, rather an
excited interest. The papers were booming her again,
and she would have been less than American had she
not appreciated her position as heroine of the most
sensational drama of the day.

In the last week of February, however, she received
information which induced her first misgiving: Miss

Beale was down with pneumonia. That superlatively healthy person loved fresh air only less than she loved the Lord, and slept with her windows open in mid-winter. Despite habit she invariably caught cold when travelling, as the one window of a small sleeping-room was likely to be at the head of her bed. She had defied Nature once too often.

When Patience told Mr. Bourke of Miss Beale's illness, the red streaked his face, as it had a habit of doing when he was disturbed. They were alone in the office.

"Will it make much difference?" she asked anxiously.

"Oh, no, I hope not; only she would have been a great card. She is known and respected throughout the county, and I should have dinned her in the ears of the jury. But you should have some woman with you. Is there no one else?"

Patience shook her head. "No one that would be of use. I have few women friends. Women don't like me much, I think. Mrs. Burr was my most intimate friend, but her husband naturally wanted to keep her out of the affair, and sent her off to Europe."

"It is odd. I cannot think of you as friendless. You attract and antagonise more strongly than any one I ever saw."

He was staring hard at her, and she turned her head away, colouring slightly. It was the first time they had been alone since the initial rehearsal, although he and the other lawyers had often lingered, after business was over, to talk with her. Apparently she and he were the best of friends, and their former acquaintance had not been recognised by a glance.

" I wonder if we really are friends," he said abruptly, then shook his shoulders slightly, as if, having made the plunge, he would not retreat.

Patience beat her fingers lightly on the desk, but did not turn her face to him.

" Our relationship is very agreeable," she said coolly. " I am delighted that Mr. Simms, for instance, is not my counsel."

There was a moment's suggestive silence, and then he said : " I understand. I can be nothing but counsel to you until I apologise. I have not done so before because there is no excuse to offer. I can only explain : you had deceived and outwitted and made a fool of me, and I was furious. Moreover, I was horribly disappointed. I am perfectly well aware that all that is no excuse. I was bitterly ashamed afterwards, and far more furious with myself than I had been with you. I have never ceased to deplore it. We might at least have been friends — "

"Ah, you forgave me then?" asked Patience, looking at his flushed face with a smile. He had never looked more awkward nor more attractive.

" Oh, yes ; my offence was so much worse, you see, I had to."

" Well," she said, giving him her hand gracefully, " we will forgive each other."

He accepted her hand promptly and evinced no disposition to relinquish it. " You are so cold, though," he said ruefully. " Your forgiveness is merely indifference. But of course," hastily, " you are absorbed in much weightier matters than friendship. I can imagine how insignificant all other episodes of your past must seem — "

"Oh, if it were not for you I might have been here before to-day, and in a much worse predicament. I doubt if I should have left him as soon as I did if it had not been for your unpleasant truths. I was drifting, and also drifting toward morbidity, where I might have been capable of anything. If I had really killed him and been arrested I should have said so, and even you could not have saved me."

"Oh, it would have been easier: I could have got you off on the plea of insanity. But am I really a link in the chain? I am egoistical—and interested—enough to be — pleased."

"Oh, yes," she said, laughing a little. "You have had a good deal more to do with forging some of the links than you imagine."

His hand was beginning to tremble, and she withdrew her own. He did not attempt to recapture it, and for a moment they regarded each other defensively. He had avoided the mistake of mistakes for thirty-six years, and the very flavour of romance about his experience with this woman made him wary. She had been mistaken twice and had ordered her imagination to sleep. Something within him pulled her, but none knew better than she the independent activity of sex. Still, like all women, fire was dear to her fingers. His eyes had a gleam in them which made her experience keenly the pleasurable sensation of danger.

"Did you know that night that I had forgotten our conversation in the tower?" he said, laughing uneasily. "Well, I will admit that I had, but I certainly remember the conversation in the elm walk—every word of it. It was a singular conversation," he continued hurriedly. "I have not found her yet, by the way. What is love,

27

anyhow? Something always seems to be lacking. I
have wanted a good many women, but there were
shallows somewhere."

Patience had taken a chair and was fanning herself
slowly. She answered with a judicial air, as of one
deciding some abstract point to which she had given
exhaustive study: "The lack is spiritual emotion.
People of strong natures who are really in love are
shaken by a passion that for the time being demands
no physical expression. It is only when it subsides, in
fact, that the other manifests itself. On the other hand,
the unimpassioned, the physically meagre, are incapable
of even imagining such an exaltation of emotion. It
is the supreme convulsion of mystery. And it must be
impossible to feel it more than once in a lifetime — for
more than one person, I mean."

"Have you ever felt it?" he asked abruptly. He
was sitting opposite her, his brows drawn together,
regarding her intently. Her cool impersonality non-
plussed him.

"No."

"Then how do you know?"

"From the organ. If one wants to read the riddle of
human nature let him listen to the organ for ten minutes. It lashes the soul — the emotional nature — up
to its utmost possibilities. One knows instinctively —
that is, if one is given to reasoning at all; for instincts
are dead letters without analysis — that only one other
force can cause a mightier tumult, a greater exaltation.
Those that do not reason mistake it for a desire to
spread their wings and fly to the throne of grace."

Bourke set his lips and looked at the floor. "Of
course you are right," he said. "A man would never

know that until he had felt it. It takes a woman to divine it. Perhaps it is as well he does n't know it — there is one disappointment the less in life if such moments never come to him ; and I doubt if they come to many. Either the savage is too strong in most of us, or we never come within range of the responsive spark. I have held that if there is any meaning at all in the progress of man out of barbarism it is that he shall become a brain with a refinement and intensity of passion which shall give happiness without disgust. But you go beyond me."

" Oh, we are both right," said Patience, rising. " We are much better off than our ancestors. I like so much to talk to you. When I am free you must come to see me often."

" I shall, indeed. How gracefully you fan yourself. I never saw any one use the fan in exactly the same way."

" I learned how from the old Spanish women in Monterey. They hold the thumb outwards, you know. That makes all the difference in the world. *Au revoir.*"

XII

THE trial began on the eighth of March. Patience slept ill the night before, and arose early. She looked forward to the day's ordeal with mingled nervousness and curiosity. Her faith in Bourke was complete, and her mind was of the order that craves experience. She could not divest herself of the idea that she was about to play the part of heroine in a great human drama.

And assuredly there has been no such theatre as the court room since the world began.

She dressed herself with extreme care, in a tailor frock and toque of black and white. The costume was becoming, but she shook her head at her reflection in the mirror: hers was not the type of beauty to appeal to the class of men in whose hands her life would be; rather they would resent its cold pride, its manifest of race and civilisation. She remembered her youthful satisfaction in the fact that "common men did not like her." Rosita or Honora would carry a jury by storm, but she was too subtle to appeal to men outside of her own social sphere. Tarbox liked her because she was game and dependent on him for comfort: it was doubtful if he thought her pretty. He came up at ten minutes to ten. He wore a new suit of clothes, and looked excited and impatient.

"There's a lot of swells come," he said without preliminary; "some from New York and some from the county. We've got 'em up in the gallery, and they look fine in their new spring clothes, I tell you. First time I ever seen swells in this court house. I rather thought they did n't go in for that kind of thing."

"They go in for fads, and you can as easily tell where lightning will strike next as what will be the next fad to possess fashionable women. Where is Mr. Bourke?"

"Up in the court room, I guess. Ready?"

A few moments later he led her up the stair at the back of the court room. A crowd of men at the door parted to let her enter, staring at her with eager curiosity. As she walked down the room to her seat beside her counsel she was conscious of a deep level of men's faces below and a tier of high-bred faces and bright spring gowns in the gallery above. She felt as if she were being shot upon a battery of eyes, and an impulse to turn and run; she looked like a black and white effigy of pride.

The large handsome room was tinted a pale blue and stencilled about the mouldings. The Bench and panelling behind it, the desks and tables, were of black walnut. Four long windows on each side of the room revealed the naked trees of March and the cheerless landscape. On the right of Patience's chair was the empty jury box, before her the Bench. In the space thus formed — flanked on the other side by the talesmen summoned for the trial and at the back by the audience — was a right angle of long study tables, three or four round tables, and many chairs. Every chair was occupied. Writing pads lay on the smaller tables. Patience recognised several of the reporters. By one of the long tables before the jury box sat Bourke, Simms, and Lansing. The former whispered to her that many of the men within the rail were eminent lawyers who had come to hear the case tried.

The judge sat alone on the Bench: an old man with pink face and head and neck, a close band of silver hair at the base of his skull. His face was narrow, his upper lip long. On either side of his mouth was a deep rut. The nose was coarse and strong, the eyes behind the spectacles humourous, severe, and a little sly. His silver chin-tuft was shaped like the queen of hearts.

Just below the Bench, beside one of the long tables, sat a man whom Patience did not notice at once, but to whom, as the judge called the court to order, she turned suddenly, conscious of a fixed gaze. He sat with one arm along the table, the other hand absently rolling a piece of paper. His narrowed eyes were regarding her with cold speculation. Patience shuddered. She knew that he was Sturges, the district attorney. Tarbox had told and retold the history of his jealousy of Bourke, and his registered vow to win one of the great legal battles of which they were occasionally chief combatants. And this was the greatest! The man's face was set. He looked like a fate.

The clerk called a name. A man shuffled into the jury box. Sturges stood up and put the usual questions. He spoke with exaggerated courtesy. Occasionally he smiled: a mechanical smile, as if an invisible string connected each corner of his mouth with a manipulator at the back of his head. His voice was soothing and cultivated, his manner almost deferential to the humble man in the box. Patience followed every motion and word with fascinated attention. When he asked the talesman if he had "any conscientious scruples regarding capital punishment as practised in this State," she felt the touch of icy fingers and her feet slipping into an open grave. Bourke, who divined her sensations, smiled encouragingly; and after she had heard the question some fifty times, she ceased to attach any personal meaning to it.

They were four days impannelling the jury. The first time Patience stood up to face an accepted juror she regarded the hairy and ill-kept farmer with such haughty and disdainful eyes that Bourke whispered hurriedly: "For God's sake don't look at them like that or they'll send you up out of spite. Remember that this class of people is always at war with its betters."

"I can't help it," said Patience. "It's humiliating to think of being at the mercy of men like that."

When the box was filled at last she regarded the occupants attentively. They were hard-featured men of middle age, with long bare upper lip and compressed mouth. Their grey skin was furrowed with lines of care and hardship, their chin whiskers grizzled and scant. Their eyebrows stood out over faded eyes in wrinkled sockets. But what excited Patience's wonder was the small size of the heads. She had never seen twelve heads so little. They were hardly an advance upon their hairy ancestors. Throughout the trial she furtively watched the twelve faces of those twelve meagre heads. Never once did their expression, stolid and set, change. At night they haunted her. She awoke in the morning with a violent start, seeing them for a moment in a row on the foot board of her bed. She speculated, at times, upon the lives of those men, those pinched grubbing lives, and felt for them a sort of terrified pity. What a mere glimpse of the world she had had, after all, and what ugly strata it had! What was the matter with civilisation?

XIII

On the fourth day the district attorney opened the case with an address to the jury which was a master-piece of temperate statement and damning suggestion. He dwelt long upon the remarkable points of the case: the youth and beauty and intelligence and social position of the defendant, the distinguished family which had been plunged into sorrow and disgrace by her crime, the extraordinary interest the crime had excited throughout the civilised world. He then gave a running account, clear and straightforward and decisive, of what the prosecution would prove, and concluded with a cold, terse, but reiterated warning that the prisoner at the bar was entitled to no sympathy because of her sex and position; that he and the jury were there for one purpose only: to consider the facts of the case and to do their plain duty, utterly regardless of consequences to the individual. Every word was chosen and weighed, and told like the ring of a steel hammer on a steel plate.

Dr. Lewis was then called to prove the fact of Beverly Peele's death, and his vigorous story weighed heavily in the scales against the defence. The moment the district attorney sat down Bourke was on his feet. For a moment he stood lifting and shaking the loose cloth of the table beside him; then asked one or two random questions which put the witness for the prosecution quite at his ease. In the course of a moment the witness began to writhe, and at the end of five minutes manifested his consciousness of the fact that he was a small country practitioner, to be regarded by any intelligent jury with contempt. Nevertheless, it was impossible to shake his testimony.

He was followed by the New York physician, a man of eminence, who had assisted at the death-bed, then by the coroner. The fact of young Peele's death being firmly established in the jury box, a chemist was put upon the stand to testify that he had found morphine in the stomach of the deceased. He was worried and badgered and ridiculed and derided by Bourke, who

temporarily infected everybody in the court room
with his scorn of the exercise of chemistry as applied
to morphine in the stomach of a dead man, but held
his ground, having been maltreated in a like manner
many times before. Following, came a civil engineer,
who described the grounds and general position of
Peele Manor to the jury; and the testimony for the
day was over.

The next morning the prosecution passed on to the
motive. Honora was the first witness called. She wore
a black frock and hat, and looked dignified and sad.
In her clear childlike voice she described to the jury
her moment of confusion and horror when awakened
from a profound sleep by the prisoner; told the mourn-
ful story of the unavailing attempts at resuscitation;
and hesitatingly admitted, in full detail, the unmistakable indifference of the wife. To the latter testimony
Mr. Bourke "objected," as he had done to similar
testimony by the doctors, but the objection was over-
ruled by the judge. She also admitted having seen
from her window the defendant returning from town
after her early visit on the morning of the " Eye "
story, inappropriately attired in grey and pink, and
having discovered the newspapers in confusion on the
library floor before any other member of the household
except the prisoner had arisen. She related Patience's
previous complaint that her husband always waited
until she was in her first heavy sleep before demanding
the morphine, and her fear lest she should some night
give him an overdose. The jury must have been small
headed indeed, to fail to understand the district
attorney's insinuations regarding the prisoner's deep-
laid scheme to avert suspicion.

As Honora gave her testimony Patience saw Mr. Bourke's eyes sparkle. She knew that some pregnant idea had flashed into that lightning-like brain. As the district attorney took his seat he rose slowly and smiled sociably at Honora. She bent her head slightly; she had always liked him.

"Miss Mairs," he said haltingly, his eyes wandering to the judge, as if in search of inspiration, his hand flirting the loose cloth of the table, "you are sure that Mrs. Peele wore a gray gown to New York that morning?"

"Yes, sir."

"And the condition of the newspapers seemed to you to indicate great agitation of mind?"

"Yes, sir."

"Yes, yes. And she returned in an hour or two, you say?"

"Yes, sir."

"Miss Mairs!" he thundered, turning suddenly upon her and pointing a rigid finger straight at her startled face, "are you sure that you were asleep when Mrs. Peele awakened you on the night of Beverly Peele's death?"

Patience drew her breath sharply. She closed her eyes. Honora had not been asleep that night! The certainty came to her as suddenly and as positively as it had come to Bourke.

For the fraction of a moment Honora hesitated. Every man and woman in the court room was breathless. Several had started to their feet.

"Quite sure," she replied finally, and that silver shallow voice did not falter.

"You are *sure* that you heard no one go to the

lavatory that night, before Mrs. Peele spoke to you?"
He hurled the words at her as the Great Judge might
hurl the final sentence on Judgment Day.

"Sure."

"Was your door open that night?"

"I don't remember."

Patience leaned over and whispered to Lansing, who
sprang forward and whispered to Bourke.

"The night was hot," continued Bourke. "Were
you not in the habit of leaving your door open on hot
nights?"

"Sometimes."

"Was it not always your custom?"

"Not always. When I thought of it I opened the
door, but I frequently forgot it."

"Yes! Yes! You are quite sure you cannot remember whether or not it was open on that night?"

"I cannot remember."

"Do you remember any other nights on which Mrs.
Peele went to the lavatory to drop the morphine?"

"Yes, sir; a great many."

"But of this all important night you remember
nothing?"

"No, sir."

"Yes! Mrs. Peele never was called upon to drop
the morphine until after twelve o'clock. Were you in
the habit of lying awake until late?"

"Yes."

"But on this night you went to sleep early?"

"Yes."

"You heard or saw — you are on your oath, remember — nothing whatever until Mrs. Peele called
you?"

"Nothing."

"You can go. — She is lying," he whispered to Patience. "Damn her, I'll make her speak yet if I have to throttle it out of her."

Mr. Peele was the witness next called. He was treated with extreme diffidence by the district attorney, and even the judge gave him a fraternal smile. He told the story of the momentous night with parental indignation finally controlled, then, in spite of repeated " objections " and constant nagging, the significant tale of wifely indifference and desertion, and read to the jury " that cruel letter written to a dying man " the day before the defendant returned to nurse her husband. He repeated with the dramatic effect of the legal actor those dark insinuations of the prisoner: "You had better let me go ! I feel that I shall kill him if I stay ! " And later in the town house when she had struck her husband in the face: " You had better keep him out of my way. Do you know that once I tried to kill my own mother ? "

He told of her eager interest in untraceable poisons one night when the subject of murder had come up at the dinner-table, her cold-blooded analysis of human motives.

Then he passed on to the painfully significant history of the day before the death : her demand for a divorce ; her fury at her husband's refusal ; her acknowledgment that she had quarrelled violently with the deceased a short time before calling the family to his death-bed.

As he spoke Patience's blood congealed. The woman he depicted was enough to inspire any jury with

horror. It was herself and not herself, a Galatea manufactured by a clever lawyer.

But it was Mr. Bourke's privilege to give the Galatea
a soul. Despite the older man's greater legal experience, his superior wariness and subtlety, he was forced
to admit that his son was a fool; that his son's wife was
a woman of brilliant intellect driven to desperation at
being tied·down to a fool; that so long as she had lived
with him she had done her duty; that when she had
returned as his nurse she had fulfilled her part of the
contract to the letter; that never had she given her
husband cause for real jealousy; that the witness himself had made a companion of her, and that he had
been bitterly disappointed in his son.

The terrible facts could not be stricken out, but Mr.
Peele, nevertheless, was made to pass the most uncomfortable hours of his life. "And in spite of these
threats," exclaimed Bourke, with the accentuation of
one addressing an idiot at large, "in spite of the precision with which you remembered them, you permitted
your family to implore her to return and become your
son's nurse; you permitted her to sleep in a room com-
municating with his, where, in a fit of passion — if she
is the woman you profess to believe her to be — she
could have murdered him in the dead of night with a
carving knife or a hatchet, before any one — even the
lightly sleeping Miss Mairs — could have flown to the
rescue; you permitted her — " he turned suddenly
and faced the jury, then wheeled about and regarded
Mr. Peele with scornful inquiry — "you permitted her
to drop morphine for your son, and to have unrestrained
access to the drug, knowing that he in his agony would
swallow whatever she gave him without question. Will

you kindly explain to the jury whether this mode of proceeding was ingenuousness on your part, or criminal connivance? "

Mr. Peele's under lip pressed the upper almost to the septum of his nose. His eyes half closed and glittered unpleasantly; but he controlled himself and answered, —

" I paid no attention to her threats at the time."

"Ah! You did not believe in them? You admit that?"

" I classed them with the usual hysterical ravings of women. That was my error."

" State, if you please, your specific reasons for your change of mind. You will hardly, as a lawyer, claim to have been converted to the defendant's capacity for crime by the mere fact that your son died of an overdose of morphine?"

And throughout the long day Mr. Bourke hectored him, fighting him, point by point, smashing to bits his testimony relative to the events of the day preceding the death, evidence to which he was not an eye-witness, which he had received at second hand from his wife and son. The " cruel letter written to a dying man " was disposed of in a similar manner.

"You believed your son to be in a precarious condition when you counselled them to send for your son's wife?"

"I did."

" But you believed with the doctors that if she returned, thereby bringing him peace of mind as well as tender care, he had excellent chances for life?"

"I did."

" And Mrs. Burr was instructed to present that phase

of the question to the defendant, with all the force of which she was capable?"

"Yes."

"And the defendant so understood it?"

"I suppose she did."

"And yet you assert that this purely business-like letter, written by a self-respecting woman, was addressed to a dying man, while at the same time you assert that this man could be cured by the gratification of a whim, and that you had taken particular pains to make the defendant aware of the fact!"

When Mr. Peele finally left the stand, he looked battered and limp.

XIV

As soon as the court had opened on the following morning, Mrs. Peele was called. She looked haughtily askance at the worn Bible as the clerk rattled off the oath, bent her head as would she whiff upon what plebeian lips had touched so often and so evidently, and took the witness chair as were she mounting a throne. She was apparelled in crape. Only her intimate friends could have told whether the backward bend of her head was due to the weight of her veil or the weight of her ancestors. At first she stared at the district attorney with haughty resentment, as, for the benefit of the humble jury, he curtly asked her several direct questions; but remembering that he was "a Sturges," and also recalling her husband's admonitions, she unbent, and even condescended to address the jury.

Her tale of the night in no wise differed from her husband's; but her accentuation of Patience's dark threats
and marital deficiencies was all her own.   Her suggestion of a lover in the case caused a sudden movement
in the jury box, although the stolid faces did not relax.
Under cross-examination much of her testimony was as
effectually demolished as her husband's had been.

Two maid servants followed.   They testified to violent quarrels between the young couple.   Then the
butler testified to the reiterant and emphatic command
of the prisoner on the day before the death to send to
New York for morphine.

The prosecution produced its trump card : the stable
boy who had spied upon the interviews between the
prisoner and the mysterious lover.   The man had evidently been carefully rehearsed — as Bourke later on
pointed out to the jury — for his memory of the eight
or ten interviews he had witnessed needed little refreshing.   His "best recollection" was given glibly and
ungrammatically.   He dilated upon the young man's
remarkable personal beauty, and observed that it far
outshone his beloved Mr. Beverly's.   They had talked
principally of books in all but the last two interviews,
but had looked perfectly happy.   His account of the last
two interviews created a profound impression in the
court room, even the jury leaning forward slightly.
The judge frowned and wheeled his chair sharply when
the man gave the gist of the prisoner's matter-of-
fact objection to living with a man who was not her
husband.

Mr. Bourke's rich voice had never rung with deeper
indignation and disgust, never shaped itself to more
cutting sarcasm than when he made the man see him-

self and the jury see him as a coward, a cur, a spy, a liar, an eager schemer for an innocent woman's life. " You felt it your duty," he concluded, " to spy upon a woman of irreproachable reputation who met a friend in an open wood in broad daylight — Yes, yes," with all the lingering scornful emphasis which only he could give that simple word. " You never felt yourself a cowardly scoundrel meddling in what was none of your business — No ! No !" He turned to the jury with the passion still upon his face, but when he took his seat he smiled encouragingly to his admiring young client.

"Would n't he make an actor?" whispered Simms: " I never saw him do the lofty indignation act with finer effect."

" Well, he would be a great actor, at least," retorted Patience, " and I am convinced that you would be a very small one."

" Just wait," said Simms, angrily. " I 've got to talk to this jury about you in a day or two, and if you don't forget I ever doubted you I 'll eat my hat. The best lawyer 's the best fakir, and a few days from now you 'll see what an ambitious man I am."

" Miss Rosita Thrailkill," called the district attorney when the court opened next morning. The audience stood up to a man.

A plump willowy Spanish figure undulated behind the jury box, kissed the Bible reverently, and ascended the witness stand. Rosita was clad in black and yellow, a mantilla in place of a hat, and many diamonds. She looked as pretty and as naughty as possible. As she met Patience's eyes, she wafted her a kiss, and the prisoner groaned in spirit. She gave her name and birthplace with melodious caressing accent and her

28

marked precision of speech. Yes, the defendant had been her dear friend, her best friend, her only intimate friend. Yes, with unaffected reluctance, Mrs. Sparhawk had been disreputable, and Patience had once attempted her life. Yes, she was the prima donna of light opera known as La Rosita. Did she appear before the public in tights and scant attire? Yes, why not? Had she not had a number of lovers? Objected to and sustained. Flashing indignation of soft Spanish eyes. Did she not have the reputation of being a woman of loose and lawless life? Objected to and sustained. Angry rattle of fan. Was it not in her house that the prisoner was arrested? Yes, it was! and she loved her Patita and would always give her shelter.

When the district attorney sat down with an ugly smile on his thin mouth, Bourke, muttering anathema, rose to his feet.

"Was there ever a whisper against your reputation when you were a school-girl in Monterey and most intimate with the prisoner?"

"No, *señor!*" cried Rosita, paying no attention to the objection. "I was a child, and could not even endure boys."

"How many times have you seen the defendant since you left Monterey?"

Rosita cast up her eyes, then tapped the sticks of her fan successively as she spoke.

"Once she came to see me just after — ah — WCTU died; then once just before she left Mr. Peele; then that day the 'Eye' came out and said she had done this so horrible thing. *Ay, dios!*"

"She has called upon you three times only, then, since you were children in Monterey, since you have been the Rosita of the public; in the last five years, in short?"

"*Si, señor* — yes, sir."

"How long did she remain upon her first visit?"

"Oh, only a little while. I told her something that shocked her, for she was always so proper."

"What did you tell her?"

"Objected to," cried the district attorney.

"Objection sustained," snapped the judge.

"How long did she remain on her second visit?"

"About a half hour. I never knew what she came at all for. She just floated in and out." Rosita waved her arm with enchanting grace.

"Did she tell you why she came the third time?"

"Because she had no other place to go to. She said no hotel would take her in."

"She said that her old landlady had refused to admit her, did she not?"

"*Si, señor.*"

"Yes, yes! — and that in her terrible extremity she naturally turned to the friend of her childhood?"

"*Si!*" and Rosita wept.

"But that she should not have gone to your house if there had been any possibility of obtaining entrance to a hotel, or if she had not been turned out of her father-in-law's house?"

"*Ay, yi!* yes."

"That is all. You can go."

During the rest of that day and the two following days the experts for the prosecution had the stand. The innumerable questions asked by the district attorney, the technical details of the cross-examinations, the constant interruptions, and the minutiæ

of the evidence emptied the court room after the first
hour, and even Patience became bored, and fell to
thinking of other things, not forgetting to pity those
twelve puzzled little heads in the jury box.

The gist of the evidence was that there was enough
morphine in Beverly Peele's stomach to kill two men.

XV

" OUR turn has come," said Lansing to Patience on the
morning after the expert testimony was concluded.
" We are confident of success now."

" But the facts are hideous, and they have painted
me black."

" Mr. Bourke scraped off a good deal, and he 'll have
the rest off before he gets through. If he could only
make that lying woman open her mouth ! You 've borne
yourself splendidly. Keep in good condition for the
witness stand. Are you frightened ? "

" No," she said, smiling at Bourke gratefully. " Not
a bit."

Simms opened the case for the defence.

He had a harsh strident voice. He gesticulated as if
practising for a prize fight, doubling back and springing forward. He cleared his throat with vicious
emphasis and rasped his heels upon the floor. His
statements were dry and matter-of-fact, his language
bald ; but he made a direct vigorous and enthusiastic
speech. The jury was informed that it was there to
save the life of one of the most brilliant and high-minded

young women of the age, — a woman utterly incapable of murder or of any violent act, a woman with the mild and meditative mind of the student. That it would be proved not only that she was far too clever to take life by such clumsy methods, but that she had no object, as she had gained her liberty, and the lover was a myth. The whole prosecution was a malignant and personal prosecution of an innocent but too gifted woman by an absurdly conceited family that had resented her superior intelligence. This and much more of fact and fancy. But Patience, with perverse feminity, liked him none the better, and would not even look at him when he sat down.

Mr. Field was the first witness for the defence. Although compelled under cross-examination to admit the prisoner's interest in subtle poisons, he managed to convey to the jury that it was merely the result of an unusually brilliant and inquiring mind, a thought born of the moment, of his suggestion. He gave the highest tribute to her cleverness, her work on his paper, and to her reputation.

Latimer Burr was called next, and spoke with enthusiasm of her "unfailing submission to a man of abominable and savage temper until submission ceased to be a virtue." He had never heard her utter any threats to kill. Yes, it was true that he had engaged counsel for defence. He believed in her thoroughly.

Miss Merrien, her landlady, and Mrs. Blair were put on the stand next morning, and the good character they gave Patience was unshaken by the nagging of the district attorney. Mr. Tarbox testified to her demeanour of innocence during her imprisonment.

"But the defence is weak all the same," whispered

Patience to Lansing. "Not a word can be said in rebuttal. Only Mr. Bourke's eloquence can save me."

"Good character goes a long way," replied Lansing. "You have no idea of its weight with a jury, particularly with a jury of this kind."

Patience was put on the witness stand next. The supreme effort to overcome nervousness gave her an icy and repellent demeanour. Never had she held her back as erect, her head as high. She kept her eyelids half lowered, and spoke with scarcely any change of inflection. She told the story of the night as she had told it in rehearsal many times. There had been a quarrel an hour before she heard the deceased get up and go to the lavatory. She offered to drop his morphine, and he replied with an oath that she should never do another thing for him as long as he lived, that he hoped she would leave the house by the first train next morning. His sudden silence upon his return to his bed excited her apprehension, and she called the family.

When Bourke sat down and the district attorney arose and confronted her she shivered suddenly. Bourke's rich strong voice and kind magnetic gaze had given her courage, but this man with his eyes like grey ice, his mechanical smile, and cold smooth voice conjured up a sudden awful picture of the execution room at Sing Sing. Her insight appreciated with exactitude the pitiless ambition of the man, knew that he stood pledged to his future to send her to her death. He made her admit all the damning facts of the evidence against her, the facts which stood out like phosphorescent letters on a black wall, and to acknowledge her abhorrence of the man that had been her husband. But all this had been anticipated: at least he could not confuse her.

Again two days and a part of a third were monopolised by experts. These two illustrious chemists testified, through the same bewildering mass of detail as that employed by their equally illustrious predecessors, that there was not enough morphine in Beverly Peele's stomach to kill a cat.

There was a short interval, after the second expert had been permitted to leave the stand, during which Bourke and Simms and Lansing conferred together, preparatory to the summing up of the former. As Bourke was about to rise, the district attorney stood up, cleared his throat, and said: " One moment, please. Will Miss Honora Mairs kindly take the stand? "

Bourke was on the alert in an instant. " The case for the prosecution has closed," he said.

" This is by special permission of the Court," replied the district attorney, coldly.

As Honora ascended the stand there was a deep murmur of admiration. She looked like an angel, nothing less. She wore a white lawn frock, girt with a blue sash ; a large white leghorn lined with azure velvet, against which the baby gold of her hair shone softly. Her great blue eyes had the clear calm serenity of a young child. Patience drew her breath in a series of short gasps. Bourke sat with clenched hands.

" We understand," said the district attorney, severely, " that you did not tell all you knew the other day, and that you have signified your willingness to now tell the truth, the whole truth, and nothing but the truth. Is this true? "

Honora bowed her head with an expression of deep

humility, as a child might that had been justly rebuked.

"You had not slept at all upon that fatal night?"

"No."

"Your door was open?"

"Yes."

"You did see somebody enter the lavatory?"

"Yes."

"Whom did you see?"

There was a moment's breathless silence, during which Patience wondered if a clock had ever ticked so loudly, or if the sun had ever shone with so vicious a glare.

"Whom did you see?" repeated the district attorney.

"The prisoner."

"What did she do?"

"She dropped some thirty or forty drops of morphine, I should say, then half filled the glass with water, as usual."

"You did not see the deceased go to the lavatory that night."

"No."

"Nor any one else until the defendant called you?"

"No."

"That is all."

Mr. Bourke sprang to his feet, his nostrils dilating, his fine face quivering with unassumed scorn and indignation.

"You admit that you perjured yourself the other day?"

"I could not make up my mind to —"

"Never mind what you had not made up your mind to do. You admit that you perjured yourself?"

"Yes," gently.

"That in other words you lied."

"Yes, sir." Her voice was like the quiver of a violin.

"What proof are we to have that you are not lying now?"

"I am not lying. My conscience gave me no rest."

"It will give you more, I suppose, if you will have succeeded in swearing away the life of an innocent woman. Yes, yes! — Exactly how long did Mrs. Peele remain in the lavatory?"

"I cannot remember. Five or ten minutes."

"State the exact time."

"Perhaps five."

"And a few moments later when she ran into your room you pretended to be asleep: Why did you assume sleep; what reason had you for lying at that time?"

"I had dropped off."

"You had been sufficiently wide awake five minutes before to note precisely all these other things, and then had promptly fallen into a sound sleep. Is that your usual habit?"

"Yes, sir."

"Did you speak to the prisoner when she came into the lavatory?"

"No."

"Were not you in the habit of holding a conversation with her upon such occasions?"

"Yes, sir."

"Why did you not address her on that night?"

"I was very sleepy, and had nothing in particular to say."

"But you were not too sleepy to note carefully all the details in the evidence you have just given. You

can go, — and to the devil," he muttered. He thrust
his hands into his pockets and wheeled about, looking
at Patience with such intensity of gaze that she moved
suddenly forward. Her face was pale, but her eyes
blazed with rage. Bourke glanced at the clock.

"It is twenty minutes to one," he said. "I would
ask your honour to adjourn until two. I must have
time to digest this new testimony. Its remarkable
glibness prevented me from giving it the running deliberation that it demanded."

The judge sulkily dismissed the court. As Patience
passed out of the room with Tarbox she heard the
word "angel" more than once, and knew that it did
not refer to her.

Patience was not conscious of fear as she ate her
luncheon. Her heart was black with rage. "I'd willingly murder *her*," she thought, "and my conscience
would n't trouble me the least little bit."

XVI

IMMEDIATELY after recess Mr. Bourke began his summing up. He commenced quietly, shaking the loose
cloth of the table in an absent manner. His language
was colloquial as he spoke to the jury of its grave
responsibilities, and complimented it upon the "unusual
intelligence which it had so far made evident." He
passed naturally to the subject in hand, and dwelt eloquently upon the character of the defendant, of her
lonely pathetic youth, her high ideals, her remarkable
intelligence, her ignorance of the world which had led

her to fall in love with the first handsome and attractive man that had addressed her.

His voice rose to tragic pitch as he dwelt upon the terrible awakening of such a woman, bound for life to such a man, — a sensual, ill-tempered, selfish brute, who was a disgrace to the nineteenth century.

He depicted two years of uncomplaining wifely devotion (until Patience became lost in admiration of the defendant), the husband's frantic rages about nothing, his unrecognition of her superiority, his ignorant determination to make her his slave — his plaything — she, a woman whom such men as James E. Field and Gardiner Peele delighted to honour.

Then he dropped again into pathos (which never for a moment degenerated into bathos) and described the desolate life of such a woman in an empty frivolous brainless society (faint murmur and indignant rustle in the gallery), a society of idle people with neither soul nor intelligence, but who squandered the money wrested from the People, the great People, of whom the Gentlemen of the Jury were twelve worthy and doubtless long suffering members.

It was not until he had emphasised and recapitulated with every resource of his splendid vocabulary, every modulation of his glorious voice, by controlled and telling gesture, by sudden tremendous bursts of indignation, the married life of the prisoner, that he passed to the day and night of the tragedy. He began with the morning, and dwelt upon every detail of the day. Before he reached midnight he had Beverly Peele in a frame of mind for both suicide and murder. He sent him to bed with black skin and white flecked nose and chaos in his heart. With a magnificent burst of scorn he quoted his shameful language when his wife had offered to get him the morphine, the oaths he had used to a "refined and elegant and patient woman." Then he took him to the lavatory, showed him jerking the stopper from the morphine bottle, and recklessly pouring a fourth of its contents into a glass. "He knew that he had to die anyhow, and he could at least die happy in a hideous revenge." In brief and vivid phrase he cited several similar instances in legal history.

Then he returned to Peele Manor and denounced the jealous woman who for five years had nursed fury in her heart, and who, on the witness stand, here, Gentlemen of the Jury, conceived, at the unfortunate suggestion of the speaker, the frightful revenge upon a woman who had treated her with unvarying kindness. She did not speak at once, partly because her lying tale needed rehearsing, partly because she believed that the case for the prosecution would win without her. But when she saw that the case for the prosecution was wholly lost she arrayed herself like an angel, that she might the better impose upon the unworldly Gentlemen of the Jury, and swore away a woman's life.

The several assertions on the defendant's part that she felt disposition to murder he tore to rags and flung in the face of the jury. Had not every high tempered person — could not the Gentlemen of the Jury recall having exclaimed in bitter moments: "I wish you were dead! I could kill you!" With deep regret and remorse he would confess that he had used similar expressions many times.

Then with consummate skill he dilated upon the impossibility of so clever a woman as the defendant doing aught so stupid as to murder in the manner of the accusation. When there was nothing left to say on this subject he expatiated upon the lack of motive with a technical and personal brilliancy which made even the cross-grained old judge lean forward with a cynical smile.

The interviews, even the final ones, with the mysterious stranger, he treated with contempt, although the contempt was sufficiently long drawn out to impress the jury with every most insignificant detail. It was the mere longing for companionship of a lonely woman : that was the beginning and the end of it. The lover, the intention of either to marry, he disposed of with a vehemence which made Simms twist about suddenly and look at Lansing ; but the young man was regarding his chief with rapt admiration.

Not so much as the scraping of a boot heel was heard in the court room. Patience glanced at the district attorney. His face was set and sullen.

After every possible point had been considered Bourke concluded with an appeal so stirring, so ringing, so thrilling that every person in the court room except the district attorney sat forward and held his breath. No such burst of passion had ever been heard in that room before. Patience covered her face with her hands. Her heart beat suffocatingly. The blood pounded in her ears ; but not one note of that wonderful voice, not one phrase of fire, escaped her.

Is there any possible condition in which a man can appear to such supreme advantage as when pleading for the life of a fellow being, more particularly of a young and beautiful woman ? How paltry all the time-worn rescues of woman from sinking ship and runaway

horse and burning house.   A great criminal lawyer
standing before the jury box with a life in his hand has
the unique opportunity to display all the best gifts ever
bestowed upon man: genius, brain, passion, heart,
soul, eloquence, a figure instinct with grace and virility,
a face blazing with determination to snatch a man or
woman from the most awful of dooms.

And all in two short hours.

If those in the court room for whom the case had no
personal interest were at Bourke's feet, hanging upon
his words, adoring him for the moment, what were the
feelings of the woman for whom he was making so desperate and manly a fight?   She forgot her danger, forgot
everything but the man, the reckless joy of loving, of
being swept out of her calm orbit at last.   Her analytical
brain was dulled, her arms ached, her heart shook her
body.

As Bourke made a few supplementary remarks calculated to take the wind out of the district attorney's
sails, — references to the young man's ambition, his
youthful eagerness to become famous, what the winning
of such a great case would mean to him, and to his
remarkable cleverness and skill with a jury, — Patience
heard Simms say to Lansing: "My God! Bourke has
surpassed even himself.   Even he never got as high as
that before."

"He's the greatest man in the country, God bless
him!" said Lansing.

As Bourke finally dropped upon his chair he turned
to Patience.   Their eyes met and lingered; and in
that moment each passed into the other's keeping.

XVII

STURGES lost no time taking his stand before the jury box. It was the hour of his life, but he was not nervous. His long thin figure leaning toward the box as he rested his finger tips on the table, showed as fine a repose of nerve as of brain. His clear-cut face with the cruel mouth and pleasant smile was calm and unclouded.

He began by defending himself against Mr. Bourke's remarks, and asserted with convincing emphasis that when he had taken the oath of office he had left his personal ambition behind him with his personal interests, and had given himself body and soul and brain to the People of Westchester County. Then he made an equally earnest statement of the grave responsibilities of a district attorney, his solemn duty to the People, the necessity to smother all promptings of humanity that he might do what was best for the People — "The greatest good of the greatest number."

Then he painted Patience as black as Bourke had enamelled her white. With masterly ingenuity he made each juror feel what an awful being a bad woman was, an unloving undutiful wife; what a curse each man of them would writhe under had Fate played him as scurvy a trick as it had played poor Beverly Peele; that no unloved husband's life would be safe were not such women exploited and punished, that if the Gentlemen of the Jury were weak enough to consider her sex they might be imperilling the lives of countless thousands. For the matter of that, he reiterated, crime had no sex.

He took up each detail of the story, and in the light of his interpretation Patience was the modern Lucretia Borgia and Beverly Peele an injured, peaceable, affectionate husband, who had been sacrificed by an abandoned woman to whom he had given his honoured name, his fortune, and his love.

He scarcely raised his voice. There was no passion in his utterance; but he manufactured a mosaic, bit by bit, each fragment fitting so exactly that the design was without crevice or crack. He demonstrated mathematically that the tardy evidence of Miss Mairs had been superfluous; that the chain of circumstantial evidence was symmetrical and complete, and that no possible motive beyond duty to her conscience could be attributed to her. With devilish adroitness, without a direct phrase, he managed to filter into those twelve small brains the secret of the inspired eloquence of the eminent counsel for the defence, — in behalf of his young and beautiful client.

While he was talking, the skeleton trees beyond the windows grew dim of outline, the mass of colour in the gallery faded. An official came out of the library behind the court room and lit the tall gas lamps on either side of the bench. The judge looked like a bas-relief in pink and silver against the dark panelling of the background. The rest of the room was in shadow. The light of the near jet fell full upon Sturges' stern face.

Patience's life from " its fiendish childhood " was rehearsed with such consecutive logic that crime at some point of such a woman's career was inevitable. The only wonder was that it had not been committed sooner.

The threats, he demonstrated, whether uttered in moments of passion or not, were the significant output of
a brooding mind.   The "cruel letter to a dying man"
was read with slow and indignant emphasis.   Then the
events of the fatal day and night, the quarrels, the
prisoner's fury at being denied a divorce, the deceased's
threat to live twenty years to spite her, her carefully
rehearsed and absurd story that her husband had
dropped the morphine himself, — something he knew
himself physically incapable of doing, — the equal ab-
surdity of his suicide when a greater revenge lay in his
hands, her brutal indifference while he lay dying, were
deliberately gone over with passionless and insidious
effect.   The quiet half-lit room was oddly in keeping
with the deadly methods of the man.

When he had made the most of her flight on the
morning of the "Eye" story, he paused a moment,
during which the rising wind could be heard in the
trees.   Within, there was no sound.   No one seemed
breathing.   Bourke and Patience were in deep shadow.
With an instinct of protection he clasped his hand suddenly about hers.

Sturges resumed, with lowered and vibrating voice :

"And — where — Gentlemen of the Jury, — was —
this — woman — arrested? ——— *In the house of a harlot!*"   He paused another half moment.   "In the
house of her oldest friend, La Rosita, one of the most
abandoned women in America."

Bourke's hand twitched spasmodically. Simms twisted
his neck, and shot at Lansing an uneasy glance.   Patience shuddered.   For the moment she forgot Bourke.
She felt as if a cobra were folding her about, — very
slowly, and gently, and inexorably.

29

When Sturges sat down the jury was told to rise. The judge stood under one of the lamps and read them his charge. He explained that unless they could find the prisoner guilty of murder in the first degree — of deliberate premeditated murder — they must acquit her. As the final quarrel had taken place an hour before the killing it was obviously impossible that she could have dropped the morphine in a moment of excitement; and a verdict of self-defence would be equally absurd. He also charged them that they were to consider the law in the case and nothing but the law, — that human sympathy must have no place in their verdict.

Bourke was too able a lawyer not to have the last word. As the judge sat down, he arose with several sheets of manuscript, and for twenty minutes asked the judge to charge the jury so and so, practically recapitulating all the strong points of the defence. The judge answered mechanically, "I so charge," and at last the patient jury was conducted out of the court room and locked up. Bourke was surrounded at once.

As Tarbox, with Patience on his arm, left the court house and its crowd behind him, he exclaimed, " By God, that was a great speech of Bourke's! There never has been a summing up like that in my time before, not even by him. But he's the smartest man in Westchester County ! Hanged if I don't think he's the smartest man in the State of New York. He'll be in the United States Senate yet."

XVIII

AFTER dinner Patience went back to the court room to remain until ten o'clock, at which time the jury, if it had not come to a decision, would be locked up for the night. She sat surrounded by her counsel and the lawyers that had taken so deep an interest in the case. Bourke sat very close to her, and once or twice as she met his eyes she forgot the terrible moment to come. Few people were in the court house. No one expected a verdict that night.

It was exactly at half-past nine that the jury filed solemnly in. Patience's knees jerked suddenly upward. She lost her breath for a moment. Bourke leaned over her and took her hand, regardless of the curious people surrounding them.

"Be brave. Be brave," he said hurriedly. "Now is the time for all your pride and disdain."

When she was ordered to stand up and face the jury, she did so with an air so collected and so haughty that even Simms murmured: "By Jove, she is a thoroughbred."

There was a moment of horrible and vibrating silence, during which Patience's brain reiterated hilariously: "Twelve little Jurymen all in a row. Twelve little heads all in a row." Then the foreman was asked for the verdict. He cleared his throat, and without moving a muscle of his face, remarked, —

"Guilty."

The district attorney sat down suddenly and hid his face with a convulsive hand. Patience resumed her seat with a mien as stolid as that of the twelve jurors. Bourke's face blanched, but he sprang to his feet and demanded that the jury be polled. Each solemn " Yes," twelve and unhesitating, sounded like a knell. Then Bourke demanded a Stay, which was granted by the impassive judge, and Patience was led through the silent crowd from the court room to her cell. Tarbox escorted her mutely, his face turned away. At the door of her cell he attempted to speak, but gave it up and retreated hastily.

Patience threw off her hat and sat down on the edge of the bed. The verdict, she knew now, had not been a surprise. But she thought little of the verdict. She was waiting for something else. It came in a moment. She heard a quick impatient step on the ground below, then a rapid ascent of stair, a word or two at the door, Tarbox's retreating step.

Bourke was in the cell. His face was white, but that of Patience as she rose and confronted him was not.

"I don't care !" she said. "I don't care ! I believe I am happier than any woman alive."

The red sprang to his face. He took her outstretched hands and held them to lips and eyes for a moment, then caught her in his arms and kissed her until the rest of the world lay dull, and all life was in that quiet cell.

XIX

A YEAR later they took her to Sing Sing. The General Term had refused her a new trial, the Court of Appeals had sustained the lower court. Bourke had won nothing but additional glory.

He did not go with her to Sing Sing. She saw him alone for an hour before Tarbox came to take her away. Her composure was greater than his. He was torn with horror and defeat, and his surpassing love for the woman. Not that he had given up hope by any means, nor the fight; but he knew the fearful odds, and he cursed the law which he had outwitted and played with so often and so brilliantly.

"I wish we were back in the middle ages," he said savagely, "when a man took his rights and regulated justice by brute force. We are not half men now that we are under the yoke of a thing that operates blindly, and strikes by chance where it should strike, in nine cases out of ten. Good God! Good God! it seems incredible that I can *let* you go, that I shall stand by and see Tarbox lead you away. Think of the combined intellect of the world and the centuries having done no more for man than that. I must stand aside and see you go to a hideous cell in the Death House — O my God!"

He had awakened the woman down to the depths; to-day he called to life the maternal instinct in her. She put her arms about him with the passionate strength of one who would transmit courage and hope through physical pressure.

"Listen," she said; "I don't mind one cell more than another — and I know, I *know*, that you will save me. I feel it. I am not going to die. You are a man of genius. Everybody says that — everybody — I know that you will have an inspiration at the last minute. And I have been happy, happy, happy! Don't forget that — not ever. I would go through twenty times what I have suffered in all my life for this past year. Don't you think I can live on that for a month or two? Why, I can feel your touch, the pressure of your arms for hours after you leave me. I shall be with you every minute — "

He threw back his head, shaking it with a brief violent motion characteristic of him.

"Very well," he said, "very well; it is not for me to be weak when you are strong. Perhaps it is because the prize is so great that the fight is so long and desperate. Oh, you wonderful woman!

"Tell me," he said after a moment, "that it has all been as perfect to you as to me. I want to hear you say that, but I know it, I know it."

"Oh, — I — I — "

Tarbox came and took her away. He looked as if he had lost home and friends and fortune, and did not speak from White Plains to Sing Sing. The details of the trip interested her less than such details are supposed to interest the condemned that look their last on sky and land; her head ached, and the glare of the Hudson blinded her; but as the train neared Sing Sing she opened her eyes suddenly, then sat forward with a note of admiration.

The river was covered with a dense rosy mist which

half obscured the opposite shore, giving it the effect of an irregular group of islands. Above was a calm lake of yellow fire surrounded by heavy billows of boiling gold; beyond, storm clouds, growing larger and darker.

As they drove, a few moments later, to the prison, the great grey battlemented pile was swimming in the same rosy glow. Patience murmured satirically :

"' The splendour falls on castle walls.' "

Tarbox looked at her in amazement. " Oh," he said, " how do you manage it ? "

" All hope is not gone," she replied ; " there is still the governor." But she knew how slender that hope was. The governor was on the eve of re-election ; public feeling was multiplied against her ; the " Eye " was clamouring for her life, and strutting like a turkey cock ; the " Eye " and Tammany Hall were one ; the governor was the creature of Tammany Hall.

The warden was in his office. He greeted her with elaborate politeness, albeit puffed with alcohol and pride. She handed him what valuables she had not presented to Tarbox, and answered his questions in a manner not calculated to placate his Irish dignity. Then she turned to say good-bye to Tarbox, but he had disappeared. The head-keeper, a big kindly man, who pressed her arm in a paternal manner, led her down long echoing corridors, past rows and tiers of cells, and yards full of Things in striped garments, and talked to her in the manner one adopts to a frightened child, until she said : —

" I am not going to have hysterics ; nor am I at all sure that I am to be executed — but please don't imagine that I don't appreciate your kindness."

"Well, I like that," he said. "To tell the truth, the prospect of having a woman here has half scared me out of my wits. But if you won't take on, I'll do everything I can to make you comfortable. We've put a woman servant in there to wait on you. I hope myself it won't be for long. The evidence is pretty black, but some of us has our opinion all the same."

"Must I go into the Death House? I think I should n't mind it so much if they'd put me anywhere else."

"I'm afraid you must, ma'am. That's the custom in these parts." He opened a door with a huge key, and Patience did not need to be told that she was in the famous Death House.

A long corridor with a high window at either end; on one side a row of cells separated from the main corridor by an iron fence sufficiently removed from the cells to make space for a narrow promenade. Where the middle cell should have been was a dark arched stone passage terminated by a stout oaken door. Patience knew that it led to the execution room. Two guards walked up and down the corridor. At the end, a sullen-looking woman stood over a stove, making tea.

"You've got the house all to yourself," said the keeper, with an attempt at jocularity. "If there'd been any men here I guess you'd have been sent to Dannemora, but it's always Sing Sing for the swells, when it's possible, you know."

He opened the gate of the iron fence and led her down to the cell at the extreme end. It was large and well lighted, but very different from the cell at White Plains.

"Are you going to lock me in?" she asked.

"Yes, ma'am, I must. If everything ain't comfortable, just let me know."

The key grated in the lock. The head-keeper with an encouraging smile walked away. Patience crouched in a corner, for the first time fully realising the awfulness of her position, her imagination leaping to the room beyond the passage. What did it look like, that horrible chair? How long — how long — the hideously practical details of electric execution — the awful mystery of it — the new death to which imagination had not yet become accustomed —

There was no sound but the monotonous pacing of the death watch. The world beyond those stone walls might have sprung away into space, leaving the great beautiful prison alone on a whirling fragment.

She sprang to her feet and clenched her hands. "I'll not go mad and make an everlasting fool of myself," she thought. "If I have to die, I'll die with my head up and my eyes dry. If I have the blood of the aristocrat in me I'll prove it then, not die like a flabby woman of the people. The people! O God, how I hate the people!"

XX

A GREAT petition was sent to the governor. It was signed uniformly by men and women of the upper class.

It is not the aristocrats that do the electing in the United States. The lower classes were against her to a man. Her personality enraged them; her unreligion, her disdainful bearing, her intellect, her position, antagonised the superstitious and ambitious masses more than her crime. Inevitable result : the governor refused to pardon.

Honora returned to Peele Manor from town in April. Bourke's attempts to see her were frustrated by a body-guard of servants. He took up his residence in the little village adjoining the grounds. He hardly knew what he hoped. But Honora Mairs was the last and only resource, and he could not keep away from her vicinity. He did not go to Sing Sing. It had been agreed between himself and Patience that he should stay away : they had no desire to communicate through iron bars.

The execution was set for the seventh of May. On the evening of the sixth, while walking down the single street of the village Bourke came face to face with the new priest of the district.

"Tim Connor!" he exclaimed, forgetting for the moment, in the sudden retrospect which this man's face unrolled, the horror that held him.

"Well, it's me, sure enough, Garan, and I've been hunting for you these two days. I heard you were here, but faith, I've been busy ! — not to say I've been away for two weeks."

" How long have you been here?"

"Six months, come June, it is since I left old Ire-land ; and I'm wanting to tell you that the creek we used to wade in is as tempting to the boys as ever, and that the bog you pulled me out of has moved on a mile and more. Twenty times I've been for going across the country to call on you and have a good grip of the hand, and to bless you again for letting me live to do good work ; but I was caught in a net here — But what's the matter — Are you ill? — Oh, sure ! sure !

This terrible business! I remember! Poor young thing!"

He laid his arm about the shoulders of the other man and guided him to his house. There, in his bare little study, he brewed an Irish toddy, and the two men drank without a spoken toast to the old times when they had punched each other's head, fought each other's battles, and shared each other's joys, two affectionate rollicking mischievous Irish lads.

The priest spoke finally.

"Nothing else is talked of here in the village," he said; "but you don't hear a word of it mentioned over at the house."

"What house?"

"Peele Manor, to be sure."

"Do you go there?"

"Occasionally — to dine; or to talk with Miss Mairs. We are amiable friends, although she doesn't confess to me."

Bourke raised his head slowly. Something seemed to swirl through his heavy heart.

"Is Honora Mairs a Catholic?" he asked.

"She is indeed, and, like all converts, full to the brim and running over."

Bourke leaned forward, his hand clinching about his chin, his elbow pressing his knee with such force that his arm vibrated. He had been raised a Catholic — he knew its grip. His mind was trained to grasp opportunities on the moment, to work with the nervous yet mathematical rapidity of electric currents. And like all great lawyers he was a great actor.

"Tim," he said meditatively, "I'm feeling terribly bad over that poor girl I couldn't save."

"Sure and I should think you would, Garan. My heart's breaking for her myself."

"Did you read the trial, Tim?"

"No, faith, I did n't. I 've been too busy with these godless folk. Sure they get away from us priests when they get into America. It 's only one more drop to hell."

"You 're right, Tim, you 're right. You always saw things at a glance. But I 've got a great work for you to do, — a great work for you and for the Church."

"You have, Garan? You have? Out with it, my boy."

"Do you remember the time when Paddy Flannagan was accused of murdering his old grandmother for the sake of the money in her stocking?" continued Bourke, in the same half absent tone, and lapsing gradually into brogue. "He was convicted, you know, and the whole town was set on him, and we two boys were the worst of the lot. Do you remember how we used to hoot under his jail window at night? And then, quite by accident, at the last minute, two days before he was going to be hanged, you discovered the man that had committed the murder, and you ran as fast as your legs could carry you to save Paddy, shouting all the way, — and that it was the happiest day of your life?"

"Yes, yes!" exclaimed the priest, his face aglow. Bourke had thrown himself back in his chair, his eyes dwelling on his old friend with a smile of affectionate satisfaction.

"It 's a grand thing to save a human life, is n't it, Tim?"

"It is, indeed; the grandest, next to saving an immortal soul."

"I 'm going to give you a chance to do both, — the soul of one woman and the life of another."

"Garan, Garan, what do you mean?"

"Just let me tell you a few things first, a few things you don't know already." He gave a concise but picturesque and thrilling account of Patience's life and of her trial. As he repeated Honora's testimony, the priest, who had followed his recital with profound interest, leaned forward with sombre brows.

"That woman lied," concluded Bourke, abruptly.

"I 'm afraid so. I 'm afraid so."

"And if she does n't open her accursed perjured lips between now and to-morrow morning at eleven o'clock, that woman up there — " he caught the priest's shoulders suddenly, his face contracting with agony — " the woman I love, Tim, will be murdered. My God, man, don't you see what you 've got to do?"

XXI

HONORA was lying on a couch in her celestial bedroom. No incense burned. The screen was folded closely about the altar. The windows were open. The pure air of spring, the peaceful sounds of night, — disturbed now and again by the hideous shriek of an engine, — the delicate perfume of flowers, played upon her irritated senses. She held a bottle of smelling salts in her hand. On the table beside her was a jolly looking bottle of Benedictine.

There was a tap at the door. Honora answered wearily. A maid entered.

"It 's Father Connor, miss, and he wants to see you particular."

"Tell him I cannot see him — no, tell him to come up."

She rose hurriedly and smoothed her hair. Mr. and Mrs. Peele had gone South. She was alone in the house, and welcomed the brief distraction of the priest's visit.

"You will pardon me for asking you to come up here," she said as he entered. "But I am in dishabille, and I did not want to keep you waiting. How kind of you to come ! "

" Sure it is always a pleasure to see you anywhere, Miss Mairs," he said, taking the seat she indicated. "What should I do without you in this godless place? "

Several candles burned. The moonlight wandered in, making a ghastly combination. Honora lay back in her chair, looking very pale and beautiful. The priest's profile was toward her for a moment after he ceased speaking, a strong lean determined profile. She watched it warily. But he turned suddenly to her and smiled, and told her an absurd episode of one of his village delinquents.

" Faith, Miss Mairs," he concluded, " you 've got to help me. They 're too much for one poor priest. I 'm not one to flatter, but your face would be enough to make a sinner think of heaven — sure it 's the face of an angel ! Between the two of us and with the Grace of God we 'll reform the village and drive the dirty politicians into the Church or out of the country."

Honora smiled radiantly, and held out her hand. " I will work with you," she said. " I intend to devote my life to the Church."

He held her hand closely, in a strong masculine clasp.

"I believed it of you. But why don't you go to confession, my child?"

The muscles under Honora's fair skin contracted briefly, and she attempted to withdraw her hand; but the priest held it closely.

"I shall go to you next week."

"To-night," he said with soft insistence; "to-night. Do you know it was that brought me here to-night? I've been knowing ever since I came that something troubled you — was eating your heart out — but I did n't like to speak. I thought every day you would come to me, and I did n't like to intrude. But to-night I said, 'I will!' I could n't get up my courage when I first came in; but I'm glad I've spoken, for I know you 'll be after confessing now. Poor girl! But remember, dear child, the comfort and consolation our blessed Church has for every sinner. Come."

Honora turned her face away, and shook her head.

The priest put out a long arm, and grasping the screen drew it away from the altar. Then he leaned forward, and laying his hands on her shoulders drew her slowly forward and pressed her to her knees. He laid his hand on her head.

"Confess," he said, solemnly.

And Honora suddenly burst into wild sobbing, and confessed that Beverly Peele had dropped his own morphine that night, that his shaking hand had refused to obey his will, and that, blind with pain, he had poured a fourth of the contents into the glass, mixed it with water, and gulped it down; that she had not gone to his assistance because she wished him to die, and the responsibility to fall upon his wife.

Then she sprang to her feet and smote her hands together.

"I did not intend to confess until all was over, but — I — Oh — it has been horrible here alone these two days — but I would not yield to superstition and go away — and you found me in a weak moment."

She walked up and down the room, talking the more rapidly, the more unreservedly, as the priest made no comment. And after all the years of immobility it was joy to speak out everything in her crowded heart and brain.

"Oh, I am not a monster, I am not abnormal, I am merely a result. It began — when did it begin? I was a child when I came here — I remember little that happened before — it has always been the *rôle* of the poor cousin, I remember no other — no other! never! never! I had to learn patience at an age when other children are clamouring for their little desires. I had to learn humility when other children — while I watched my cousins take all the goods and joys of childhood as their divine right. While their little world was at their feet I was learning to cringe and watch and wait and smile upon people I hated, and listen to people that bored me to death, and suffer vicariously for all the shortcomings of the Peele family when my aunt was in one of her cold rages. It was early that I learned the lesson that if I would occupy a supportable position in life I must 'work' people; I must cultivate will and tact — how I hate the loathsome word — and study the natures of those about me, and play upon them; that I must acquire absolute self repression, be a sort of automaton, that, being once wound up properly, never makes a false move. I believe that was one thing which drove me to the Catholic Church, — the unspeakable relief that I should find in confession, — that and one other thing — "

She paused abruptly, and pressed her hands to her face, to which the blood had sprung.

"I loved Beverly Peele," she continued violently. "I do not know when it began; when I was old enough to fall in love, I suppose, and that is young enough with a woman. When we were children we used to play at being married. Even after he was grown and was rather wild, he used to come back to me in the summer time and tell me that he cared for no one else. I knew all his faults, his weaknesses, his limitations, mental and moral and spiritual, — none better. But I loved him. I worshipped him. He was not even a companion to me, for I was always intellectually ambitious. Not a taste but music did we have in common. I have seen him in raging tempers that would make any other woman despise him — when he seemed an animal, a savage. But nothing made any difference to me. A woman loves or she does not love — that is the beginning and the end. There is no more relation between cause and effect in an infatuated woman's mind than — Oh, well, I can't be finding similes.

"One night he came in here. The next night I kissed the pillow his head would lie on. For a year I was happy; for another I alternated between joy and anguish, jealousy and peace, despair and hope. Then a year of misery, during which he brutally cast me off. It was that which drove me to the Catholic Church — not only the peace it promised, but the knowledge that with baptism my sin would be washed away — for when

happiness went remorse began.   I have not a brain of
iron, like that woman he married.   She could snap her
past in two and fling it behind her.   She could snap
her fingers at moral laws, if it suited her purpose, and
know no regret, provided she had had nothing to regret
meanwhile.   That was one reason why I hated her.

"Oh, how I hated her!   How I hated her!   Beverly never had any reserve, and he made love to her
before my eyes.   He was infatuated.   His affection for
me was an incidental fancy compared to his mad passion for that woman.   And month after month!   Month
after month!   And I loved him still!

"I never dared say to myself that when the time
came I should have vengeance, for such a resolution I
should be obliged to confess; and the priest would
make me promise to thrust it out, or refuse me absolution.   But down in my heart I knew that when the
hour came the temptation would conquer.   It came
first when I let him drink the morphine.   And when I
saw her in court, when her lover gave me that sudden
suggestion, when I knew that I could send her to that
horrible chair —" She threw out her arms and laughed
hysterically, "O God, I was almost happy again."

The priest rose and stood before her.   There were
tears in his eyes.

"Poor woman!" he said.   "Poor woman!"

Honora's face convulsed, but she shut her lips reso-
lutely and tapped the floor with her foot.

"There is pardon and peace in the Church," he continued softly; "and not only for the sake of that poor
girl at Sing Sing, battling to-night with horror and terror, sleepless, listening to the solemn tramp of the
death watch, counting the hours that are marching her

to that hideous death, but for the future peace of your own soul, speak out and save her. Think of the years of torment, of remorse, when you will not have the excitement of the present, the pressure of your wrongs to sustain you. Speak out, and I will give you absolution, and your soul shall know peace."

But Honora threw back her head and laughed.

"No! No!" she said. "I am not so weak as that. I have no intention of going to pieces at the last moment. It is only her death that will give me peace."

He bent his long body backward, drawing himself up to his full imposing height.

"And have you thought of what will be the penalty?" he said, in a low voice, and with an intonation that was almost a chant.

She shuddered, but dragged her eyes away.

"I don't care!" she said passionately. "I don't care!"

"You are sure?" he said, in the same voice.

She drew two short breaths. "Oh, go away and leave me," she said. "Why did you come here? I did not intend to confess until all was over."

"And you expected absolution?"

"I would have done any penance. I would have burnt my flesh with red-hot irons —"

He gave a short, scornful laugh.

"The Church wants no such makeshift penances," he said passionately. "It has no use for the sinner that commits deliberate crime to-day and comes cringing and triumphant to the confessional to-morrow. We have no use for such as you," he suddenly shouted, flinging out his arm and pointing his index finger at her. "You are a disgrace to the Church, a pollution; you are the lips of the leper upon the pure body of a Saint. We have no place for such as you. We have only one method by which to deal with you and such as you—" He curved his body, and his voice fell to a hollow monotone: "Ex-commu-nica-tion."

The woman stared at him with pale distended eyes, no breath issuing from her dry lips, then sank to the floor, a miserable, collapsed, quivering heap. The priest went to the window and called to a man who stood on the walk below.

XXII

BOURKE was pacing up and down among the trees, his eyes seldom absent from the man standing motionless in front of the house, or from the light in Honora Mairs' window. He struck a match every few moments and looked at his watch. He lit a cigar, then found himself biting rapidly along its length with vicious energy. He flung it away and lit another, puffed at it violently, then let it fall to the ground as he pressed his hands suddenly to his eyes, shutting out the picture of Patience in her cell.

All the agony and doubt and despair of the past year were crowded into this hour. Would the priest succeed? Was he clever enough to outwit a clever and implacable woman? If he had only caught her in a moment of weakness. But was there any weakness in that organisation of knit and tempered steel? "He'll blarney her," he thought, with sudden hope,—"but bah! you can't blarney a snake. That will go so far with her and no farther. Only acting can save us. If he can act well enough to fill the stage on which this terrible tragedy is set, and conquer that woman's imagination, he can save my poor girl, but not otherwise."

His hands clutched the bushes as he passed. He kicked the gravel from his feet. He cursed aloud, not knowing what he was saying. He felt an intolerable thirst; his eyeballs burned; his heart hammered spasmodically.

He looked at his watch. It was twelve o'clock. His spinning brain conceived the wild project of forcing himself up to that lighted room at the corner of the house and putting the woman to the torture. And at that moment he saw the priest lean out of the window and speak to the notary public, who immediately entered the house.

A half hour later the priest came out of the front door and toward him. He held a paper in his hand.

Bourke was waiting at the door. He took the affidavit from the priest, glanced over it, and thrust it into his pocket.

"Come," he said. "I'll get one of the men here to hitch up a team and drive us to the One Hundred and Twenty-fifth Street station. There we'll take the train for Forty-second Street, and at the Grand Central the train for Albany. No south bound local will pass here for an hour. I happen to know that the governor is in Albany to-night attending a banquet."

XXIII

PATIENCE had given up hope at last. Its death had been accompanied by wonder rather than by despair. Her remarkable experience with Bourke had led her to idealise him even beyond the habit of woman, and her faith in his ability to save her had been absolute. Nevertheless, woman like, she wove elaborate excuses for him, and loved him none the less.

The day had dragged itself into twenty years. The chaplain had called and been dismissed. The warden had visited her and uttered the conventional words of sympathy, to which Patience had listened without expression, loathing the coarse ungrammatical brute. The head-keeper she liked, for she was the first to recognise true sympathy and nobility within whatever bark. Miss Beale had come and wept and kissed her hands through the bars.

"Patience! Patience!" she sobbed. "If it could only be said that you died like a Christian!"

"It can be said that I died like an American gentlewoman of the nineteenth century," replied Patience. "I am quite satisfied to know that they will be obliged to say that."

Miss Beale shook her head vigorously. "You will fail when the time comes," she said. "Only the Lord can sustain you. Please, Patience, let me pray with you."

"Please let me die in peace," said Patience, wearily, "and consistently. I shall not make a spectacle of myself. Don't worry."

After Miss Beale had gone the prison barber came and shaved a bald spot on the back of her head. She kept her face in the shadow, her teeth set, her skin thrilling with horror.

She sat on the edge of her bed until midnight. In the past two months, despite her faith in Bourke, she had deliberately allowed her mind to dwell upon the execution until fear had worn blunt. She was conscious of none to-night. Moreover, she had the poise of one that has lived close to the great mysteries of life. Were she free she might have a lifetime of happiness with Bourke, but in degree there were many hours of the past year that in mortal limitations could never be surpassed. The people had won their fight, but she felt that she had cheated them at every other point. For, after all, happiness is of kind, not of quantity. They could strike from her many years of life, but had she not lived? And a few years more or less — what mattered it? One must die at the last. She had realised an ideal. She had known love in its profoundest meaning, in its most delicate vibrations. A thousand years could give her no more than that.

Suddenly she lifted her head. The rain was dashing against her high window and against the windows of the corridor. She flushed and trembled and held her breath expectantly. In a moment she lay along the bed, and in a moment more forgot her evil state. Memories without form trooped through her brain: snatches and flashes of childhood and adolescence, glimmers of dawn, and stirrings of deeps, vistas of enchanted future, the rising and receding, rising and

receding of Mystery, the vague pleasurable loneliness
— the protest of separateness.

Then she pressed her face into the pillows, weeping
wildly that she should see Bourke no more.   The rain
gave him to her in terrible mockery.   Every part of
her demanded him.   She cared nothing for the morrow;   she had thought of no to-morrows when with
him.   Morrows were naught, for there was always the
last; but the present are always there to fulfil or torment.   She shuddered once.   The rain had given her
back the power to long and dream; and to longing
and dreaming there could be no fulfilment, not in this
world, now nor ever.

She beat her clenched hand against the bed, not
in fear, but in passionate resentment that she with
her magnificent endowment for happiness should be
snuffed out in her youth, and that there was no power
on earth to assuage her lover's agony.   She wondered
where he was, what he was doing.   She knew that
there was no sleep for him.

Her philosophy deserted her, as philosophy will
when the sun is under the horizon.   She ceased to be
satisfied with what had been;   the great love in her
soul cried out and demanded its eternal rights.   And
her fainting courage demanded the man. . . .

Her thoughts suddenly took a whimsical turn.   What
should she be like in eternity shorn of her stronger
part? — for assuredly in her case the man and the woman
were one.   Was space full of those incomplete shapes?
— roaming — roaming — for what? — and whither?   She
recalled a painting of Vedder's called " Identity " and
Aldrich's verses beneath : —

> " Somewhere, in desolate, wind-swept space,
>   In Twilight land, in No-man's land,
> Two wandering shapes met face to face,
>   And bade each other stand.

> " ' And who are you ? ' cried one, agape,
>   Shuddering in the gloaming light,
> ' I know not,' said the second shape,
>   ' I only died last night.' "

The picture had fascinated her profoundly until she had suddenly noticed that one of the shapes looked as if she had left her teeth on her death-bed.   She laughed aloud suddenly. . . .

For the first time she felt curious about the hereafter. Poetry had demonstrated to her that hereafter of some sort there must be : the poet sees only the soul of his creations, makes the soul talk as it would if untrammelled of flesh, and in unconscious forecast of its freedom.   Browning, alone, would have taught her this. His greater poems were those of another and loftier world.   No wonder poets were a mad unhappy race with their brief awakenings of the cosmic sense, their long contemplations of what should be, in awful contrast to what is. . . .

Patience suddenly turned from the thoughts of the hereafter in shuddering horror.   Then, as now, she should be alone.   Perhaps it would be as well, if she were to look like that shape. . . .   But she should know soon enough !

Whimsies deserted her as abruptly as they had come. She realised with terrible vividness all that she was leaving, the sweetness of it, the beauty of it — and the awful part allotted to the man.

She had imagined that in her last night on earth — if it came to that — her mind would dwell on the great problems of life ; but she cried herself to sleep.

XXIV

BOURKE and the priest arrived in Albany at two minutes past eight in the morning.   A hack carried them to the governor's house in less than ten minutes.

Bourke's ring was answered immediately.   He had his card ready, also that of the priest.

"Take these to the governor," he said to the butler. "We must see him at once."

"The governor took the 8.13 express for New York."

Bourke uttered an oath which the priest did not rebuke.

"Did he leave an answer to a telegram he received between two and five this morning?"

"No, sir ; no telegrams are ever sent here — by special orders, sir.   They are all sent to the State House."

Bourke's skin turned grey ; his eyes dulled like those of a dying man.   But only for a moment.   His brain worked with its customary rapidity.

"Come," he said to the priest.   "There is only one thing to do."

To the hackman he said : "Twenty dollars if you get to the station in five minutes."

He and the priest jumped into the hack.   The driver lashed the horses.   They dashed down the steep hills of Albany.   Two policemen rushed after them, shouting angrily; but the horses galloped the faster, the driver bounding on his seat. People darted shrieking out of their way. Other teams pulled hastily aside, oaths flying.

They reached the station in exactly four minutes and a half. Bourke had little money with him, but he was well known, and known to be wealthy. In less than five minutes the superintendent, in regard for a check for two hundred and fifty dollars, had ordered out the fastest engine in the shop. In ten minutes more it was ready, and the message had flashed along the line to make way for "45."

By this time every man in the yard was surging about the engine in excited sympathy. As the engineer gave the word and Bourke and the priest climbed in, the men cheered lustily. Bourke raised his hat. Father Connor waved them his blessing. The engine sprang down the road in pursuit of the New York express.

Despite the flying moments, the horror that seemed to sit grimacing upon the hour of eleven every time that he looked at his watch, Bourke felt the exhilaration of that ride, the enchantment of uncertainty. The morning air was cool; the river flashed with gold; the earth was very green. They seemed to cut the air as they raced through fields and towns, dashed and whizzed round curve after curve. People ran after them, some shouting with terror, thinking it was a runaway engine.

Father Connor had bought some sandwiches at the station, and Bourke ate mechanically. He wondered if he should ever recognise the fine flavour of food again.

The priest put his lips to Bourke's ear and spoke for the first time.

"Where do you expect to catch the train?"

"At Poughkeepsie.   It waits there ten minutes."

"And what shall you do if you don't catch it?"

"Go on to Sing Sing, and do the best I can.   I have made one fatal mistake: I should have telegraphed to Sing Sing.   But I was mad, I think, until I reached Albany, and there it is no wonder I forgot it.   The regular time for — that business is round eleven o'clock, about a quarter past; but if the warden happens to be drunk there 's no telling what he will take it into his head to do.   But I dare not stop."

Suddenly they shot about a curve.   The engineer shouted "There!   There!"   A dark speck was just making another curve, far to the south.

"The express!" cried the engineer.   "We 've side-tracked everything else.   We 'll catch her now."

An hour later they dashed into Poughkeepsie, the express only two minutes ahead of them.   Amidst a crowd of staring people, Bourke and the priest, be-grimed, dishevelled, leaped from the engine and boarded a parlour car of the express.   Alone, Bourke would probably have been arrested as a madman, controlled as was his demeanour; but the priest's frock forbade interference.

The governor was not in the parlour car, nor in the next, nor in the next.

Yes, he had been there, a porter replied, and would be there again; but he had left the train as soon as it had stopped.   No, he did not know in what direction he had gone; nor did any one else.

There was nothing to do but to wait.   Bourke sent a telegram to Sing Sing, but it relieved his anxiety little: he knew the languid methods of the company's officials in country towns.

There were five of those remaining seven minutes when he thought he was going mad. An immense crowd had gathered by this time about the station. Nobody knew exactly what was the matter, and nobody dared ask the man walking rapidly up and down the platform, watch in hand, gripping the arm of a priest; but hints were flying, and no one doubted that this sudden furious incursion of a flying engine and the extraordinary appearance of Bourke had to do with the famous prisoner at Sing Sing.

At exactly three minutes to starting time the governor came sauntering down the street, a tooth-pick in his mouth, his features overspread with the calm and good-will which bespeak a recently warmed interior. Bourke reached him almost at a bound. He was a master of words, and in less than a minute he had presented the governor with the facts in the case and handed him the affidavit.

" Good," said the governor. " I 'm glad enough to do this. It 's you that will understand, Mr. Bourke, that I would have been violating a sacred duty if I 'd slapped public opinion in the face before."

He wrote rapidly on the back of the affidavit.

" This will do for the present," he said. " I 'll fix it up in style when I go back. You 're a great man, Mr. Bourke."

But Bourke had gone. Whistles were sounding, train men were yelling. He and the priest barely had time to jump on their engine when they were ordered to clear the track.

Bourke glanced at his watch as they sprang out of the station. The time was twenty minutes past ten. It was barely possible to reach Sing Sing in three quar-

ters of an hour.   Lead was in his veins.   His head felt
light.   The chances for his last and paramount success
were very slim.

But the great engine dashed along like an inspired
thing, and seemed to throb in sympathy.   There was a
note of triumphant encouragement in its sudden piercing shrieks.   It tossed a cow off the track as lightly as
the poor brute had lately whisked a fly from its hind-
quarters.   It whistled merrily to the roaring air.   It
snorted disdainfully when Bourke, refusing to heed its
mighty lullaby, curved his hands about his mouth and
shouted to the engineer : —

" For God's sake, go faster ! "

XXV

THE town of Sing Sing was awake at daylight.   It was
the most exciting and important day of its history.
The women, even the pitiful ones, arose with a pleasurable flutter and donned their Sunday frocks.   The
matrons dressed the children in their brightest and best,
and laid the gala cover on the baby carriage.   The
men of the village took a half-holiday and made themselves as smart as their women.   The saloon keepers
stocked their shelves and spread their counters with
tempting array of corned beef, cold ham, cheese, crack-
ers, pickles, and pretzels.

By ten o'clock a hundred teams had driven into the
town, and were hitched to every post, housed in every
stable.   A number stood along that part of the road
which commanded a view of the prison towers.

The women sat about on the slope opposite the prison, pushing the baby carriages absently back and forth, or gossiping with animation.   Other women crowded up the bluff, settling themselves comfortably to await, with what patience they could muster, the elevation of the black flag.

The reporters and witnesses of the execution sat on a railing near the main entrance, smoking cigarettes and discussing probabilities.   Inside and out the atmosphere of intense and suppressed excitement was trying to even the stout nerves of the head-keeper.   The assistant keepers, in bright new caps, moved about with an air of portentous solemnity.

Never had Sing Sing seen a more beautiful day. The sky was a dome of lapis-lazuli.   The yellow sun sparkled down on the imposing mediæval pile of towers and turrets, on the handsome grey buildings above the green slopes near by, on the graveyard with its few dishonoured dead, on the gayly dressed expectant people, as exhilaratingly as had death and dishonour never been.   The river and the wooded banks beyond were as sweet and calm as if the great building with the men in the watch towers were some feudal castle, in which, perchance, a captured princess pined.

The head-keeper walked once or twice to the telegraph table in a corner of the office, and asked the girl in charge if any message had come.

" It 's the wish that 's father to the thought," he said to the warden ; "but I can't help hoping for a reprieve or a commutation or something. Poor thing, I feel awful sorry for her."

" Damn her," growled his chief.   " She 's too high-toned for me. When I read the death warrant to her this morning she turned her back on me square."

"She's awful proud, and I guess she has a hard time keeping up; but it ain't no time for resentment. I must say I did think Mr. Bourke'd save her, and I can't help thinking he will yet."

"Time's getting short," said the warden, with a dry laugh. "It's 10.40, and the execution takes place at 11.12 sharp."

"Could n't you make some excuse to put it off a day or so? It ain't like Mr. Bourke."

"Not much. Off she goes at 11.12." And he got up heavily and shuffled out.

The head-keeper took a decanter of brandy from the sideboard and placed it, with a number of glasses, on the table. Then he called in the newspaper men and other witnesses.

He wandered about restlessly as the men entered and drank in silence. He carried a stick of malacca topped with silver. One or two of the newspaper men shuddered as it caught their eye. They knew its hideous portent.

"Guess we'd better go," he said, after one more fruitless trip to the telegraph table. "It takes time to go through those underground passages."

As the great gates were about to close behind them he turned suddenly and called a guard.

"If it should so happen that Mr. Bourke should come, or telegraph, or that anything should happen before — 11.16 — I can delay it that long — just you be on hand to make a bolt. It ain't like Mr. Bourke to sit down and do nothing. I feel it in my bones that he's moving heaven and earth this minute."

XXVI

It was five minutes after eleven. Patience sat on the edge of her bed, her hands clenched, her face grey. But she was calm. The horror and sinking which had almost mastered her as the warden read the death warrant, she had fought down and under. And she had drunk a quantity of black coffee. She had but one thought, one desire left, — to die bravely. Even Bourke was forgotten, and hope and regret. She was conscious of but one passionate wish, not to quail, not for a second. Perhaps there was a slight touch of the dramatic instinct, even in this last extremity, for she imagined the scene and her attitude again and again. In consequence, there was a sense of unreality in it all. She felt as if about to play some great final act; she could not realise that the climax meant her own annihilation. Physically she was very tired, and should have liked to lie down for hours, although the coffee had routed sleep. Once she half extended herself on the bed, then sat erect, her mouth contracting spasmodically.

Suddenly she heard the noise of many feet shuffling on a bare floor. She knew that it came from the execution room. She shuddered and bit her lips. Now and again, through the high windows, came the shrill note of a woman's voice, or a baby's soft light laugh.

A moment later she sprang to her feet, quivering in every nerve, her hands clenched in a final and successful attempt at absolute self-mastery. On the door sep-

31

arating the Death House from the main building, resounded three loud raps, slow and deliberate. They reverberated in the ears of the condemned like the blast of the last trumpet.

The door opened, and the head-keeper entered, walking slowly, and stopping once to hold whispered converse with the death watch. Patience controlled an impulse to call to him to hurry and have it over.

He came forward at last, tapping his malacca stick on the floor, unlocked the door of her cell, and offered her his arm. He bent to her ear as if to whisper something, then evidently thought better of it, and led her slowly to the passage facing the execution room. Again she wanted to ask him to hurry, but dared not speak. The death watch turned away his head. The lace of her low shoe untied, and she stooped mechanically and fastened it.

The head-keeper asked her if she would like some brandy, — he would send and get it for her. She shook her head emphatically. The exaltation of heroism was beginning to possess her, and she would give no newspaper the chance to say that she owed her fortitude to alcohol.

They walked down the narrow vaulted way through which so many had gone to their last hideous moments. The head-keeper fumbled at the lock. The door swung open. For a moment Patience closed her eyes; the big room of yellow wood was a blaze of sunlight. Then she opened them and glanced curiously about her.

The execution room was large and high and square and cheerful. On the left, many feet above the floor, was a row of windows. At the far end a number of men that had been sitting on stools stood up hurriedly as the prisoner entered, and doffed their hats. They were the newspaper men. She recognised most of them, and bent her head. At the opposite end near the door leadïng to the Death House was a chair. Patience regarded it steadily in spite of its brilliancy. It was a solid chair of light coloured oak, like the room, and supported on three legs. Two were at the back ; in front was one of curious construction, almost a foot in breadth. This leg was divided in two at the extremity. Half way up there was a cross piece which spread the full width of the chair. To this was fastened the straps to hold the ankles of the condemned. The chair stood on a rubber mat to ensure perfect insulation. It was studded with small electric lamps, dazzling, white-hot.

Behind the chair was a square cupboard in which stood the unknown, who, at a given signal, would turn on the current.

Two prison guards stood by the chair, one behind it and one on the right. The State electrician, two surgeons, and a man in light blue clothes stood near.

Patience turned her eyes to the reporters. The young men were very pale. They regarded her with deep sympathy, and perhaps a bitter resentment at the impotence of their manhood. One looked as if he should faint, and turning his back suddenly raised something to his lips. Even the " Eye " man still held his hat in his hand, and had not resumed his seat. Only one watched her with eager wolfish curiosity. He was the youngest of them all, and it was his first great story.

Patience wondered if she looked ugly after her long confinement, and possibly ridiculous, as most women look when they have dressed without a mirror. But there was no curve of amusement on the young men's faces, and they were shuffling their feet uneasily. Her hair hung in a long braid. She looked very young.

She dropped the head-keeper's arm and walked deliberately to the chair; but he caught her hand and held her back.

"Wait a minute," he said, with affected gruffness. He went to the chair and examined it in detail. He asked a number of questions, which were answered by the electrician with haughty surprise. In a moment the reporters were staring, and like a lightning flash one brain informed another that "something was in the wind."

When the head-keeper had lingered about the chair as long as he dared he returned to Patience, who was standing rigidly where he had left her, and drawing a short breath said, —

"If you have any last words, ma'am, you are at liberty to speak."

"I have nothing to say," replied Patience, wondering if her mouth or brain were speaking.

"Yes, yes, speak," exclaimed several of the reporters. They had out their pads in an instant; but, for once, it was not the news instinct that was alert. The most quick-witted men in the world, they realised that the head-keeper was endeavouring to gain time. Their stiff felt hats dropped to the floor and bounced about. Their hands shook a little. For perhaps the first time in their history they were more men than journalists.

"I don't wish to speak," said Patience, and again she walked toward the chair. The newspaper men sprang forward with an uncontrollable movement, but the guards waved them back.

"Be careful, young men," said the head-keeper with pompous severity. "Any more of that, and you go out." Taking advantage of the momentary scraping of boots, he whispered in Patience's ear, "For God's sake speak — and a good long one. You must have something to say; and it 's your last chance on earth."

"I have nothing to say," she replied, her brain closed to all impressions but one. "Can't you see that I need all my strength? If you have any mercy in you put me in that chair and have done with it."

"Oh, you are not the kind to break down — my God!"

The silence of the prison, the hush without the walls, was pierced by a single shriek, a shriek which seemed shot from earth to heaven, a mighty shriek of furious warning.

Every man in the room jumped. The newspaper men drew their breath with a hard sound. Only Patience gave no heed.

"It 's an engine," stuttered the head-keeper, "and there 's no train due at this hour — "

The outer door was flung violently open. The warden stamped heavily into the room. His face was purple.

"Why in hell has n't this execution taken place?" he roared. "Get to work!"

The head-keeper's face turned very white. His hand shook a little. The men stared at him with jumping nerves. Patience and the warden were the only persons in the room unaffected by the inexplicable excitement which had taken possession of the atmosphere.

"Get to work," repeated the warden.

Patience walked to the chair and seated herself, extending her arms in position. Once more her brain relaxed its grasp on every thought but the determination not to scream nor quiver. She closed her eyes and set her teeth.

The guards began to fasten the straps, but slowly, under the significant eyes of the head-keeper.   The warden stamped up and down. The electrician came forward. The surgeon went into an adjoining room and cast his eyes over his instruments, laid out on a long table.

The brain works eccentrically in such moments. Patience's suddenly flung upon her consciousness a picture of Carmel tower. She speculated upon the fate of her owl. She recalled that the Mission had been restored, and wondered if Solomon, that proud and elderly hermit, had turned his haughty back upon civilisation to dwell alone in the black arbours of the remote pine tops of the forest. She saw the spray toss itself into scattering wraiths, as when she had knelt there — a thousand years ago — a little lonely girl in copper-toed boots, dreaming dreams that were pricked with no premonition of life's tragic horrors.

She frowned suddenly, recalling her long-lived determination to take life as a spectacular drama.   Life had gotten the best of her! Assuredly there was nothing impersonal about this ignominious and possibly excruciating death. The thought banished Carmel tower. Her mind was a sudden blaze of light — white light she thought with a stifled shrink — in which every detail of the room was sharply accentuated. She opened her eyes, but only a trifle, lest these men see the horror in them. Her blood was curdling, but she knew that she was making no sign.

Her sensitised mind received the immediate impression that the atmosphere of the room was vibrating with excitement. She saw the head-keeper's neck crane, his furtive glance at the outer door. He expected some one. Bourke!

She set her teeth. She had believed up to last night that he would save her. Why had she doubted him for an instant? She understood now the diplomacy of the head-keeper. Why had she not spoken when he had implored her?

It seemed to her that the men fastening the straps were racing each other. She wanted to whisper to them to lag, but pride stayed her tongue.

The warden was striding about and swearing. The electricians and surgeons were whispering in a group.

She looked at the newspaper men. She met their gaze of excited sympathy, understood at last the spirit that animated them, and bowed her head. She dared not speak.

But in a moment indignation routed gratitude. Why did they not rescue her, these young vigorous men! They knew her to be innocent. They outmatched in number the guards. Where was their manhood? What had become of all the old traditions? Then her anger left as suddenly as it had come. They were not knights with battle axes, but the most exaggerated product of modern civilisation. It was almost a miracle that they passionately wished to save her.

Her head was drawn gently back, her eyes covered. Something leapt and fought within her. Horror tore at her vitals, snarling like a wolf-hound. But once more her will rose supreme. Then, as she realised that her last moment had come, she became possessed by one mighty desire, to compel her imagination to give her the phantasm, the voice, the touch of her lover.

The wrench with which she accomplished her object was so violent, the mental concentration so overmastering, that all other consciousness was extinguished.

Suddenly her ears were pierced by a din which made her muscles leap against the straps. Was she in hell, and was this her greeting? She felt a second's thankfulness that death had been painless.

Then, out of the babel of sound she distinguished words which made her sit erect and open her eyes, her pulses bound, her blood leap, hot and stinging, her whole being rebound with gladness of life.

The cap had been removed, the men were unbuckling the straps. The head-keeper had flung his cap on the floor and run his hands through his hair until it stood up straight. Round her chair the newspaper men were pressing, shouting and cheering, trying to get at her hand to shake it.

She smiled and held out her hand, but dared not speak to them. Pride still lived, and she was afraid that she should cry.

Then she forgot them. A sudden parting in the ranks showed her the open door. At the same moment the men stopped shouting. Bourke had entered. He had followed the guard mechanically, neither hoping nor fearing until the far-reaching cheers sent the blood springing through his veins once more.

He was neither clean nor picturesque, but Patience saw only his eyes. He walked forward rapidly, and lifting her in his arms carried her from the room.

THE END.